HER BODYGUARD

BY
MALLORY KANE

AND

PREGNESIA

BY
CARLA CASSIDY

D1422063

MILLS &
BOON

HER BODYGUARD

MALLORY KANE

First published in Great Britain 2011
by Mills & Boon, an imprint of Harlequin (UK) Limited,
Eton House, 18-24 Paradise Road, Richmond, Surrey TW9 1SR

© Rickey R. Mallory 2010

ISBN: 978 0 263 88525 5

46-0511

Harlequin (UK) policy is to use papers that are natural, renewable and
recyclable products and made from wood grown in sustainable forests. The
logging and manufacturing processes conform to the legal environmental
regulations of the country of origin.

Printed and bound in Spain
by Blackprint CPI, Barcelona

Mallory Kane has two very good reasons for loving reading and writing. Her mother was a librarian, who taught her to love and respect books as a precious resource. And her father is an amazing storyteller who can hold an audience spellbound for hours. She loves romantic suspense with dangerous heroes and dauntless heroines, and loves to incorporate her medical knowledge for an extra dose of intrigue. Mallory lives in Mississippi with her computer-genius husband, their two fascinating cats and, at current count, eight computers. She loves to hear from readers. You can write her at mallory@mallorykane.com or via Harlequin Books.

For the members of Magnolia State Romance Writers.
Thanks for all your support.

Chapter One

Lucas Delancey eyed the shelf of DVDs next to the flat-screen TV in the French Quarter apartment's living room. The fake movie looked remarkably like all the others. As long as she didn't decide to watch *Charade*, she'd never know she was being watched.

He'd had to get creative in the tiny kitchen. He couldn't embed the state-of-the-art spy cam in the spine of a cookbook because they were stored in a cabinet. So he'd finally stuck it inside the smoke detector. Of course, that meant he'd had to deactivate it.

"Don't burn down the house, Ange," he muttered as he retrieved his screwdriver, wire stripper and pliers from the end table.

He glanced across the small living room toward the bedroom and bathroom, wondering if he was going to regret not setting up cameras in those two rooms, but it didn't matter. He would not spy on Angela Grayson in her bedroom, much less her bathroom.

No way. He was violating her privacy in too many ways already.

He looked at his watch. Fifteen minutes to spare before she was due to be home, according to her class schedule. He took a last look around. No sign he'd been there.

He was almost to the door when his cell phone rang. It was Dawson.

Damn it. The only reason Dawson would call was if he'd spotted Angela.

"Yeah?" he snapped. "Don't tell me—"

"Yep. You're lucky I took a stretch break and looked up the street. She just came out of the market. You've got two minutes."

"Great." He'd have been home free in four. *Crap.*

He ran out, slamming the door behind him, and bounded down the stairs four at a time. At street level, the back door of the building opened onto a quaintly decorated alley, with iron benches and Boston ferns. Rain sprinkled down on his head and shoulders as he glanced toward the Chartres Street entrance, then he turned the other way and loped down the alley to Decatur Street. He circled the block and emerged back onto Chartres below Angela's apartment building, prepared to sprint across the street.

Instead, he ran into her—literally. Something clattered to the pavement. He caught her arm to keep her from falling head over heels.

"Whoa! Sorry."

Son of a bitch! Why had she bypassed her building? For a split second, he considered bolting. But he'd never get away before she recognized him. He might as well face the music. "Are you okay?" he asked, grimacing inside.

Angela Grayson stiffened as a jolt of recognition hit her. *That voice.*

Her first thought couldn't be right. Lucas Delancey was a police detective in Dallas. He wouldn't be walking in the French Quarter in early June.

When she looked up, she caught the full impact of those familiar intense green eyes.

"Lucas?"

"Hi, Ange," he said, giving her a sheepish grin.

She jerked her arm out of his grasp. "What are you doing here?" Heat crawled up her neck to her cheeks. She couldn't believe it. *Lucas Delancey.* Literally the last person she'd ever expected to see. It had been twelve years since she'd last looked into those devilish eyes.

"Uh—" he looked down and then picked up the DVD she'd dropped. He met her gaze as he handed it to her. "How...how've you been?"

"Why aren't you in Dallas, detecting something?" Now that she'd come down from the initial shock of seeing him, she noticed how uncomfortable he seemed. She'd never seen him this ill at ease, except around his dad.

He was out of breath, as if he'd been running, and his hair was tousled, too. It really was Lucas. Hot and tanned and as handsome as she remembered, to her chagrin.

Still looking sheepish, he shrugged. "I'm taking some time off. A buddy lent me his apartment for a few days."

Angela frowned. He was lying. She'd always been able to tell when he was dishing out bull. Okay, truth to tell, she once could, back when they were kids. Nowadays, who knew?

"Your buddy's apartment. Please tell me it's not around here—" She gestured vaguely.

"No. No. I was just walking." He stepped backward. "What about you? Are you still living in Chef Voleur?"

"No way! I didn't want to stay in our hometown any more than you did."

"You and Brad gave up your mother's home?"

She shook her head. "We're renting it out." She took a half step backward. "I've got to go."

"You live around here?"

"That building back there, with the red shutters." She saw the faint puzzled look that arose in his eyes. "I was going down to the newsstand to get a magazine."

"Ange?"

Something inside her twisted at his use of her nickname. "It's Angela," she said coldly. "I'm all grown up now."

He nodded, watching her intently. "I see that. You look good."

"Do I? And the punch line is—?"

His brow wrinkled slightly. "No punch line. Still can't take a compliment, I see."

She met his gaze and was surprised. The twinkle she remembered hadn't appeared in his eyes.

"Like you'd know," she shot back, suppressing a smile. They'd always been good at the banter.

"Things going okay with you?"

And there it was. Just what she'd wanted to avoid. She didn't want to try and make small talk with Lucas Delancey. Even twelve years later, she was too embarrassed.

"Things are fine." Defensiveness edged her tone. She cleared her throat softly and continued. "You?"

He nodded and smiled—with his lips. His eyes remained serious. Something wasn't right with Lucas—not that she cared. Or at least, not that she'd admit it.

"Okay, good. So—" She glanced around.

"We should get together sometime," he ventured. "Catch up."

"Sure. That would be—" *Nice?* No, it wouldn't.

"Let me give you my phone number."

"Listen Lucas, I don't—" She stopped. Suddenly, irritatingly, having Lucas Delancey's number at her fingertips sounded like the best idea ever. Probably because of the paranoia that had been growing inside her over the past few days.

"Okay," she finished lamely. "That sounds great." She dug her cell phone out of her purse and entered the numbers as he recited them. She didn't offer him hers.

"Okay then," he said. His gaze flickered downward, toward his feet, for an instant. Then he looked at her from under his brows.

"Take care, Ange. I'll see you around." He turned and headed back toward downtown.

For a couple of seconds, she watched him. In some ways he hadn't changed since high school. That eyebrow still rose as if he knew a secret nobody else knew. And he still had that same cocky attitude.

No one would consider him skinny these days—*cut* was a better term. And his walk held more confidence than swagger. All things considered, he was still the best-looking guy she'd ever seen.

"Lucas," she called out, not sure why.

He stopped and turned.

"It was—you know—good to see you."

He nodded and smiled, as if he'd known she was going to say that, then kept walking.

Annoyed, she abandoned the notion of getting a magazine and turned on her heel, back toward her building. At the door, she glanced up the street, but he'd disappeared.

She frowned. What had he said? He was in town for a few days staying at a buddy's apartment.

That was a lie. She had no idea what he was doing in

New Orleans, but it wasn't just a vacation. Her earlier thought had been right on the money.

Something was wrong. And whatever it was, Lucas was in the middle of it.

LUCAS ENTERED HIS BUILDING through the rear door, still cursing himself. All he'd have had to do was pause for five seconds to make sure Angela had gone into her building, before heading across the street.

Now she knew he was here. It wouldn't take her long to figure out why. He'd seen how her eyes narrowed when he'd spun the vacation story. Those chocolate-colored eyes should be declared a lethal weapon.

Chocolate. The word conjured the scent he'd picked up when they'd collided. She'd been eating chocolate.

Chocolate and old movies. Her favorite guilty pleasures.

A thrill of lust slid through him as his mind flashed back twelve years to the night she'd kissed him. She'd been eating chocolate then, too. And ever since, he'd avoided it—tasting it was like tasting her lips.

He growled and forcibly shut down that part of his brain as he pushed open the door to the barren second-floor loft.

In front of the window across the room, his cousin Dawson was plugging a computer monitor into a black box. Four other screens were lined up on a long folding table.

"So, how's Angela?" Dawson said. "Leave it to you to go all the way around the block and still manage to run into her."

Lucas ignored the barb. "Are the cameras in her apartment working?"

"Of course. But you've got a problem."

"What now?"

Dawson nodded toward one of the monitors. "Look at her door."

Lucas looked at the monitor just as Angela came into view. The camera he'd set up over the transom opposite her apartment showed a perfect view of her entry door.

It was ajar.

"Ah, hell. I know I closed it. The lock should have caught."

He watched as Angela stopped and stared at it.

"Maybe it doesn't always catch," Dawson offered. "Maybe she's found it open before."

Lucas shook his head. "Nope. She hasn't. Look how rattled she is. And she'd never forget to lock it. Angela doesn't make mistakes like that."

He watched her glance around and knew exactly what she was thinking.

Do I go inside or find the building super and call the police?

"Damn it. Don't go inside. You know better than that." He tapped his fist against the table top. "She knows somebody's been in there, because she knows she locked the door this morning. But I hope to hell she doesn't call the police. If she does, we're sunk. They'll find the cameras."

She finally made her decision and pushed the door open.

"That's my Ange. Diving right into the middle of danger." He glanced toward the other monitors. "Which one's the living room?"

Dawson plugged the last monitor in and turned it on. "Right here."

"What's that?" He pointed at the box that all the cables ran to.

"A UPS. Uninterruptible power supply. Finest kind. It'll run the computer for four hours if the power goes out. Take a look."

The last monitor lit up. Lucas took in the array. The five monitors gave him a clear view of the street in front of her building, the front lobby, the hallway leading to her apartment, a wide-angle shot of her kitchen and her living room, where she was turning the lock on her door.

He watched as she scrutinized every inch of the room. She was looking for signs that someone had been in there.

"Only the kitchen and living room cameras pick up sound," Dawson commented. "Keep it turned low. They're powerful and sensitive."

The high-definition monitor clearly showed the tense line of her jaw and her white knuckles. She looked toward her bedroom, then toward the French doors that led out onto the balcony, her teeth scraping her lower lip.

"That's not the fearless bratty kid I remember. I don't think I've ever seen her this shaken by anything."

Except once, his brain was quick to remind him. Again, the memory of her soft lips and chocolate scent assaulted his senses. He immediately shut off those thoughts. He needed to concentrate on protecting her.

She tossed her purse, her leather tote and the DVD onto the couch and headed for the balcony.

Lucas turned his gaze from the monitor to the streaked, spotted window. Her balcony was almost directly across the street. She opened the balcony doors and peered out. Her face was pale, her mouth set.

After a quick look up and down the street, she closed the doors and flipped the latch.

When he looked back at the living room monitor,

all he saw was her sexy backside disappearing into the bedroom.

"You should have put a camera in her bedroom," Dawson commented.

"What the hell is she thinking, living in a place like that?"

"You mean a place where someone can install cameras in her home without her knowledge?"

Lucas growled. "You know what I mean."

"Thousands of people live in New Orleans in perfect safety."

"Thousands of people don't have ruthless Chicago crime families out to kidnap and kill them."

"You can't blame her. She doesn't know she could be a target, right?"

"Right. But look at that place. I could fly a 747 through the holes in security. Anybody could climb up the balcony. Those French doors are an open invitation to burglars. And there's no security at all in the lobby. The doors are unlocked 24/7. I got in her front door with a credit card."

"A credit card? I thought her brother gave you a key."

"He did. But when I saw that lock—it's ancient. I mean, how long has it been since you unlocked a door with a credit card?"

"Let's see. *Forever.* Why would you even try to do that?"

"Because those locks are so old that—never mind. The point is, she needs deadbolts."

"If she had deadbolts, you wouldn't have been able to get in."

"Fine. I'll give you that. But at least I've got the surveillance system in place, thanks to you. And it looks good. I appreciate it."

"Yeah. Don't mention it. Seriously, don't. Particularly when you're arrested for breaking and entering, not to mention stalking. I've taken all the Delancey Security logos off the equipment."

"Thanks for the support."

"Why didn't your buddy Brad hire a private investigator to bodyguard his sister until he can put that crime boss behind bars? Or just make her move to Chicago, where he could keep an eye on her himself? Didn't you tell me that the police there have his family under an order of protection?"

"Two reasons. First, since Angela's last name is different from his, he figured she'd be safer if he didn't do anything formal. He didn't want to tip off Picone's goons that he has a sister. And the second is the same reason he doesn't want her to know she has a bodyguard. She'd have a tantrum and do her best to prove she doesn't need protecting. And if she knew it was me—" Lucas shook his head "—hell, she'd probably paint a bull's-eye on her back just to spite Brad and me."

"Which brings up another question." Dawson scrolled through several screens on the main monitor and nodded to himself. "Why *is* it you?"

"Brad asked me to find someone. I was available." Lucas heard the irony in his voice.

Dawson nodded. "Lucky you, getting suspended for excessive force at just the right time."

He grimaced. It rankled that his lieutenant hadn't gone to bat for him against Dallas P.D. Internal Affairs. The domestic dispute had gotten violent long before Lucas and his partner had shown up. And if the husband hadn't been the son of a Texas state senator, it would have been a routine call.

But Junior hadn't appreciated Lucas conking him on the head to stop him from whaling on his wife. So he'd called his daddy, and suddenly, despite the wife's black eye and strained shoulder, Junior was home free and Lucas was on suspension for three months.

"Gives me something to do. When Brad called, I'd already been on suspension for six weeks. Why wouldn't I jump at the chance to do something other than stare at the walls?" Besides, how could he refuse? It was Angela—Brad's little sister—who needed protecting.

He saw movement on the living room monitor. Angela was coming out of her bedroom. She'd changed into a sleeveless top and shorts and pushed her hair back from her face with some kind of headband.

"Okay. You're all set up here. I've got other clients to see—paying clients." Dawson stood. "Take care, Luke. If there really is a hit man after her, you could find yourself in the line of fire."

Luke stood, too, and held out his hand. "That's why I'm here. Thanks, cousin. I really do appreciate your help." His gaze slid back to the monitor. "Look at her. She can't settle down. She keeps looking at the door. There's got to be something else going on." He frowned. "Damn, you reckon she's noticed someone watching her?"

"Maybe you should talk to her—tell her it was you in her apartment. It might make her feel better."

"Are you kidding me? To her, that would be worse than finding out she's being targeted for a hit. Angela Grayson hates me."

ANGELA SLAMMED THE BOOK SHUT and drained her glass of sweet iced tea. Her watch read 11:15.

She groaned and rubbed her eyes. She'd been trying to study for two hours, most of which she'd spent staring at indecipherable words. So much for cramming for tomorrow's Business Ethics exam.

Hopefully, she'd gleaned enough from the lectures to pass, because no way was her brain going to process anything tonight.

She could only think about one thing—okay, two if she counted Lucas Delancey, and both of them were making her crazy. But the one that scared her most was that someone had been inside her apartment.

And not for the first time, either.

A week ago, after going to dinner with friends, she'd come home to find the living room light on and a torn slip of paper on the hardwood floor.

She'd called Mr. Bouvier, the super. Sure enough, he'd had an electrician checking the wiring in 1A downstairs, but he didn't think the guy had gone into any of the other apartments. So she'd written that one off with a request for Bouvier to put deadbolts on her doors. He'd promised her he'd get to it. But of course he hadn't yet.

Now it had happened again. Damn Bouvier and his cut-rate handymen. She'd had it with them invading her space and interrupting her life.

She opened the book again, but it might as well have been written in Greek. She growled under her breath and managed not to throw it across the room.

As soon as exams were over, she'd buy the deadbolts herself. Maybe she'd even get an alarm system. Didn't one of the Delancey boys own a security company?

Of course, if she didn't pass the exams, she might not be able to keep the apartment. Not to mention she could kiss her career plan goodbye. Even with a PhD in hospitality management, she needed the specific postdoctoral courses she was taking during the June mini-semester to qualify for the kind of position she wanted with a premier hotel chain.

She carried her glass to the sink, doing her best to ignore the frisson of fear that slid down her spine when she passed her hall door.

It must have been Mr. Bouvier who'd been inside her apartment and left the door open. As her super, he had a key. But that rational explanation did nothing to make her feel better.

To avoid looking at the door she glanced in the other direction, toward her balcony. There she spotted her broken reflection in the multiple glass panes of the French doors. Her heart skipped a beat.

For the first time since she'd moved in, she was conscious of what someone looking in her window could see. She shivered, feeling exposed. How many times had she walked to the kitchen in skimpy pajamas? Or next to nothing?

With a huge effort, she managed to walk calmly across the room and turn out the lights. Now she could see out while she was hopefully hidden by darkness.

Directly across the street from her balcony was a dirty window. In the past eight months she'd never once seen lights in there, much less anyone moving around. But tonight, her imagination was running wild.

She squinted. Did she see a faint blue glow behind the streaked glass? Or was it just a reflection? Were the deep shapeless shadows hiding a dark figure whose eyes followed her every move?

She really needed to get curtains.

She took a deep breath and, ignoring the trickle of fear

that slithered down her back, stalked deliberately over to the French doors and checked the locks.

On the way to her bedroom she packed up her Business Ethics book. She might as well take it with her. She was pretty sure she wasn't going to sleep tonight.

She wasn't fond of studying into the wee hours of the morning, but it would be better than lying awake in the dark. Then a second thought had her reaching for her purse. She grabbed her cell phone to carry with her into the bedroom.

"Whoever you are," she said out loud to the faceless person who had violated her privacy. "Are you trying to make me afraid in my own home? Well, it won't work."

Whoever was sneaking around in her apartment while she wasn't home was a coward. So why was she the one who felt terrified?

LUCAS HEARD HER brave words through Dawson's state-of-the-art equipment. He also heard the quiver in her voice. Just like he remembered.

When they were kids, there was no dare Angela wouldn't take. She'd stick that stubborn little chin out and flash those brown eyes. It didn't matter if her chin trembled and vulnerable fear lurked behind her cutting glare. She'd never balked at anything.

She had a nasty scar above her right knee to prove it. He'd bet her that she couldn't follow him across a deep drainage ditch. He'd barely made it to the other side. But before he could turn around and warn her not to try it with her shorter legs, she'd jumped—and fallen.

"Damn it, Angela," he whispered. "Be careful." Her attitude had earned her more scars than that one—

both physical and emotional. A couple of each were his fault.

He'd been both reluctant and glad to take on this job when Brad asked him to. He'd thought Lucas was doing him a favor. But he wasn't doing it for Brad. He was doing it because he owed Angela.

Brad Harcourt was the assistant district attorney in Chicago, and Angela's half-brother. He'd asked Lucas to make sure she was safe until Nikolai Picone's trial was over and the crime boss was behind bars. He'd outlined for Lucas the extent of Picone's influence. Nikolai Picone headed one of the biggest crime organizations operating in the Midwest.

Lucas knew a man with that much power would have no trouble tracking down an innocent young woman who had no reason to hide. He couldn't let down his guard for even one instant.

If he did, Angela could end up dead.

Chapter Two

At least the Business Ethics exam was over. Who knew if she'd passed or not? When she'd turned it in a half hour ago she'd felt pretty confident, but now her brain was racing, questioning every single answer.

Angela hurried along the sidewalk, hoping to beat the rain. Usually she enjoyed the two-block walk from the streetcar stop to her apartment on Chartres Street. She liked to stop at the market for vegetables or fruit, French bread, a DVD from Sal's private collection of classic movies and maybe a chocolate truffle.

But today was different. The air was heavy with humidity, she hadn't slept the night before and there was a man behind her following way too closely.

She'd felt funny on the streetcar, like someone was watching her, but she'd chalked it up to nervousness about the exam and the paranoia that had been growing inside her over the past several days.

She should have stopped in at Sal's, where she'd be surrounded by people in case the man really was following her. She wasn't really sure why she hadn't. For some reason, at the last second, she'd decided she'd rather be home, inside her apartment with the doors locked.

Stupid.

A few drops of rain penetrated her thin shirt, so she

sped up. To her alarm, the footsteps behind her sped up, too. And was it her imagination, or could she hear the man's harsh breaths in her ear, sawing in and out—in and out?

She wanted to turn her head and look back, but if he was following her, she didn't want to look into his eyes.

When had she become such a wimp?

Before yesterday, she'd have stopped and whirled, eyeing him with a pugnacious stare until he walked on past her or crossed the street. She might be afraid, but she'd never let him know it.

Today, however, everything was different.

Today terror clawed its way up her throat, like it had when she was a child and a nightmare would wake her. She swallowed hard and gripped her umbrella like a weapon.

"Angela, hi!"

She almost tripped.

It was her downstairs neighbor, Billy Laverne, walking his Afghan hound toward her, or, more accurately, being walked by the gigantic dog.

"Hi, Billy." The wash of relief that coursed through her ticked her off. Since when did Billy, whose head barely reached her eyebrows, who weighed less than she did and who definitely had a better manicure, represent safety to her?

"So," he drawled. "Tell me. How're the exams going? I'm sure you're doing fabulously."

She reached out a hand to pet Alfie. The friendly dog licked her knuckles. "I hope you're right. Can I ask you something?"

She half turned, but when she did, the only person close to her was turning to head across the street. All she saw was the back of a loud Hawaiian print bowling shirt and a blue baseball cap. She couldn't tell anything about the man except that he was not much taller than her five feet seven inches.

"Honey, you can ask me anything."

She kept her hand on Alfie's head. "Do you know that guy?" She gestured toward the retreating back of the man in the Hawaiian shirt.

Billy shook his head. "Heavens no. That is a nasty excuse for a shirt. Why?"

She laughed weakly. "It's nothing. For a few minutes I thought he was following me. So, did Bouvier send someone to work on your electricity last week?"

"Yeah. My stove went out—again."

"Was it the greasy guy with the shaved head?"

Billy nodded and shuddered. "Ugh. And the baggy work pants? Yes."

"Did he go anywhere else?"

"I don't know. What's wrong?"

Angela thought better of telling Billy what had happened. He could be dramatic. She didn't want to cause a panic among the other residents of her building.

"Nothing," she lied. "I needed him to look at my kitchen light."

Alfie whined and pulled on his leash, jerking Billy's arm. "Oops. Gotta go. Alfie's got to have his afternoon constitutional."

"See you later." She liked having Billy as a neighbor. He was funny and sweet, and he made great jambalaya. But right now she wished he was eight inches taller and forty pounds heavier. Although she'd never admit it to anyone, she could use a knight in shining armor.

Oh please. Get over yourself. She no more needed a knight—shining armor or not—than she needed a second head. Either one of them would be too high-maintenance. All she needed was something to distract her from this damn paranoia. As soon as she was done with finals, she was going shopping for a deadbolt and a pair of opaque curtains.

And then it would be time for a trip to Chicago, to see her brother, Brad, his wife and her two adorable nieces. The thought of seeing the girls made her feel better immediately. She headed on toward her apartment, glancing back for one more glimpse of the man in the blue cap, but she didn't see him anywhere.

Before she got her attention turned back to where she was walking, her foot caught and she nearly went head over heels. She steadied herself by grabbing the back of the wrought-iron chair that she'd tripped over.

The man sitting in it reached one hand for his mug and the other to help steady her. "Whoa there."

Without letting go of her arm, he stood. "You okay? Sorry my chair got in your way." He laughed. "I hate it when it does that."

"Oh, no."

"Crap," he said at the same time.

It was Lucas Delancey. She glared at him. "You again. Your apartment *is* around here," she said accusingly.

"It's in the area, but you gotta admit, this place has the best café au lait on this side of the Quarter." He cocked his right eyebrow. "Can I buy you a cup?"

"No!" She heard the harsh panic in her voice. She took a deep slow breath and tried again. "No, thank you," she said evenly. "If I run into you one more time I'm going to be convinced I have another stalker."

"You've got a stalker?" His gaze turned sharp as an emerald.

She winced. "No, I didn't mean that. It was—" She shook her head. "It was a joke."

He stared at her. "I don't think so, Ange."

There was that nickname again. The single syllable sent nostalgia surging through her. He'd always called her Ange, when he wasn't calling her *Brat*.

"Well, you don't know, do you?" she retorted, making a show of looking at her watch. "I've got to go."

He caught her by her wrist. "Who is he?"

"Nobody you know. Anyhow, I was joking."

"You've got my phone number. Call me if you need me."

She looked down at his hand. It was big and well shaped, with long, strong fingers. It looked like a hand that could wield a mean sword. Like a knight in—

Stop it! she commanded herself and jerked away from his grasp. Lucas Delancey was a lot of things. Maybe to the people of his precinct in Dallas he was a knight in shining armor, but in her experience, he'd be better cast as the Artful Dodger.

Still, the idea of having someone like him on her side was tempting. It would be so easy to tell him about the odd occurrences of the past week or so. Her certainty that someone was going into her apartment when she wasn't home. Her sense that someone was watching her, following her.

But seeing him twice in two days flung her back in time. To when she was sixteen and knew she'd die if she never got to kiss him. Her insides turned upside down at the memory of her hesitant naïve kiss and his bold, sensual response.

She'd never been kissed like that since.

"Ange?"

She blinked and realized she was staring at his mouth. What had he said?

Call me if you need me.

"I won't need you," she said coldly and headed in the direction of her apartment.

Behind her, he spoke. "Don't be so sure about that, Ange."

She stalked away, praying he wasn't watching her. The idea of him checking out her butt was horribly embarrassing. After a dozen steps or so, she stopped and glanced back over her shoulder.

He was nowhere in sight.

Irritated with herself for looking back, she whirled—and ran into someone else.

"Hey, Angie. Careful."

"Oh, no," she muttered. Not Doug, too. She'd thought she'd finally convinced him she wasn't interested in dating him. Apparently this was destined to be her week from hell. Exams, intruders, high school flames and creepy ex-boyfriends. What else could happen?

Doug's arm snaked around her shoulders. "Steady. Are you okay?"

She pulled away from him as smoothly as she could, not quite able to suppress a shudder. "I'm fine, Doug. What are you doing here?"

"I had a delivery to make in this neighborhood, so I thought I'd run upstairs and see if you were okay. I've been worried. You haven't answered your phone in the last several days."

Angela cringed inwardly. No, she hadn't, on purpose.

"I'm glad you're okay. You're certainly looking good."

"Thanks. I'm kind of in a hurry."

"Who was that guy you were talking to?" Doug's words were casual, but his pale blue eyes narrowed as he scrutinized her.

"An old friend from high school." She started to walk away but he caught her arm.

"Have dinner with me. I miss you."

She stepped away, tugging her arm away from his grasp. "I'm sorry, Doug, but no. You need to stop calling me. I'm in the middle of final exams and—"

"After exams then."

"No, that's not what I meant—"

But he was walking away.

Angela practically ran the rest of the way to her apartment. She locked the door behind her.

"Finally!" she sighed. What a bizarre day. At least it was over now and she was back in her apartment. *Safe*.

She tossed her things onto the couch.

And froze.

There, on the corner back cushion, was a smudge. A tiny smudge—hardly noticeable, even on the pale beige fabric. But it hadn't been there last night or this morning.

Dread settled beneath her breastbone and tears prickled behind her eyes. "No," she muttered. "Not safe."

She frowned. Could it have been Doug? He had no reason to be in this neighborhood, except to check on her. He'd said he had a delivery in the area, but his office supply store was out in Metairie. She doubted he had many clients down here in the French Quarter.

Before she could decide whether to call the super or storm downstairs and bang on his door, her phone rang.

She looked at the caller ID, and the dread in her chest

lifted. "Brad, hi—" Her voice gave out. She cleared her throat. "Calling to make sure I'm studying?" she asked, smiling.

Her brother didn't call often. He was too overworked. And he never, ever called during the day.

"Studying? Oh. Your exams," Brad said. "No, I just wanted to see how you're doing."

"I'm fine," she answered automatically, turning her back on the sofa. "You, on the other hand, sound a lot more distracted than usual. How's Sue? And my two gorgeous nieces?"

"Good. They're good. So how are you doing?"

She laughed. "You just asked me that. Somebody was talking about you the other day. Let's see—oh, I know. Hank Percy. He'd heard your name on the national news—some case you were trying. He wanted to do a piece on you for the *Chef Voleur Weekly Record*. I'm supposed to ask you if you would talk to him." She paused for dramatic effect. "So, ADA Harcourt, I guess you've finally hit the big time. You're going to have a write-up in Hank Percy's column."

There was a pause, barely enough to notice. "I guess."

"Brad? Is everything all right?" The sinking feeling came back. "Is Sue okay? The girls?"

He sighed. "Seriously, sis. Can't I call and check on you without you getting paranoid?"

"Interesting choice of words," she said wryly. "It's been a weird day. But my last exam is Monday, and I'll have a whole six weeks before summer classes start."

Suddenly, she missed her brother. He and Sue and her nieces were her only family since their mother had died. "I was planning to fly up there for a long weekend this summer. Why don't I come next week, or the week after?"

Another pause. Longer this time. "Now's not a good time. That big case Hank Percy called you about has put me behind on several others, and—and the girls have a virus."

Angela felt hurt. Brad was putting her off. She could hear it in his voice. "Are you sure there's nothing wrong?"

She heard him take a breath. "Absolutely. It's just hectic. Maybe in about a month. How about the Fourth of July?"

"Okay then. Now's not really a good time for me, either. I'm probably going to sleep for a week after my last test on Monday. Why don't you give me a call when things settle down—if they ever do?"

"I will. I promise. Things are just crazy right now. Listen, sis. Watch out for yourself. New Orleans can be dangerous."

"Don't worry about me. I'm tough. See, when I was a kid, my brother and his best friend picked on me all the time. I had to learn to stand up for myself."

Brad chuckled. "You *are* tough. There's no denying that."

"Speaking of your best friend, guess who I ran into today?"

There was nothing but silence on the other end of the phone.

"Brad? Are you there?"

"Yeah. What—you don't mean Delancey, there in New Orleans?"

"Who else? How many best friends have you had?"

"So you saw Luke. I thought he was in Dallas."

"Well, apparently he's taking a vacation." She frowned. "It's funny. He didn't ask about you."

"Hang on a second," Brad said.

She heard him talking to someone.

"Sis, I've got to go. I've got a meeting in two minutes. Good luck on the rest of your tests."

"Love you," she said, but Brad had already hung up.

She realized she was oddly close to tears.

"That was weird," she whispered. As she swiped her fingers across her cheeks, her gaze lit on the smudge on her sofa.

Her fist tightened around her cell phone and she shivered.

"HOW IN THE HELL DID YOU let Angela see you? I thought you were good at this stuff."

Lucas cringed at the fury in Brad's voice. He'd seen Angela on her cell phone a few moments ago. She must have been talking to him.

"Hey, I'm a detective, not a cat burglar. I was bound to run into her sooner or later. I was grabbing a quick café au lait. Who knew she'd finish her exam in just over an hour? Isn't that record time?"

"*You* should have known. Have you forgotten how smart she is? What did she do when she saw you?"

"What do you think she did? She got pissed off. Wanted to know what I was doing here. I told her I was taking some time off." He sniffed. "The years haven't mellowed her much."

"So what now? You're going to have to find me somebody to take your place."

"Nobody's taking my place. She just thinks it's her bad luck that she ran into me. I could see it in her face.

Nope. I've got cameras set up everywhere—the street in front of her apartment, her hallway and door and her living room and kitchen. Anybody even goes near her building, I'll see them."

He paused for a beat and then took a deep breath. "Somebody's going into her apartment when she's not there, Brad."

"Oh, God. You've seen him? I knew it. It's got to be Picone. He's sent someone down there after her. A hit man."

"Who? Who would he send?"

Brad grunted in frustration. "That's the $64,000 question. Picone's organization is a family business. He's got four sons and two daughters. Word is Nikki Jr. is being groomed to take over someday. Milo and Paulo have been linked to several suspicious deaths. And the son-in-law, Harold, was convicted of manslaughter about six years ago. The younger daughter isn't married. She's in her twenties. I've heard she's a technology whiz."

Lucas filed the names away in his brain. "What about the fourth son?"

"Tony. The youngest boy. He's totally clean, from all the information I've got. The police have a confidential informant who says he's *Mama's* baby, and not in the business."

"So which one's out of town?"

Brad laughed wryly. "I wish it were that easy. None of them have been seen for the last couple of days."

"Have you got pictures?"

"I'll have to get my secretary to check the newspaper archives. Why? Have you spotted someone hanging around?"

"Not really. There is this one forgettable type who

seems to hang around the building a lot. He's kind of dumpy and pale as a fish's belly."

"Doesn't sound like any of the family I've ever seen."

"Maybe that's the point. Forgettable is probably a job requirement for a hit man. I'm keeping an eye on him."

"Think he's the one getting into her apartment? Have you talked to the super?"

"Not yet. This guy's never done anything that I've seen. He just hangs around like he's waiting for somebody. But the next time the intruder goes into her apartment, I'll be watching. And trust me, I'll be all over him—"

"The next time?"

"Don't worry, Brad. I'm going to get Ryker to talk to Chicago P.D. and maybe get a handle on who your big crime boss might have sent."

"You can't do that. I don't want to broadcast that I've got a sister, much less where she is."

"I said don't worry. Look up the word *discreet* in the dictionary and you'll find Ryker's face."

"Yeah, but Ryker's so by-the-book. I'm afraid that'll trump his discretion. He'll be concerned with chain of command. And by the time he gets to someone who knows something, he'll have spread the word about my sister all over the Chicago P.D. Besides, he's in Chef Voleur, and that means even more links in the chain. Maybe Ethan could get one of the senior detectives in New Orleans to call up here, maybe talk to somebody he knows. Discreetly."

"That's not going to happen. My hot-headed younger brother isn't happy with me right now. Ryker'll handle it. He's not such a stickler for chain of command these days."

"Okay, if you're sure. But do it today. That hit man's on a deadline. I'm doing closing arguments on Monday. The case should go to the jury no later than Tuesday. I doubt it will take them a day to convict. Until then, Angela's in danger."

"Brad, you trust me, right? I'm on it. Nothing's going to happen to Ange. Not on my watch."

"Thanks, Luke. How are the accommodations?"

"Well, at least this place has a working toilet. I bought a portable refrigerator. Dawson found me a cot, and there's a market three doors down."

"Anything you need, just ask."

"I could use an air conditioner, but other than that, I'm fine. There's nothing I'd rather be doing right now than spying on Angela—okay wait. That didn't come out right."

Brad chuckled. "Don't worry, Luke. I know what you meant, and I know I can trust you with my sister. I *can* trust you with my sister, can't I?"

"Hey, she's practically my sister, too." *Liar.* That might have been true when he and Brad were eleven, but now—

As Angela had told him, she was all grown up now. And so was he. And there had been nothing brotherly about his reaction to her.

"Thanks, Luke. I knew I could count on you."

Lucas hung up with a frustrated sigh and dialed Ryker's number.

Yeah, Brad could trust him completely. He'd watch

her every move and be on alert in case anything happened.

He'd keep her safe. Even if it meant taking a lot of cold showers.

Chapter Three

It was after ten when Lucas tossed half a sandwich into the trash. He made a mental note to take the bag out in the morning before it started to smell. He was going to get real tired of ham sandwiches before this bodyguard detail was over.

And right now he'd sell his vintage Mustang Cobra for a café au lait. At least he had the refrigerator, so his bottled water wasn't the temperature of his unair-conditioned room.

As he drained the last of the water, his eye caught a movement on Angela's living room monitor. She'd finally gotten up from the table, where she'd been hunched over her books for the past three hours.

He yawned. That was dedication. And determination. Those qualities were more appealing in grown-up Angela than they had been in bratty kid Angela.

They weren't the only qualities that had gotten better with time, either. She had on shorts and a T-shirt that read *Laissez les bon temps roulez*, with *bon temps*— good times—stretched across her breasts.

Lucas swallowed. Those *would* be good times.

Her long legs, which had made her as awkward as a newborn colt when she was a kid, now made his mouth water. That dark brown hair that was always getting in her eyes now fell in soft waves to curve inward at her neck. And her pugnacious chin and too-short nose were now part of a face that had turned out just about perfect.

She walked into the kitchen, giving Lucas a unique stereo view of her front and back through the two monitors.

That did it. She officially looked hot from every angle.

As she poured herself a half glass of wine, Lucas grabbed another cold plastic bottle from the refrigerator, quelling the urge to splash some of it on his face—not to mention other parts of his body.

Back in the living room, she stopped in front of her shelf of DVDs and perused them as she sipped her wine.

Lucas's pulse sped up. She was looking for a movie to watch. *Just don't pick* Charade. He'd chosen the 1963 Audrey Hepburn/Cary Grant movie because it wouldn't stand out on her shelf of old movies, but he hadn't stopped to see if she had another copy of it. Still, out of her hundred or so titles, the chances were slim that she'd pick that very one.

Watch the one you rented, Ange. It's right there on the couch.

But she didn't pick up on his telepathic plea. Her fingers slid across the cases' spines, until she was dangerously close to his mini-spy cam, so close that the shadow of her hand obscured the lens.

Holding his breath, he reached for his cell phone. As a last resort, he'd call her. He could say he got her number from Brad—and it would be true. He wasn't going to tell her *when* he'd gotten it. He started dialing.

A sharp knock sounded on her door.

She jumped—and so did he. Her head snapped around and her hand went to her throat. Then she set her wine glass down directly in front of the camera lens.

Lucas pocketed his phone and reached for his Sig Sauer. He seated it in the paddle holster at the small of his back. He scrutinized the monitors and cursed as only a Delancey could. He'd been so intensely concentrated on her that he hadn't noticed someone coming into the building.

The hall spy cam picked up on a dark figure, barely visible in the wan light of the inadequate 40-watt bulbs that lined the corridors. The camera aimed at her door showed the back of a man's bald head.

Lucas shoved his arms into his long-sleeved shirt and fastened a couple of buttons. He couldn't see a damn thing through the living room monitor. The stem of the wine glass was blocking it. He had to rely on sound and what little he could see through her French doors.

ANGELA'S HEART BEAT a staccato rhythm as her fingers closed around the glass door knob.

"Who is it?" she said sharply.

"Electrician," came the terse reply.

She jerked her hand away as if the knob were hot. A repairman this time of night? That didn't feel right.

Billy must have told Bouvier what she'd said about her kitchen light. But why would Bouvier send the guy up here at night? He normally went around the world to avoid paying overtime.

"I'm sorry, but it's late. Please come back tomorrow," she called through the door.

"Look, lady, I get here when I get here. Now do you want your light fixed or not?"

"It—it's working now. It was probably just a burned-out bulb."

"Awright," the electrician growled. "No skin off my nose. I'm billing Bouvier anyhow."

She listened as his heavy footsteps echoed down the hall. Once she could no longer hear them, she slumped and hugged herself, her hands shaking.

"What's wrong with me?" she muttered. She was becoming too paranoid. She pressed her palms against her hot cheeks. Overreacting to every little thing.

Was it the pressure of exams causing her to make mountains out of mole hills? Sure, a few odd things had happened in the past few days, but every single one of them had a reasonable explanation, didn't they?

Her gaze lit on the smudge on her sofa. *No.* Not all of them. In the eight months she'd lived here, Bouvier had never sent a repairman during the evening, and he'd never gone into her apartment when she wasn't there.

At least not to her knowledge.

She sucked in a deep, shaky breath. First thing tomorrow, she was going to march down there and demand he change her locks and install deadbolts.

But what about tonight? She twirled slowly, looking around the room.

"I know," she whispered. She grabbed a dining chair and dragged it over to the door. She braced it under the knob. Then she fetched her broom and slid it through the dual handles of the French doors.

For a few seconds she stood in the middle of the room, feeling appalled by her makeshift locks.

She'd always prided herself on her fearlessness. And now look at her.

She sighed. At least if anyone tried to get in, she'd

hear them. She grabbed her cell phone and headed into her bedroom.

Then she stopped. What had she done with her wine glass? A quick glance around and she spotted it on the shelf of DVDs. Retrieving it, she headed into the bathroom to take a shower.

By the time she got out of the shower and dried her hair, she was yawning. It wasn't that late. Barely eleven. But she couldn't study any more tonight. Not only was she really tired, but she wouldn't be able to concentrate. That meant she'd have to study all weekend if she wanted to do well on Monday's exam. So maybe getting to sleep early tonight was a good idea.

After she finished brushing her hair, she put on her red pajamas and climbed into bed. Just as she reached to turn her light out her phone rang.

It was Doug. She was tempted not to answer, but she was afraid if she didn't he might show up at her door, *just to check on her.* He'd done it before.

She answered.

"Angela, I'm sorry. I meant to call earlier. Now you're in bed."

"Oh, I just—" She stopped. Why had he said that? "I'm studying, Doug. What did you want?"

"Studying? Really? It was nice seeing you today. It's been so long since we've seen each other face-to-face, much less had a good talk."

"I just saw you today. Have you been drinking?" He always tended to ramble, but tonight he wasn't making any sense.

"Oh, I've had a little wine. Just sitting here thinking about you."

She grimaced and rubbed her temples. "This isn't

a good idea, Doug. You need to move on. Go out with someone else."

"I don't want to go out with someone else, Angela. I want you."

"Please, Doug. Don't—"

"Don't try to deny it, Angela. We were perfect together. I felt it, and I know you did, too."

"No, we weren't. Don't make it more than it was. We went out three times. I'm sorry, but I have to insist that you don't call me again. If I have to, I'll change my number."

"Oh, Angie. You don't want to threaten me. You're just tired from all your exams. I'll let you go to sleep. We can make plans later." He laughed softly. "By the way, I really love you in red pajamas." He hung up.

Angela frowned at the phone as her brain processed what he'd just said.

Love you in red pajamas.

Oh, God. She looked down at the red silk pajamas she'd put on after her shower—put on right here in the bedroom.

Her blood froze in her veins as the ominous implication of his words sunk in.

Now you're in bed.

Love you in red.

Her gaze flew to her bedroom window. The blinds and the curtains were closed. There was no way anyone could see in.

She frowned as she looked around the room. Window, closet, bathroom doors, door to living room. There was no way he could possibly see, unless—

The answer that hit her like a slap in the face was inconceivable. It couldn't be, could it?

"Oh, no," she moaned. It was the only answer.

"No, no, no." Her breath caught and her scalp burned with panic.

She wanted to scream. Wanted to vault out of bed and run. But if what she was thinking were true, he was watching her, waiting for that very reaction.

With her skin crawling and her insides knotted with fear, she reached out as quickly and smoothly as she could and felt for the switch on the bedside lamp. It took several tries with her terror-numbed fingers before she turned it off.

With the lamp off, the room was dark, except for the pale light seeping in around the window curtains. She stood on shaky legs, the hairs literally standing up on the back of her neck, and her shoulder muscles cramping.

She felt like someone was right behind her, breathing down her neck, about to grab her.

Moving slowly, as if it would keep her from being seen, she slipped out from under the covers and fled into the living room. For a few seconds, she just stood there in the dark while gigantic shudders shook her body.

Finally, she turned on the overhead light. She'd rather be seen through the balcony doors by half the population of New Orleans than consider what her brain was telling her.

"It can't be—" she breathed. "Oh, God, what do I do?"

Her brain felt as frozen as her blood. She couldn't think of anything except the awful implication of Doug's words. How had he—? Surely he couldn't have—

Yes. He could.

She had evidence that someone had been inside her apartment. Not to mention her feeling that someone was watching her.

And what he'd said.

"Police!" she said aloud. "I've got to call the police."

Where was her phone? Staring down at her hands, she tried to make her brain work. She didn't have it. That meant it was still in the bedroom. She'd dropped it, either on her bed or on the floor.

She had to go back in there.

"Oh, God, no. I can't. He's *watching* me!"

ANGLEA WAS IN TROUBLE.

Lucas jerked awake and almost tipped over his chair. He'd dozed off leaning back in it.

"He's *watching* me!" Her voice was pitched high with panic. "Got to call the police!"

He blinked and focused on the monitor screen. She was standing in the living room in slinky red pajamas with her hands over her mouth, as if to stop herself from screaming.

Oh crap! She'd found the cameras.

How in hell—? He vaulted up, sending his chair flying across the room, and headed for the door.

He bolted down the stairs four at a time and hit the street door running. He had to get to her before she called the cops.

If the police came and found the cameras, a three-month suspension would be the least of his worries. His career would be over—hell his whole life. Not even Brad's testimony would keep him from being thrown in prison.

And if Angela hated him before, she'd despise him after this.

He sprinted across the street and up the stairs, digging in his pocket for her key as he ran. With everything else that was about to explode, he sure didn't want to wake up the whole building by crashing in her door.

He unlocked the door and pushed on it. It barely gave, and he heard the creak of wood scraping across wood.

Damn it! She must have blocked the door with a chair. He pushed as hard as he could against the wooden chair without shattering it.

"Ange!" he called. "Angela, it's me, Lucas."

"What—?"

"Let me in, Ange."

"What's—what are you doing here—?" Even though she was breathless and choked with fear, she got the chair moved and unlocked the door.

He came bursting in and grabbed her by the arms. "Listen Ange, let me explain—"

"Lucas, what are you—?"

"Calm down. Everything's going to be okay."

"Oh, Lucas! Help me!" She pointed toward the bedroom. "He's watching me. He knew everything. It's a camera—it's got to be!"

Lucas cringed, but then what she said sunk in. *He's watching me.*

She was pointing toward the bedroom. He didn't have a camera in her bedroom.

"What? No, not in the bedroom," he said.

She stared at him. "It is. You have to believe me. He knew I was in bed. Knew what I was wearing. He was—he was—"

She wasn't making any sense. "Okay, okay." He pulled her close, to try to soothe her panic. "Shh. Let's get you calmed down and then we can figure out what to do."

"No, you have to call the police. My phone's in there. I couldn't go back in there—I couldn't."

"I know, sugar, I know." He slid his palm up her back and cradled her head. Her warm breath stuttered against his neck as her arms slipped around his waist. For a second, he was lost in the sensation of her soft, firm body pressed against him.

Then she pulled away. "Police," she muttered. "We've got to call the police."

Lucas forced his brain back to his problem. He needed a couple of minutes to think. To figure out why she thought there was a camera in her bedroom. And he needed to get her terror under control—fast.

"Come on," he said gently, leading her to the kitchen. "Let's get you a glass of water. Sit down." He quickly fixed a glass of ice water and handed it to her.

He watched while she drank it. Her pale cheeks had regained a little bit of color by the time she'd downed about half of it.

"That's good." He sat on his haunches in front of her. "Now tell me why you think there's a camera in your bedroom, and who you think put it there."

She choked a little on the water and coughed.

"Shh. It's okay. Take your time. Is the bedroom camera the only one you've found?" Some protector he was. She was terrified and his first thought was to cover his ass. He held his breath, waiting for her to answer.

"The only one? Oh, my God. Do you think there are more?"

"No." He took the glass and set it on the table, then held her hands in his. "No. Shh. I was just checking. You said he called you. Who?"

"Doug Ramis. He called me and he knew I was in bed. And then he said he liked me in red pajamas." Her cheeks lost color again. "He could see me, Lucas! He could *see* me. How else would he know? Please! Tell me I'm wrong. Tell me he couldn't see me. I can't believe anybody would do that. It's so perverted." She shuddered again.

Lucas couldn't quite sort out what she was talking about, but he did hear her say, "It's so perverted."

She was going to despise him. "Who's Doug Ramis?"

"I dated him a few times. Three. Three times. He thinks we're—" she gestured aimlessly "—soul mates or something."

Could he be the bland guy who'd been hanging around her building? Lucas made a mental note to show her a photo of him.

"Maybe he's seen your pajamas before? Maybe he was just guessing?"

"No! No. Of course he hasn't seen my pajamas." For an instant, indignation overcame her panic. "He couldn't have just guessed. *He. Saw. Me.*"

"Okay, shh. Here. Finish your water." He handed the glass back to her, then looked toward the bedroom. "You turned the light off?"

She nodded. "So he couldn't see me." A brittle laugh escaped her lips. "You think I'm crazy, don't you?"

"No. I'm going to get your phone. You said it's in there?"

She nodded. "I dropped it on the bed."

"Do you have any idea where the camera might be?"

"No." She shuddered. "I never thought about where it was."

"That's okay. Wait right here." He rose and started toward the bedroom.

"Lucas?"

"Yeah?"

"How—how did you show up just in time?"

That took longer than he thought it would. She was

too smart. He put on a grin. "Hey, sugar. That's what knights in shining armor do, right?"

His lame joke didn't earn him a smile. Her chocolate eyes went wide and something he couldn't identify shone from their depths.

He went into the bedroom and closed the door, shutting out the light from the living room. He wished he had an infrared light, so he could see without being seen through the camera. But he didn't, so he stood still until his eyes adapted to the darkness. He wasn't about to turn on the light and risk the guy seeing him.

He felt around in her bed for her phone. To his body's delight and his brain's dismay, the sheets were still warm from her heat. He took a deep breath, hoping to tamp down his body's automatic response. But he only succeeded in filling his nose with the scent of chocolate. He shook his head. That had to be his imagination.

His fingers closed around the phone and he pocketed it. Staying low, he swept the room with his gaze. If there was a camera, it would be positioned on the wall opposite the bathroom. At least that's where he'd mount it.

It was damned hard to see with only the dim light from the curtained windows, but he scrutinized the chest of drawers and dresser that sat against the wall.

A decorative clock hung on the wall above the chest. He looked from it to her bed to the bathroom door. That would be *his* choice for the best vantage point. He carefully took it down and opened the back.

And there it was. Lucas stared at the familiar shape. It was state of the art, almost as sophisticated as the ones Dawson had loaned him. He didn't see a microphone. So it was visual only.

Anger hit him like a hot blast of wind. The slimy skunk who was spying on her deserved to spend the rest of his life in prison for stalking. Quelling his urge to smash the clock and the camera inside it against the wall, he pried the camera loose and lifted it out using his handkerchief. He made sure the clock still worked and then repositioned it on the wall.

"Try to spy on her now, you bastard!" he muttered as he pocketed the camera and headed back into the living room.

"Did you find it?" She met his gaze. "You did!" Her hands covered her mouth again. "There really was a camera."

Lucas wiped a hand down his face. "This Doug guy— that's who you were talking about, isn't it?"

"Talking about?"

"When you said *another stalker*, it's him?"

She bit her lip and nodded.

Son of a bitch.

Angela was under a double threat. Not only was she in danger from a Chicago crime boss who wanted to use her as leverage against her ADA brother, but she was also being stalked by an obsessed ex-boyfriend.

He had his work cut out for him now. He'd given her a throw-away answer to her question of how he'd shown up just in time, but as Brad had said earlier, Angela was smart—and quick.

She'd ask him again, as soon as she was over the worst of her fear.

And what was he going to say?

Sugar, your brother sent me here to protect you from a hired hit man. The deranged ex-boyfriend is just a bonus. You know, lagniappe. Oh, and by the way, I've been watching you through hidden cameras, too.

"Yeah," he muttered under his breath. "That'll work."

Chapter Four

Angela frowned at Lucas, trying to make sense of what he'd just muttered. "What did you say? What will work?"

He looked surprised. "Nothing. I need to get you out of here."

"Out of here? But where?"

"Someplace where I can keep an eye on you."

"I can't—" She looked down. She had on a little satin pajama set that wasn't fit for going out in public. Not even at night in the French Quarter. "I need to change clothes."

"Okay, but make it fast." He nodded toward the bedroom.

Angela swallowed. "You got rid of the camera?"

"I've got it with me. I'll give it to Dawson to check out."

"Where was it?"

"In the clock over the chest."

"In the clock." She nodded, hardly able to believe what she was hearing—what she and Lucas were talking about. Doug Ramis had put a camera—a *camera* inside her apartment. In her bedroom.

He'd watched her.

Revulsion and fear made her scalp burn.

"You can go in and get some clothes now."

She took a deep breath.

"Want me to go in there with you?"

"No," she said quickly. "No. I can do it."

He put a hand on her shoulder. "Hey, Brat, you don't have to prove anything to me. Just tell me what you want and where to find them."

Brat. His other childhood nickname for her. Fraught with all the reasons she *had* to do this herself. Neither he nor Brad had ever thought she was capable of handling anything on her own. What they obviously didn't realize was that it was because of them that she *could* take care of herself.

She shook her head, a deep breath fueled her determination. "No," she said firmly. "No."

He studied her for an instant, an odd little smile lighting his expression, then he nodded.

She forced herself to walk steadily through the door, but no amount of determination could stop her from looking at the clock. Or from shuddering. Again.

She grabbed underwear, Capri pants and a short-sleeved top, and went into her bathroom. Lucas had assured her that the camera aimed at her bed was disabled, but it didn't matter. There was no way she could undress in that bedroom. *Ever again.*

She ran to the bathroom, changed in record time and rushed back to Lucas's side.

"Ready?"

She grabbed her cell phone and stuck it in her purse with shaky hands. "What about my things? I've got a test Monday."

"Don't worry about that. Right now we need to get you someplace safe."

"But—where are we going?"

He sent her an unreadable glance. "Not far. You'll see." He took her hand and pulled her toward the door.

"Lucas, how did—"

"No time right now, Ange. If your boyfriend shows up, I don't want him to see us."

"Don't call him that," she said stiffly.

He stopped and looked at her. "I'm sorry," he said gently.

To her surprise, once they were outside, Lucas didn't herd her toward a car. Instead he pulled her with him across the street, where he unlocked the door to the abandoned building that faced her apartment.

She dug in her heels, the hot fear washing over her again. "What is this? Why are we—?"

Lucas slid his arm around her waist and urged her inside. "Come on. It'll be all right."

Stunned by all that had happened in the past half hour or so, Angela let him guide her inside. He used the same key to unlock a door at the top of the stairs and then stood back for her to enter ahead of him.

She walked into a darkened room lit only by one large window that faced the street. And her apartment.

It was the window she'd studied earlier, fantasizing that there might be a sinister figure lurking behind it.

Was that sinister figure Lucas?

Then she saw the table and the array of computers and monitors lined up in front of the big window. Beyond the glass, not fifty feet away, were her French doors.

Lucas had left the light on in her living room, and she could see everything, crystal clear. She stared in horror as the full implication of what she saw sank in.

"Oh, God," she muttered. Her knees went weak and she had to steady herself with a hand against the wall.

Behind her, she heard him shift. When she looked at him, his expression was sheepish and his cheeks were pink.

"I don't understand. What's going on here? This looks like—?" her throat closed up. She couldn't even form the words.

Lucas opened his mouth, but apparently he was having trouble speaking, too, because nothing came out.

Angela tore her gaze away from the window and looked at the monitors lined up on the table.

And moaned.

"Wh-what is this?" she asked, but he didn't have to answer. It was obvious what she was looking at. There on the screens, in high definition, were her kitchen, her living room, the building's lobby—

Her hands flew to her mouth as the meaning of everything she was looking at, everything that had happened, finally coalesced into a clear, cohesive picture. She gasped and gulped in air in huge sobs.

Dear God, Lucas was watching her?

"Y-you?" she stammered. "It was you? Spying on me?"

"No, Ange. Not—not really."

"Oh, God. But Doug knew—what I was wearing. How?"

"Ange, come here."

His voice sounded like it was coming through an echo chamber, barely discernable over the sawing of her breaths. "No," she mouthed.

"Here. Sit down. You're hyperventilating."

"No, no, no—don't touch me." She backed away, pressing her cupped hands more tightly over her nose and mouth, trying to hold in the screams that wanted to escape.

She glanced toward the door.

"No, Ange." He spread his arms and held his hands palm up. "Don't panic. You don't want to do that. You're safe here."

An hysterical laugh escaped her lips. "Safe—?"

She bolted for the door, but he caught her easily and pulled her back against him, pinning her arms.

"No!" She gathered as much breath as she could, in preparation for screaming, but he fastened one arm around her and clamped his other palm over her mouth.

"Listen to me, Ange. I need you to stay quiet and listen."

She tried to bite him, but his hand held her too tightly.

"Ange, you've got to trust me. You've got to calm down. I'm not going to hurt you. All I want to do is protect you."

She exerted all the effort she had to pull against his hold on her. He let her go and she backed away, feeling behind her for the door. She knew it was back there. They'd come straight into the room. The room was dark—all the better to see her with, she figured.

"It's okay, Ange. It's me. You know you can trust me."

She watched him warily. This was Lucas. She didn't understand what was going on. But he *had* rescued her.

She glanced cautiously around. The room appeared to be a warehouse space with no interior walls. The only light was from the window. The only furnishings she could see were the long table, two chairs and a cot. If there was a bathroom somewhere beyond the reach of the pale light, she couldn't see it.

"Ange," he said gently. "Come over here and sit down."

She took several cautious steps toward him. He gestured toward the other chair, but she didn't take it. She stood her ground.

"Tell me what happened," she said flatly.

He shrugged. "Some of it I don't understand myself. I was surprised as hell—"

"Lucas!" she snapped. "Don't give me your charming excuse." Those few words depleted her breath. Her heart was still beating so fast that she could barely get enough air. "Just tell me the truth. Please."

Lucas grimaced internally as he took in Angela's pale face, the shine of unshed tears in her eyes and her horrified expression. He'd scared her half to death, but he'd had no choice. The fact that someone else had gotten into her apartment without her knowing meant she was in more danger than he'd realized

"Okay," he said and drew in a fortifying breath. "I'm here because your brother asked me to watch over you."

Angela's arms tightened around herself, and a tiny wrinkle appeared between her eyes. "My brother? Brad?"

"He's the one." Lucas sent her a small smile, but it only earned him a narrow-eyed frown.

"Brad wanted you to *watch* me?" She shook her head. "That doesn't make any sense. What does he think I'm going to do, that I need watching?"

The color was coming back to her face. That was good.

"It's not what you're doing."

"Then what is it?"

"Remember him telling you about his big case? The one you heard about from Hank Percy?"

"How do you know about that? Oh." She looked at the monitors. "You weren't just watching me. You were listening, too? Oh, this is unbelievable." She dropped into the chair and pushed her fingers through her hair, then covered her face.

"Please just tell me everything," she mumbled.

"Brad is prosecuting a racketeering and murder case against Nikolai Picone. He's a huge crime boss in Chicago. Until Picone is convicted and sentenced, Brad and his family are under an order of protection."

Her head shot up. "Brad? The girls? Are they all right?"

He nodded. "That's what an order of protection is for. They're under twenty-four-hour surveillance, for their safety, and armed security guards are staying in their house and escorting them whenever they leave."

"They think that this Picone might try to hurt Sue or the girls?"

"He's made threats."

"Threats? Why isn't he locked up?"

"He is. He's remanded, but he has a long reach, long enough to give orders from prison."

"Orders? You mean, he *ordered* a *hit* on them?" Her face drained of color again. "I can't believe what I'm hearing."

Lucas clamped his jaw. "Well, believe it."

"Why in *hell* didn't Brad tell me this? Damn him *and* you. Neither one of you have ever thought I could take care of myself. Well, I'm doing quite well, thank you. I don't need your sneaky secret protection. I'm calling Brad right now." She began to dig in her purse.

Lucas caught her hand in his. "No, you're not. You

need to listen to me. Brad didn't want to risk exposing your existence by asking the police to extend the order of protection to you. He felt like it would be putting a bull's-eye on your back. He thought the best solution, since you two have different last names, was to just keep quiet, and make sure you stayed under the radar. Picone's men might never know about you."

"So why are you here? And how, by the way? What about your job?"

"Brad called me to see if I could recommend somebody to watch over you for a week or two, just until the trial is over and Picone is behind bars. He's asking for solitary for Picone, considering his far-reaching influence. I had some time on my hands, so I told him I'd take care of it."

Angela stood and turned away, looking out the streaked, dirty window. "So you came here, wired my apartment with all the latest greatest surveillance equipment and didn't bother to tell me?"

The pale light etched her face in shadow, like a chiaroscuro painting. Her chin went up and her lips flattened. Her fists clenched at her side. She was furious.

After a couple of seconds, she turned her attention to the monitors, studying them. "You got into my apartment? Put all those cameras in there? Did Bouvier let you in?"

"No. The locks on your doors are pathetic. You need new ones."

"I know that. Which one shows the bedroom camera?"

"I didn't put a camera in your bedroom."

She tilted her head and looked at him. "What do you mean? Why not? You put one everywhere else."

He shook his head. "I guess I should have. But I just

couldn't. I'd invaded your privacy already." He pushed his fingers through his hair. "If I had though, I'd have found Doug's spy cam and you wouldn't have had to go through that scare. I'm sorry now that I didn't."

She arched a brow and her chocolate eyes turned to black.

"*You* didn't put a camera in my bedroom. And yet there was one in there. Doug's camera, your camera. Seems to me like there are an awful lot of cameras." She turned to face him. "Do you actually expect me to believe that two spy cams were placed in my apartment at the same time by two different people for two different reasons? Isn't that a little far-fetched?"

She propped her fists on her hips. "So tell me, Lucas, is Doug Ramis working for you?"

Chapter Five

"Come on, Angela," Lucas said, his voice harsh with exasperation. "Of course Doug Ramis isn't working for me. That's absurd. I don't even know him."

"It's a wonder. You seem to be two of a kind." Angela was glad for the anger that was burning in her chest and making her scalp tingle. She needed it to offset the mind-numbing horror of what Lucas had just told her.

He'd been spying on her. Of course, he'd had a very good reason.

There was a hit man after her.

She shook her head and sank back into the chair. "I need to call Brad. He's overreacting, right? Why didn't you tell him? You've never overreacted to anything, ever. I mean, seriously. Hit men don't go after people in real life."

She started to reach for her cell phone, but Lucas put his hand over hers. The look on his face told her he didn't think Brad was overreacting at all. Brad feared for her life. And so did he. And that meant she was in danger.

Suddenly, she felt paralyzed. Her limbs felt too heavy to lift. "Fine," she said, trying to pretend her voice wasn't shaking, "I'll wait till tomorrow to call Brad. Trust me, I'll still be just as mad."

"I believe you. Here," Lucas said, twisting in his chair

to retrieve a bottle of water out of his little refrigerator. "Drink this."

When she didn't reach for it, he put it in her hand. She relished the shock of cold against her palm. "So where is this hit man? Is he already here?"

"I don't know. We don't even know if there actually is one. I've only been here since Monday. But that camera—" he indicated the monitor that was recording the street directly in front of the apartment building's door "—was the first one I set up. So it's been recording every person that passed in front of your building since Tuesday evening."

"Have you seen someone?"

"I noticed one guy hanging around, but my guess is he's your—your ex." He dug through a stack of papers and handed her a poor-quality photo printed on plain paper.

She held it so the light from the window shone on it. The quality was awful, but she had no doubt who it was. "That's Doug."

"He's been walking past your building at least twice a day."

A shudder of aversion shook her.

"My guess is he's trying to catch you on your way out or coming home. He never went inside while I was watching." He gestured toward another monitor. "I have a camera on the rear entrance, too."

"This is so unbelievable," Angela muttered. Her head was pounding and she still felt shaky.

"I know. I burned the feeds from the front entrance camera onto DVDs. I need you to look at them and tell me if you recognize anybody."

"Recognize, as in if I know who they are? Like my neighbors? My friends?"

He shook his head. "More like if you recognize someone you've noticed hanging around."

"Oh." With a start, she remembered the man who'd followed her off the streetcar. "I thought someone was following me. I kept feeling him breathing down my neck on the streetcar. But when I finally worked up the nerve to turn around and look, he'd turned away. He had on a blue baseball cap."

"Yeah? What did the cap say?"

She frowned. "I don't know. I didn't really get a good look at the front."

Lucas inserted a disk into a DVD player and turned the monitor toward her. "I'm going to put this on fast-forward. If you see anything—anything at all that catches your attention—stop it and tell me. We'll look at it. You might be surprised at what your subconscious has noticed."

She nodded. "Okay." She rubbed her temples and squeezed her eyes shut.

Lucas laid a hand on her shoulder. "I know you're tired. Just watch for an hour or so, then you can get some sleep. I'll make up the cot for you."

ANGELA FELT LIKE HER EYES were about to drop out of their sockets. They burned and ached. She'd watched the recording of the people passing by her building for almost an hour, hardly blinking, and the pounding in her head had become a painful drumbeat.

Then she saw him.

"Oh, my God," she muttered.

Lucas looked over at her. "What is it?"

"How do you stop this thing?"

He scooted his chair over, took the remote from her

hand and paused the picture. Then he pressed Rewind. "Tell me when to stop."

Angela blinked and tried to focus on the rapidly reversing pictures. "Okay," she said.

Lucas pressed Play and the two of them watched the screen together.

"There!" she cried.

He rewound and pressed Play.

"There. Stop. That's him. That's Doug."

On the screen, someone walked up and started talking to Doug.

"Oh, no," she whispered.

"What? Who is that?"

"It's Billy Laverne, my neighbor. I had no idea they knew each other."

As she watched, Billy told Doug something, and they both looked around, then Doug nodded and Billy went in the door.

Doug pulled out a cell phone and made a call, then hung up and followed Billy into the building.

"You've never seen them talking before?"

"No. I'm not sure I've ever even seen them on the same day, until yesterday." She read the time and date stamp on the screen. "Wednesday afternoon at four twenty-three. This is after I ran into Billy and Doug on the way home."

"Well, he's either following Billy, planning to sneak into your apartment or meeting with your building superintendent. Speaking of which, how much do you know about your super?"

"Mr. Bouvier? He's a cheapskate, but he seems nice enough."

"Anton Bouvier has several arrests for drug charges. Mostly possession, rather than intent to sell."

"Really?" She was surprised. She didn't like Bouvier, but she'd never had the impression that he was a criminal.

"Really. And didn't you notice his arm? Those are prison tats."

"What?" She had no idea what he was talking about.

"Prison tattoos."

"They let them get tattoos?"

Lucas stared at her for a second with his brows lowered, then he raised them and gave his head a shake. "No. The inmates do them themselves."

"Oh. It's hard to imagine Doug being involved with an ex-con."

"I'm going to have Dawson do a background check on Doug, Bouvier and your neighbor, Laverne. I wouldn't be surprised if at least two of them have a history."

Lucas was right. She shouldn't be living in that building. She needed to find another apartment.

"I don't understand," she said. "Do you seriously think that they're in a big conspiracy to do something to me? Why would they? It makes no sense."

Lucas shook his head. "Maybe not. But if someone in the Picone family is after you, there's no telling what lengths they'll go to."

"So you think the Picone family somehow recruited Mr. Bouvier and Doug and Billy to help spy on me? Isn't that a little preposterous? I mean, Doug probably never did anything overt in his life." She licked her dry lips and tipped the water bottle, but she'd emptied it.

"You're probably right about him. He might never do anything on his own. Plus I'm thinking your super, Bouvier, could walk all over him." As he spoke, Lucas produced a new, ice-cold bottle.

She accepted it gratefully and took a long swallow. The cold liquid eased her parched throat. "I'm getting really scared."

"Good. You need to be scared. I don't want you to underestimate the danger you could be in." He handed her the remote again.

"Watch a little while longer. See how long Doug stays in there. I'm going to take a look at the lobby cam. Whatever he was doing in there, we've got it on disk."

"Okay." Angela pressed Fast-Forward and watched the screen for a few minutes, until the water bottle slipped out of her fingers.

Lucas scooped it up. "Okay. That's enough. You're about to fall asleep sitting there."

She couldn't deny it.

"Here. Lie down." He pointed to the cot. "It's not much, but I can promise you it's more comfortable than it looks."

She eyed the cot skeptically. "It would have to be. What are you going to do?"

"Sit right here. I'm going to see what Doug was up to in your building."

The cot looked like a camp cot, made of aluminum and canvas, but there was a pad on it, covered by a snowy white sheet. And a plump pillow that looked very inviting. Suddenly Angela found it hard to keep her eyes open, even though her whole body was trembling.

"I don't think I can sleep," she said.

"I give you two minutes once your head hits the pillow," Lucas said, touching her shoulder to guide her toward the cot. As warm and comforting as his touch felt, she shrugged it off and leaned backward, away from him.

She didn't want him close to her. Didn't want him

touching her. The first time she'd seen him on the street the other day, she'd realized that, for her, nothing had changed. She was still smitten by her big brother's best friend.

Even though she'd found out that Lucas had been spying on her without her knowledge, just like Doug. Did the fact that he was doing it for her own safety and at the request of her brother make it less heinous? Less creepy?

She didn't think so. The very fact that his touch made her feel safe creeped her out.

He sent her an odd look and then turned toward the monitor. "Go ahead. Try to sleep for a while. I'll be awake."

She slipped off her shoes and sat carefully on the cot, then lay down. The camp bed felt sturdier than it looked. Of course, it would have to be to hold Lucas's long, powerful body.

A big sigh escaped her lips as she let the pillow take the weight of her head.

"Maybe all this won't seem so horrible after I've had some sleep."

Lucas didn't say anything, but his shoulders, silhouetted against the streaked window, stiffened. Her gaze lingered on the nape of his neck. His hair was short, but still long enough to slide over the collar of his pullover shirt. The streetlights shining through the window played over the muscled planes of his biceps and forearms and outlined his long lean body.

Lucas Delancey was as sexy and attractive as he'd always been. And as dangerous.

Deliberately, Angela closed her eyes and tried to wipe her mind clear of the all the dangers that lurked around her. Doug Ramis stalking her. The likelihood that a hit man might be after her. And the very close proximity of the only man on the planet whose kiss had left her longing for more.

LUCAS FROWNED AS HE WATCHED the figures on the screen prancing around in fast-forward. He wished Angela could understand that everything he'd done was for her protection.

But those chocolate eyes had held nothing but disgust when she looked at him. She'd put him in the same category as her ex-boyfriend. In her opinion, they both were perverted creeps.

And he couldn't blame her. He hadn't given her one bit of proof that he was any better than Ramis.

Okay. Sure, he'd rushed over to rescue her, but by now she'd probably figured out that the reason he'd been so Johnny-on-the-spot was because he'd been afraid the camera she'd found was one of his.

Behind him he could hear her soft, even breaths. She'd fallen asleep. He was reluctant to move a muscle for fear of waking her up. But he did want to look at her.

For some reason, it was all he'd wanted to do from the moment he'd first seen her early on Tuesday morning as she headed out to her classes at Loyola. Truth to tell, in some ways, it was all he'd wanted to do for twelve years, since the night she'd surprised the heck out of him by kissing him.

It was why he'd taken this job instead of doing what Brad had asked him to do—what he should have done— recommend someone. He'd taken the job himself, even knowing that once Angela found out what he was doing, she'd hate him.

There was a part of him that had hoped seeing her

again would prove to him that his memory of that kiss was way overrated.

It hadn't. Of course, he could still hope that if he kissed her now it would be a disappointment.

He stole a glance, holding his breath in case she was awake and caught him.

But no, she was sound asleep. Her lips were slightly parted, and her chest rose and fell with her even breaths. Her eyes were closed, the dark lashes resting gently against her cheeks. The only indication that there was anything wrong in her life was the tiny wrinkle between her brows.

His thumb twitched to brush away that frown, but since it was his fault, it would only come back. At least she was sleeping for now.

He turned back to the computer screen and ran the lobby disk up to Wednesday afternoon. He fast-forwarded until he spotted Doug coming through the door from the street. Billy was nowhere in sight.

Sure enough, Doug went up to the door labeled Office and knocked. Within seconds, Bouvier opened the door. He was in an undershirt, and his left upper arm was covered with crudely drawn tattoos—prison tats.

Doug spoke to him for a few seconds, and the super nodded and glanced upward, toward the second floor. Then Doug took out his wallet and handed him some bills.

"Well, creep, whatever you're up to, I've got proof," Lucas muttered. "I'll be damned if I'll let you hurt Angela."

ANGELA WOKE TO THE UNMISTAKABLE smell of café au lait. She turned over and almost ended up on the floor.

"Whoa, Ange," a familiar gravely voice said. "You've got to move slowly on that cot."

She froze. That voice. Her eyes flew open and she saw Lucas. It wasn't the first time in the past twelve years that she'd woken up dreaming about him. But it was the first time she'd managed to conjure him up in the flesh.

"Here," he said. "I got you some coffee."

In the flesh with café au lait. Nice dream. She took the paper cup and sipped it.

"Lots of sugar, right?"

She smiled and took a bigger sip. By the time the warm liquid hit her stomach, she remembered everything.

Doug. Lucas. Cameras. Danger. All the terrifying events of the night before.

She was here in the abandoned building across the street from her apartment because Lucas was hiding her from someone who wanted to kill her. She shivered.

And now she was watching him do what he'd been doing for the past several days—watching her through spy cams.

"You okay?" he asked.

"Don't," she grated. "Don't talk to me."

His eyes narrowed for a second, then he nodded and swiveled around to face the computer screen. He was fast-forwarding through one of the disks. The disks he'd recorded through cameras her brother had ordered set up—to catch a hit man.

She got up and moved to the other chair. She didn't want to watch the figures on the screen, but it was impossible to look away. She sat there, clutching the cup with both hands, until she'd drunk the whole thing. Finally, fortified by the caffeine and sugar, she felt a little less fuzzy-headed. Even slightly less terrified.

Lucas didn't say anything else. He appeared to be

totally concentrated on the computer. He had on a light-weight jacket over a white shirt this morning. His hair was damp and he was freshly shaven. But his eyes were red. She wondered if he'd slept at all.

She focused on the image on the screen. "That's the street camera," she said. "Oh." She chafed her arms. "I can't stand this. The idea that Doug—and *you*—were watching me."

He didn't comment, but the straight line of his back underneath the lightweight jacket he wore this morning seemed to tighten. "This one's yesterday morning. Thursday." He paused the screen and then rewound it a bit.

"That's me." She watched herself leaving her building, her purse and book bag slung over her arm, headed southwest toward the streetcar stop.

It was a bizarre feeling, watching herself.

Lucas muttered a curse.

"What?" Then she saw what he'd just seen. "Oh, my God!" she cried. "That's him! Do you see him? It's the man from the streetcar. Go back."

He was already rewinding.

"There. Stop." Angela swallowed hard, feeling nauseated. "Look at him. He's following me."

Lucas hit Pause, freezing the guy in his tracks, then rewound and played, rewound and played, until he had the best view of the man.

"I thought he was bigger than that," she said.

Lucas nodded. He pulled a small pad out of his pocket and wrote something on it and then clicked the mouse. A couple of seconds later a printer started up.

"He was waiting out there Thursday morning. He must have followed me to Loyola and back. Oh—" she took a deep breath "—I think I'm going to be sick."

Lucas shot her a quick glance and then retrieved a bottle of water out of the refrigerator.

She accepted it gratefully and pressed the chilled bottle against her temple for a few seconds before she opened it and drank. It helped a little.

"How long has he—?"

"I've watched the feed from this camera since we turned it on Tuesday night, and this is the first time I've seen him."

"Are you sure?" But she knew he was. He'd already spotted the guy before she'd said anything. Suddenly she realized he'd been watching this screen all night, looking for him.

"Can you tell anything about his face? I never got a good look. But that's him. I'm sure of it. He's the guy who followed me off the streetcar."

"Watch how he keeps the brim of his cap down over his face. He's used to hiding his face from security cameras. Can you make out the logo on the cap? I'm thinking it's a Chicago Cubs cap. And I'd bet real money that he's hiding a gun under that shirt."

"Gun? He's got a gun?" She sucked in a shaky breath.

"Yeah." He studied the screen for a few seconds. "It'll be easy to determine his height and weight. And if he hangs onto that shirt, he'll be easy to find."

"What are you going to do now? Can you have the police arrest him?"

"For what? Loitering in a tasteless shirt? No. But I'm going to send this disk to Dawson and see if he can get an angle on his face."

"Your cousin Dawson helped you set up the spy cams, didn't he?"

"Yep. He loaned me the equipment from his company."

"What about this building? How'd you manage this?"

"There are several abandoned buildings on this street, which, by the way, makes it pretty unsafe for someone like you."

"Someone like me? You mean, like a *girl*?"

"No, Brat. Like any ordinary civilian. There are reasonable precautions anyone should take. One is choosing a safe neighborhood to live in."

"This neighborhood is just fine. But please. Keep going. Is there anything else you'd like to criticize about my life?"

He cocked his head and that ghost of a smile flitted across his features again. "Yeah, but instead, I'll finish answering your first question. Dawson found this building for me. A developer is about to turn it into condos. Dawson called him, and it turned out he'd worked with his dad, my uncle Mike, on a project or two."

"Convenient."

He nodded and his mouth quirked wryly. "Sometimes it helps when everybody in the state knows your family's name. Even if it is infamy rather than fame."

"Oh, I know that." She took a long swig of cold water. Amazingly, she was becoming inured to the horrific situation she found herself in. She glanced at Lucas and saw that his wry smile had softened, and his green eyes held a spark of amusement.

"What?" she snapped. Suddenly, she felt stiff and uncomfortable. The legs of her pants were twisted and her shirt had ridden up while she was asleep. She stood and straightened her clothes.

"Feel better now?" He nodded toward the water bottle.

"Better? You mean better than last night, when I found out that everybody I know has been watching me through spy cams in my apartment? *My* apartment."

"Yeah. Better than that."

"I need to get back to my apartment. I have to study. I have to return that DVD to Sal. I want to talk to Mr. Bouvier about installing deadbolts—" her voice broke and she shuddered.

"Right. That's not going to happen. You're staying with me until I get all this sorted out."

She pushed her fingers through her hair, trying to pretend she didn't notice them trembling. It didn't work. "But I have a final on Monday."

His brows lowered and his green eyes turned dark. "I'm not interested in whether you pass your test, Ange. Because you definitely won't get the kind of job you want if you're *dead.*"

Chapter Six

The man sitting at the outdoor café nursing a cup of black coffee looked less uncomfortable than he felt. He hated the ridiculous-looking orange and yellow bowling shirt. But it was either that or an even sillier oversized T-shirt, so he could conceal the Glock 22 tucked in his belt.

So now at least he was dressed a little more like the people around him, but he still felt conspicuous. He was used to silk shirts and suits custom-tailored to hide the gun that had been a part of his wardrobe since he was twenty, but which he'd never used outside the shooting range, thanks to Mama. He'd figured he'd be even more conspicuous in a custom-tailored wool gabardine suit. Not to mention he'd probably melt.

He took off his baseball cap and wiped sweat off his forehead. He hated the South. He figured God must, too, because he'd made it hot as hell.

Give him Chicago, where the heat generally stayed where it belonged, in the month of August, and there was no such thing as humidity.

And what was with the streets? They were narrow enough to begin with, and then people parked all up and down them, so there was no room to squeeze one car in, much less two going in opposite directions. The big Lexus he'd rented at the airport was useless here.

He looked around for the waiter. He couldn't drink any more coffee. He needed a bottle of cold water. And he needed to piss. But he wasn't moving, not until he saw her.

He'd been tailing her for two days, since Wednesday, on the hot campus of Loyola University, the steaming streets of the French Quarter, even back and forth on that suffocating streetcar. Both days she'd left her building by eight-thirty, stopped to get a cup of coffee right here at this café and headed toward the streetcar stop.

Not today. He'd been here since seven and it was after nine, and she still hadn't shown. That put a crimp in his plans. He'd decided that neither the Loyola campus nor the streetcar would work for his needs. He liked the idea of catching her walking by an alley at dawn or dusk. That would be quick and clean.

His chest tightened with anxious anticipation. He was going to do it this morning. His first hit. And it would be a doozie. Popping the sister of the ADA who was prosecuting his father. Papa was going to be so proud. See if his brothers teased him about being the baby— Mama's boy—now.

A familiar figure caught his eye.

There she was. The ADA's sister, coming out of the abandoned building across the street from her apartment—with a man.

What the hell?

Not the soft guy who'd been hanging around her apartment building, either. This guy was tall, and nobody would ever call him soft. He looked like he could handle himself.

As he watched, the guy checked out the street, up and down, before he led her to an old red Mustang Cobra and held the door for her. He guided her with his hand at the small of her back.

The way he touched her, the way he looked at her, Tony figured they were lovers.

That explained the change in her routine. *Damn it!*

He sighed as he reached in his pocket for his cell phone. There was no way he'd make it back to Chicago in time for his son's soccer game tomorrow. He'd figured it would be a quick, easy trip. Everything he'd observed in the past few days told him she lived alone and didn't have a boyfriend.

But now she'd acquired a protector. It was going to take longer than he'd thought to eliminate Angela Grayson and scare the ADA into throwing the trial. He knew his plan would work, because if Nikolai Picone's family could find and kill Brad Harcourt's half-sister a thousand miles away, not even an order of protection could keep his wife and daughters safe.

The thought that popped into his brain gave him pause. It was awfully convenient that the guy had shown up when he did. Had Brad Harcourt hired her a bodyguard?

It made sense. He was staying in an unoccupied building across the street from her apartment. He could have been there the whole time, watching, waiting.

Looking for Tony. Well, he wouldn't find it easy to catch Tony Picone. Being the youngest and the smallest of four brothers had its advantages. He'd learned early how to sneak around to find out what he needed to know to hold his own with his older brothers. He'd relied on stealth and blackmail rather than strength. It had worked, to a certain extent.

His brothers gave him a wide berth, but they didn't respect him, either. They respected brawn, not brains.

A smile spread his lips as he watched the vintage Cobra pull away from the curb. Now that he thought about it, this was much better than a classic hit. He didn't have to take Angela Grayson out in the same clumsy, distasteful way the others handled their assignments.

He had a better idea. He'd show his brothers what brains could do. His degree in electrical engineering would come in very handy for what he was planning.

She and her convenient protector would be back soon enough. In the meantime, he had a few purchases to make. Then all he needed was the cover of darkness. His new plan was going to be more elegant than a messy gunshot in an empty alley that could be dismissed as a mugging gone bad.

This message would be loud and clear.

Very clear.

And very *loud*.

ANGELA'S PHONE RANG AGAIN. Both Lucas and Dawson looked at her. She shrugged at Lucas, then excused herself and skipped out of Dawson Delancey's office, and into the reception room. She didn't have to look at the display. She knew who it was. Doug Ramis. It was the third time he'd called in the past hour.

"Oh, no," she muttered, staring at his name as her ring tone played. She didn't want to answer it, but it was torture to listen to the ring and do nothing.

She could feel Dawson's receptionist looking at her. Finally she hit the Reject button to turn off the sound.

She knew Lucas wouldn't be much longer. He and Dawson were winding up their conversation. He could tell her what to do about Doug. Whether to answer and let Lucas listen in or just ignore his calls. Although, if she didn't answer eventually, she knew what would happen. Doug would go by her apartment looking for her. And if he didn't find her there, then what would he do? Call the police? Report her missing?

Just as she reached for her purse to put her phone away, the door to Dawson's office opened and Lucas came out. He was grinning.

She gasped, then quickly covered it with a pretend cough. Dear God, she'd forgotten about that grin.

The Delancey grin. All three of his brothers—hell, the whole Delancey clan—had it.

It lit up the room—the entire world. Lucas Delancey was gorgeous no matter what he was doing, but that grin was worth a million words in any language.

He walked over to where she was sitting. "Everything all right? I'm guessing by your expression that was Doug calling."

She nodded.

"You didn't answer it, did you?"

"No. I didn't know what to do."

"That's the third time he's called since last night, right? He'll call back."

"That's what I'm afraid of."

"I'll deal with him. But first, let's get some breakfast—" he looked at his watch "—or lunch if you'd rather, and then head back."

"I'm not hungry," she said automatically, as she stood.

"Yes, you are. How about Lou-Lou's?"

She tried to shake her head. Tried to say no, that she really wasn't hungry. But Lou-Lou's Café had the best breakfast in the world, bar none. Huge fresh biscuits with butter and homemade jelly, fluffy omelets golden with cheese, thick slabs of smoked bacon and coffee that must have been made in heaven. Her mouth watered just thinking about it.

Lucas sent her a quick smile over the roof of the Cobra. "I can hear your stomach growling from here. I'll take that as a yes."

"I thought you didn't want anyone in Chef Voleur to know you were back here. If we go to Lou-Lou's, the word will be out before she brings the coffee. And my stomach's not growling."

"Oh, yes it is. Lou-Lou'll let us eat in the kitchen. She's really good at keeping secrets."

LOU-LOU WAS THRILLED to see Lucas, and she made Angela bring her up-to-date on Brad's daughters. She sat them down at the big wooden table in the café's kitchen and fed them breakfast and gossip in equally large, mouth-watering portions.

About the time Angela had finished her second cup of coffee, her phone rang again. She looked up at Lucas.

He shook his head.

She ignored the ring, but it wasn't easy. "He's going to keep calling."

"No, he won't. He'll give up eventually."

"Not before he goes by the apartment to see why I'm not answering. What if he gets worried and calls the police or something?"

"If I see him going by your apartment, I'll talk to him." Lucas stood and reached in his back pocket for his wallet.

Lou-Lou waved her ample arms. "Uh-uh," she said. "No. You don't pay in this kitchen. I know you didn't forget that."

Lucas smiled and inclined his head. "I beg your

pardon, Miss Lou-Lou. It was habit—living in the big city, you know." He bent and kissed her plump cheek.

"Next time you come in the front door and sit like regular customers, and I'll have some bread pudding for you."

"Miss Lou-Lou, you're going to ruin my figure."

Lou-Lou cackled as they left the kitchen and headed for Lucas's car. "Okay. When we get back, you can tell me where your books are and I'll go get them. If Doug shows up, I'll make sure he understands not to bother you again."

The lump that had grown beneath her breastbone began to dissipate. "Really? Do you think that'll work?"

He reached around her to open the passenger door. "What do you think?"

With your arm brushing mine? She couldn't think at all. She leaned slightly away as she nodded. She believed him. When he was that close to her, she believed every word he said. The lump shrank.

As he straightened, his gaze zeroed in on the corner of her mouth. He brushed at her lip with his thumb. "Biscuit crumb. You always were a messy eater, Brat."

Her tongue flicked out automatically—and encountered his thumb. Their gazes locked, and for a few seconds neither one of them moved. Finally, she looked down, and he took a step backward.

"Wow," she said, trying to pretend that whatever had just happened between them hadn't. "If I'd realized you could take care of Doug that easily, I'd have called you to come and rescue me ages ago."

He shook his head and gestured for her to get into the car. His face had lost all traces of amusement. "This isn't a joke, Ange. Don't forget that Doug's not your only problem." His eyes turned dark.

"There's a good chance there's a man out there whose mission it is to eliminate you."

BY THE TIME THEY GOT BACK to Chartres Street, Angela's phone had rung three more times.

"He's going to be there," she said flatly. "If I ignore his calls, he'll show up at my door eventually. He's done it before."

Lucas glanced at her sidelong as he squeezed the Cobra into a parking place half a block from his building. He didn't like the tone her voice was beginning to take when she talked about Ramis.

He'd heard it before, in women who were victims of domestic abuse or stalking. There was no way his Ange was going to become one of those women. Not on his watch.

"He might be there, but you won't," he reminded her. "I told you. I'll take care of him."

She nodded, but she didn't seem convinced.

"Hey." He touched her hand briefly. "Trust me, okay?" As he got out of the car, his phone rang. It was Dawson.

"Got something on your boy Ramis," he said.

"Already?"

"You'll see why. I got Ryker to run his name. Apparently he's had a couple of restraining orders, one arrest for assault and one attempted suicide. The suicide attempt was less than a year ago and came only two months after the second restraining order."

"Damn. Thanks. What happened on the assault?"

"The woman dropped the charges."

"Okay. Later." He hung up.

Angela looked at him wide-eyed. "Assault?" she echoed. "Are you talking about Doug? What has he done?"

"Sounds like he can be dangerous. Here's what we're going to do. As soon as Brad's trial is over and we know you're safe, I'll help you move out of that apartment. We'll find you a new one, somewhere other than the Quarter. I think you ought to move back to Chef Voleur. Get rid of the renter and fix up your parents' house. One thing you can say for our nosy little hometown, the folks there take care of each other."

"Angie!"

Angela started and gasped.

Lucas whirled around and saw Doug stalking toward them from across the street.

"Angie, I've been worried sick," he cried as he got closer. "I was about to break into your apartment."

"About to?" Lucas said, maneuvering so that he was between Doug and Angela. He lifted his chin, emphasizing his six-inch height advantage.

"Who the hell are you? And what was that crack supposed to mean?"

Doug's voice rose half an octave. Lucas wasn't entirely successful in suppressing a sneer. The little jerk was scared of him. Of course, he ought to be.

"Angie?" Doug turned his attention to her. "What's going on? Are you all right?"

"Angela has asked you to leave her alone," Lucas said quietly.

"What? No she hasn't. Angie, is this man bothering you?"

Lucas laughed. "Hardly. You're the one bothering her. And I'm going to tell you once, and once only, to stop."

Doug huffed. "I don't know who you are, bud, but Angie and I are together. Tell him Angie."

"Doug, please. You've got to stop this."

Doug sidestepped, trying to get past Lucas to talk directly to Angela, but Lucas moved right along with him.

Doug backtracked and spread his arms. "Okay, okay." His seersucker sport coat gaped open and the unmistakable glint of sunlight on blue steel.

Gun. Lucas reacted quickly and smoothly. He pushed Angela aside and shifted his weight to the balls of his feet, ready for anything. He moved his right hand so he could easily reach his own weapon, which was tucked into his paddle holster at the small of his back, under his jacket.

"Freeze, Doug," he said conversationally. He didn't want to rile the guy any more than he already had.

"Freeze?" Doug cried. "What are you, a freakin' cop?" His hands were still spread, as if he were carrying double six-guns in a B western. He wasn't advancing. That was a good sign—maybe.

"Take it easy." Lucas raised his left hand slowly, holding out his keys and his cell phone. "Angela, take these and go inside. Check in with my cousin for me." He didn't take his eyes off Doug as he willed her to understand that he wanted her to call the police.

Doug's eyes snapped to Angela. His face was pale and he was sweating. Lucas was afraid he was going to panic and draw that gun any second.

Angela reached out and took the keys. Out of the corner of his eye, he saw her ease backward.

Good girl.

"Doug," he said evenly, trying to keep the man's attention on him and away from her. "Doug, you and I need to talk."

Doug whirled on him. "You! You're poisoning her mind. You're scaring her."

"No I'm not. You are the one who's scaring her." *Go, Ange! Get inside!*

"You're a liar! Angie?" Doug didn't see her. "Angie!" He staggered backward and fumbled at his side.

Lucas dove, not daring to take the time to draw his own gun. He aimed for Doug's knees, hoping to take him down before he got a shot off.

He didn't quite make it. A hot streak skimmed down Lucas's back at the same time as the report cracked in his ears. An immeasurably small fraction of time later he slammed into Doug, who was already stumbling backward. They hit the ground hard, rolling. Doug squealed. The gun went flying. Metal scraped noisily against pavement.

Lucas forced the roll to continue, jerking Doug along until he managed to maneuver on top of him. Then Lucas did what he'd wanted to do since the first moment he'd realized that the perverted slimeball was stalking Angela.

He slammed his fist into that pasty, ugly face.

Just once. Not even enough to hurt him—much. Then he stood and drew his weapon. He nudged Doug in the ribs with the tooled toe of his cowboy boot.

"On your stomach," he commanded.

"Somebody! Help me!" Doug whined. He might have been trying to scream, but he was too out of breath and too scared. "You broke my nose!"

"Shut up and spread your arms." Lucas heard sirens. Good. Angela had called them. "Now!"

"Help! I'm hurt!" Doug cried. "He's assaulting me!"

"Spread 'em."

A police car roared up, sirens blasting and lights flashing. Two uniformed officers jumped out. Lucas didn't know the older, shorter cop, but he sure as hell knew the lanky kid who unfolded himself from behind the wheel. He was just a couple of inches shorter than Lucas's six feet four.

Lucas holstered his Sig and stood back out of the way so they could cuff Doug. Once they were done, the taller cop leveled a hostile green gaze at him.

"Ethan," he said with a nod.

His younger brother shook his head, frowning. "Lucas. Why am I not surprised? You couldn't find enough trouble in Dallas? You had to come all the way back to New Orleans just to interrupt my day?"

"Good to see you too, kid."

Ethan's frown deepened and he nodded toward Doug. "What happened here?"

Lucas gave him the facts, including Doug's rap sheet and the information about the camera he'd put in Angela's bedroom.

"Angela? Angela Grayson? Brad Harcourt's kid sister?"

"That's the one."

Ethan looked at him thoughtfully. "Are you going to tell me how you're involved in all this?"

"Sure. But not right now. Dawson's got the camera and the disks that prove he was stalking her. That alone should be enough to put him away."

"Dawson? What's he doing with them?"

"Holding them for me," Lucas said noncommittally. "Then when you add assault with a deadly weapon on a police officer to this lowlife's charges, he should be gone for a long time. That'll make Angela happy."

"Deadly weapon?" Ethan had been making notes on a PDA, but at Lucas's words his head snapped up. "Are you hit?"

Lucas suppressed the urge to arch his right shoulder, where his skin was stinging and he could feel a sticky warmth growing. He wasn't about to tell his brother he'd taken a bullet. It would add attempted murder to the charges against Doug and bury Lucas in paperwork. "Nah. Not because he didn't try though. The runt's runty little gun is over there."

Ethan squinted in the direction Lucas indicated. "Not that runty. It's a Glock 22.

"What about Angela? Is she okay?

Lucas nodded. "I sent her inside."

"So you don't have any witnesses?"

"I don't. You could talk to the crowd though."

Ethan glanced around at the three tourists who'd stopped to see what was going on. Lucas followed his gaze. A little farther down, the magazine shop's owner peered out his door. Up the street in the other direction at the sidewalk café, a man in a bowling shirt sat drinking a cup of coffee and watching idly, while a waiter stood with a tray of dirty dishes, in no hurry to take them to the kitchen.

Ethan sniffed audibly. "Yeah. I'm sure I'll get a lot out of them," he muttered, then turned to check on his partner.

The older cop had deposited Doug in the backseat of the police car. He looked at Ethan and nodded.

"You need to come down and make an official statement," he said to Lucas. "Follow me to the station in your car."

"Listen, kid. I need a few days—"

"Ah, hell, Luke. Give me a break."

"I'm serious. I can tell you this much. Brad called me in to protect Angela. He's prosecuting Nikolai Picone, a major crime boss in Chicago. The family has threatened Brad, so he and his family are already under an order of protection."

"So is this guy—?"

Lucas shook his head. "Nope. I'd stake my reputation on it." He ignored Ethan's raised eyebrow and went on. "He's just lagniappe—a little something extra. Brad's worried that Picone may have found out Angela's his sister and sent someone after her, either to use as leverage to get Brad to throw the case, or to kill her as a warning."

The raised eyebrow was joined by its twin as disbelief spread on his younger brother's face.

"Hey, call Brad. I'll give you his number. But I need a few days. I can't take my eyes or my concentration off her for an instant."

Ethan's jaw flexed and he leveled a gaze at Lucas. "Do you know how much flack I'll get if I let you off the hook? I'm being considered for detective. I won't get another chance for at least three years."

Lucas blew out a frustrated breath. *Damn it.* Ethan had played the detective card. Lucas knew how seldom those opportunities came around. He rolled his eyes. Besides, he owned Ethan for running out on him and Harte, years ago. "Fine. But help me out. Don't make us wait all afternoon."

Chapter Seven

Tony Picone was having a great time watching the scene being played out before him. He'd seen the pale, soft-looking guy who hung around Angela's apartment, waiting for a chance to run into her.

From the moment the guy had stopped Grayson and her protector, Tony had known there was going to be trouble. But he'd figured the big man would just beat the other guy to a pulp and leave him in the street.

He hadn't counted on the pudgy guy having a gun. Or getting a shot off.

As soon as Tony had realized what was going to happen, he'd placed a mental bet. *A thousand bucks the big man takes him before he gets a shot off.*

He'd have lost.

Even from his distance, he'd seen the puff of fibers and the instinctive reaction of the big man's body as the bullet hit his back. He'd dived to clip the smaller guy's knees but hadn't gotten completely under the bullet.

Tony grinned to himself. He probably had a nice flesh wound. It couldn't be more than that, because it had hardly slowed him down at all. He'd still overpowered his opponent and, to Tony's delight, smashed him in the face.

Tony watched as the cops stuffed the shooter into the

back of the police car. It looked like the excitement was about over.

He checked his watch. Five o'clock. He had time to grab some dinner and finish his project before dark.

Just as he reached for his wallet, his cell phone rang. It was his brother Paulo.

"Tony? Where are you? Mary says she doesn't know."

"She doesn't, and what's with asking my wife about me anyhow?"

"Papa's worried, and Mama's about to have a stroke."

Tony fumed. "How come Mama knows I'm not there?"

"Because Papa wanted us all in court today since we missed the past couple of days. And nobody could find you."

Tony didn't answer.

"God, Tony, you're gonna break Mama's heart. You went to Louisiana didn't you? Whaddaya think you can do down there?"

"Shows what you know. That ADA has a half-sister down here. I'm going to take her out. That'll show Harcourt that his family won't be safe until he lets Papa go."

"You're chasing the half-sister? By yourself? You gonna put Mama in the hospital worrying about you."

"She's not sick, is she?"

"Not yet."

"Listen, Paulie. I got a plan. You wait and see. Tomorrow Angela Grayson's death will be all over the news. And I'll bet you the ADA will make sure Papa gets out."

"Whaddaya think you're gonna do? You never shot nobody in your life."

"Remember how I always tried to get you and Milo

and Nikki Jr. to try out some of my ideas? Well, just wait and see what I've got in store for that ADA's sister. It's better than shooting."

"Come on, Tony. Don't tell me you're trying out one of your complicated ideas. Milo's gonna snatch one of Harcourt's kids. When the hired security guards take them to school."

"And you talk about my ideas? How's he planning to get past the armed guards?"

"There's about two minutes when the kids stand outside the car, with only one guard. It's a simple grab-and-go. Takes care of the ADA, and it won't get Mama's baby boy killed or put away for the rest of his life."

"You don't think I can do it, do you? Well, just watch. And tell Mama not to worry." Tony jabbed the Off button, his ears burning in fury. By tomorrow Paulo and Milo and Nikki Jr. would be singing a different tune.

What Paulo had said about Mama bothered him, though. The last time she was in the hospital, she'd gotten pneumonia and almost died. Tony's heart pounded with alarm and he fingered his phone, wondering if he should call her.

But Mama had to learn sometime that Tony was no longer the baby. Hell, he was thirty-six and married, with kids. He loved his mama, but she'd stifled him long enough. She needed to be concentrating on her grandchildren.

He sucked in a deep breath and drained his water glass. And he needed to be concentrating on his plan.

He looked at the building where Angela and the big guy were staying, then at the last couple of rubberneckers as they headed down the now-empty street.

He was pretty sure Angela and her protector wouldn't go anywhere else today. She'd probably be bandaging his wounds—taking care of him.

The way he was hovering over her, Tony figured if he hadn't gotten into her pants yet, it wouldn't take him long. Especially now. What woman didn't like taking care of a man's wounds? Taking care of all his needs. Tony licked his lips and signaled the waiter to bring his bill.

Yeah, he was sure they'd be busy—all night.

IT WAS FIVE O'CLOCK BEFORE Ethan and his partner had dispersed the small crowd of curious bystanders that had gathered to see what all the fuss was about and headed off with Doug Ramis in tow, followed by Lucas and Angela in Lucas's car.

Lucas glanced up and down the street as he pulled away from the curb, but he didn't see anything out of the ordinary.

Chartres was its normal quaint and quiet self now that the excitement was over. The little sidewalk coffee shop where he'd run into Angela the day before was nearly deserted. The single patron, dressed in that ridiculous bowling shirt, was digging for his wallet.

Lucas did a double take. Who wore those things, anyway? They were usually made of nylon or polyester, which made them completely inappropriate for the muggy New Orleans summer. The guy had to be a tourist.

Lucas took a deep breath and arched his neck, then grimaced as the material of his shirt pulled against his stinging back. Thank God no one had seen any blood, or the hole that had to be somewhere around the collar of his jacket.

"Are you okay?" Angela asked.

Lucas nodded. "Yeah, sure. Just landed a little hard on my shoulder when I dove at your *boyfriend's* knees." He knew what he was doing by calling Ramis her boyfriend again, after she'd asked him not to. And it worked. Her chin lifted, and she folded her arms and turned away. For the rest of the trip she stared out the passenger window.

Better than staring at him.

At the police station, Ethan directed them to an interrogation room, where he asked them each to write a statement of the events that led up to Doug drawing his gun.

"I don't have two separate rooms to put you in, so do me a favor and don't collaborate on your stories, okay?"

Lucas snorted.

Ethan turned to Angela. "Okay, Angela?"

"Of course, Ethan."

Lucas sat with his back to the wall. He didn't want to take a chance that any telltale blood had seeped through his jacket. It was bad enough that he had to spend an hour or more on witness statements. But there was no way he'd allow himself to be forced to go to the hospital for a mere scratch. Granted it stung, but scratches did sting.

Lucas wrote rapidly and quickly finished his statement. He sat back and watched Angela as she pored over hers.

"You need any help?" he finally asked.

She shook her head without looking up.

Just then Ethan stepped into the room. "How's it going?"

"I'm done," Lucas said. "I want to talk to Ramis."

Ethan shook his head in resignation. "How many ways can you buck the system, Luke? You have no authorization to talk to anyone here."

"You could get the detectives to let me interrogate him if you wanted to. It's a serious matter. So what if it's not my jurisdiction."

"So what if you're on suspension."

Lucas felt like his younger brother had hit him. He should have expected Ethan to find out, but it didn't mean he had to like it.

He felt Angela's reproachful gaze. He hadn't exactly lied to her, but he certainly hadn't been forthcoming about how he happened to be available to play body-guard. It took all his willpower not to duck his head.

Instead, he scowled at Ethan and went on the attack. "Dawson tell you that?" he snapped.

"No. I called your precinct out in Dallas."

Ethan's shadowed gaze met his. He'd let his kid brother down again. He'd done his best, but he was a poor substitute for Robbie. Their oldest brother had been their protector all through their childhood, until he'd joined the service when he was eighteen.

Eight months later he was dead, and Lucas, only thir-teen, had taken Robbie's position as the fortress that stood between his dad and his two younger brothers. Ethan had looked up to him, until he left. At least the old man had never whaled on his only daughter, Cara Lynn.

For a split second, Ethan's hard gaze turned quizzical, but then he blinked and glanced toward the window.

"You didn't think I'd assume you were just taking a few days off, did you?"

There was no future in trying to explain anything, so Lucas got back to the issue at hand. "I need to talk to Ramis. I need to find out if he could be involved with the Picone family."

"The Picone family. Your big Chicago crime family who's after Angela."

Lucas nodded.

"I talked to Brad. He confirmed your story."

Lucas frowned. "Thanks for believing me," he said wryly.

"You'd have done the same thing if our positions were reversed."

He couldn't argue with that. Still, Ethan was acting more like their cousin Ryker every day. *By the book.* He'd make a good detective. Tight-assed, but good.

A sliver of pride nicked the corner of Lucas's heart. Maybe—hell, probably—a better detective than Lucas himself was. He smiled wryly to himself—not such a stretch these days.

"Let me talk to the detectives on the case. Do I know any of them?"

"Dixon Lloyd is the lead. James Shively's his partner."

"I don't recognize the names. Can I talk to Lloyd?"

Ethan opened his mouth but immediately clamped it shut and shrugged. "Sure. I'll let you and Dixon duke it out."

ANGELA WATCHED LUCAS AND ETHAN leave the room together. If she remembered correctly, Ethan was three years younger than Lucas. He had inherited more of their father's Irish fairness than Lucas, who was dark-haired like his beautiful mother. But both of them possessed the angular lanky grace of the Delancey clan.

And for all their differences, they looked remarkably alike.

Probably neither one of them would be happy to hear that.

She quickly finished her statement and read it over before she signed it. Even though this was her own description of events as she'd experienced them, as she read them over she found them difficult to believe.

It seemed inconceivable, even now, that Doug had really spied on her, had been in her apartment while she was away. He'd set up that spy cam. What else had he done while he was there—alone?

She shuddered.

Then today he'd apparently gone crazy. He'd pulled that gun and waved it at Lucas. It amazed her that Lucas had stayed so calm. That he'd managed to bring Doug down without getting hurt or letting Doug hurt anyone else.

She dropped the pen onto the table and pushed her fingers through her hair. For a few moments she sat, her elbows propped on the table, her head in her hands.

She was tired. It was an odd weariness, bone deep, caused not by long hours or lack of sleep, but by nerves. Last night, in that abandoned building with Lucas, had been the first time she'd slept well in several weeks.

She straightened and rubbed her eyes, then arched her neck. Just as she started to massage a knot of tension with her fingertips, the door to the interrogation room opened. It was Ethan.

"I thought you might like to hear what Ramis has to say." He stood in the doorway, his hand on the knob.

Angela stood and reached for her statement.

"Leave it," Ethan said. "One of the secretaries will get it."

He led her through another door, into a darkened closet-like space with glass covering one wall. The lone occupant, a tall, dark-haired man with classic features and an air of elegance, nodded to her.

She gave him a small smile.

"This is Detective Dixon Lloyd. Dixon, this is Angela Grayson."

Angela held out her hand, and Lloyd grasped it firmly and briefly, then nodded toward the glass. Through it Angela saw Doug sitting at a plain wooden table. He shifted uncomfortably and pulled on his left arm, which was handcuffed to his chair. He looked miserable, and a little wild. His clothes were dusty and spattered with blood. His lip was cut and swollen and blood dripped from his nose.

Where Lucas had hit him. She didn't know that—not for sure. But she'd noticed that the knuckles of Lucas's right hand were abraded. It wasn't hard to put the pieces together, especially knowing Lucas. He'd always been quick to defend her, or anyone else who needed it.

At that moment Lucas appeared through a door. He slammed a file folder down on the table out of Doug's reach and then walked over and shoved Doug's chair back from the table with the toe of his boot.

Angela could tell by the look on his face that he was pissed.

She pressed her lips together.

Ethan must have noticed the same thing because he muttered, "Watch it, Luke. Just watch it."

On Angela's other side she felt Detective Lloyd send a questioning glance Ethan's way, but Ethan didn't respond.

"So, Doug. Tell me. How many women have you terrorized, stalking them and spying on them because you don't have the *cojones* to face them?"

"Get away from me." Doug turned and looked at the glass. Angela knew from that side it was a mirror, but Doug's swollen eyes seemed to seek out her gaze. "Get him away from me. He broke my nose. He hit me."

Lucas nudged his chair again. "Talk to me, Doug. Or maybe you'd get your kicks by watching me through a spy cam?"

Doug's eyes narrowed. "I don't know what you're talking about," he said.

"Sure you do. We found that camera you set up in Angela's bedroom. Must have been pretty exciting stuff. Watching her undress. Watching her come out of the bathroom. Watching her sleep."

Angela's fists clenched at her sides. Lucas's words made her feel ill. What was he doing? *Don't talk to him about me like that*, she wanted to shout.

"Listening to her soft, even breaths…" Lucas went on.

Doug shook his head furiously. "No! I didn't have sound!"

Lucas stayed near the door, so that Doug had to turn his head to see him. He leaned against the wall and crossed his arms across his chest.

When he did, Angela noticed a brief grimace cross his face. His shoulder. He'd said he'd fallen hard when he dove to stop Doug from shooting.

"What?" he asked Doug. "You didn't have what?"

"Sound. I couldn't—" Doug stopped. "I don't know anything," he finished lamely.

"Right. So tell me, Doug, who're you working for? Who told you to put a camera in Angela's bedroom?" He looked toward the mirror.

Angela saw a gleam in his eyes that she recognized. It was the same triumphant look he'd always gotten when he was about to run the ball for a touchdown, or sink the winning basket, or tease her unmercifully.

His gaze met hers through the glass, although she knew he couldn't actually see her. He winked and her heart leapt in her chest. Then he reached for the file folder and opened it, making a big deal out of paging through it until he finally found what he was looking for.

"Right here, it says that two years ago, you were arrested for voyeurism after a woman spotted you watching her through her apartment window using binoculars."

"No. She misunderstood."

Lucas laughed. "She misunderstood why your binoculars were pointed at her?"

"Don't—laugh at me. She thought it was dirty, but it wasn't. I wasn't doing anything. I was just watching."

"And a year ago when a woman came home with her young daughter and found you in her bedroom going through her underwear drawer?"

Angela moaned softly. How could she have gone out with such a sick pervert even once? Why didn't she know just by looking at him, by talking with him, what kind of person he was? Maybe Lucas was right. Lucas and Brad. Maybe she really couldn't take care of herself.

Ethan answered her as if she'd spoken aloud. "You couldn't have known, Angela. Don't beat yourself up. These guys manage to do what they do because they appear so harmless. It's only when someone can finally expose their ugly underbelly that people realize they've been fooled."

"Thanks," she said dully.

"From what Lucas told me, you already knew there

was something wrong with him. You'd already told him you didn't want to see him anymore."

"Small comfort."

"No," Dixon Lloyd said. "That should be a very big comfort to you. Sadly, a lot of people don't realize what's happening until it's too late."

On the other side of the window, Lucas was talking again. "No answer for that one, Doug? Because it says right here that you knocked her down and pushed the little girl out of the way and ran like the coward you are."

"I was—I was in the wrong apartment."

"Yeah? So it was a mistake that you broke into the apartment of the woman who'd been warning you for weeks to leave her alone?"

Doug didn't answer.

Lucas closed the folder and set it down. "Here's what I want to know, Doug. Why were you talking to Billy Laverne yesterday? And why were you handing cash over to Angela's building super a few minutes later?"

Doug stared at the table.

Lucas kicked his chair again. He leaned over until he was in the other man's face. "I asked you a question, Doug. What was the money for?"

"Take—take these handcuffs off. You're holding me against my will. Am I under arrest?"

"You bet you are. For assault with a deadly weapon. And in case nobody told you, you have the right to remain silent." Lucas leaned even closer.

"But I gotta tell you, Doug, if you choose to remain silent, I'm going to wipe this floor with you. By the time I'm done you won't be able to taste anything but dirt for the next five years, which, coincidentally, will be the same amount of time you'll be spending in prison. You're going to enjoy prison, *Doug*."

Doug was white as a sheet by the time Lucas straightened.

From beside Angela, Dixon said, "He's good."

Ethan sighed. "Yeah. Not exactly by the book, though."

Dixon chuckled. "By-the-book's not all it's cracked up to be, kid."

"Yeah? Well, neither is being a cowboy."

Lucas took a deep breath. "So, Doug, what do you know about a man named Picone?"

Doug's white face scrunched into a perplexed frown. "Picone? Nothing. I never heard the name."

Lucas walked around behind Doug's chair. He looked up at the glass and raised a brow.

"Luke believes him," Ethan said.

Then Lucas grabbed the arm of Doug's chair and swung him around. "I tell you what, Doug. I'll see what I can do about your sentence if you tell me just exactly what was going on between you and Bouvier. I'll know if you're lying, and you'll get to enjoy the pleasures of prison for as long as I can possibly get you in for."

"I swear, all I was doing was getting Bouvier to scare Angie a little. I was hoping she'd come to me to protect her."

Lucas waited.

"I got him to hire one of his repairmen to knock on her door late at night, wanting in. He was supposed to scare her. That's all."

"And Billy?"

"Billy was the one who told me she was asking if a repairman had been working in the units. He figured she was afraid someone had gone into her apartment while she wasn't there."

"So you're claiming that's what the money was for?" Lucas crossed his arms.

"Yeah," Doug said eagerly. "Just to pay the repairman."

"Where'd you get the gun?"

"I, uh—from a guy." Doug's forehead was spouting beads of sweat.

"A guy. Would that be a guy we've already talked about?"

Doug's eyes widened and snapped to Lucas.

"Well I'll be damned," Dixon drawled. "Lucas sunk it in one."

"What?" Angela whispered.

"Listen," he muttered.

"Let me guess. Not Billy Laverne."

Doug swallowed visibly.

"That leaves Bouvier. So how'd you know he'd be open to getting you a gun?"

No answer.

Lucas got in his face again. "How, Doug?"

"I-I'm thinking I might need a lawyer."

Both Dixon and Ethan stiffened.

"Yeah? You think so?" Lucas pushed a pad of paper over to Doug and took a pen from his pocket. "And here I was just about to offer you a deal."

"He doesn't have the authority to do that," Ethan protested.

"A deal?" Doug's face lit up a bit.

"Yeah. Tell you what. You write out your complete confession, including Bouvier and the gun, the cameras in Angela's apartment and anything else you think you need to confess."

"And you'll keep me out of prison?"

Lucas laughed. "I kind of doubt that, Doug. But I'll see what I can do. Let's just say that the more you tell us, the easier it'll go on you."

Angela breathed a sigh of relief and heard similar sighs from the two men in the room with her.

Lucas had broken Doug. Not that she'd doubted him, but it was still a relief to know that Doug Ramis would be behind bars for the next several years.

Watching Lucas as Ethan went into the room to receive Doug's statement, she found herself believing, as she had when she was a child, that Lucas could do anything.

Chapter Eight

Lucas hung back as he and Angela left the police station. So far he'd managed to keep anyone from noticing the slight rip in the back collar of his jacket made by the bullet that had streaked across his back.

Thank goodness.

He hadn't had a chance to check the wound, but apparently blood hadn't seeped through his shirt to his jacket, or someone would have commented on it by now.

If Ethan or Angela even guessed that he'd been hit, he'd never get away without being forced to go to the emergency room. And that meant more paperwork, more delays and, if the wound was worse than he thought, possibly an overnight admission. He couldn't take the chance that he'd be separated from Angela for even short time. He held his breath until the automatic door closed behind him and he climbed into his car. Once his stinging back pressed against the leather seat, he was home free.

He started the car, and as soon as Angela closed the passenger door, he pulled away and headed back for Chartres Street.

"Thank you," she said.

He sent her a quick glance. "For what?"

"For what you did in there. The way you took care of Doug. I feel—safer now."

He shifted and clamped his jaw as the material of his shirt tore at the stinging place on his back. He felt sticky warmth and knew he was bleeding again.

"All in a day's work, sugar."

For some reason, that answer irritated her. She crossed her arms and turned away to look out the window, just as his phone rang.

It was Brad. "Hey, Harcourt. What's up?"

Angela turned back.

"Luke, I've been stuck in court all day, and I have a meeting starting in two minutes, but I wanted you to know that all the Picone kids showed up in court today, except for Tony."

"Tony. So you think he may be the one who's after Ange?"

"Who?" Angela said. "What's he saying?"

Lucas gestured for her to stay quiet.

"I guess," Brad answered. "Until two days ago, he was in court every day. Those two days, the brothers must have been having some kind of pow-wow. And now today, Nikki, Milo and Paulo, and even the brother-in-law, were there, but no Tony."

"Okay. Can you get me that picture?"

"I'll ask my secretary. I've gotta go. I'll let you know if I find out anything else."

"Brad, one more thing. Why would Picone send the baby for this kind of job?"

"You got me. I'd have thought he'd send Paulo. Word is that he's a crack shot with a long-range rifle."

"Long-range? Are you serious?"

"Things are changing. Paulo is suspected of picking

off a rival lieutenant in broad daylight with a sniper rifle, but we couldn't prove anything."

"I see. Well, keep me posted. Talk to you later." Lucas hung up. So the hit man who was after Angela could be Tony Picone, the youngest of the brothers. The one who supposedly wasn't involved in the family business. Had he struck out on his own? Or was he just the scout? Maybe Paulo was heading this way.

"That was Brad? You didn't tell him anything about Doug and the shooting."

"Nope." And he wasn't going to tell her about Tony and Paulo, either. He figured the less Angela knew about the hit man or men, the better.

"Why not? Don't you think he needs to know?"

Lucas pulled over to the curb in front of their building and parked. "No. I don't think he needs to know. He was on his way to a meeting, and the trial is winding down. What he needs to do is concentrate on putting Picone away. Knowing about Doug would just worry him."

She nodded. "I guess you're right. But what was that about long-range?"

"Plans," Lucas lied. "He knows I've got to get back to Dallas soon." He felt her suspicious gaze. She'd always been able to tell when he was lying. "I'll call Brad on Monday and let him know what happened. Meanwhile, you go on inside. I'll be up in a few minutes."

"What are you going to do?" Before the words were out of her mouth, her face changed. "You're going to talk to Bouvier, aren't you? Detective Lloyd said he was going to do that."

"I just want to check him out. See what he knows."

"Then I'm coming with you."

Lucas opened his mouth to protest, but the look on Angela's face stopped him. He didn't feel like arguing.

And it didn't matter. She'd never have to deal with Bouvier again. She was never going back to that apartment. After all this was over, he was going to make sure she moved into a safer place.

"Fine," he said. "Let's go." He guided her across the street with his hand on the small of her back. Inside the lobby, he headed straight for the door labeled Office and rapped sharply.

He could hear someone moving around inside. He knocked again. As the door opened he stood back, leaving Angela in Bouvier's line of sight. He didn't want to take the chance that Bouvier would spot him and slam the door.

"Angela," Bouvier said. "Can I help you with something?"

"You can help me," Lucas said, stepping forward and setting his foot against the bottom of the door. "I'm Detective Lucas Delancey." He flashed his badge, too quickly for Bouvier to focus on it. "I'd like to ask you a few questions."

Bouvier's dark brows lowered. "Questions? About what?"

"Let's do this inside."

"Angela? I don't understand. Is this about the deadbolts? 'Cause I was going to get them today." Bouvier suddenly looked extremely nervous.

"Inside?" Lucas said again.

Bouvier looked behind him, then opened the door wider and stood back.

Lucas let Angela precede him into the office. Bouvier sat stiffly behind a scratched wooden desk and Angela sat in a straight-backed chair. Lucas stood with his injured back to the door.

"You're the super for this building? Who owns it?"

Bouvier shifted in his chair and rubbed the crudely etched tattoo on his left biceps. "A company that owns several apartment buildings around New Orleans. What's this got to do with—?"

"And you've got a couple of side businesses, right?"

"I don't understand—"

"Guns."

Bouvier stopped fidgeting and stared at him.

"Guns. You want to tell me about it?"

"You think I'm selling guns? That's crazy."

"Is it? What about Doug Ramis?"

Bouvier's eyes narrowed. "Ramis? What'd he tell you?"

"It's time for you to stop asking questions and start answering them. I'd be happy to take you downtown if you'd be more comfortable talking there."

"No. I can tell you this. Doug said he'd been mugged. He wanted to be able to protect himself, but he didn't know how to shoot. I loaned him a gun so he could practice at a shooting range."

"You loaned him a gun. And he *loaned* you money in return."

"What?" Bouvier's gaze wavered.

"We've got you on a surveillance camera, accepting money from Ramis."

"You've—" he turned pale.

"Clear as a bell. I can run you in for trafficking in illegal arms. I'm sure you know the gun Ramis was caught with was not street-legal. And with your record—"

"Okay, okay. I—accepted money from him. He insisted. But that's the only time. Swear to God."

"Sorry, Bouvier. I don't believe you. But I tell you what. I'm not interested in Ramis. He's small potatoes. Who else have you sold guns to in the last week?"

"Nobody! I swear."

"No? How about a guy in a Cubs cap?"

Bouvier's face changed, and Lucas felt a jolt of triumph. Maybe his hunch was going to pay off. He waited. There were very few criminals who could sit in silence for very long while a cop stared at them and said nothing. For some reason, they always felt compelled to fill the silence.

"Okay. A few days ago a guy in an orange shirt and a Cubs cap stopped me on the street asking directions. Then he started feeling me out about where to buy—you know—stuff like that."

A Cubs cap. Lucas waited. Angela turned toward him, her expression shocked, but he didn't look at her.

"He gave me three Benjamins, so I gave him a couple of names."

"Why you?" Lucas asked him, but he already knew the answer. The Chicago Cubs baseball cap cinched it. The man was her hit man. Apparently whoever he was, he was a pretty good judge of people. It hadn't taken him any time to tap Angela's own building super as a source for his weapon.

Bouvier shrugged. "No idea."

"No kidding? Are you sure you didn't know him from somewhere?"

"I never saw him before—or since."

Lucas stared at him some more.

Bouvier fidgeted and rubbed his thumb over his tattoo. "He might have noticed my tats."

"That's what I'm thinking. Where'd you serve?"

"Big Muddy."

Lucas nodded. Big Muddy River Prison was located in southern Illinois, not far from St. Louis, Missouri.

"Did you two have a nice talk about your mutual friends in Chicago?"

Bouvier didn't answer, but the panicked look on his face told Lucas all he needed to know.

"What'd he look like?" Lucas growled.

Bouvier shrugged. "Medium. Medium height. Medium build. Maybe a little on the skinny side. White. He kept his hat and his sunglasses on, but he looked Italian or something. You know, dark."

"Anything else you noticed?"

"Nah. Just that he was nervous."

"Nervous how?"

"He was always wiping his mouth and his forehead, probably not used to sweating."

"Did you ever let him into Angela's apartment?"

"No!" Bouvier wiped sweat off his forehead as his eyes darted back and forth from Angela to Lucas. "No, I swear. Look, I don't know nothing about him, except his name is Tony and he needed a connection for a gun. That's all."

"Have you seen him since?"

Bouvier shook his head. "I haven't been paying attention. I don't like to be involved in the—other side of the gun business. You know?"

"Right." The longer he talked to Bouvier, the more irritated he got with Angela. What was she doing living here, around all these lowlifes?

He stood and pulled out a card. "Tell you what, Bouvier. If you see your friend Tony again, you call me." He stuck a finger in Bouvier's face. "You say one word to him and I'll drag you in as an accessory to attempted murder. Got that?"

Bouvier swallowed.

"Have you *got* that?" Lucas growled.

"Yeah. Yeah. I swear."

"And another thing. You put a padlock on Angela's apartment and hold her stuff until we come and get it. Don't turn it over to anyone. *Anyone*, but me. You got that?"

Bouvier held up his hands. "Yeah, I got it. Swear to God."

LUCAS MANAGED TO STAY BEHIND Angela until they got inside the lobby of the abandoned building.

"I can't believe what Mr. Bouvier did," she said as she climbed the stairs ahead of him. "He sells guns? And I actually thought he was a nice guy who'd watch out for me."

"How did you decide *he* would watch out for you?"

"He told me he would."

Lucas laughed. "Yeah, well, you've always been a little gullible."

"I have not."

"Oh, yeah? What about the time Brad and I convinced you that bats fed off bat trees, and if you followed one, you could find a tree that grew baseball bats."

"I was *eight*."

"And now you're—what? Twenty-eight? And you still believe a guy is nice, just because he tells you he is." Climbing the stairs aggravated the stinging and burning of his wound, but not so much that he couldn't appreciate Angela's backside in the snug-fitting pants. He hung back so it stayed at his eye level.

He probably ought to enjoy it as much as possible while he had the chance. Because once the danger to her was over, and he was reinstated, there was a chance he'd never get to see it again.

"There's nothing wrong with believing the best of people." She threw the remark over her shoulder.

"There is if it could get you killed. Try being just a little suspicious when something seems too good to be true."

She turned and caught him staring at her butt. To her credit, she didn't mention it. "Too good to be true. Like how you happened to show up at the very moment I discovered Doug was watching me? And never once thought it would be appropriate to mention that you put spy cams in my apartment, much less that you'd been *suspended* from the Dallas police force! What did you do?"

"Nothing. Just tried a little too hard to stop a guy from putting his wife in the hospital. It was my bad luck that the abuser was the son of a Texas senator."

She stared down at him. "What do you mean 'a little too hard'?"

"*That's* the part you heard?" Lucas snorted.

"I heard all of it. So they suspended you for excessive force. Is that why Ethan called you a cowboy?"

"He called me a cowboy?"

Her gaze traveled slowly down his legs to his tooled cowboy boots. "I don't think he was referring to your boots, was he?"

He shrugged. "Who knows. Are we going to stand here and talk about it on the stairs?"

She sniffed and whirled around. And Lucas was pretty sure she swayed her hips more than absolutely necessary as she stalked up the stairs.

For Lucas, it was all good. He got to watch her very nice butt—an innocent pastime, considering that there was no way in hell he'd ever act on any attraction he felt for his best friend's kid sister.

Plus, the madder she was at him, the less likely she was to notice bloodstains on the back of his jacket before he could slip into the bathroom.

He decided to add a little more fuel to the fire. "By the way, speaking of my little brother, it's quite a coincidence that he showed up to take that call, isn't it? Why didn't you call 911?"

"When you gave me your phone? You *said* to call your cousin." Her voice sounded defensive.

"If I'd said to call 911, Doug might have panicked and used that gun."

"Well, I called Dawson. He must have called Ethan."

"Yeah. I figured that out." He laughed shortly. "You'd think he might have been busy or off duty or something. There should still be a few cops around who aren't kin to me."

"What's the problem between you and Ethan?"

"When I moved to Dallas, he felt like I abandoned him and Harte." Lucas felt the sting of guilt in his gut.

"Abandoned them? Why would he think that?"

"He had good reason."

"What good reason?" she persisted.

"Never mind. It was probably a good thing Ethan did take the call. I might not have been able to convince another cop to let me question Doug. Or to get his bail hearing put off until Monday."

"Monday? Are you expecting all this to be over by Monday?"

He hated to burst her suddenly floating bubble of hope, but he didn't believe in lying to people just to make them feel better. He shot straight from the hip. Forewarned was forearmed.

"There's no telling. I doubt it, actually." He took a

deep breath. "Even with the information from Bouvier, I'm no closer to finding your hit man than I was. Doug sort of threw a monkey wrench into the works."

At the top of the stairs, Angela headed toward the refrigerator.

Lucas paused on the landing. He needed to get to his duffle bag and grab a clean shirt, then escape to the bathroom before she had a chance to notice that anything was wrong. But the bag was on the other side of the cot. And the cot was on the other side of her. There was no way he could reach it without turning his back to her. And that was a calculated risk.

He'd been doing this dance all afternoon without having any idea whether there was blood on his jacket. Hell, there probably wasn't. But if he could just get into the bathroom and get cleaned up, then he'd no longer have to worry about it. He could stick his head out and ask her to hand him the bag, as if he'd forgotten to get it.

He sidled toward the bathroom door.

"Want some water?"

God, yes. Suddenly, his mouth was so parched and dry that he couldn't swallow. And he felt slightly woozy, as if his head were encased in a soap bubble. A hot, suffocating soap bubble.

There's water in the bathroom. He just needed to get there.

"Lucas?"

"No." He turned, hoping the shadows in the corners of the room were dark enough to hide any blood. Hoping that she wasn't looking. Hoping the increased stinging on his back didn't mean he was bleeding again.

He's almost made it to the bathroom door when a metallic clatter echoed across the wooden floor. He looked down automatically, but didn't see anything.

"What was that?" Angela asked

"Don't know."

She headed toward the sound, toward him, looking around on the floor. He didn't care what had made the noise or where it had come from. All he cared about was getting to the bathroom before Angela saw any blood.

"Here it is," she said, bending down to pick it up. "Lucas? Oh, my God! It's a bullet."

Chapter Nine

"Lucas! Where did this bullet come from? It has blood on it." She started toward him. "Wait. What's that on your collar?" she cried.

Lucas didn't stop. He reached the bathroom door in two strides and slammed it behind him.

Make that *almost* slammed it. She caught it before it closed and shoved it open. It hit the wall with a bang.

"You're bleeding. You *did* get shot. Why didn't you tell me?"

He fingered the torn back of his collar. "It's nothing," he growled. "Would you bring me my bag? It's on the other side of the cot."

"Nothing? That's blood!" She held out her hand. "And this is a bullet."

He shrugged carefully. "Doug pulled his gun and I dove for his knees. I wasn't fast enough."

He felt her measuring gaze, almost as hot as the sting of the bullet, on his back. "So if you hadn't moved he'd have shot you in the stomach? Oh, my God! Lucas!"

"Or missed. I'd have probably been better off just stepping out of the way. I'm pretty sure hitting me was an accident."

"Take your coat off. I need to see how bad it is."

"It's not bad."

Bending over the sink, he splashed cold water on his face. He suppressed a groan as the material of his shirt pulled at his wound. "Get my bag?"

"Don't you dare lock me out. If you do I'll call Dawson and tell him and Ethan that you've been shot."

He lifted his head and looked at her reflection in the mirror. She knew him well enough to know that threat would work. "Okay. I won't."

She harrumphed but turned around and went to grab his bag.

He reached for the towel he'd bought when he set up camp here. It hung on the handle of an old-fashioned hand-cranked paper towel dispenser.

By the time Angela was back with his bag, he'd dried his face and neck and swallowed a couple of mouthfuls of tepid water from the tap.

"I brought you a bottle of water, too."

He grabbed it and downed half of it in one gulp. "Thanks."

"Now take off your jacket."

"Listen, Ange, I can handle this. I just—"

"Is there a first-aid kit in here? Because I've got one in my apartment. I can go—"

"Ange!" He grabbed her arm. "Slow down. I'm fine. I just need to get this shirt off and clean up a little. I saw a kit in the big office on the first floor. Toward the back. The lights work down there, but don't leave them on any longer than you have to. I'd rather nobody know we're here."

She nodded and left.

Lucas turned around to look at the back of his jacket. The collar was stained with blood, and there were a few spots down his spine where blood had seeped through the jacket. He shed it then looked in the mirror again.

His white shirt had a dark red streak nearly a foot long running down it, just to the right of his spine. It started at the base of his neck and stretched across his shoulder blades. The material of the shirt was puckered along the edge of the red stain.

He unbuttoned the shirt and grabbed the lapels to ease the material away from the wound, but it was stuck fast. He pulled at it gently and felt a searing pain as the fabric tore at his skin.

"Wait!" Angela came hurrying into the room. "Don't do that. Let me wet the shirt."

He didn't protest.

She sat the first-aid kit down on the back of the toilet and put the seat cover down. "Sit."

Lucas wanted to laugh, to act like the wound was no big deal, but Angela was serious, her face crunched into a frown of concentration. So he stayed quiet and followed her instructions.

She ran water on the towel until it was sopping wet. Then she applied it to his back.

He shivered in spite of himself. The water had been tepid and flat on his tongue, but it seemed both cold and hot at the same time as it soaked his shirt and trickled down his skin.

"Damn, you're getting my pants wet."

"Do you want to take them off? Because I'm not done yet."

"No." He clamped his jaw and sat still while she slowly, meticulously pulled the soaked shirt away from the wound.

Finally he heard her sigh. "There." She slid his shirt down his arms and tugged the tail out of his pants. "Oh."

"What? What is it?" He craned his neck to look at her.

"Take off your belt."

He uttered a quiet chuckle. "The bullet didn't go any farther, Ange."

"I know. It hit your belt." Her gaze raised to his and he saw the horror in her eyes.

He understood. As cavalier as he was acting, he was unnerved by just how close the shot had come to his head. If he listed all the times he'd come close to being killed or maimed—well, it didn't bear thinking about.

He unbuckled his belt and pulled it off. "I'll be damned. The belt did stop the bullet. It hit that metal stud right there." The one that was mangled. He suppressed a shudder. Like his body would have been if the bullet had penetrated rather than skimmed him.

"Sit down. I need to finish cleaning your wound."

"Fine. But maybe you could hurry. I'm not used to being fused over."

He certainly wasn't used to so much gentle, tender personal attention. The last relationship he'd had was with an attorney in Dallas. It had been a casual relationship anyway, and when she found out he was being suspended, she'd turned cold pretty fast.

Apparently a detective on his way up was good for her career, but a detective on suspension was not.

Angela's warm, capable hands roamed over his bare back as the faint scent of chocolate filled the close space of the bathroom. Her touch was quickly turning from antiseptic and clinical to intimate and sensual, at least in Lucas's mind.

He had to think about something else—quick.

"Ow! Crap!" he cried, as cold liquid turned to blazing fire sizzling down his back.

That worked.

"Don't be such a baby. I needed to disinfect it."

"With—hot lava?" he gasped.

"Iodine. This is a very old first-aid kit."

He heard suppressed laughter in her voice. It reminded him of when they were kids and he'd do or say something she thought was funny.

A pang hit him in the center of his chest. She'd always thought he was funny. She and Brad. Two people in his life who'd stuck by him no matter what. No expectations. No disapproval. No disappointment. And no punishment.

Just love and acceptance. At least until he'd kissed her.

"At least it has some sterile strips. I can use them to close the wound."

"Close the wound? How bad is it?" He stood and backed up to the small mirror, craning his neck to see. There was a red strip with ragged edges down the right side of his upper back. It still oozed blood. "Looks to me like there's not much to pull together. Just bandage it."

"Will you let me take care of it? I know what I'm doing."

"Do you?" he sent her a crooked smile.

"I've tended my share of scrapes and scratches. Even a broken bone or two. I'm certified in first aid. I was a lifeguard at the Chef Voleur Country Club, in case you've forgotten."

"That must have been after I graduated."

Her gaze faltered. "That's right. It was. Turn around and I'll finish up."

He obeyed. Her fingers slid sensuously over his skin as she dried his back and applied the sterile strips. With his eyes closed, he could fantasize that she was massaging warm, chocolate-scented oil into his skin as a prelude to sex, and soon she would turn him toward her and slide her fingers across his chest, his abs and further, until she was—

He shook his head to rid himself of the wayward, lustful thoughts.

"What? Did I hurt you?"

"No," he said shortly. He clenched his jaw and closed his eyes again.

Within a couple of minutes she had finished bandaging his back. "There. How do you feel? I wish I had some aspirin or something to give you—"

"I'm fine." He caught her gaze in the mirror. "Now, I need to clean up and change clothes, if that's okay with you."

Her face turned pink. "Sure. Okay." She backed out of the bathroom, clutching the first-aid kit.

"Ange—"

She stopped, and her chocolate eyes met his in the mirror.

"Thanks. I appreciate your help."

"Of course. No problem." Then she fled.

As soon as she'd gone round the corner, Lucas kicked the bathroom door closed and turned back to the mirror. He took a deep breath and grimaced—not from the pain of his wound but from the pain of unquenched desire.

He hadn't dared to turn around, or she'd have known how turned on he was by her touch, even with the sting of the iodine.

He narrowed his eyes and gave himself a stern stare. "Keep your head where it needs to be. You are *protecting* her. Not trying to get her in the sack."

He closed his eyes and shook his head. Now that she'd

touched him, it was going to be harder than ever to remember that it wasn't his job to lust after her. It was to keep her alive.

ANGELA SAT DOWN AT THE TABLE in front of the big window and packed everything back into the first-aid kit. She left it sitting on the edge of the table. Who knew when they might need it again.

The sight of Lucas's bloody back had scared her half to death. Thank God it was nothing more than a flesh wound. It might sting like hell, but at least it was just a scrape. The bullet had nearly missed him.

Nearly.

The picture in her head of him diving at Doug was lit by the bright imaginary path of the bullet as it slid along the flesh of his back. If he hadn't ducked his head—she shuddered.

He could have died.

She was a little surprised at the depth of horror and sadness that enveloped her at the thought of him dying. She loved Lucas. She always had. Almost as much as she loved her brother. Lucas had always been as much of an older brother to her as Brad had.

Until that night.

She still didn't know even now, twelve years later, why she'd kissed him that night. All she remembered was that suddenly, the idea of him graduating from high school and leaving Chef Voleur was unbearable.

Unbearable and very different from the way she had felt about Brad, who was also graduating and leaving. She would miss Brad, of course. But he was her brother. His father was married to her mother. She'd see him again. Often. And anyhow, he wasn't leaving the area. He was going to law school at Tulane.

On the other hand, Lucas had been heading out to Dallas. He'd told her he wanted to get as far away from Chef Voleur and his family as he possibly could.

Somewhere the name Delancey means nothing, he'd said. *I'm going out to Dallas to become a cowboy.*

When she'd found out that he really meant it, she'd kissed him. She'd had nothing to lose, or so she'd thought.

She hadn't known she'd lose her heart.

"Okay," Lucas said behind her, startling her. His bare feet had made no noise on the hardwood floor. "I feel a whole lot better now. Thanks."

She nodded without looking at him. "No problem."

He glanced at the refrigerator. "Although, I'm starving and I'm sick of ham sandwiches. What do you say we go out tonight. Get a real meal?"

"Are you sure you feel like it?"

"I'm starving. I guess bleeding works up an appetite."

"That's not funny." Angela looked at the clock in the corner of one of the computer screens. "It's after seven. And I think you need to rest. What if we just walked up to the café and got a sandwich? Or maybe some bread pudding and a café au lait. I've been thinking about bread pudding ever since Lou-Lou mentioned it."

"Sure. That'll work. I'll put on a shirt. I didn't bring another jacket."

"I could wash the blood off yours. But it's got that—you know—bullet hole in the collar."

"Yeah. I trashed it. I'll need to pick up another one somewhere. But for now, I can wear a long-sleeved shirt to hide my weapon."

"You're going to take your gun to the café." She didn't even bother to make it a question. The reminder turned her stomach upside down and killed her appetite. He was here because Brad thought her life was in danger. And he agreed.

Since the incident with Doug this afternoon, and the admissions Bouvier had made, it wasn't as difficult for her to believe that as it had been.

He sent her a look. "You'd better believe I am," he said. "I'm taking my weapon everywhere until I'm sure nobody's out there looking for you."

TONY HEARD THE LOCK on the door to the abandoned building just in time. He ducked back into the alley as the big man and Angela appeared. If they'd have been two seconds later, they'd have caught him.

Damn it. Damn it. Damn it. They were going somewhere. No telling how long he'd have to wait before they got back. *If* they came back.

He hoped like hell they weren't leaving the building permanently. They didn't have any bags, so he was optimistic. There was no way he'd have time to retrieve his Lexus from the parking garage and follow them.

He huddled there in the shadows, clutching the backpack filled with the tools and supplies he'd bought earlier against his side, and held his breath, waiting.

The big man looked around. Tony had already figured out that he didn't miss much. Tony hunched further back against the wall and tried to breathe normally, quietly. It wasn't easy with the smell of decaying garbage and mildew tickling his nostrils. He prayed there were no rats in the dirty alley. He hated rats.

Angela and her bodyguard skirted the Cobra and walked up the street toward the sidewalk café.

Tony breathed a sigh that was part relief, part frustration. They weren't taking the car. They were just out to get a sandwich or some coffee. They'd probably be done in an hour. But from the café they'd be able to see him if he approached the car.

He retraced his steps to the opposite end of the narrow alley, crossed Royal Street and came out on Bourbon, a few blocks from his hotel. Then he swung the backpack over his shoulder, dug his baseball cap out of his back pocket and strolled up the street with his head down, as if he were a tired student heading home after a late study session.

There was no way he was going to hang around Chartres Street waiting for them to finish eating and go back inside. It was too risky. The bodyguard might see him.

He'd come back later. Much later. After they had retired for the night.

LUCAS RUBBED HIS EYES and squinted at the clock in the corner of the computer display. Five o'clock in the morning. He groaned quietly. He'd seen the same display at twelve midnight, at 2:20, at 3:27, and at 4:11.

He couldn't sleep. Partly because it just wasn't that easy to sleep sitting up in a straight-backed chair, partly because he kept hearing noises in the street below and partly because something was niggling at his brain and he couldn't figure out what.

He stood carefully, trying to stay quiet as he stretched and yawned. Angela was asleep on the cot with her back to him. She'd fallen asleep around midnight. He'd detected the change in her breathing. And as far as he could tell, she'd been asleep ever since.

Outside the window, he heard something metallic hit the pavement. He stepped over to the glass and looked across at her apartment. It was dark. No sign of anyone inside.

He thought about Angela's bed, her sofa, her air conditioning. There was probably no reason they couldn't stay over there. If Picone's hit man was here in New Orleans, he had certainly already spotted them. And at least on her sofa he could stretch out—okay, *almost* stretch out, if he rested his feet on the arm.

He endured another jaw-cracking yawn and took a look up and down the street. The faint glow of coming dawn dusted the sidewalks and storefronts with a misty blurriness.

In less than an hour, the café would open and he could run down and get a café au lait. That would help. In the meantime, he'd have to make do with cold water.

Just as he started to turn from the window toward the mini-fridge, a movement on the sidewalk below caught his eye. Someone was standing at the passenger-side door of his car.

He squinted. "Son of a bitch!" he growled. "He's stealing my car!"

Angela started and then sat up. "What? What is it?"

Lucas grabbed his weapon and headed out the door. "Stay here!"

He heard her voice behind him as he ran toward the stairs.

"You're barefoot!"

He vaulted down the stairs three at a time and landed at the bottom with a quiet thud. He flaunted his weapon in his right hand and the keys to the street door in his left. He couldn't see the guy through the dirty glass door, but he could tell that the passenger-side door, the one facing the curb, was open.

The punk was hot-wiring his car. He reached out and inserted the key into the door's lock and turned it.

And all hell broke loose.

Later, he would remember it as if it were being re-played on a TV screen in slow motion. His beautiful red Mustang Cobra transformed into a yellow and white and red ball of fire. For an instant, there was no sound. Just light.

Then came the bang.

Somehow, he managed to turn and crouch before the blast sent him flying across the room. He slammed headfirst into the wooden stairs. Stars shot back and forth across his field of vision as sharp pain peppered his whole body.

From somewhere far away, he heard Angela scream his name.

Chapter Ten

At first, Angela couldn't figure out what had happened.

Something had exploded. Something big. Like a transformer blowing when struck by lightning. But lower, deeper. It shook the floor under her, and she suddenly realized it had been preceded by a flash of light. Light that didn't fade. A fire.

She jumped up and screamed for Lucas as she ran out the door and down the stairs.

She saw him crumpled against the bottom step, his body glinting in the harsh orange light from the street.

It took a few seconds for Angela's brain to process what her eyes saw. She knew she needed to be doing something for Lucas, but the sheer unbelievability of the scene before her kept her paralyzed.

She raised her gaze to the street door. Through the glass she could see fire. Something was on fire.

A car. Lucas's car.

On fire.

Then she realized she wasn't looking through the door. Because the door wasn't there. It was—gone.

She looked back down at Lucas.

Glass was scattered all around him. All over him.

Glass. From the door.

At that instant, everything made sense.

"Oh, no," she whispered.

Lucas's car had exploded. It had shattered the glass in the door and windows of the building and thrown Lucas across the room.

She dropped to her knees. "Lucas! Lucas, answer me!"

He groaned.

Angela sobbed with relief. He was alive.

"Don't move!" she warned him. "You're covered with glass. I'll be right back. Oh, Lucas, please be all right. And please don't move!"

She turned and ran up the stairs, hardly noticing a sharp pain in her left heel. Back in the room, she grabbed her cell phone and shoved her feet into her running shoes. When she did, the sharp pain stabbed her heel again. She must have stepped on a piece of glass, but she didn't have time to check. She had to call for help.

As she ran down the stairs she dialed 911, but before she finished punching the numbers in, she heard sirens. Someone was on their way. Police or fire department.

At that instant, a voice asked her what her emergency was. She screamed for them to send an ambulance. To hurry. The voice asked her the address, and somehow she was able to tell them.

The next hour flew by in a blur. The fire department arrived first and extinguished the blaze.

Then police cars and ambulances roared up.

The EMTs took charge of Lucas. She followed behind them as they rolled him on a gurney through the growing crowd of onlookers that gathered around the ambulance.

She tried to walk on her left tiptoe to keep the piece of glass in her heel from digging in deeper.

Even though the crowd parted for the EMTs, they immediately closed in behind the gurney again, jostling her. She stepped down on her heel more than once and nearly fell, only to be pushed and pawed and set upright by anonymous hands in the crowd.

After they made sure Lucas was okay, one of the EMTs removed the shard of glass from her heel. As he was applying the bandage, Ethan climbed in through the back doors.

"Get me out of here," Lucas demanded as soon as he saw him.

"No way in hell," Ethan responded evenly.

Angela could tell Ethan was shaken by the sight of his older brother. She understood perfectly. Even though she knew from the EMTs that Lucas's injuries were superficial, he was covered with blood and dirt.

He had a cut at his hairline that was going to leave a scar and nasty scrapes on his cheek and both elbows, where he'd slid across the floor. But the worst of it was the hundreds of small nicks and cuts that marred his beautiful body. They were all over his neck and face and torso. The EMTs had cleaned all the wounds, but they hadn't even tried to bandage them. Most were shallow, but the totality of them was a horrific picture.

Lucas uttered a colorful curse. "Kid, you're just trying to bully me. I don't have time to go to the hospital just so they can tell me I'm fine. Get me out of here."

"Tell me what happened," Ethan said, ignoring his brother's plea.

"Damn it, kid!"

"Luke, I can actually take you in and hold you as a material witness. You know I can. So if you don't want to be buried in a load of paperwork you'll never be able to climb out of, you'd better start talking."

"I couldn't sleep," Lucas said grudgingly, "so I was staring out the window when I saw a guy trying to break into my car."

"A guy—" Ethan echoed in a strangled voice. "There was someone in the car?"

"Oh, God!" Lucas sat up. "Did you find a body?"

"No." Ethan's face grew pale and he thumbed the radio attached to his right shoulder.

"Bill, who's there from the fire department? Tell him there may be a body in the vehicle." He paused to listen to the squawking voice coming through the mike.

"Repeat please," the voice crackled. "Did you say *body*?"

"Body. Casualty. Affirmative. May have been trying to hot-wire the vehicle. Out."

Angela had been listening to the two of them and feeling as if she were two steps behind them, just like she'd felt as a child following Brad and Lucas around. But with Lucas's words, her brain had suddenly raced forward.

Hot-wiring the car.

"It was a bomb," she whispered, stunned.

Lucas glanced over at her. "Yeah," he said, then turned his gaze to Ethan. "It could have been set by the hit man."

"The hit man. All right Luke. That does it. I think we need to take steps to keep Angela safe."

"No!" Lucas snapped. "Absolutely not. Brad doesn't want anything formal. That's why he called me. He knew I'd guard her with my life."

Angela stared at Lucas—at the cuts and bruises and scrapes. It was shocking and humbling to realize he really was willing to risk his life to protect her.

At that instant, the back door opened and the EMTs reached in to slide the stretcher out.

Lucas rolled off onto his feet. "I'll walk in," he said.

Angela shook her head in frustration and sent a glance Ethan's way. Ethan just shrugged.

Angela watched Lucas's straight proud back as he walked into the Emergency Room.

Even though Lucas was a bloody mess, not to mention a bully and an altogether annoyingly arrogant man, she felt safer with him than with the entire police force of New Orleans.

It made no sense.

TONY PICONE WAS BREATHING so hard he was afraid his lungs might collapse as he let the dispersing crowd carry him back across the street to the sidewalk café. He looked at his watch, but he didn't have to wonder if they were open yet. The heavyset waiter who always worked the early shift was ogling the crowd and exchanging theories of what had happened with two people standing in the doorway of the café.

When the waiter spotted him, the excitement in his eyes turned to resignation. Tony was still too out of breath to speak. The waiter opened his mouth, then closed it and went inside.

Good damn thing he did, too. If he'd have waited for Tony to get his breath so he could order the exact same black coffee he'd ordered every time he sat down, or if he'd tried to sell him a "cafay o lay" again, Tony would have to shoot him.

If he could. His trembling fingers touched the handle of the Glock in the pocket of his hoodie. He hadn't known how hard it would be. His fingers spasmed involuntarily as he relived that awful moment. He'd pushed through the crowd, congratulating himself on his ingenuity. The bomb had failed, but the huge crowd it had attracted offered an excellent cover.

He'd held the gun, hidden in his pocket, against Angela Grayson's side, but he hadn't been able to pull the trigger.

By the time the waiter got back with his coffee, Tony's breathing had almost returned to normal. But the panic squeezing his chest hadn't.

He'd risen early and headed down to Chartres Street to be there when Angela and her bodyguard got into the car. When he'd leaned around the corner of the building and spotted the two-bit carjacker breaking into the passenger door of the Cobra, he'd reached for his Glock, but it was already too late.

Tony had watched in dread fascination as the thief climbed into the car and ducked his head below window level. He'd put a hell of a lot of explosives under the chassis, more than enough to kill whoever was inside it. He couldn't stop the guy—couldn't get any closer, for fear of being caught in the blast that was inevitable, as soon as the two live wires touched.

He'd cringed, unable to avert his eyes—unable to so much as blink. All he could do was wait. Then it happened.

The car exploded.

He'd ducked back, holding his breath until the blast of heat and the crackling roar of the flames finally subsided.

Tony's lungs spasmed again as that terrifying instant replayed in his head. Then nausea twisted his gut and he broke out in a cold sweat. He'd killed someone, and not even the right someone.

Don't let Papa hear about this, he prayed. His papa considered it a disgrace to kill an innocent bystander. Not that the car thief was exactly innocent, but that wouldn't matter to Papa.

He wrapped a hand around the hot mug of coffee and slurped it. After a few more swallows, his chest loosened up a little, his gut unclenched and he could finally concentrate on what was going on in front of the abandoned building at this very moment.

The police and fire crews were standing by as a wrecker lifted the car onto a low trailer. He wondered if they knew they had a body—or at least what was left of a body—inside. Tony wiped his forehead with a paper napkin.

Whether they did yet, they would. Their forensics people would quickly put together what had happened. The thief had hot-wired the car, triggering the spark that set off the bomb. He also knew they would quickly figure out how the bomb was built.

They'd be impressed with the workmanship. He was good at bomb-making. It was his favorite hobby.

He smiled to himself. They'd quickly reconstruct it, but they wouldn't be able to trace it. He'd driven all the way down to the Ninth Ward to buy the supplies he'd needed. He'd gone to five different stores, and he'd paid cash at each one. He'd also changed his shirt prior to each purchase. And kept his face away from the surveillance cameras.

Wait until Paulo heard how he'd planned and built a perfect, untraceable car bomb. It was brilliant.

The police probably already knew who the car belonged to, but even if they didn't, they could run the license plate. It was black with soot, but still readable.

However, one thing the forensics people wouldn't find

among the burned wreckage was the vehicle registration, because Tony had taken it.

Now he knew who the big guy was who'd latched onto Angela. His name was Lucas Delancey. Address somewhere in Dallas, Texas.

Tony didn't know what Delancey was doing here in New Orleans, but he didn't need to. He gulped the last of his coffee, pleased with himself now that the gut-wrenching fear had subsided. He might not have been able to shoot Angela Grayson at point blank range, but he *had* managed to institute his back-up plan. He'd made sure he could find the ADA's sister, no matter where she and her convenient protector went.

As he sipped on a second cup of coffee, Tony watched a young uniformed cop walking toward him. He set the cup down. He was calm now. Ready. He understood that the cop had to question everybody. And he'd hung around on purpose, so he could find out as much as he could about what the cops had discovered. He smiled to himself. Once again, he'd proven that brains were better than brawn.

He was calm and confident as the cop showed him his badge. "Been here awhile?" he asked.

Tony nodded pleasantly. "I saw the explosion. Terrifying."

"What were you doing up and about that early?"

"I have coffee here every morning," Tony answered. "Pretty days like today, if I wake up early, I come down here and sit until they open."

"So what did you do when the car exploded?"

Tony gave a small laugh. Better to stick as close to the truth as possible. "Nearly jumped out of my skin. It was awful to watch, you know? But I couldn't look away."

"You didn't run over there?"

"Sure. I tried, but I couldn't get close. The fire was too hot, and then I heard the sirens. I figured it was best to stay out of the way."

"Mind if I ask you a few questions about what you saw?" the cop asked. "I'm Officer Ethan Delancey."

BY NOON, ANGELA FOUND herself sitting beside Lucas in Ethan's car, headed for the north shore of Lake Pontchartrain. She looked across at Lucas. His face was marred by at least a dozen tiny nicks from the exploding glass. The backs of his hands were similarly pocked with small cuts. The sight of them sent cold shivers across her skin. Any one of those small pieces of glass could have been a giant shard. Any one of them could have killed him.

He glanced at her sidelong. "Are you all right?"

She swallowed. "I'm fine." He'd made it clear how tired he was of hearing her tell him how he could have been killed, so she changed the subject.

"What kind of car is this?" she asked. "It looks even older than yours."

Lucas grinned. "It's a '64 Corvette. Nice, isn't it?"

"What is it with you Delanceys and your ancient cars?"

"Vintage, sugar. Ethan will kill me if I let anything happen to it."

"When you said you'd abandoned Ethan and Harte, what did you mean?"

Lucas's jaw muscle flexed. "Family stuff," he said shortly.

"Your dad?"

He didn't answer.

"I remember you coming to school with black eyes and cut lips. You don't think it was a secret, do you?

Chef Voleur's a small town." Angela saw the pain in his expression.

After driving in the silence for a few moments, Lucas spoke. "When Robbie left for the service, he told me to take care of them. I shouldn't have gone to Dallas."

And that was it. The essence of Lucas Delancey. His sense of responsibility, of honor. His need to protect those around him from harm. It was the reason she trusted him. The reason she loved him.

"Why not?" she countered. "Robbie went into the service."

Lucas shot her a glare. "That was different."

"No it wasn't. Besides, by the time you went to Dallas Ethan and Harte were old enough to take care of themselves. "

"You don't know anything about it."

Angela heard the cold warning in his voice, so she stopped talking. After a few miles, the muscle in his jaw stopped flexing.

"Where are we going? she asked.

"The fishing cabin."

Angela had been to the Delanceys' fishing cabin lots of times, years ago when they were kids. It had always been fun to stay there.

The Delancey family's definition of *fishing cabin* was a gigantic log house built back in the forties, with a fireplace that stretched across one entire wall of the main room, a fully stocked kitchen and enough rooms to support a never-ending water pistol war.

"What if someone's there?"

Lucas shook his head. "Nobody has time these days. I just hope Marie-Jean is still taking care of the place."

"Marie-Jean?"

"Claude's wife. You remember them, don't you? He

runs the bait shop about two miles from the cabin. As long as I can remember, she's cleaned the place once a month, checked for leaks, restocking supplies and tested the generator."

"Oh. I never even thought about where the electricity and food came from. Kids are so oblivious."

"Me neither, until I got out on my own and realized all that stuff costs money."

"So who pays her?"

"My granddad provided for it in his will." Lucas maneuvered the car along the winding dirt road and took a sharp right turn.

"Here we are." He pulled the car up close to the back door. As he unfolded his tall frame to climb out, he groaned quietly.

She got out on the passenger side and eyed him over the roof. "Are you okay? Are you dizzy? The doctor said to take it easy."

He glared at her. "I'm fine. I guess my muscles took more of a beating than I thought."

"Right. Your muscles. Not to mention the huge bump on your head, and the bullet wound down your back and the ten thousand cuts from all that glass." She gave an ironic laugh. "I doubt I could find a place on your body that's not sore."

Lucas muttered something Angela didn't catch. She replayed it in her head as she grabbed her purse and slammed the car door. Had he really said, *You could try*?

Surely not. Throwaway lines like that were used by guys who were flirting. Lucas didn't flirt—not with her. He never had.

That wasn't to say he didn't know how. All through middle school and high school she'd watched him teasing girls, making them giggle and blush like nobody else could. At school dances, he danced with them all, paying particular attention to the wallflowers. That alone was enough to make Angela love him.

But he'd never danced with her. She'd always been the *Brat*. Brad's kid sister.

He opened the trunk and retrieved the bags of groceries and supplies he'd bought, then headed up the steps to the cabin door. She followed him.

Shifting all the plastic bags to one hand, Lucas dug inside the base of the porch light and pulled out a key.

"Really?" she said as he unlocked the door. "Among you and all your cousins you have, what, five cops in the family, and *that's* where y'all keep the key?"

"Four cops, and yes. That's where we keep it."

"How many times has this place been cleaned out by burglars?"

"Let's see," he answered as he replaced the key, then led the way through the dark hallway past the big front room and the bedrooms on to the kitchen. "I'm thinking—never."

"Hard to believe. Shouldn't you let Marie-Jean know we're here?"

He set the bags on an enormous pine table that was scarred with the initials, names and rude comments of dozens of kids.

"No. I don't want anyone to know we're here. Better for them and better for us."

He took the top off a ceramic cookie jar and reached inside, pulling out another key.

He tossed and caught the key, then unlocked the kitchen door. "I'll be right back." He said. "I'm going to fire up the generator. I hope there's plenty of diesel."

The kitchen and dining room took up the entire back

of the cabin and had windows on three walls, so it was bright and sunny even without electricity. It was also hot.

Within a minute, Angela heard a humming sound and felt cool air on her face. It was the air conditioner. Lucas had gotten the generator going. Behind her a second different hum started. The refrigerator.

She dug in the plastic bags for the cream and butter and a carton of orange juice. When she opened the refrigerator, half grimacing at the expected smell, she was pleasantly surprised. It was fresh and sparkling clean, with baking soda on each shelf.

"Must be nice to afford a housekeeper for your *fishing* cabin," she muttered. She could already feel the cool air flowing through the wire shelves.

Behind her, Lucas opened the kitchen door. He put the key back in the cookie jar. "See," he said. "Even if burglars did find the front door key and get inside, they wouldn't have any electricity. They'd never find the key to the generator."

She looked up to see his lips spread in that slow Delancey grin that could knock all sense out of her head.

She smiled back and returned to putting away the groceries. "Right. First of all, they obviously couldn't steal anything in the dark. And second, of course they'd *never* think to look in the cookie jar."

"Burglars like things easy. Where's that orange juice?"

"Right here." She picked it up and turned just as he peered around her into the fridge.

They collided. Her breasts flattened against his chest, and the carton of juice slipped from her hands to plop onto the floor.

For an instant neither of them moved. She gasped, inflating her lungs and pressing her breasts even more tightly against his chest. A thrill slid through her.

He stared down at her, his chest rising and falling in strong steady rhythm against her increasingly sensitive breasts.

"The orange juice—" she murmured, unable to tear her gaze away from his.

"It didn't break," he responded softly. His gaze flickered downward, toward her mouth, and suddenly for Angela, breathing was totally out of the question. Her throat tightened. So did her nipples. Tightened and ached as the memory of his warm, firm lips against hers washed over her, along with the memory of how exciting, how disturbing, the feel of him so close to her had been when she was sixteen.

Now she was nearly twenty-eight and more experienced than she'd been back then, but the sensations rising inside her were exactly the same.

His brows drew down in a frown, two pink spots appeared in his cheeks and he recoiled slightly, enough that she got the message. He'd noticed her reaction. And was embarrassed by it. He was pulling away.

Chagrin sent heat flaring up her neck to her own cheeks. She tried to step backward, but the refrigerator door stopped her.

His gaze darkened, intensified, and for one crazy second, she thought he might actually lean forward and kiss her. But he didn't. He did what he should have done, what any gentlemanly bodyguard would do. He withdrew.

And she plunged back into reality. Of course he wasn't about to kiss her. That was her own wishful thinking.

To keep from having to look at him, she bent down

to pick up the orange juice and nearly bumped his head with hers.

"Whoa! Careful." He grabbed the juice and straightened, inspecting it for damage. "It looks okay, but we ought to pour it into a pitcher, in case there's a slow leak."

"Right. Good idea." Angela straightened, too, and sidestepped Lucas. "I'll wash a pitcher. Want a glass?"

He put the carton on the counter. "Not right now. I'm going to walk around, make sure everything's okay. You keep the doors locked, and if anything happens, give me a call on my cell."

"What do you think might happen?"

"Nothing. Just playing it safe."

"Sure." She opened a couple of cabinets, making a show of looking for a pitcher. "I'll get the rest of the groceries put away."

Lucas went out through the kitchen door and waited until she locked it behind him. He gave her a thumbs-up through the paned glass before he headed down the back steps.

She watched him for a few seconds. The cuts and bruises didn't detract from the harshly beautiful planes of his face one bit. His slight favoring of his sore right shoulder and leg didn't make him seem any less capable or strong, either.

It scared her to death to think about what could have happened had Lucas not been somewhat protected by the building's door and walls when the car exploded. A shudder racked her body.

He could have died.

Chapter Eleven

Lucas walked around the cabin, checking to be sure nothing looked out of place. In the small outbuilding the generator was working perfectly, and the diesel tank was nearly full. He and Angela could stay here all summer if they needed to.

But staying here for one night, much less all summer, was a very bad idea. He'd already nearly embarrassed himself at the refrigerator when he'd stepped up too close, looking for the orange juice.

When she'd turned unexpectedly, her breasts had ended up pressed tightly against his chest. So tightly that he'd felt her distended nipples through their clothes. His body had immediately responded, so he'd had to back away before she became aware of his lust.

He wished he knew if her breasts' taut peaks had been a reaction to his closeness or just a physical response to the collision.

It didn't matter.

The hell it didn't!

He pushed his fingers through his hair and gave his head a shake, trying to rid himself of the dark delicious scent of chocolate that always surrounded her. Some day he was going to have to ask her how she managed to always smell like chocolate. *Did she bathe in the stuff?*

He unlocked the kitchen door and stepped inside, where she was bent over, working to fit a six-pack of beer into the refrigerator. The sight stopped him in his tracks. That backside was easily the finest one he'd ever seen. His fingers twitched as he imagined how firm and curvy it would feel if he grabbed it right now.

Cool air slid across his hot sweat-dampened skin, raising goose bumps and reminding him that her backside was none of his business.

"Ah, summer in New Orleans," he said. "Heat and humidity. Dallas is a desert by comparison."

"Any place is a desert by comparison," Angela replied as she straightened, smiling. "Want a beer instead of juice? I need to get rid of two. They won't fit."

"Sure."

She handed him one. "I'm going to have a sandwich. Want one?"

He nodded as he popped the top and drank. Just then, his cell phone rang. He pulled it out of his pocket and looked at the display.

It was Brad. Lucas needed to talk to him about several things, preferably without Angela hearing. So he set the beer down and headed for the back door again. "I need to take this," he said to her. "Could you make me a sandwich? Turkey and Swiss. Mayo. No mustard."

Outside, he answered the phone. "Brad."

"Lucas. Everything going okay down there?"

Something was wrong. He could tell by the tone of Brad's voice. Had Ethan told him about the explosion? "Everything's fine here. Why?"

He could hear Brad's shaky breath even through the phone.

"Brad? What's wrong?"

"That rat bastard Picone tried to kidnap Ella."

Brad's younger daughter. The six-year-old. "Is she all right?"

"Scared half to death. But not as scared as Sue and me. God, Lucas. Wait until you have kids. You can't imagine. A guy attacked the policewoman as she was putting Ella into the backseat. He knocked her down!"

Lucas's mouth went dry. He sank to the steps. "Son of a bitch. He didn't get to Ella, did he?"

"The officer drew her weapon and winged him before he was able to."

"Thank God. Is he in custody?"

Brad took another shaky breath. "Yeah. But Ella hasn't stopped crying. And neither has Sue. And I'm damn close myself."

"What about Dawn?" Brad's other daughter. The nine-year-old. "Where was she when the guy tried to grab Ella?"

Behind him Lucas heard a gasp.

Damn it.

He hadn't heard Angela open the kitchen door. He stood and turned.

Her face was white as a sheet, her eyes were wide, and her hand flew to her throat. "Did something happen to Ella? Or Dawn? Are they all right?" Her words sounded strangled.

"Angela, keep your voice down. They're fine. Go back inside." He caught her arm, but she wrenched it out of his grasp.

"Luke!" Brad's voice shouted through the phone. "Don't tell Angela what happened. She'll be terrified."

"I heard that. I'm not afraid. Let me talk to him." She reached for his cell phone. He had to hold it out of her reach.

He caught her arm again. "Once you're inside," he

said through clenched teeth. "I don't want anyone hearing us." He guided her firmly up the steps and into the kitchen, pushing the door closed with his hip.

She whirled on him. "*You* were out there."

"*I* wasn't yelling."

She huffed and stiffened. "Give—me—the—phone."

He grabbed her hand. "Listen to me. Do *not* tell him where we are. Do you understand?"

"Why—?"

"Do? You? *Understand*?"

She nodded.

Angela's conversation with her brother was a long one. Before it was over, she had sat down at the table. She'd grabbed a paper towel to wipe her eyes and blow her nose, and she'd told Brad all about the car bomb. The way she described it, Lucas had nearly been killed.

He set his jaw and busied himself by making a couple of sandwiches and drinking his orange juice.

Then he heard Angela say, "Where?" She paused. "Well—"

He whirled and scooped the phone out of her hand. "Brad," he said. "Sorry, but I can't tell you where we are. And this call has gone on way too long. I don't know how high-tech the Picone organization is, but you said Picone's youngest daughter was a tech whiz, and I'd rather not take any chances. I'm turning off my phone and we're moving. We'll be in touch."

"Wait, Lucas," Brad demanded. "What happened? Was there really a bomb?"

"Let's just say you owe me a vintage Mustang Cobra and a bottle of Excedrin Migraine."

"Damn it, Luke. Picone put a bomb in your car? I've got closing arguments Monday, but after this morning and now this, I'm about ready to throw the trial."

Angela overheard him. "Don't you dare!" she cried. "Tell him we're fine, Lucas. Tell him to put that lowlife away for good!"

"Did you hear that? Ange is just fine right here with me. I'm hanging up now. You need to talk to me again, call my cousin."

He heard Brad say, "Which one?" as he cut the connection.

He glanced at Angela. "You okay?"

She pushed her hair back from her face with both hands and squeezed her eyes shut for a couple of seconds. "Okay? You want to know if I'm okay?" She gave a short laugh, a high-pitched, hysterical sound, and shook her head.

"Sure, I'm fine. My six-year-old niece is seeing and experiencing things no one, much less a child, should ever have to go through. My brother is half crazy with fear for his family, just because he's trying to do the right thing. And I'm—I'm running for my life with—with a—with *you!*"

Lucas heard the disgust in her voice and saw the sparkle of unshed tears in her eyes. He couldn't blame her. To her mind he'd brought her nothing but trouble from the moment she'd first seen him.

He'd promised Brad he'd protect her, but he hadn't done a very good job of it. Sure, she was unharmed, but danger had come way too close to her twice now, and that was two times too many.

"Angela, you've got to trust me. I swear I'll keep you safe. You heard Brad. He's got closing arguments tomorrow. No matter what he decides to do, it'll all be over in a few days."

"Not if he decides to stop the trial."

"Come on, Brat. You know your brother. Do you really think he'd stop the trial, even if he could?"

She paused for a second, then shook her head. "No. He can't. It's not in him."

"That's right. And once it goes to the jury, it won't take them any time to convict Picone. You know Brad didn't prosecute Picone without knowing full well that he had enough to put him away."

She nodded, beginning to look less panicked.

"He'll be in prison—probably in solitary confinement, where he won't be able to talk to anybody, and all of you will be safe."

She stared at him, hope dawning in her brown eyes, then fading immediately. "Can you guarantee that?" She shook her head. "I don't think so."

At that moment, Lucas wished he could lie and make her believe what he himself didn't fully believe. But he knew her almost as well as he knew himself, and he knew, even if he could say the words, she wouldn't believe them.

"Ange, I'll protect you with my life. It's all I can offer. I will die before I'll let anything happen to you."

A little color returned to her face, and she nodded and wiped at her eyes.

At least he'd reassured her a little. "You want a sandwich?"

She shook her head wearily. "Maybe later. Are we really moving to another location?"

He shook his head. "No. I was just being careful. This is the best place for us. It's nice and isolated, and yet we get good cell phone service because we're within thirty miles of New Orleans."

She nodded, but he could tell she wasn't really listening to him. "Is it okay if I take a shower and lie down for a while?" she asked.

"Sure. Go ahead. There should be hot water by now. Take the master suite. The big bedroom at the front of the house, across from the living room. You'll be comfortable there."

"Oh." She stopped. "I don't have any clothes. I guess I'll have to put these back on."

"No, you won't. Mom always kept some clothes here. I'm sure Aunt Edina and others kept clothes here, too. You'll be able to find something to fit you. If all else fails, there are some men's and boys' clothes in some of the drawers."

She nodded. "Great, thanks." Then she looked at him and shook her head. "Wait. What am I doing? I'll stay up. You're the one who needs to sleep. I don't think you've slept in two nights."

He grabbed the rest of his sandwich and his glass of juice and sat down at the table. "Don't worry about me. I'm fine. We can pick up satellite here. I might watch a little TV while I eat. We're going to have to go to bed and get up with the chickens, because once the sun goes down, I don't want the lights on." He paused. "Ange, don't open the blinds. And don't go out on the deck, okay?"

She glanced back at him. "I won't. Lucas—"

"Yeah, sugar?"

A tiny smile lightened her serious countenance. "Thanks."

He nodded and saluted her with his glass. "No problem, Brat. No problem at all."

He listened until he heard the bedroom door open and close, then he got up and splashed cold water on his face. He was tired. And sore. But he had the rest of his life to rest and heal.

He'd be damned if he'd sleep until Angela was out of danger.

ANGELA CLIMBED OUT of the shower and wrapped herself in a big white towel and blew out a long breath. She felt so much better now that she was clean.

She glanced at her underwear hanging on the towel rack and dripping onto the wooden floor. There was probably a washer and dryer somewhere in the house. She couldn't see Lucas's prim and proper mother staying here without all the comforts of home. But she'd undressed before she'd thought about it and she hadn't wanted to dress again in her dirty clothes to go ask Lucas. So she'd rinsed them out in the sink.

Her shirt and Capris were dirty too. She'd worn them for the past two days. There was no way she was putting them on her clean body. So she fastened the towel around her body and went exploring for clean clothes.

A walk-in closet was filled with pants and tops, all of which were too small for her. On the other hand, the men's clothing was much too big.

She rooted around in the dresser among sweaters and too-small panties and bras, and finally came up with an orange print caftan. It was a little short, but at least it covered her and wasn't indecently tight. On the floor of the closet was a pair of flip-flops that fit fairly well.

She caught a glimpse of herself in the full-length mirror on the bathroom door. Not too bad. At least she was covered until her underwear was dry. Later she'd find a pair of pants and a shirt.

Once her hair dried she'd be almost presentable. She tousled it with her hands. There wasn't a hair dryer in the bathroom, which surprised her. She couldn't imagine Lucas's mother letting her hair air-dry.

Speaking of air-drying, she squeezed water off the ends of her hair and fluffed it again. It would be a cloud of waves once it dried. Not the worst thing that had—or would—happen to her this week.

She folded the comforter down to the end of the bed and turned down the blanket and sheet. The white sheets smelled fresh.

She climbed into bed and settled back, sighing. She knew Lucas had lied when he said he wasn't tired. The toll his injuries had taken on him was clearly outlined on his face. Lines of pain dug furrows between his nose and mouth, and the corners of his lips were white and pinched. But he was trying to be the big brave protector, and she appreciated that.

She swore to herself that she wouldn't rest for more than an hour. Then she'd find him and make him take a nap while she fixed something for dinner.

With a yawn, she relaxed and closed her eyes.

For about two minutes.

Long enough for the image of her niece Ella to rise in her mind—Ella watching as a bad man attacked the woman who was trying to keep her safe.

Angela sat bolt upright. Panic seized her chest and wouldn't let go. Panic and a hot, terrifying claustrophobia. Her lungs felt paralyzed. She kicked off the covers and launched herself off the bed.

Sweat pricked her forehead and the back of her neck. She had to get out of there. Even with the air conditioner, it was too hot, too close, too terrifying.

Her hands clutched at her chest. Everything that had happened hit her at once. Doug with his gun, the faceless man out there following her, blowing up Lucas's car, men trying to kidnap her nieces—

Desperately, she gasped for breath. The knotty pine walls were closing in. As she cast about wildly, her gaze lit on the double doors that led out to the cypress deck.

The late afternoon sun shone through the trees, making pretty, delicate shadows on the gray, weathered wood. Beyond, the sparkling water of Lake Pontchartrain reflected the fading sunlight like cool ice crystals.

She rushed over to the doors and flipped the latch. She needed to breathe in fresh air, to feel the cool lake breeze, just for a few minutes.

When she threw open the doors, the air off the lake lifted her hair. She closed her eyes and sucked in a lungful.

It helped.

Stepping out onto the deck, she took in the familiar area around the cabin. The shell driveway that circled the entire house, the worn path that stretched into the woods in one direction and down to the lake in the other.

On the deck were two Adirondack chairs and a glider made of the same weathered gray cypress as the deck. She thought about sitting for a while, until her heart and her brain stopped racing. But the path toward the lake enticed her.

Pleasant childhood memories replaced the dreadful images in her brain. She recalled running along the path as a child. It had seemed endless, winding back and forth down the hill toward the muddy banks of Lake Pontchartrain. She recalled the crunch of shells and gravel under her feet, the faint brackish smell of the air, growing steadily stronger as she'd approached the lake.

She and Brad and Lucas had played on the warm, smooth boards of the old pier and had sat with their legs dangling and fished with old-fashioned cane poles using crickets for bait.

It wouldn't take five minutes to walk down to the pier and soak up a few happy childhood memories. Five minutes to calm down a bit.

Lucas had brought her to the cabin because he knew it was safe. Nothing was going to happen to her here.

Chapter Twelve

Lucas stared at the two rib-eye steaks. Damn it, he'd forgotten to pick up a bottle of his favorite steak marinade. He shook his head. He'd just have to make do. He'd bought butter and a head of garlic. In a pinch that would be enough, along with salt and pepper.

He opened the pantry door and smiled. The first thing that caught his eye was four bottles of Louisiana Hot Sauce. A staple in any pantry in this neck of the woods. But not for steak.

He grabbed a few bottles and set them out on the counter. He quickly concocted a marinade of olive oil, soy sauce, crushed peppercorns, oregano, basil, a pinch of tarragon, plus a few garlic cloves and some sea salt. He laid the steaks out in a flat pan, poured the mixture over them and set them in the refrigerator. In about an hour, they'd be ready to go on the grill.

He'd bought greens for a Caesar salad and a loaf of genuine French bread.

His mouth watered. They wouldn't go hungry.

He figured they'd eat around seven, which meant putting the steaks on about twenty minutes before. If he started the coals now, they'd be white and ashy by six-thirty.

He opened the bottle of wine he'd bought, so it would have time to breathe.

He grabbed two plates and two bowls, then reached in the drawer below for the silverware.

Just as he finished setting the table, he heard the unmistakable boom of a shotgun.

Close.

He froze. Then his rational mind reminded him that everybody around here carried weapons. For the locals, it was the best way to dispatch a water moccasin or a vulture. For those used to living in the city, the land around Lake Pontchartrain was wild and fraught with danger. Anyone could run into an alligator or a wild boar or snakes.

Another shot. Despite his knowledge of the area, fear squeezed his chest. He quickly checked his weapon and seated it in the paddle holster at the small of his back. Then he headed for the master bedroom. If the shots had woken Angela, she'd be terrified.

If they hadn't, and she was asleep and totally oblivious to whatever was going on outside, he'd probably scare her half to death when he burst in. But he'd rather be safe than sorry.

He eased open the bedroom door and saw the pile of covers on the big king-sized bed. Stepping quietly into the room, he circled the bed until he could see the other side.

It was empty.

He turned toward the bathroom, but its door was open and the lights were off.

"Ange?" he called, just as another shot rang out—followed immediately by a startled cry. A feminine cry.

He vaulted toward the doors. They weren't locked.

He slammed them open and launched himself across the deck and down the cypress stairs.

"Angela!" he shouted, stopping dead still at the bottom of the stairs to listen.

He heard her yell his name.

And then a colorful string of curse words in the unusual dialect peculiar to native New Orleanians. Accompanying the curse words was a chorus of barks and yelps and a couple of howls.

He knew that voice and those sounds. It was Felton Scruggs, the bootlegger, and his pack of dogs.

"Felton!" he yelled. "Yo, Felton!"

"Who's there?" came the guttural reply, barely heard over the chorus of howls and barks.

A round little man stepped out from behind a stand of trees, holding a wad of leashes wrapped around his left arm and a big blue over-under shotgun cradled in his right.

Lucas stared. Felton looked just like he had twenty years ago. He had to be in his eighties by now. He'd been bootlegging all his life, just like his papa before him.

It didn't matter a bit that liquor was legal in Louisiana these days. Felton still produced his pure grain alcohol, and just like when Lucas was in high school, people still came from all around the state—indeed the entire Southeast—to buy it.

"Felton, it's me, Lucas Delancey. Stop shooting!"

Felton jerked on the leashes and seven dogs ranging from a tiny terrier to what looked like a cross between a Great Dane and a shepherd, with a couple of Doberman mixes and some hounds in between, immediately quieted.

"Angela!" Lucas called. "Answer me. Are you okay?"

"Over here." Her voice, small and scared, came from the other side of the road.

He turned in time to see her rise from behind an old, rusted car with no wheels. She ran straight to him and crashed into his side. He wrapped his left arm around her shoulders.

"It's okay," he whispered. "He was just trying to scare you."

Angela's whole body was trembling. "He did," she muttered.

"Lucas Delancey, as I live and breathe." Felton Scruggs slung his shotgun over his shoulder, yelled at his dogs and then shuffled up to Lucas.

He thumbed his faded, dirty hat up off his forehead. "I heard you went out West. Are you a cowboy now? I see you got the boots anyhow." He talked out of one corner of his mouth, because he had a cheek full of tobacco in the other corner.

Lucas shifted. "I went to Dallas, but I became a cop."

"A cowboy cop," Felton muttered, then he leaned sideways and spit. "Well, I hope you didn't come down here to run me in, 'cause I can't go." He lifted up on the leashes. "I got dependents—seven of 'em."

Lucas laughed. "No way. I've got my own problems. I don't need anything more to do."

Felton's pale blue eyes flickered toward Angela, who still cowered at Lucas's side.

"Ain't she a pretty thing. Where'd you pick her up?"

Lucas grinned and tightened his grip around her shoulders, hoping she wouldn't take offense and say something. "Down the road a piece," he joked. "She's a friend of mine. I'd appreciate it if you wouldn't shoot at her. She's no danger to you or your business."

"Aw hell. I figured she was city folk, snooping around. Thought I'd scare 'em away. If I'd know she was with you… No problem."

"Listen, Felton. Like I said, we've got a problem. Maybe you can help."

Felton jerked on his leashes and growled loudly. All seven dogs sat. "You need some *paint thinner*? 'Cause I can keep you supplied with all the *paint thinner* you want. Just like back when you were in high school."

"No, I'm too old for that. It'd probably burn a hole in my gut these days."

Felton nodded and his mouth stretched into a one-sided grin that revealed tobacco-stained teeth. "All right then. What can I do you for?"

"We're hiding out here. There are some bad people looking for my girlfriend."

"Bad people? Like what kind of bad people?"

"Real bad. They're trying to stop her brother from putting their dad in prison."

Felton spat again and wiped his mouth on his sleeve. A couple of the dogs stirred restlessly. "Heeyah," Felton growled, and they settled back down. "That bad, eh?" he said, staring thoughtfully at Angela. "Whaddaya need?"

"Is it still true that you can't see anybody on the road until they're already up here behind our cabin?"

"Yep. If I climb up into my attic I can see 'em when they turn onto the road and again when they top the ridge right before they get to your cabin. You can't see 'em because your cabin's down the hill from mine."

"That what I remembered. Can you be a lookout for

us? If you see anybody headed this way, can you let me know?"

Felton spat and then grinned. "Course I will," he answered. "Gimme your cell number and I'll call you."

Lucas was surprised. "You've got a cell phone?"

The older man shrugged. "My customers get cell phones. I get a cell phone. Hell, with my GPS locator, I can keep up with my still—that is—my *locations* all around here."

Lucas and Felton exchanged numbers.

"Well, my girls have gotten their exercise," the bootlegger said, "so I best get back to work." He touched the ragged brim of his hat. "I apologize for scaring you, miss."

Then he gave the dogs an order and they all jumped up and headed back down the road with Felton hanging onto the leashes.

Lucas held Angela at arms length and peered down at her. "Are you okay?"

Her eyelashes were wet from tears and her hair fell in soft, dark, cloud-like waves onto the delicate curve of her neck. She nodded.

He turned and, without a word, guided her back up the road to the cabin, up the steps to the deck and on through the doors into the bedroom. He closed the doors behind him and turned to her.

"What the *hell* were you doing out there?"

She cringed, making him regret yelling at her.

"I tried to sleep, but when I closed my eyes, all I could see was Ella in that car, watching some man attack the policewoman who had promised her she'd be safe." She pushed her fingers through her hair, then swiped them across her cheeks, as if she could erase all signs of tears.

But she couldn't. Her eyes were red. Her cheeks looked chapped, and the way she was standing with her arms wrapped around herself tore at his heart.

"Hey, sugar. Ella will be fine. Kids are resilient." He should know. He'd had to be. He and his brothers.

"I couldn't breathe in here. Lucas, I don't know what to do. What to think. I'm living in a nightmare. People are trying to kill my family. They're trying to kill me—" A sob cut off her words.

Lucas stepped closer and pulled her into his arms, cupping the back of her head in his hands. "It's okay. You're here with me," he murmured gently. "Didn't I promise I wouldn't let anything happen to you?"

She shook her head against the thick cotton material of his T-shirt. "But look what's happened to you. You've been hurt twice because of me. And how long is this all going to last? Can we—can Brad ever be sure the danger is over? Even if he convicts Picone—"

"Listen to me, Ange," he whispered in her ear. "I know you're scared, but remember what I told you. Brad's good at his job. You know he is. He's going to get Picone put away so far in the back of the prison that the man will never have an unmonitored conversation with anybody, not even a prison guard, for the rest of his life."

She relaxed minutely and her arms slid around his waist. Lucas groaned inwardly as her breasts pressed against his chest.

Here he was back in the same position he'd been in earlier, when he'd gotten too close to her at the refrigerator.

Only this time, she was wearing nothing but a flimsy orange gown. The thin material did nothing to disguise the sweet round shape of her breasts.

As soon as they came in contact with his chest, they tightened, the nipples erecting into tiny, hard buds that scraped disturbingly against his skin through the T-shirt he wore.

She took a deep breath, which pressed those pebbled buds more fully against him. Then she gasped and lifted her head.

Her eyes glistened like chocolate syrup and her lips parted. Luscious, sexy lips—not thin, but not too full, either. Perfect.

He remembered them, their cool softness changing to heat as he'd deepened the kiss on that innocent night twelve years ago. And the small, round O they'd made when he'd pulled away, mirroring her wide, round eyes that glittered with hurt.

He couldn't do that again. He couldn't indulge himself by kissing her, not now. He needed all his senses, all his focus about him if he was going to be able to protect her from the man who was after her.

All at once, to his surprise, she lifted her head and touched her lips to his, just like she had that long-ago night when she was sixteen and he was a few weeks away from his eighteenth birthday.

Her mouth was cool and soft, just like he remembered. He bent his head and pressed his parted lips to hers. She gasped quietly, then exhaled. Her delicate breath was suffused with the scent of chocolate.

"How do you always taste like chocolate?" he whispered against her lips.

"Trade secret," she whispered back, then stood on tiptoe and wrapped her arms around his neck. "Last time we did this you tasted like cigarettes."

"I was an idiot back then."

"In more ways than one," she agreed. Then she slid her tongue along the soft inner flesh of his lips.

Without thinking, he tightened his arms and kissed her, responding not like a kid but like a man. He met her flirtatious tongue with a deep sexual response—a mimicry of the act of love itself.

His body reacted, but not with the hot, desperate, explosive lust that he'd felt back in high school.

What he felt now was a slower, deeper burn, not as frantic, yet far more erotic. More erotic than anything he'd ever felt, in fact.

Stunned, he pulled back and stared at her. What was it about her?

"Lucas?" Her mouth was open, her eyes dewy and heavy-lidded. She was turned on, too.

Don't kiss her again, his brain warned him. But he wasn't about to listen to reason. Reason would prevail soon enough. Right now his libido was in charge. And his libido insisted that once was not enough to taste those chocolate-flavored lips. It demanded he taste them again.

So he did.

He held her head between his hands and kissed her long and hard, soaking up her taste, her scent, the exquisite inconsistency of her cool lips and her hot tongue. He held her there until they were both breathless.

"Oh, Lucas," she whispered. "It's been so long—"

And like a race car slamming against a wall, everything stopped dead still.

Reason. That bitch.

He pulled away. "This is stupid," he muttered. "I'm sorry, Angela. I'll get out of here so you can get dressed."

He held his hands up, palms out—as if he could shield himself from her attraction. Then he bolted for the door.

Chapter Thirteen

Angela stood in the middle of the bedroom, her lips and her breasts and her sexual center throbbing. She looked at the bedroom door. The sound of it slamming shut still echoed through the room.

She pressed her suddenly cold hands against her hot cheeks. Lucas had rejected her—again. Just like twelve years ago.

Twice, she'd opened herself to him, and twice he'd turned away. Tears pricked her eyelids.

Fine. Maybe she was a little slow. Maybe it had taken her twelve years, but she'd finally gotten the message.

This is stupid, he'd said. Harsh words. Cold words. But she knew they were true. It was stupid. *She* was stupid. She should have gotten the message way back then.

After all, what red-blooded high school senior would turn down a chance to have sex with a reasonably attractive sophomore? Okay, she didn't know from personal experience, because back in high school she'd extended that invitation to one person and one person only.

From everything she'd seen back then and since, the odds of any man turning down a sure thing were enormous. A guy would be nuts to walk away.

But Lucas Delancey had done just that.

And now he'd done it again.

She stumbled into the bathroom and splashed her face with cold water, then let the water run across her wrists. Finally, her tears stopped and the heat of embarrassment and humiliation let up.

As she dried her face and hands with a towel, Angela swore to herself that there would be a blizzard in hell the day she ever made any sort of overture toward Lucas Delancey again.

She knew him. He'd given Brad his word, and he would keep it. He'd stick by her side until he was sure she was safe. Or until he was reinstated by the Dallas Police Department.

As soon as he could, he'd go back to his life in Dallas and leave her and Louisiana behind.

She'd known from the beginning how much he hated New Orleans and Chef Voleur. He'd always said that as soon as he could he was going to leave Louisiana behind and find a place where nobody knew who the Delanceys were. Or at least where nobody cared.

He had. He'd high-tailed it out of there the day after graduation. And he'd never looked back. Not once.

She knew that as soon as he was certain she was out of danger and he'd made good on his promise to Brad, she'd never see him again.

Fool me once, shame on you. Fool me twice—

"Shame on me," she whispered.

TONY SPENT SATURDAY afternoon watching his GPS device as it tracked Angela and Delancey. They ended up stopping on a ridiculous-sounding and unpronounceable river spelled Tchefuncte. They were near a place called Pleasure Beach, a couple of miles from the town of Madisonville on the north shore of Lake Pontchartrain.

He shook his head. Over half the names in this wretched state were unpronounceable.

As soon as he decided they weren't going anywhere else, he traded his big rented Lexus for a midsized four-wheel-drive vehicle, stopped at a local discount store and bought some heavy-duty work boots. Because even on the white-and-blue GPS map, the area looked muddy. His lip curled in disgust. If there was anything he hated more than rats, it was mud.

He'd had an early dinner, and now he was back in his hotel room, figuring out the best way to get from his hotel on Bourbon Street to the town of Madisonville on a Saturday night or Sunday morning. It looked like the fastest way was to head across the Lake Pontchartrain Causeway. Then it was two miles from Madisonville to Angela.

He jotted the directions on a piece of hotel notepaper. Just as he finished, his phone rang. It was Paulo.

"I didn't see no announcement of the ADA's sister dying. Harcourt wasn't broken up at all in court, neither."

Tony grimaced. "Not my fault. I set a beautiful car bomb, but a car thief set it off."

"A car bomb? Your big, fancy idea for killing the sister was a *car bomb*? I thought you said you had new ideas. Damn it, Tony. You're gonna end up in jail in Louisi-freakin-ana."

"You wait and see. They'll never trace it back to me. I made sure of that. You need to start respecting my talents. I can't help it if some loser decided to hot-wire the car and blew himself up. That was bad luck."

"Yeah, well you're gonna learn that you can't count on luck in this business, little brother. Now where in this steaming hellhole city are you?"

"What?" Tony blurted. "You're here?" He felt a mixture of irritation and relief. "Listen up, Paulie. If you're here to take me home, then forget about it. I've got 'em."

"I'm not here to take you home. I figure if you're dumb enough to do this, I better help."

"Where are you? D'you fly?"

"Naw. How could I bring my rifle if I flew? I drove, and I'm whipped. I hope you got a nice hotel."

Tony's pulse leapt in anticipation. Paulie was here. They could take out Angela and her big protector together. "I got the nicest." He gave him directions.

This was going to be good. He could leave Delancey to Paulie, while he grabbed the girl. Once Delancey was dead, they'd have no problem getting Angela to call her brother and force him to fix it so Papa could go free.

Tony grabbed a bottle of bourbon and poured himself a double shot. When Paulie got here, they'd have a toast—a toast to Nikolai Picone's freedom, and Tony's first hit.

DINNER WAS STRAINED. Angela had found a pair of boys' jeans that weren't indecently tight and a man's white shirt that was almost indecently loose. But with it buttoned all the way to the top button and the sleeves rolled up, it served its purpose.

She'd come out to the kitchen when she couldn't reasonably avoid it any longer. She'd smelled the coals burning and knew Lucas was cooking dinner.

She'd planned to do that for him while he napped. Something else she'd failed at.

She couldn't bring herself to meet Lucas's gaze. He grilled the steaks and she fixed the salad. They sat across from each other at the kitchen table and ate in near silence.

At first, Lucas tried to make conversation. He mentioned a couple of pieces of gossip his mother had told him the last time they'd talked. Mitzi Ingerman had divorced her husband and was living *in sin* with a younger man in Baton Rouge. The Baptist preacher had been called to a higher-paying church. Lucas's youngest brother, Harte, had decided he wanted to try politics, like their father and grandfather.

Angela tried to pay attention. She murmured at what seemed to be the appropriate times, and smiled occasionally, but she was miserable. Humiliation, fear and self-consciousness seemed to paralyze her.

Finally, Lucas picked up his plate and took it to the sink.

"Can I fix you something else?" he asked, eyeing her nearly untouched plate.

She looked down. "I'm sorry. It's delicious. I just don't have an appetite." She stood and picked up her plate just as Lucas reached for it.

Their fingers touched. Another close encounter. She froze and slipped her hand out from under his. "I'll do the dishes," she said.

"No, that's okay."

"Lucas." Her voice was sharper than she'd intended, but she'd had all of his altruistic care that she could stand. "You've been shot. You've been blown up. You haven't slept. What's it going to take to get you to rest?"

He opened his mouth to protest.

"I swear Lucas—" She held up her hands. "I don't know how you think you're going to protect me if you can't hold your head up. Isn't it dangerous to be too tired? Aren't you liable to make a mistake?"

His jaw muscle flexed.

"I don't want you to make a mistake."

The jaw muscle was still moving. "I might be able to get some sleep if I could be sure you wouldn't run outside as soon as I closed my eyes."

She propped her fists on her hips. "I have no intention of going outside alone. I panicked," she added grudgingly. "It won't happen again."

He tried to cover a yawn but was unsuccessful. "I need to be able to count on that." He assessed her. "I tell you what," he said. "You and I will both get some sleep tonight. We'll sleep in the master bedroom in the king-sized bed."

Together? Angela thought. Oh no. *No. No. No.*

"I'll sleep in my clothes and keep my gun at my side, in case anything happens."

"You want me to sleep in that bed—with you?"

His face grew solemn. "Not with me. Just in the same room in the same bed as me. It's a good idea."

Right, she thought. Except for the part where he and she were sleeping in the same bed. She wouldn't close her eyes all night, she was sure.

"Okay. I'll wash these dishes and then I'll come in there and lie down."

"Nope. Leave the dishes. I'm ready to go to sleep, and if I'm in the bed, you're in the bed. We go to bed together."

Angela swallowed hard and ducked her head to keep him from noticing the pink that stained her cheeks. Every word he said sounded suggestive. Why couldn't he have decided to sleep on the couch in the living room? She could curl up in one of the massive recliners. That way, every sentence he uttered wouldn't contain the words *bed* and *together*.

As a matter of fact, that was a good idea. She opened her mouth to suggest it, but he cut her off.

"Let's go."

"Why don't you lie down on the couch in the living room?"

"Too hot. And it's on the wrong side of the house."

"Too hot? We could open the windows—"

"No." He set his jaw and glared at her.

"But—"

"Ange." The warning in his voice and eyes was clear. She wasn't going to win this argument. It was over.

So she followed him into the bedroom. He grabbed his duffle bag on the way.

"Okay, it's cool in here. And with the blinds closed it's fairly dark. The sun's gone down so the light will be fading fast." He stepped over and lifted one of the slats on the blinds to peer out. "Looks like it might rain."

He turned. "I've got to take a shower. Can I trust you not to get into trouble?" He sent her a mischievous grin. "Or am I going to have to cuff us together?"

Her cheeks flamed with heat. "No. No. I promise. I'll sit right there in the middle of the bed. You don't have to worry about me. I've learned my lesson." *All my lessons,* she added silently.

"Just to be safe, I've got the keys to all the doors with me."

Irritation sent heat along her nerve endings. "Right. Typical. You can't possibly trust me. It's insulting that neither you nor my brother think I have sense enough to take care of myself or to stay out of trouble. I mean, what if there's a fire while you're in the shower, and you've got all the door keys?"

Lucas shook his head and clamped his jaw again. If she didn't know just how irritated he was at her, she'd think he was struggling not to smile. "First of all, that's not going to happen. Second, if there is a fire, you come into the bathroom and get me, and we'll escape through the window in there." He gave a brief nod. "Okay?"

Angela scraped her teeth across her lower lip. "I still wish you'd consider for one moment that I can take care of myself."

"Listen, sugar. Brad and I both know you can take care of yourself, normally. But this isn't a normal situation. Your *life* is in danger. And your life is not something either Brad or I take lightly. We love you, and in spite of your stubbornness, we *are* going to take care of you."

By the time Lucas finished his shower and emerged from the bathroom in khaki shorts and a white T-shirt, Angela had changed back into the orange caftan. She'd turned back the comforter and the blanket and climbed beneath the sheets.

He had his duffle bag in one hand and was finger-drying his hair with the other. In the dim light filtered by the closed blinds, his skin shimmered a dusky gold color against the white of his T-shirt. His bare arms and legs were sleek and toned. His shoulders were broad, and the loose T-shirt barely hinted at the planed abs beneath.

In high school, his fresh good looks and slender body had promised powerful, virile manhood.

They had delivered, with interest.

He went around to the other side of the bed and set the bag on the floor and then rooted in it. Angela leaned up on one elbow, curious to see what he was looking for. She heard the clattering of keys.

He set a key ring and several individual keys on the bedside table and then dug again. A cell phone went beside the keys. He dipped into the duffle bag a third time and came up with a gun. It seemed to be the gun he'd drawn from underneath his shirt. But as he ejected the magazine and checked it, then reinserted it with that unmistakable sound, it looked twice as big. Even in his large, long-fingered hand.

"Do you have two of those?"

He shook his head. "I put it in the bag while I showered. Safety." He laid it on the bedside table.

"But now you're keeping it right out there on the table?"

"That's right."

She swallowed.

He pushed his hands through his damp hair one more time and lay down on top of the sheet.

She lay back down and studied his profile across the expanse of white sheets.

He closed his eyes, the lids sweeping down as they fanned the longest lashes she'd ever seen.

"You doing okay over there, Brat?"

"I'm okay. I'd be happier if there wasn't a lethal weapon less than three feet away from me, but yeah, I'm fine."

"I'm going to nap awhile. I'm sure I won't sleep long." He turned his head and looked at her, a twinkle in his green eyes. "Don't go anywhere."

She shook her head in frustration and sighed. "Yes, dear."

For a second his gaze held hers, then he turned over. "Say good night, Gracie."

Her chest fluttered with a chuckle and something else as her gaze traced the slightly ragged line of his hair along the nape of his neck. What was it about a man's nape? It looked so innocent, so vulnerable, so—sexy.

She swallowed. "Good night, Gracie," she whispered, because his breaths already sounded even and strong.

He was asleep.

A DEEP, SHARP CRACK split the air. Angela sat bolt upright, gasping. The room was shaking. She tried to scream, but she didn't have enough breath.

Blinding light flashed in her eyes and another crack rattled the windows. She pushed herself back against the headboard. Her breath rasped in her ears.

"It's just thunder," came a rough sleepy voice from right beside her.

"What?"

"Ange? Sugar, wake up. It's me, Lucas."

"Lucas?" *Lucas?* But it was dark. She was in bed.

She reached out blindly just as another bright flash and resounding boom filled the air. She saw his silhouette sit up. He turned and loomed over her, then she felt his arm around her, pulling her close.

The sky continued to rumble as rain beat down noisily on the tin roof of the cabin, but suddenly she didn't mind it so much. Lucas's body was sleepy-warm and big enough to shield her from any threat.

"I thought it was another ex-explosion," she stammered.

"Nah. Just thunder. I told you we were in for some rain." He pulled her head down to rest against his chest. His voice rumbled through her like the thunder.

And like the thunder, it scared her.

His voice, his body, his very presence, was like a drug—a dangerously addictive drug. And she knew if she ever gave in, she'd be hooked.

His palm slid up and down her arm, petting and comforting her. He laid his cheek against her hair. "How're you doing?" he whispered.

And there it was again, that urge to kiss him. Apparently, it was never going to go away. It would be so easy. All she had to do was lift her head.

She'd raise it slowly. He'd wait. Then when they were looking into each other's eyes, all she'd have to do was press her lips against his.

Easy.

Except that she'd kissed him twice before, and both times he'd rejected her. What if he rejected her a third time?

"I like your hair like this," he muttered. "It's soft. Why don't you let it curl like this all the time?" His left hand still caressed her arm. He touched her hair with his right hand, then brushed it back from her face. Let his fingers trail along her cheek to her neck.

She gasped quietly at the feel of his warm, rough fingers. Was he coming on to her? Or just comforting her?

The sky exploded again and she jumped. She couldn't help it. "Sorry," she whispered.

His arm tightened around her and he wrapped his other hand around the nape of her neck. "Don't be. I remember, you were always afraid of thunderstorms."

She nodded, her eyes closed. "They're always so big, and you can't get away from them."

He laughed softly. "I'm going to go out on a limb here and guess that your fear of thunderstorms is not because you can't get away from them, Brat. You're afraid of them because you can't control them."

His thumb slid along her jawline. The simple gesture made her entire body ache with unbearable longing.

"Because being in control is what you're all about,

isn't it? It doesn't matter if it's the weather, or your brother, or a stalker, or me—you refuse to give in. It's in your nature to fight."

She squeezed her eyes shut and swallowed. Every slight touch, every word that rumbled up from his chest, was stoking her desire.

"Comes from—from having a big brother and his best friend who were always two steps ahead of me," she stammered. A pulse fluttered in her throat.

His thumb pressed gently on her jaw, urging her head up. She met his gaze, and the fire in his eyes sent a spear of yearning all the way through her, down to her sexual core.

She'd gotten a fleeting glimpse of that green fire before—twice. But this time, the fire didn't die as quickly as it appeared.

This time it stayed.

This time, *he* was going to kiss *her*.

And in that instant everything changed. Protector became lover. Safety morphed into danger—danger to her heart.

Angela knew all she had to do was lift her head another millimeter and his lips would cover hers.

After that, who knew what would happen? She didn't know, nor did she care.

She was consumed with need. She throbbed with desire. And it was far too late for second guesses. So she threw caution to the thunderstorm outside and lifted her head.

Lucas made a soft sound deep in his throat and kissed her. At first it was a soft, short pressing of lips on lips. Then he paused, he lifted his head and stared into her eyes.

She wanted to close them, to block out the inevitable

sight of those brilliant emerald eyes fading to opaque jade as he realized, once again, that he didn't want her. But she couldn't.

Whatever happened between them this time, she was going to meet it head-on.

So she tilted her head back a little more and reached for his mouth with hers. His mouth came down again, softly. But almost immediately, the pressure increased and his tongue traced the seam of her lips until she parted them. Then his hand on her nape slid up to cradle the back of her head and his mouth took hers, seeking her tongue with his.

When her heart was racing so fast that she thought she couldn't breathe, and her entire body was pulsing with desire, he left her mouth and trailed his tongue down her jawline, down her neck, all the way to her collarbone, where he nibbled lightly.

His fingers slid down her neck to caress the skin he was kissing. Then further, until they trailed fire along the curve of her breast. When his hot, questing fingers brushed her nipple, she arched, pushing her breast into his hand as liquid fire burned all the way to her core.

He arched, too, and she felt the length of his erection through his khaki shorts. Tentatively, fearfully, she touched him. Lightning flashed again and a roar of thunder shook the room.

Lucas gasped as the touch of her hand sent shudders through his body. He strained, forcing his length more fully against her hand. The stiff fabric of his khaki shorts rubbed against his flesh, creating a nearly unbearable friction that only ratcheted his need higher.

Angela's breasts were barely covered by the thin cloth of the gown she wore. Her nipples puckered, perfectly visible through the gauzy fabric. Was she naked under the gown? Lust stabbed him at the thought.

He kissed her again, as his hand slid lower, lower, until he felt the swell of her hip.

Her hand still stroked him through his clothes. Her breathing had changed, now coming in short, sharp bursts, just like his.

She was turned on. She wanted this as much as he did. And that was a lot. More than anything he'd ever desired in his life.

Only, he shouldn't.

For a split second, reality triumphed over desire. He was betraying her trust. Acting purely on hormones, when he ought to be detached and focused on the important problem—stopping the man who was trying to kill her.

He realized that he'd gone still when Angela looked up at him, fear and inevitability almost drowning out the desire in her eyes.

He didn't want to watch that desire die.

So he covered her hand with his and guided it to the button fly of his shorts. Her gaze held his.

He nodded, and her chocolate eyes widened slightly.

Then, one by one, her fingers nimble and sure, she undid the buttons. With each success, she slid her fingers along the exposed flesh.

By the time all the buttons were undone, Lucas was holding onto the last dregs of his self-control with all his strength. She tugged at his shorts. Ignoring the last passing reminder of the inevitable regret he'd feel when morning came, Lucas pushed his shorts and briefs down and off, saving her the trouble.

Then he bunched the material of her gown in his hand and slid it up her body.

Within seconds, they were both naked and he was holding her slender, supple body pressed tightly to his and kissing her senseless.

When he slid his hand up her thigh and delved into her with a finger, she cried out and clutched him closer.

"Lucas," she whispered. "Please—"

He knew what she was asking. Her hand closed around him, squeezing, rubbing, caressing, and she whispered again. "Please—"

He raised himself above her and pushed into her silken waiting core. And groaned.

Angela cried out softly, then arched her hips, giving him full access, which he took. For a few seconds he didn't move, allowing her time to get used to him. He tortured himself by staying perfectly still until he thought he might explode. Then when he did move, it was excruciatingly slowly.

But she wasn't having slow and easy. His chest rumbled slightly with laughter. Not his Brat. Even in bed, she fought to be in control.

"Stop trying to be on top," he whispered in her ear, then he kissed his way from her ear to her lips. "You're not going to win this one."

Then he thrust inside her—hard. Hard and long. He moved in and out, in and out until he saw her expression change from determination to surprise to ecstasy.

He thrust again and came in a burst of inner light that rivaled the storm outside. Within a split second, she gasped and arched and he felt the full extent of her orgasm as she pulsed around him.

He buried his face between her neck and shoulder, breathing hard. As his breathing slowed, he heard her soft sigh and felt her fingers tracing his forearms, his biceps and triceps, his shoulders.

He'd satisfied her. He knew that. What he didn't know was how she was going to feel about him when morning came.

He lifted his head and brushed his lips across hers, then gently rolled away, pulling her into the crook of his arm.

She settled in with a soft sigh, as if she were made to fit there.

With the super-attenuated clarity of second thought, he understood that he was going to regret this. A few moments of indulgence may have cost him the most precious necessity for keeping her safe.

Her trust.

Chapter Fourteen

Lucas's cell phone woke him. He came awake completely aware of everything around him. He'd learned that trick early on, when his dad would come home late and drunk.

The bed beside him was empty, only a small indentation in the pillow indicating that Angela had been there. He grabbed the ringing phone with one hand and his briefs with the other, as his eyes swept the room.

The bathroom door was closed, and he realized he heard the shower running. He let out a sigh of relief.

"Yeah?" he said into the phone.

"Luke! Why didn't you answer?" Brad asked sharply.

"I was asleep," he said, glancing at the phone's display. "It's not even seven o'clock."

The bathroom door opened and Angela emerged through a fast-dispersing cloud of steam. She had the orange gown on, and her hair was wet.

He held up his hand in a warning to stay quiet.

"Asleep?" Several explicit curse words told Lucas what Brad thought about that.

"Lucas, do you have any toothpaste?" Angela asked, missing or ignoring his upraised hand.

"Is that Angela?" Brad snapped.

Lucas grimaced.

"What the hell? You said you were asleep. Listen you SOB, you'd better not—"

"Brad, come on. She just came in looking for tooth-paste. I wouldn't—" But he had.

Angela froze and her face turned red.

Lucas pointed at his duffel bag but didn't move to help her. He couldn't. He was naked under the covers, and he was pretty sure she wouldn't appreciate him jumping up.

She sidled over to the bag, grabbed the tube and rushed back into the bathroom.

"Yeah, sorry," Brad said. "I know you'd never take advantage of my little sister. I'm just really on edge. I got this number from Dawson. Listen, Luke. There was a note in our mailbox this morning. One of the cops watching the house saw a kid leave it. It was written in block letters. It said 'Too late, Mr. ADA. Your sister's already dead.'"

Fear arrowed through Lucas's gut. "Good God, Brad!"

"I know," Brad responded. "It scared the crap out of me."

"Did they catch the kid?"

"Yeah, but of course he knew nothing. Some guy gave him twenty bucks to put it in the box. What do you think it means?"

Lucas thought fast. Obviously, the hit man had reason to believe he knew where Angela was. That was the only thing that made sense. "Listen to me, Brad. That's scary as hell, but I think they're just trying to put pressure on you. Trust me. I haven't seen anything that would make me think they know where we are."

"Well, listen to this. Nikki and Milo showed up at the

prison to see their dad, but Paulo wasn't with them, and neither was Tony."

"Okay. So big brother Paulo may have taken off down here to help baby brother Tony. We'll be ready for them. I'm going to hang up now, in case they're monitoring your phone. Next time send a text."

Lucas hung up and quickly pulled on his briefs and shorts. When he turned around, Angela was standing in the doorway to the bathroom, the toothpaste in her hand. Her chocolate eyes were wide and worried.

"Who are Paulo and Tony?" she asked.

How much had she heard? He stepped over and took the tube, noticing that she let go as soon as his fingers touched it. He took his cue from her.

"Nobody," he said without looking at her.

"So now you think the hit man who's after me is nobody? Because it sounded to me like he's somebody you need to be *ready* for."

"Don't worry about it. Nothing's happening this weekend. We'll know more after the trial reconvenes on Monday."

"So Brad only called to tell you the hit men were in New Orleans? Right. *That's* nothing to worry about."

"He was just letting me know what's happening up there." Lucas was breaking his own rule by lying to her. But nothing good could come from her knowing about the cruel note.

"And you still think they're monitoring his phone, too. How can that be? I mean, Brad and the whole family are in protective custody."

He shrugged. "Can't take any chances. It's easy to track a cell phone these days."

"As easy as setting up a spy cam?"

There was an edge of recrimination to her voice. He

couldn't even feel indignant about her attitude. He deserved recrimination and more for his monumental lapse in judgment. He never should have made love to her the night before.

He turned, his mouth quirked up at the corner. "Probably every bit as easy. I'll go make coffee."

He skirted the end of the bed, doing his best to stay as far away from her as possible. He needn't have bothered. As soon as he moved, she stepped, out of his way.

In the kitchen, he put the coffee on and paced as he waited for it to brew. He did his best not to think about the night before, but his brain wasn't cooperating.

She already regretted their lovemaking just like he knew she would. He regretted it, too, but probably not for the same reason she did. Once he'd realized that he didn't have the willpower to stop himself from making love to her, and had accepted that she wasn't going to stop him, he'd hoped at least he'd finally be able to get her out of his system.

No such luck.

Nothing worked. Not splashing cold water from the sink on his face. Not gulping half a quart of orange juice.

Twelve years ago, Angela's innocent, soft kiss had shocked the hell out of him. And not only because he'd never suspected that she felt anything but a big brotherlike hero worship for him. He'd always been a friend to her, a buddy, just like he was to Brad.

Or at least that's what he'd always told himself. But her kiss had shocked him to the core. Suddenly, Brad's bratty little sister wasn't a kid. She was a woman.

If Lucas hadn't already had a really good reason to get out of Chef Voleur, she'd given him one that night.

He'd run like hell away from his hometown not only

to escape the infamy and scandal of the Delancey name but also to deny the terrifying truth that he suddenly lusted after a girl he'd known since they were kids. A girl who'd trusted him, just like she trusted her big brother. Until he'd betrayed her trust by kissing her.

Staring out the bank of windows that faced Lake Pontchartrain, Lucas shook his head. As of last night, kissing Angela wasn't the worst mistake he'd ever made.

Making love with her was.

"Lucas?"

He whirled.

She stood in the kitchen doorway, dressed in the enormous man's shirt and tight jeans she'd worn last night. She had a pair of pants in her hand, and she looked terrified.

"What is it?"

"These are the Capri pants I've been wearing ever since the other night when you found the camera."

He frowned. "Yeah?"

"There's something on them." She held them out in a trembling hand.

"You mean like blood?"

She shook her head.

He took the pants from her. "What am I looking for, Ange?"

She pointed. "The waist. There. I'm not sure what it is, but I'm afraid—"

He looked at the waistband of the pants.

And saw it.

There, stuck to the left back of the waistband, was a small plastic disk. It was light enough that it wouldn't weigh down the pants but large enough to notice, unless the person it had been planted on was under a tremendous amount of stress.

Like Angela had been.

"Lucas—"

He nodded. "It's a GPS tracking device. Son of a bitch!" He grabbed a paper towel and covered the disk with it to preserve the fingerprints before he ripped it away from the material.

He squeezed it in his fist. "I ought to—" *No.* It was too late to destroy it. Whoever had planted it on her already knew where they were. They'd had—how long? He opened his fist and studied the small disk.

"When did this happen?" he muttered.

"It must have been after the car exploded," Angela replied. "The EMTs were pushing your gurney through the crowd and I was following you. I almost fell more than once. People in the crowd caught me and set me upright."

That made sense. The crowd had been as tight as sardines.

"If he was close enough to plant this GPS on you, why didn't he just—" He stopped.

"Why didn't he just kill me? She shrugged. "Maybe he's a coward. Maybe he doesn't know how to shoot a gun. You said he's the baby of the family, right?"

Lucas nodded. She could be right. Maybe Tony had planted the device and now he was waiting for his sharpshooter brother Paulo to come in and finish the job. "He's had more than a day to track us." He put the paper-wrapped plastic disk in his pocket, cursing himself for not suspecting something like this. "No wonder they said you were already dead."

"What?" Angela's face drained of all color. She swayed and caught hold of the back of a kitchen chair.

"Damn it!" He had to focus. He was making mistakes right and left. He was getting what he deserved for taking his mind off his purpose.

Trouble was, Angela was in the crosshairs, which was exactly why he should have never allowed himself to let down his guard, not even for one kiss, much less a full night of pleasure.

"They? Who said I was al-already dead?" Her knuckles were white where she held onto the back of the chair. "What—are you talking about?"

He set his jaw. No more giving in to his feelings. He was her protector. Her bodyguard. And that was all.

"Brad got a note," he said in a measured tone. "It said, 'Mr. ADA, your sister is already dead.' That's what he called about."

Her face grew ashen. Her throat moved as she swallowed. "You—didn't think I needed to know that?"

He shook his head.

The indescribable fear that held her in thrall was his fault. He'd sworn to keep her safe—to Brad, to himself and to her. And he'd failed.

"I don't understand. Why would they write a note like that? What does it mean?"

It meant she wasn't safe with him. And once he answered her question, she'd realize that. She'd know that even though he'd promised her she could trust him, she'd been stupid to do so.

"It means they've found you."

ANGELA STARED AT LUCAS, not wanting to believe her ears. She'd known in the rational part of her brain what the disk was as soon as she'd seen it. But the emotional side, the terror-filled side, had tried to deny it. Had hoped that Lucas would have some other explanation for what it was.

"You're saying the hit man—put that thing on me."

Lucas nodded blandly, as if he'd been asked if he wanted a drink. No concern. No reassurance. No emotion of any kind.

Within the space of a few seconds, he'd changed completely. He was no longer her brother's best friend. And even though just a few hours ago they'd shared the most intimate experience two people could possibly share, he was not the lover who'd held her so tenderly and made her feel beautiful and loved and secure in his arms. He wasn't even the cop who'd promised to protect her.

He was a stranger. A cold, aloof stranger just doing his job. Even as that thought slid through her mind she knew it wasn't true.

She knew him. He wasn't a distant, cold man. Certainly not about responsibility. Lucas was passionate, determined, focused. Never detached.

So what was he doing?

And then the answer hit her. Of course. He was afraid he'd failed her, and he was trying to hide his fear.

"Lucas?" she said tentatively.

"You need to eat something. I'm going outside to look around." He half turned. "Don't leave the house."

"What about you? You need to eat, too."

He didn't answer her. He just opened the kitchen door and stalked through it, slamming it behind him.

Angela watched him until he was out of sight. His back was straight. He strode purposefully down the back steps and across the lawn toward the lake, moving with a powerful grace, like a lion or a tiger—like a predator. Then she saw him reach behind under his T-shirt and pull his weapon.

When she saw that, she realized it didn't matter whether he regretted what they'd done. It didn't even matter if she never saw him again after all this was over.

Nothing mattered, except that he was prepared to give his life to save hers.

He was her hero.

LUCAS FELT THE SLIGHT WEIGHT of the disk in his pocket as he surveyed the area around the cabin. The words from the note Brad had read him rang in his ears.

Your sister's already dead.

It took every ounce of his willpower to quell the urge to throw the GPS locator on the ground and stomp it into dust. He was second-guessing himself—never a good idea. His instincts had always been good.

But his brain kept on anyway. What if it wasn't too late? What if the hit man hadn't tracked her to this location yet?

He might still have time to get her away from here, leaving the locator behind as a decoy.

He shook his head. Anyone savvy enough and with enough chutzpah to plant a locator in a crowd was certainly smart enough to have already pinpointed their location and be on their way, and he didn't want to meet them on the narrow road that was the only way to get to the cabin.

He wanted to be prepared. Find a vantage point from which he could pick them off as they arrived.

Pulling the disk out of his pocket, he stared at it. The hit man had been right next to Angela. He'd touched her.

The thought of Tony Picone being that close to Angela, the image of him pressing the sticky back of the disk against her pants, sent chills down Lucas's back. Tony had been close enough to kill her.

So why hadn't he?

Either he'd been ordered not to, or he'd chickened out. If the latter was the case, then what Brad said made a lot of sense. If it was Tony, the baby, then this was his first hit.

But the question he'd asked Brad still plagued him. Why would the crime lord have sent his wife's baby boy on such an important mission? Lucas couldn't think of a good answer. But maybe that was because the elder Picone *hadn't* sent him. What if Tony had taken it upon himself to free his father?

Lucas liked those odds.

He pulled out his cell phone and dialed his brother's number. "Ethan, it's me."

"Are you okay? Has something happened to my car?"

"The car's fine. And by the way, so are we. Listen. This is important. Tony Picone planted a tracking device on Angela's clothes. He knows where we are."

"Tracking device? How the hell did that happen without you seeing it? And when?"

"Had to be in the crowd after the explosion."

"Damn. If he was that close to her—"

"He could have shot her. But this is his first hit. Either the old man's given orders not to hurt her, or Tony's here on his own, which means anything could happen."

"Seen any sign of him?"

"No, but I'm expecting him any minute. I figure he waited until daylight, since he doesn't know anything about the area around here." As Lucas spoke, he heard Felton's dogs howling.

"And around here is—?"

"The fishing cabin."

"Good idea."

Lucas smiled wryly. "Yeah, when I thought he couldn't find us. I'm thinking I'd like to have some backup. What do you think? Can you or your boss call the Madison local law enforcement?"

There was a slight pause. Was Ethan weighing the advantages of helping the brother he'd been angry at for so long?

Now's not the time, kid. They could go head to head about their personal differences when Angela's life was no longer in danger. He opened his mouth to say as much.

"Why don't you get out of there? You can't see the road from the cabin."

"He's had plenty of time to get here. I don't want to run into him on the road with Angela in the car. I'd rather stay up here and meet him on my turf. Felton's watching the road for me."

"Okay," Ethan responded. "I'll give Sheriff Lessard a call and see if he can send a couple of deputies. You want them now?"

"Now would be good. Maybe post a car down at the road and send a couple up here."

"Sure, if you think you can handle him yourself."

There it was. The attitude. The kid brother who'd never gotten over being left behind—twice. First by Robert, who'd gone and gotten himself killed in Afghanistan, and then by Lucas, when he'd headed for Texas after graduation.

"That's right kid. I've decided I could use some help keeping my—keeping Ange alive."

"I'll call Lessard now."

"Have him approach silently, okay? But ready to take

the guy down." Just as he spoke, Lucas's phone beeped. It was Felton, the bootlegger. He hung up with Ethan.

"Felton? What's up?"

"Lucas, there's a car behind your house. I went down to feed the girls out back and didn't see it. Didn't hear it either. The girls were howling."

Damn it! He hadn't heard anything either. "I got my shotgun, "Felton continued. "We're on our way."

"Thanks. Try not to shoot the good guys."

The old man chuckled as he cut the connection.

Lucas sprinted back toward the house.

As he started across the short expanse of lawn, a shot ricocheted off the trunk of a tree right beside his head.

He dove instinctively, reaching at his back for his weapon. Had that shot come from inside the house?

Angela!

Chapter Fifteen

Tony Picone heard the rifle shot. Good. Paulie had his sights on Delancey. With any luck, that one shot had taken the big man down. Paulie was the best shot by far, of all Papa's men.

He turned back to Angela, who was sitting in a kitchen chair staring at the barrel of his Glock.

He brandished the roll of duct tape in his other hand. "I said hold out your hands, or would you rather have a matching knot on the other side of your head?"

"Go to hell." She shook her head, dislodging a small trickle of blood from the cut where he'd hit her with the butt of his gun. Her brown eyes were filled with fear and hatred.

He didn't care. He wasn't trying to win a popularity contest. His sole purpose was to show Papa that he wasn't a baby. That he could handle himself in the family business as well as any of his older brothers. Better, in fact. Because he had the brains.

He holstered his Glock in his side holster and yanked a long strip of tape off the roll. He trussed Angela's wrists and forearms, winding the tape all the way up to her elbows. Then he wound another long strip around her torso and shoulders, securing her hands tightly against her chest. Finally, he wrapped the end of the tape around her neck.

He'd demonstrated that method for his older brothers. Paulie had seemed mildly interested, but Milo had laughed and Nikki Jr. had echoed his Papa. *Forget about it, Tony. You'll break Mama's heart with that talk. You're not in the business.*

"Now see?" he said to Angela. "My brothers shoulda paid attention to me. See how effective that is? You can't move your arms *or* your head. No biting the tape and getting free, right?" He giggled. "Go ahead. Try it."

She glared at him.

"Okay, but you gotta admit it's a good design. Now, stick out your feet."

She sucked in air in preparation for screaming.

He backhanded her. "You think I'm kidding, or what? See. Now you got matching bruises. It's what you call symmetrical. I like symmetrical. Now, Angela, if you don't keep your mouth shut, I'll cut your tongue out. Do you believe that?"

"Coward," she spat. "Who are you anyway? One of Picone's sons? I'll bet you're Tony, the baby. I've heard about you. Apparently you don't take after your father, because you are a pitiful excuse for a hit man."

He slapped her openhanded, twice. "Didn't I tell you to keep your mouth shut. As soon as Paulo is finished with your big convenient bodyguard out there, I'll get him to come in and hold your mouth open so you don't bite me when I go to slice your tongue. See this?" He set the duct tape down and pulled a switchblade out of his pocket.

He pressed a button and the blade sang open. "It's double-sided. You don't see many of those these days. Take a look at that stainless steel. It's sharp."

Angela just stared at him without speaking. But her face turned pale and she didn't say anything else. He knew he'd gotten to her.

"Let me show you."

He pointed the blade at her left nostril and slowly inserted the tip of it.

Her breath caught, but to her credit, she didn't move. Her eyes never left his. "You think this little pointy blade could slice right through your nostril?"

She swallowed but remained perfectly still.

"Do you?" He smiled. "Oh, that's right. I told you not to talk. Be sure not to shake your head either. It wouldn't be a good idea." He left the blade there for another few seconds. "I wonder how long you could sit there without moving, Angela? A few minutes? A few hours?"

A tear formed in her left eye and slid over the lid to trickle down her cheek.

"Good answer." He removed the knife and snicked it shut. "Now, like I said before. It's time to do your *feet*, Angela. Stick 'em straight out in front of you."

As he wrapped duct tape around her ankles, he congratulated himself. He'd seen some of the things his brothers had done. Some of their particular techniques. Most of them were crude but effective.

He'd sat for hours in his engineering classes at the university, sketching out ideas to make their techniques more effective, once Papa made him part of the family business.

He'd designed the methods on paper, and he'd tried a couple out by himself, like the bombs, but he'd never gotten a chance to use them for real. It was a heady victory to know that this one worked.

Outside he heard another rifle shot.

"Damn it," he muttered. He'd hoped Paulie had taken

out Delancey on the first shot. Paulie had the skill, but he was used to working in the concrete jungle of Chicago or in the area around Lake Michigan. This place, this ungodly hot, overgrown marsh, was an entirely different world.

Then as he finished binding Angela's ankles, the silence was split by a burst of shots—from a handgun.

That had to be Delancey.

"Come on, Paulie," he muttered as he pocketed his knife. "How hard can it be to take him out with that fancy rifle?"

"Paulie. Oh, right. Paulo. One of your older brothers? He's the real hit man, isn't he?"

"You shut up!" he shouted. "I didn't tape your mouth, but I will. Just as soon as you call your ADA brother and tell him to drop the case against Papa. And if you don't shut up about me and my family, I'll do a lot more than just cut your tongue out."

"You put that GPS locator on me, didn't you? In the crowd after the car you rigged exploded."

"Shut up. Where the hell is your phone?"

"You were close enough to shoot me with that brand new, shiny gun. Why didn't you?"

She gasped. "Like that," she panted. "You couldn't, could you? I'll bet you had the gun out. Had your finger on the trigger. But couldn't kill me then, and you can't kill me now. "

"Shut! Up!"

"So you called Paulo, didn't you? He had to come down here to help his little brother, the coward."

Tony's scalp and ears burned with panic and fury. He shoved the gun's barrel deeper into the soft tissue of her breast. "What's the matter with you? Do you *want* me to shoot you?"

Outside, the unmistakable blast of a shotgun rent the air. Tony jerked upright. *What the hell was going on out there?*

Angela tried not to gasp at the sickening pain of the gun barrel bruising her breast. It didn't take a cop to understand that a scared guy holding a gun represented a very dangerous situation. Tony was scared, but he was also smart.

Yes, he might have panicked in the crowd and balked at shooting her then. But now...his plans had changed. Tony had an agenda. He was much more interested in freeing his father than killing her outright. His whole purpose in coming down here had been to prove to his papa that he was as good as his brothers.

The question remained—was he? She didn't know.

What she did know was that all the gunfire from outside was ominous. She'd told Tony that the shots meant that Paulo was hurt, but inside she was terrified that it was Lucas who was getting the worst of it.

Whatever was going on out there, it was obvious that Lucas had his hands full. She couldn't count on him to save her. Him or anyone else.

She was on her own. She carefully tried to strain against the tape binding her wrists and ankles. She had to admit, Tony was right about the way he'd trussed her. There was no way she could move as much as a fingertip to save herself. All she had were her wits and her mouth. So until he got mad enough to gag her or, God forbid, cut her tongue, she had to use them. Maybe if she could rattle him, she could somehow get away, or stall him until Luke get here. If he *could*.

"What's Papa going to think of you when you get yourself thrown in prison, Tony?" she taunted. "You might scare my brother to throw the trial and letting your papa out of jail. That's admirable. A son taking care of his papa. Nobody can deny that you're a good son. But what about when he's out and you're behind bars for kidnapping, attempted murder or even murder? What's Papa going to do then?"

She took a shaky breath and wondered if she was wasting it. Tony was barely listening to her. He'd backed away finally and removed that steel-hard bruising barrel from her breast.

He sidled over to the windows to look outside. Her heart sped up in hope. Maybe Lucas would see him through the window and shoot him.

Dear God, was she actually hoping that a human being would be killed?

She was.

Once he got to the window, Tony crouched down and slunk back to stand in front of her.

"Where's your phone?"

"Don't you have one?" she retorted.

"We're using yours. You're going to call your brother and tell him to let my papa go."

Angela swallowed hard. "Like I said, your papa is going to be free as a bird and you're going to be locked up behind bars. What do you think he's going to do then? Is he going to stop his illegal activities and spend all his time and resources to free you, like you're working so hard to do for him?"

Tony growled in exasperation. "I said—"

"He's not, is he? He doesn't care a thing about you, does he? You're just a big mama's boy. Your mother probably whined and pleaded with him not to let you get involved in the family business. Your brothers probably think you're a sissy, don't they?"

"I said shut up!" Tony swung the pistol around and

aimed it right at Angela's head. His eyes were fiery and black, like smoldering volcanic rock. He stalked over until the barrel of the gun was pressed against the center of her forehead.

She swallowed bitter bile. Had she gone too far? Was her desperate attempt to rattle Tony Picone going to get her killed?

"Don't you breathe another word about my mother. Now where is your god…damned…purse?"

He pushed the barrel into her forehead with each of the last three syllables.

"In-in the chair on the other side of the table," she stammered. Despite how hard she was trying to sound tough and unafraid, her insides were churning and her head was spinning with fear.

Tony moved sideways and reached for her bag. With one hand he dumped its contents out on the table, never once taking his gun off her.

Outside, more shots shattered the silence. Different shots, coming from different directions.

Please God, don't let Lucas get shot. He was tired and hurt, and she wasn't sure how long his strength would hold out.

Tony scattered the contents of her purse until he spotted her cell phone. He grabbed it and pressed a couple of buttons.

"Here he is. *Brad.*" He punched the number and listened.

"It's ringing." He held the phone up to Angela's ear, and sure enough, Brad answered.

"Brad! Don't listen to him!" she shouted.

Tony jerked the phone away and swung at her head again. This time it was his knuckles that impacted with her cheek, rather than the butt of the gun.

It still hurt. She grunted with pain.

"Shut up, bitch!" Tony held the phone to his ear. "This is Tony Picone, Mr. ADA. If you don't make sure my father is back home with no legal problems hanging over his head by tomorrow morning, I'm going to kill your sister."

He stopped and listened.

Angela could make out Brad's voice, shrill with fear, but she couldn't tell what he was saying.

"Oh, yeah? Well, you're way up there in Chicago with not a lot of options, and I'm standing right here with a gun aimed at your sweet little sister's head. So who do you think is in charge?"

He paused, listening. "That's right. Matter of fact, I'm starting now, with a few cuts and bruises. I'll get to the bigger stuff later on this evening."

Brad shouted something.

"You just call me back with the exact time my papa will be released. You'd better figure out some way of verifying that Papa's free, because I'm not letting your sister go until I'm sure you've fixed it so he can never be arrested again—for *anything*!" He paused.

"I don't care if it's impossible. It's your job to make it possible. Meanwhile, your sister and me are going to get to know each other. Got it?"

Brad's frenzied words crackled through the air.

"My brother Paulie, the sharpshooter, is taking care of him. Lucas Delancey won't be an issue very much longer."

Whatever Brad said next infuriated Tony. "Don't count on it. You better spend your time getting my papa out of jail. If you don't call me back here on your sister's phone no later than nine o'clock this evening and tell me what's been done, your sister is going to be a lot worse for wear. By ten o'clock, she'll never be able to talk to you again. Then by eleven—well, I think you get the picture."

Tony flipped the phone shut and turned his black eyes to meet her gaze. "Your brother seems to be sufficiently scared for your life."

He grinned. "While I wait to hear what your brother's gonna do to make sure Papa is set free, I'm going to cut the tape on your ankles, because you and me, we're going into the bedroom. It'll be a lot more comfortable to wait in there until Paulie takes care of your bodyguard."

He leered at her. "A *lot* more comfortable."

LUCAS CRINGED AS THE BULLET ricocheted off the tree next to his ear. He darted out, fired off three rounds, then ducked back.

Another loud crack, another bullet zinging past his head. Whoever was shooting at him was good. Damn good. And that rifle was no pea-shooter, either.

Of course, neither was Felton Scruggs's shotgun, he thought, as a deep boom reverberated through the air. As far as Lucas could tell, Felton was east of the house. He had to be close, and he had to have a bead on the sniper. Felton had never wasted a shot in his life. So the sniper wasn't *inside* the house.

Lucas didn't know what that meant, and not knowing was eating him up inside. Was the sniper Tony Picone? Was he alone?

Lucas was sure the answer to both questions was no. Someone who'd rather plant a GPS locator on his target than go ahead and shoot her wouldn't be able to handle a long-range rifle so competently. And Brad had told him Tony's brother Paulo was the expert sniper.

Another shot grazed the tree trunk next to his

shoulder. Lucas angled out and shot again. That had to be Paulo shooting the rifle. And that meant Tony was inside.

Bile churned in Lucas's gut. He'd left Angela alone. He'd failed her. The very thing he'd tried to prevent had happened.

Tony Picone had Angela. To get to her, Lucas had to get the sniper out of the picture.

Felton's shotgun boomed again, and as the thunder faded, Lucas heard something that turned his blood to ice.

A scream. From inside the house.

Chapter Sixteen

Angela's scream ripped through Lucas like a sniper's bullet. His fingers went numb and his heart stopped dead in his chest. Angela wasn't a screamer. She never had been. He couldn't imagine what Tony was doing to make her scream like that.

At least she was still alive. But that thought didn't reassure him. He flexed his hands. Then with a growl he whirled and emptied his magazine in the direction of the rifle shots.

He ducked back behind the tree and ejected the empty magazine. He refilled it as quickly as he could and slapped it back into his Sig Saur. Then he turned and fired again.

Another cry reached his ears, this one muffled and pained. That bastard was hurting her, while he and the sniper and Felton were playing shoot-'em-up. This stand-off could last for hours.

Angela didn't have hours.

Sweat broke out on his forehead and his gut clenched in impotent rage and frustration. He had to get to the cabin, even if it meant taking a bullet.

At that instant, Felton's hounds howled, and the plan that had eluded him now flashed in front of him.

Dogs. That was it! He dug into the pocket of his khaki shorts and retrieved his phone.

He hit the button that dialed the bootlegger. "Felton," he whispered.

"Luke, we ain't getting nowhere," Felton whispered.

"Can you see the sniper?"

"Yep. He's on this side of the house, having a ball with that fancy rifle."

Lucas heard the sound of Felton spitting tobacco on the ground.

"What if you let the dogs have a go at him?"

"My girls?" The bootlegger paused. Lucas knew he was thinking about that rifle and those penetrating bullets. "That pretty little girl—you like her, I reckon."

Lucas's eyes stung. "I like her a lot," he said, his voice choked.

Felton sighed. "Awright then, son, I believe you've got a plan. Just say when you're ready."

"When I say go, you count to three, then let the dogs go and I'll make a run for the back door."

"Your tail better be on fire, 'cause if I give my girls the word, I can't control 'em until the frenzy dies down."

"Count to three, Felton. Got it?"

"Got it."

"Go!"

Lucas shoved his phone in his back pocket as he pushed away from the tree and sprinted through the underbrush toward the house. He held his weapon in his right hand, ready to shoot.

A split second later he heard the unmistakable howls of seven dogs on a scent. He pumped his legs as hard as he could.

Felton had ordered the dogs to attack, and attack they

would, without regard to who were the good guys and who were the bad.

He heard the sniper's squeal and knew he'd sighted seven sets of bared teeth. Under the noise of the dogs, Lucas heard the double blast of Felton's shotgun. It excited the dogs, who growled and howled even louder.

Just about the time the sniper's squeal died down, Lucas spotted movement out of the corner of his eye. He was already running as fast as he could, but at the sight of three dogs bearing down on him, he pushed harder.

Growls and yelps filled his ears until he heard nothing else. Felton was probably still firing, but all Lucas heard was his own breath, the pounding of his heart and the dogs. As he crossed the last few yards toward the back steps of the cabin, he was sure he felt the hot breath of the hounds on his heels.

As he vaulted up the steps and slammed open the screen door, another sound joined the cacophony. It was the piercing squeal of sirens.

Damn it. He'd told them no sirens.

His shoulder hit the wooden porch floor first. He rolled, coming up hard against the kitchen door with a grunt of pain.

But there was no time to stop and lick his wounds. He had to get through the kitchen door before the dogs caught him. He rolled to his feet and grabbed the knob, twisting it open.

Two huge Doberman mixes slammed through the screen door as if it were paper and hit the thick wooden kitchen door just as Lucas had it almost shut. He put all his weight against it.

The Dobermans nearly outweighed him. It was pure luck that one of them backed up to charge again at the very instant he exerted his last ounce of strength to close the door.

Without stopping to glance back through the glass panes, Lucas whirled. The kitchen was empty, as he'd expected. If Picone had been in the room, Lucas wouldn't have made it this far.

In the back of his mind he registered several separate yet almost indistinguishable sounds—sirens, screams, frenzied yelps and barks, as he moved with quiet stealth into the long hall that stretched the entire length of the house.

Where the hell are they?

He triple-checked his weapon and held it ready as he slipped from one doorway to another down the hall. He checked the rooms on the other side of the hallway— the dining room and the living room—as he made his slow way down the hall. He rounded the facings of each bedroom door as he passed, but nothing.

Finally, there was only one room left—the master bedroom. The room where he and Angela had made love just last night.

The lowlife had her in there—waiting for him. After all the commotion, he had to know that Lucas was in the house.

Lucas stopped at the edge of the door, pressing his back against the wall and holding his gun ready to angle around and take a bead on the bastard who was holding Angela—hurting her.

He stood there, trying to control his breathing as he pictured the layout of the room. Angela had screamed twice, but suddenly the house was ominously silent.

What if they weren't in there? What if Tony had taken Angela outside? What if he was even now headed toward his vehicle?

If Tony tried to get away, he'd be facing the dogs, Felton's shotgun and the police. But Lucas knew there was another possibility. A real, grim possibility.

What if Picone had already killed her?

A pain worse than anything Lucas had ever felt in his life pierced his chest at that thought.

No. Focus!

She was alive. She had to be. He'd know if she were gone.

With a deep breath, he whirled around the door facing, his weapon pointed at the head of the bed. The image in front of him stole what little breath he had left in his body.

There, on the bed, was a grotesque sight. Angela, bound with duct tape, lay with her back against a small dark man Lucas recognized. He'd seen him at the sidewalk café. He was still dressed in that outrageous bowling shirt and blue baseball cap.

With stunning clarity, Lucas realized what had bothered him about the man when he'd seen him at the café. He'd seen a baseball cap on the table. That blue Chicago Cubs cap. And Lucas had missed it.

The little jerk held a switchblade, the point of which was inserted in Angela's left nostril. And he was smiling.

Lucas froze with his gun pointed at Picone's head.

"Lucas Delancey. We've been waiting for you. Haven't we, Angela?"

Angela's dark irises were completely surrounded by white. Her chest was rising and falling rapidly. But she didn't move a muscle.

Lucas could see that if her head moved even a fraction of an inch, the switchblade would slice through her nostril.

"Oh, that's right. You don't want to take the chance of speaking. Do you, Angela? If you move your head, it might hurt." He looked at Lucas. "Why don't you relax a minute while I fill you in on what your girlfriend and I have been talking about. You'll be more comfortable if you drop that gun."

The man's voice was calm, conversational—maddeningly so. Lucas's trigger finger twitched. He wanted nothing more than to shift his gun the millimeter or two it would take to get a bead on his head and squeeze the trigger.

But Tony was poised, ready to jerk Angela's body into position in front of him.

If Lucas tried to shoot him, he could easily shoot Angela.

"I can't do that, Tony. I'm going to need it."

Picone's left arm moved on Angela's body until it rested on her right breast.

A tear formed in her eye and slipped down her cheek. She never took her gaze off Lucas.

"If you don't, I'll have to slice her nose off. You'll scream for me again, won't you?" Picone stage-whispered in her ear.

The son of a bitch had made her scream.

Lucas wished with all his heart he had some kind of reassurance to give her, but he didn't. He was helpless. No matter what he did, he was going to end up getting her horribly injured or killed.

"The police are outside," he said in what he hoped was an authoritarian voice.

"I heard them. Do I look like I care?" the man replied.

"What are you planning to do? It's not like you can just get up and walk out."

"I'm not planning to. I'm sitting right here until I get word from Chicago that the charges have been dropped against Papa, and he has walked out of prison a free man, with—what do they call it?—jeopardy attached, so they can never try him again."

"You know that's not going to happen."

Picone slid the tip of the switchblade out of Angela's nostril.

She sighed in relief just as Picone moved the knife to rest against her neck. Lucas stared at the glistening length of steel. He hoped Angela didn't know that the sharp blade was near her carotid artery.

She might be breathing easier, but she was in no less danger than she had been—more in fact. If Picone slit her nostril, it would be horrifying, but not lethal. If he slit her carotid, she'd die.

Lucas sighted down the barrel of his Sig and took a bead on Picone's head. "How long do you think you can hold that knife like that?"

"As long as you can hold that gun like that."

Lucas frowned to himself. There was something not quite right about Tony Picone. He really seemed not to care about the cops outside or Lucas's gun pointed at his head.

"I can call ADA Harcourt and see what's going on with your father."

"Right. You can do that, and good old Brad'll say anything he has to say to save his sister, right?" Picone shook his head. "No. I'm staying right here until somebody proves to me that Papa is free."

"What then?" Lucas asked. "You'll never get out of here. Whether you let Angela go or not, you're either a dead man or you're going to prison. Just put the knife down and we can all walk out there. I'll testify that you cooperated."

The knife pressed harder against Angela's neck. Lucas saw infinitesimal beads of blood appear on the bright metal of the knife. Impotent fury sent nausea crawling up the back of his throat.

"Nope. Can't do that," Tony said. "You don't get it, do you? I don't care what happens to me, as long as Papa knows I'm the one who got him set free."

"Do you care what happened to your buddy outside?"

Tony's eyes darted past Lucas for a split second. He *did*.

"He's sure good with that rifle. I heard somewhere that your brother Paulo is a crack shot." Lucas paused. "Ah. I get it. Papa sent your big brother to babysit you."

The black eyes snapped. Lucas had him. "Did you hear the dogs?" he said conversationally. "A friend of mine has them trained to attack."

Picone's gaze darted toward the back of the house, then back to meet Lucas's.

"So if there is anything left of your brother after the dogs got through with him, the police have him in custody—or in a body bag."

Lucas dared to meet Angela's gaze. Her eyes flickered—could have been with abject fear, he didn't know. He nodded his head no more than a half millimeter. He hoped Angela saw it. He hoped she believed his implied lie—that everything was okay, that he was going to save her.

"I'm tired of listening to you, Lucas," Tony said. "You offered to call Harcourt. Do it. See if he has any news for me."

Lucas shook his head. "I'm waiting for the police. As

soon as they load up your brother, they'll come storming in here and it'll be all over for you."

Tony shook his head and laughed. "Don't you get it? It's all over for me anyway. But you're not going to be able to stand what will happen when the police come charging in, because at that instant, it will all be over for your girlfriend here."

Lucas's throat was dry as a bone. He wanted to swallow, to lick his lips, but he knew those were classic body language signs of nervousness, and the last message he wanted to send to Picone or to Ange was that he was deathly afraid that Picone was telling the truth.

The sound of heavy boots echoed on the hardwood floors.

Tony jerked and Angela cried out in pain as two more beads of blood appeared on her neck.

"That's the police," Lucas said, gritting his teeth. Tony Picone was going to pay for hurting her.

A shadow caught his attention from the area of the deck. He did his best not to move a muscle—not even an eye muscle. He hoped like hell Tony didn't notice the policeman who had stepped up onto the deck. Not until Lucas was ready for him to.

Trust me, he silently begged Angela. *Trust me.*

"You're surrounded, Tony. The cops are coming in the back door, and they're all around the cabin. That means Paulo's dead. What's your papa going to think when he finds out you got Paulo killed?"

Tony's eyes widened and his knife-hand shook. "That's a lie. Paulo's not dead. He can't be—" he stopped as his gaze snapped to the French doors. He'd spotted the cop. Sweat popped out his forehead.

It was Lucas's only chance. Praying for the strength to hold his hand steady, he squeezed the trigger. A tiny red hole appeared in the center of Picone's forehead. He made a small, guttural sound and the knife nicked Angela's skin, drawing more blood.

Wood shattered as the policeman broke in the cypress door from the deck.

A keening cry erupted from Angela's throat. Tony's body went slack and the switchblade tumbled to the bed beside her.

Two uniformed officers stormed through the hall door. Lucas didn't even look at them. He vaulted toward the bed and lifted Angela away from Picone's dead body. He carried her out of the room and down the hall to the kitchen.

Her entire body was stiff with tension, and beneath her skin, Lucas could feel the uncontrollable trembling of her muscles. He whispered to her.

"It's okay, Ange. He's dead. You're safe."

But all she did was stare at him. Then when he took out his knife to cut the duct tape, she cringed.

"Ange, don't," he pleaded softly. "I've got to get this tape off you, okay? The longer it stays the worse it will tear your skin."

He worked quickly, dismayed that she just sat without moving, without a single protest other than a gasp of pain when he had to jerk a piece of tape as he cut and peeled the duct tape away from her skin and clothes. In several places, the adhesive abraded her skin.

He worked in silence, until one of the officers came into the kitchen and ordered him to stop.

"You're tampering with evidence," the officer said.

"I'm Detective Lucas Delancey, Dallas P.D.," Lucas answered. "I'll hold the duct tape for your forensics people, but Ange—Angela Grayson is the victim. I'm not about to make her sit her all tied up for hours."

"Yes, sir." The words were faintly grudging. "The crime scene investigators and the coroner are on their way. They should be here in a few minutes."

"What about EMTs?"

The officer nodded.

"And the sniper outside?"

The officer shook his head. "Damnedest thing. We originally called the EMTs for him. Apparently he tangled with Felton's dogs. Of course, there's no sign of the girls or Felton out there. But if that's what happened, he's lucky to be alive."

The officer glanced quickly at Angela. "How's—"

Lucas nodded briefly. "She'll be okay," he said, knowing he was lying. In truth, he had no idea how she was, because she still hadn't spoken.

Once he'd disposed of the last of the tape, her hand tentatively touched her neck, where rivulets of blood marred her skin. She met his gaze and opened her mouth to speak, but the only sound that came out was a small gasping sob.

"Shh," he muttered, giving her an encouraging smile. "It's just a scratch. Won't even leave a scar."

Then, with dread and fear clogging his throat, he took her hands in his. "Ange? Are you hurt anywhere else? Did he—hurt you?"

She met his gaze, her chocolate eyes swimming with tears.

Lucas couldn't breathe as he waited for her answer.

She shook her head and relief washed over him. Just then, the kitchen door slammed open and an emergency medical technician carrying an emergency kit came in. Lucas moved aside as the technician pulled a chair up and began examining Angela.

Then the local police captain entered, and Lucas was

forced to leave Angela with the EMT and head back to the bedroom, where he was questioned about everything that had happened.

By the time he got back to the kitchen, Angela was gone.

Chapter Seventeen

Angela stood in the middle of her living room, looking around her. Nothing was out of place, but nothing looked right, either.

She shook her head. When she'd moved in to this apartment, she'd loved it. The hardwood floors, the French doors, the quaint balcony and the view of the French Quarter.

Now, there was no way she could stay here another night. And she wasn't sure if she was going to be able to look at that couch, or her bed, or that clock over her dresser ever again. She might as well just leave everything here and start over, with new furniture in a new place that nobody had ever watched through a spy cam.

She shuddered at the thought and touched the bandage on her neck. She'd come here to get her book bag and some clothing to take back to the hotel with her. It was unbelievable that it was only Sunday evening. She'd been spied on, shot at, nearly blown up, kidnapped, had a knife held to her throat and been three inches from the bullet that had killed the man who was trying to kill her, and yet she still could make her last exam tomorrow morning, if she wanted to.

A bone-cracking shudder racked her.

No. That cushy job with a premier hotel chain would have to wait. There was no way she'd be able to even hold a pen steady enough to write, much less answer questions.

Taking a deep, shaky breath, she picked up the book bag and the small suitcase she'd packed and turned toward her open hall door.

Lucas was standing there.

"May I come in?" he asked.

Angela braced herself for the familiar aching desire that accompanied her every glimpse of him. It hit her, just like always.

But this time the ache felt deeper, stronger. Not only did she lust after Lucas, as she had ever since that long-ago kiss, but now a sweet knowledge colored the sensations with richer, more complex tones. Now she knew how it felt to make love with him. And she knew, because of that, it was going to be that much harder to watch him walk away.

"Sure," she said a little belatedly. "Are you doing okay?"

"I came here to ask you that. You look good. Those bruises almost match your pink shirt. Too bad they couldn't have given you pink tape."

"Yeah." She looked down at herself. "Color-co-or-di-nated bandages. Good idea. Maybe I should go into business."

This was awkward. *Please, just say what you want to say and go.* The longer he stood there, looking all handsome and strong and wounded, the more deeply his image would be implanted in her brain, and the harder it would be to forget him.

"Ange? Are you all right? Do you need me to do

anything?" Lucas's green eyes were soft as the sea as he scrutinized her.

"Fine. I'm fine. And I can—"

"Take care of yourself. I know." A brief shadow darkened his gaze. "It's just—you've been through a lot."

"Me? What about you? I didn't get shot or knocked down by an explosion or showered with broken glass or—"

"No. You just got pistol-whipped, trussed with tape and cut. You just got nearly killed."

She shivered and gave a weak laugh. "We're a pair, aren't we? I'd rather not talk about all that, Lucas. It's done. I'm fine."

Lucas took a couple of steps toward her. "I'd rather not talk about that, either. I've got something to tell you."

Angela's heart leapt. Was he about to tell her that making love with her had changed his life? That he couldn't possibly live without her? Because if she could, that's what she'd tell him. Only she never would, because to reveal all that to him would open herself up to him, and she didn't think she could take his rejection—not a third time.

So she met his question with the most logical, unemotional answer she could think of.

"Your suspension's been lifted."

He laughed. "No such luck. Although a buddy of mine called me earlier and said he'd heard there was going to be a hearing tomorrow, and the scuttlebutt is that I'll have my job back by the end of that hearing."

"I'm so glad," Angela lied. Now she knew what people meant when they said their heart sank. She tried to force brightness into her voice. "So you're leaving."

"Yeah." He paused. "You don't have to sound quite so happy about it."

"Oh, Lucas, I'm not! I mean, I just know you'll be glad to get your job back."

Again, his eyes intensified. "I just hate to leave you."

Dear God, if only he meant it. "No. I'm fine," she rushed to reassure him. "I can take—"

"All right, stop it!" he snapped. "You know, Ange, it's really annoying to listen to you say that, over and over and over."

She frowned. "What? That I can take care of myself. But I can. Usually, that is. I mean, do I say it that much?"

To her surprise, Lucas looked down at the toe of his boot. "Not today. Not yet. You know—"

He took a long breath. "I never wanted anything to do with family. Especially not the Delancey kind. Big, close and destructive."

She blinked. That was a strange change of subject. "I know. It's why you went to Dallas."

Suddenly she understood. This was it. The big good-bye. Although she wasn't quite sure why he was bothering. They'd hopped in the sack one time. It wasn't like they'd made some kind of commitment to each other.

To her horror, Angela felt a prickling behind her eyes that signaled tears. She blinked, determined not to cry.

All through their childhood, she'd never cried in front of Lucas. And she wasn't about to start now. Right now it was more important than ever to make sure he understood that she really could take care of herself, because right now she felt more vulnerable, more lonely, more at a loss than she'd ever felt before.

"Suddenly, I've got all these ridiculous notions in my head. Weird things." Lucas stopped and swallowed.

"Like a house. Like a hon—" He cleared his throat. "A trip, you know. Someplace special."

"Lucas, what are you talking about?"

He put a hand on the door facing and looked at it, scrutinizing his fingers as if he'd never seen them before. "What do you think of Dallas?"

"Dallas? I don't—" All at once an odd thought hit her. *A house? A trip?* A *special* trip. She took a step forward, then another, until she was within arm's reach of him.

"Lucas, why does it matter what I think about Dallas?" Her heart was pounding so fast she felt like she couldn't get her breath. She watched him warily.

Come on and say it already, she wanted to shout. *Before I make a fool of myself.*

Lucas's gaze lowered from her eyes to her mouth, then back up. "Why'd you kiss me?" he asked.

"Why—what?"

"Why did you kiss me. Back in high school. Why?"

Now it was her turn to look down at her shoes, but a gentle fingertip urged her chin up until she was looking into his eyes. "Because it was the last thing I ever expected you to do. And I want to know why you did it."

She closed her eyes for an instant. Okay, here was her chance to prove once and for all that she could take care of herself. Because if she fell apart because Lucas didn't love her, then he would be right. Lucas would finally have definitive proof that she couldn't take care of herself in any situation.

Sucking in a deep breath, she took the plunge. "Because I wanted to see how it felt. I wanted to know if I was in love with you." Her voice sounded a little strangled at the end of that sentence, but at least she'd made it through.

Lucas's eyes glittered like emeralds. "And—?"

She shrugged. "I was."

He moved a little bit closer. "Was?"

She caught her lower lip between her teeth.

"That's a relief," he said softly.

"A relief?"

"Yeah, because if I had to do all the loving *and* all the taking-care-of, I'd be exhausted."

"All the loving? All the—Lucas?" Her heart leapt.

He gave her a solemn nod. "When we're married, Ange, I expect you to take care of yourself."

Before Angela could say anything, he kissed her, good and hard. And long.

Much later, as their lips parted, Angela couldn't stop smiling. "When we're married, I'll not only take care of myself, Lucas Delancey. I'll take care of you."

Lucas grinned at her. "And there she is. That's the stubborn Brat I love." He swept her back into his arms, where she'd always known she belonged.

* * * * *

PREGNESIA

BY
CARLA CASSIDY

All the characters in this book have no existence outside the imagination of
the author, and have no relation whatsoever to anyone bearing the same name
or names. They are not even distantly inspired by any individual known or
unknown to the author, and all the incidents are pure invention.

First published in Great Britain 2011
by Mills & Boon, an imprint of Harlequin (UK) Limited,
Eton House, 18-24 Paradise Road, Richmond, Surrey TW9 1SR

© Carla Bracale 2009

ISBN: 978 0 263 88525 5

46-0511

Harlequin (UK) policy is to use papers that are natural, renewable and
recyclable products and made from wood grown in sustainable forests. The
logging and manufacturing processes conform to the legal environmental
regulations of the country of origin.

Printed and bound in Spain
by Blackprint CPI, Barcelona

Chapter One

Lucas Washington stared at the darkened house across the way from where he stood on a quiet residential Kansas City street. Although everything was silent and it appeared the occupants of the house were sleeping, Lucas knew this was the most dangerous time in the job he had to do.

He was about to repossess the two-year-old Buick in the driveway, and he didn't know if there might be a crazy man with a rifle in one of those darkened windows ready to protest the repossession.

Lucas didn't believe in favors, giving them or getting them. Still, it was repaying a favor that had him standing on the street on a cold November night at two in the morning. Repossessions were usually done in the middle of the night when hopefully the deadbeat was sleeping and there was less of a chance of a confrontation.

As the third partner of Recovery Inc., it wasn't unusual for Lucas to be repossessing some kind of vehicle. But the business dealt in big-ticket items, speedboats and airplanes and such, and they often ventured into dangerous territories to get back whatever was necessary.

A two-year-old Buick wasn't their usual kind of job, but when Bob of Big Bob's Used Car Sales had called and asked Lucas to repossess the car, Lucas had reluctantly agreed.

Big Bob had given Lucas's sister a heck of a deal on her car and had overlooked the fact that Loretta's credit wasn't exactly stellar.

Besides, business had been slow lately and Lucas had been out of sorts. Maybe it had something to do with the fact that in the last four months his partners had both found love and suddenly had a life that didn't include him.

He scowled and pulled his collar up against the cold night air, then reached into his pocket and grabbed the key that Bob had provided him. All he wanted to do was get this car to Big Bob's, then go back home to his apartment.

According to Bob, who had financed the deal, the man who'd driven it off the lot hadn't made a single payment in four months. Bob's phone calls to try to work something out had gone unreturned, and so he'd called Lucas.

"No pay, no play." Lucas muttered. He hoped there wouldn't be any drama, that Mr. Deadbeat would wake up in the morning and wonder what in the hell had happened to his ride.

He approached cautiously, checking the windows of the house a final time then heading across the street. He crouched behind the back fender and listened, but heard nothing to cause him alarm.

Pulling the key from his pocket, he edged around to the driver's side and tried the handle. It was unlocked. Sweet. Mr. Deadbeat had made it remarkably easy.

He opened the door, slid into the seat and breathed a sigh of relief. He put the key into the ignition, cranked the engine and yelped as a hand fell on his shoulder.

He whirled around, expecting Mr. Deadbeat with a gun. Instead he found himself staring into the biggest, bluest eyes he'd ever seen. Female eyes. They belonged to a blonde who looked as if she'd just gotten the hell beat out of her.

A nasty gash decorated one side of her forehead. It had bled down her face and onto her white blouse.

"Please, if you're stealing the car, just let me out now." Her voice was thin and reedy and her face was pasty white.

"I'm not stealing the car, I'm repossessing it. What are you doing back there?" As he asked the question he backed out of the driveway.

He wasn't about to sit and talk with a bloody woman in the backseat with the engine idling when Mr. Deadbeat might come outside.

He pulled out onto the street and headed in the direction of Big Bob's. He glanced in the rearview mirror and saw her slumped in the corner, a perplexed frown on her pretty face.

"What are you doing in the car? Is it yours?" he asked. What in the heck was going on? "What happened to your head? Did somebody beat you up?" The questions snapped out of him. He didn't like surprises, and a banged-up woman in the back of the car was definitely a surprise.

He also didn't like the fact that she wasn't talking, wasn't offering any explanation for her presence. He frowned and shot her another glance in the rearview mirror. Maybe she was seriously hurt.

"Do you need to go to a hospital?" he asked more gently.

"No!" The word shot out of her like the report of a gun. "No, please." Her eyes were shiny with tears. "Just drop me off someplace. I'll be fine."

A domestic issue? he wondered. Maybe she was afraid that if she went to the hospital, whoever hurt her would find her. He tightened his hands on the steering wheel. There was nothing he despised more than a guy who abused women.

"Look, if your husband or boyfriend hurt you, then you really should go to the police."

"Please, no police, no hospital. Wherever you're going I'll just get out there and everything will be fine."

"What's your name?"

His question was met with silence and once again he looked at her in the rearview mirror. She met his gaze, then quickly looked out the side window. "My name isn't important," she finally said.

"Is this your car? Your husband's car?"

"No, I don't know who it belongs to. It was the only one on the block that wasn't locked and I was cold. I was just going to sit in it for a little while and try to warm up before leaving."

Something definitely wasn't ringing true. She wasn't telling him her name or what had happened to her. He'd get the car to Big Bob's, then figure out what he was going to do with the young woman.

What he'd like to do was drive her straight to a police station or to a hospital, but he'd heard the absolute panic in her voice when he'd mentioned either option.

His quick, easy favor for Bob was turning into something much more complex, and that was the last thing Lucas wanted or needed.

He breathed a sigh of relief as the car lot came into view. He told himself that he wasn't a part of whatever drama the woman in the backseat had going on and yet there was no way he could just dump her at Big Bob's.

She was obviously in some sort of trouble. He needed to get a closer look at the gash on her forehead to see if she needed medical attention.

He turned into the lot and pulled through a gate that led to a secured area. He'd park the car, drop the keys into a lockbox, then close a gate that would make it impossible for Mr. Deadbeat to retrieve the vehicle using the key he still had in his possession.

He glanced to the backseat where the woman lay, her eyes closed and looking as pale as the winter moon. He pulled through the gate, parked the car and cut the engine. Only then did she open her eyes and stare out the window as if terrified of what might happen next.

"I won't hurt you," he said softly. "I need to leave this car here, but mine's parked close by and I'll be glad to take you wherever you need to go."

He opened his car door and got out, then opened the back door. She stepped out of the backseat with obvious reluctance, and as she did, he gasped in stunned surprise.

She was pregnant.

Very pregnant.

The idea that somebody had beat up a pregnant woman caused a wealth of unexpected protectiveness to surge up inside him.

She was only about five-two, dwarfed by Lucas's six feet. And when she looked up at him, her blue eyes were once again filled with the threat of tears.

"Maybe you could drop me at a motel? And maybe I could borrow enough money to pay for the night? I promise I'll pay you back. If you'll give me your name and address I swear you'll get every penny back." Her voice held a ring of desperation and promise.

"I can't do that," he said. "You're obviously in trouble. Tell me what's happened. Tell me your name."

Her lower lip began to tremble and her eyes filled

with tears. "I can't." The two words were a mere whisper.

She drew a deep, tremulous breath and leaned back against the Buick. "I can't tell you because I don't know." She raised a hand to her forehead and winced. "I don't know who I am."

Lucas narrowed his eyes and stared at her, wondering if she was for real. She could be lying through her straight, white teeth.

She shivered and he knew he had to make up his mind quickly. She was coatless and pregnant, and somebody needed to clean that wound on her head. He'd do what he could to help her tonight, but in the morning she'd have to be on her way.

She might not be telling him the truth about having amnesia, but there was no way he could just abandon her in her present condition.

"Look, my apartment isn't far from here and my sister lives down the hall from me. She's a nurse. You need somebody to look at that cut on your forehead. Why don't I take you there and we'll figure out what to do with you after that?"

She eyed him warily and placed her hands on her protruding belly. "I don't know you," she finally said.

"My name is Lucas. Lucas Washington." He raked a hand through his long, shaggy hair. "I don't know about you, but I'm freezing and just want to get home. You're obviously in trouble, and if what you told me is true, then you need to trust somebody. It might as well be me."

"You'll take me to your sister's?" she asked. Lucas nodded. "And she's a nurse?"

"That's right."

"Okay," she agreed, although there was still more than a little wariness in her voice.

As Lucas walked to his car with her following just behind him he told himself he'd see her safely through what was left of this night, but tomorrow she had to go. He wasn't about to get any more involved in whatever drama she had going on in her life.

COULD SHE TRUST HIM? She didn't know. He seemed all right even if he did look like what she'd assume a car thief might look like. At least he wasn't a car thief. She just wasn't sure what else he might be.

As she got into the passenger side of his sports car, she shot him a surreptitious glance. His black hair hung nearly to his shoulders and framed a face that was lean and slightly dangerous looking. The black leather jacket he wore stretched across broad shoulders and his dark jeans hugged slender hips and long legs.

On some level she found him intensely attractive, but could she trust him? Her head pounded with nauseating intensity. But the pain couldn't touch the frantic terror that clawed inside her.

Why didn't she know her name? How had she gotten hurt? Why couldn't she remember anything? She was pregnant and she didn't even know if she was married or not. She wasn't wearing a ring, but that didn't necessarily mean anything.

"You all right?" Lucas asked as he turned into the parking lot of an apartment complex.

At least he hadn't driven her to some field where nobody would hear her scream. "I guess," she replied. "To be honest, I'm terrified."

He pulled into a parking space, then turned to look at her, his eyes dark and enigmatic. "You don't have to be terrified of me. I promise I won't hurt you."

"I think that might be what all serial killers say just before they murder somebody," she replied.

A rumble of deep laughter escaped him as he turned off the engine. "I guess I never thought about that before."

He got out of the car and she did the same, comforted by the fact that if he did try to hurt her and she screamed, surely somebody in one of the apartments would hear her.

She had to trust somebody. She had no money, no identification and a headache that threatened to topple her to her knees. The night was cold, and she was beyond exhaustion. Even if she didn't care about herself, she cared about the baby she carried.

Surely after she slept she'd remember who she was and what had happened to her. All she needed was a couple of hours of rest and everything would become clear again.

She followed him into the building and down a long hallway. Not a sound came from any of the doors they passed. It was almost three in the morning and the building held the silence of a tomb.

"This is my place," he said softly as they passed apartment 104. "My sister's place is at the end of the hall."

When they reached the apartment numbered 108, Lucas knocked softly on the door. There was no reply and he rapped harder.

"I feel terrible," she whispered. "It's the middle of the night and you're waking her up."

"Loretta won't mind," he replied, and knocked once again.

The door cracked open and a pair of sleepy dark eyes that looked remarkably like Lucas's peered out. "Lucas, what are you doing here at this hour of the night?" The door closed again and there was the sound of a chain being removed and then the door opened all the way.

Loretta Washington was as petite as her brother was broad. She had the same rich, black hair and dark eyes, and those eyes widened as they saw her. She opened the door wide enough to allow them entry and then belted her short blue robe more tightly around her waist.

"What's going on?" she asked.

"Jane here has a problem," Lucas said.

Jane? As in Jane Doe. She supposed for now the name would serve her as well as any. "I'm sorry to bother you in the middle of the night," she said.

"Nonsense, come into the kitchen where I can get a look at that head wound." Loretta had a calm efficiency about her that put Jane somewhat at ease.

She allowed herself to be led through a tidy living room and into a small kitchen with a round wooden table. "Sit," Loretta instructed, pointing to one of the chairs at the table.

Jane complied and fought an overwhelming desire to weep with relief. She sensed safety here, at least for the moment. Lucas sat in the chair across from her and eyed her with the same wariness that she'd used on him. Looking into his dark eyes, that sense of safety was more tenuous.

"What happened?" Loretta asked as she got a first-aid kit from under her kitchen sink.

"She doesn't know," Lucas said, but his tone indicated that he didn't quite believe her.

"I wasn't talking to you," Loretta exclaimed. She got a damp cloth and began to wipe the side of Jane's face. Jane closed her eyes against the gentle touch. "What happened, honey?"

"I don't know." She winced as Loretta began to clean the cut. "All I remember is running and running. Then I was tired and cold, so I crawled into the car where your brother found me."

"She says she has some kind of amnesia or something. She doesn't know her name," Lucas said, and once again his voice was laced with a touch of suspicious disbelief. "For the time being I'm calling her Jane."

Jane met his gaze. Those dark eyes of his seemed to look inside her soul, but there was nothing there for him to see.

"You don't know your name?" Loretta asked gently. "Do you know what day it is?"

"November second or third." Jane knew she must be right because Loretta nodded with encouragement. Loretta asked her several more questions, about the year and who was the president.

"I know all that," Jane said. "I just don't know who I am and what's happened to me." Again fear bubbled up inside her and she fought against it, refusing to show either of them just how terrified she really was.

As Loretta checked Jane's blood pressure and pulse, Lucas continued to watch her with hooded eyes that gave nothing away.

"Well, the good news is your vitals are all normal and you don't need stitches on your forehead," Loretta said. "But you really need to go to the hospital to be checked out for other head injuries."

Panic swelled in Jane's chest. She wasn't sure why, but she felt that if she went to a hospital or to the police, she'd only be putting herself in more danger. "No, I'm sure I'll be fine if I can just get some rest." She looked at Lucas once again. "Maybe you could take me to that motel we talked about earlier?"

"Nonsense," Loretta exclaimed. "It's almost morning now. There's no reason for you to go anywhere. I have a spare room where you'll be perfectly comfortable for the night and we'll sort out everything else in the morning."

"Oh, I couldn't impose anymore," Jane said, offering a weak protest.

"Don't bother arguing with her," Lucas said. "Loretta might be small, but she's as stubborn as the day is long."

Loretta cuffed him on the back of the head and gave him an affectionate grin. "Why don't you get out of here and let us women get to bed?"

"Walk me to the door?" he said to his sister.

Loretta nodded, and as she followed Lucas out of the kitchen, Jane slumped forward and cradled her belly in her arms as she felt the baby move around inside her.

At the moment the only thing she was certain of was that she loved the baby she carried. She had no idea who the father was, or what her relationship might be with that man, but it didn't matter. She had a feeling she'd loved the baby from the moment of conception.

What would she have done if Lucas Washington hadn't stumbled upon her? Where would she be at this moment? Still in the backseat of that car, slowly freezing half to death? And what would she have done in the morning when she had to leave the car?

She shivered and again a low pulse of fear filled her. It was more than the fear of not knowing her name. It was some innate knowledge that she was in danger. And the most frightening part was not knowing who might be after her and why.

Chapter Two

Lucas sat at his kitchen table and watched the morning sun peek over the horizon. He'd only slept for a couple of hours, but felt rested. He'd never needed much sleep. Not sleeping too soundly or too long had been a survival mechanism learned in his youth, with his father's explosive temper that could erupt anytime day or night.

He tightened his fingers around his coffee mug as he thought of those nights of terror. If it hadn't been for his younger sister, he wasn't sure he'd have survived his childhood.

Initially he'd worried about leaving a stranger with Loretta for the night, but he'd realized a very pregnant woman with a head wound didn't pose much risk. Besides, Loretta was tougher than she looked.

Jane.

She'd haunted what little sleep he'd gotten. Once Loretta had cleaned the blood off her face, Lucas had gotten his first real look at her. She was stunning, with her heart-shaped face and big blue eyes. Her complexion was smooth and her skin had looked soft and supple.

He'd been surprised by the tiny kick of pure male lust in the pit of his stomach. He was thirty-three years old and rarely felt that particular feeling. And he'd certainly never felt it for a pregnant woman suffering from amnesia.

He consciously willed himself not to get interested in any woman. He had his work and his sister and that's all he'd ever really needed.

Getting up from the table, he stretched with his arms overhead. He needed a shower. By the time he was done his sister would be awake and he could check in on Loretta and her patient.

As he stood beneath a hot spray of water he thought about the mysterious Jane. He suspected she might be lying. Even though there had been genuine fear in those gorgeous eyes of hers, he wasn't convinced that her amnesia was real.

What he thought was that she'd probably had a fight with her boyfriend or husband and had concocted the amnesia story to buy her a little time. As long as she didn't go to the police or to the hospital, the man in question couldn't find her or go to jail on domestic abuse issues.

Surely by this morning she would have "remembered" her name and found forgiveness in her heart for the guy who banged her up. It happened all the time. It was a story Lucas knew intimately.

He dressed in his customary jeans and pulled on a ribbed, long-sleeved navy shirt, then returned to the kitchen for another cup of coffee before heading to his sister's apartment.

He needed to call one of his partners and let them know he wouldn't be in to the office until later in the afternoon. He needed to figure out where to bring Jane and wasn't sure exactly what to expect.

Lucas and two of his ex–navy SEAL buddies had started Recovery Inc. when they'd gotten out of the service. The company dealt in recovery of both items and people in sticky situations and had been successful beyond their wildest dreams.

Despite the financial rewards, Lucas lived a simple life. He used most of his money to help pay Loretta's student loans and was determined to help her pay for medical school next spring. Her dream had always been to be a doctor, and Lucas wanted to make sure she achieved that dream.

He pulled his cell phone from his pocket and punched in the number for Micah Stone, one of his partners and his best friend.

Micah answered on the first ring. "Hey, partner, what's up?"

"I just wanted to let you know that I won't be in this morning. I've got some things to take care of, but I should be there sometime this afternoon."

"That makes two of us. It looks like Troy will have to hold down the fort by himself," Micah replied.

"I'm being fitted for a tux this morning. Have you been fitted yet?"

Micah's wedding was less than a month away and Lucas was serving as his best man. "Not yet. I'll try to get in before the end of the week."

"If you don't, then you know Caylee will be chewing on your backside. And trust me when I tell you she has very sharp teeth."

Lucas laughed. Caylee was Micah's fiancée. She was definitely a spitfire, but Lucas had never seen his friend so happy.

"Then I guess I'll see you sometime this afternoon," Lucas replied, and the two men hung up. Lucas was glad Micah hadn't asked him why he'd be late. He wasn't sure why, but he wasn't eager to share the night's events and his mysterious Jane with anyone.

If she'd taken advantage of their kindness, as he suspected, then he sure didn't want his partners to know he'd been taken for a fool.

He finished his coffee and checked the clock. Just after seven. Loretta would be up by now and he was eager to see what Jane had miraculously remembered this morning.

When he reached Loretta's apartment door he rapped lightly and his sister answered almost immediately. She was dressed for the day in blue-flowered scrubs and held a cup of coffee in her hand.

"I've been expecting you," she said, and motioned him to the kitchen. "My houseguest is still asleep."

"Did you talk to her after I left last night?" Lucas leaned against the counter.

"A little, but not much. She was exhausted and I figured the best thing for her was a good night's sleep. I take it you don't believe her story."

Lucas raised an eyebrow. "Do you?"

Loretta sat at the table. "I don't know. I do think she had a trauma of some kind and she seemed genuinely afraid and confused. She looks to be around eight months pregnant. If some man whacked her upside the head, he should be hung by his manly parts for the rest of her life."

Lucas grinned. "Ah, Loretta, tell me how you really feel." Love for his sister surged up inside him. Loretta was six years younger than him. With both their parents dead and the history they shared, the two siblings were particularly close.

"What I feel is that you need to put your overactive cynicism aside when you talk to her. She may not have amnesia, but she's obviously in trouble." Loretta drained her coffee cup and got up from the table. "I've got to get to work."

Lucas walked with her to the front door where she turned to look at him once again. "Feed her something, Lucas. And if she needs to stay here a couple more days, it's fine with me." She reached up and kissed Lucas on the cheek, then left.

Lucas returned to the kitchen, poured himself a cup of coffee and then sat at the table. He wasn't surprised by his sister's generous offer to a stranger. Loretta made a habit of helping people.

Sometimes it amazed him how his sister had survived the dysfunction of their past with such a goodness of spirit, such a pure, sweet soul. Too bad he couldn't say the same about himself.

He had his cup halfway to his mouth when Jane appeared in the doorway. She was clad in a white nightgown that stretched taut across her breasts and her belly. Her blond, curly hair was tousled, and it was obvious by the widening of her eyes that she'd expected to find Loretta, not Lucas, in the kitchen.

"Oh!" She instantly hunched her shoulders and crossed one arm over her breasts. Her lower lip trembled and her eyes looked as if she'd been crying. Once again Lucas felt a strange surge of protectiveness. "I'll just...I'll be right back." She darted out of the kitchen and back down the hallway.

It was only then that Lucas realized he'd been holding his breath. He took a sip of his coffee and tried to forget the vision of her, so soft and feminine, and so utterly vulnerable.

She returned moments later, this time clad in the jeans and the dirty, bloodstained white blouse she'd worn the night before.

"Doesn't Loretta have something you can wear?" he asked.

"Your sister is tiny." She placed a hand on her stomach. "And right now I'm not. She didn't have anything big enough to fit my stomach."

"Sit down and I'll get you a cup of coffee," he said.

He got up as she sat. He poured her a cup of coffee and carried it to the table, where he set it before her.

"How are you feeling this morning?" he asked.

To Lucas's horror, she burst into tears. "I thought everything would be all right this morning," she said between sobs. "I thought I'd wake up and I'd know who I was and what happened, but I don't know any more now than I did last night."

The sobs were painful to watch. Lucas grabbed a handful of napkins and handed them to her. She was either the greatest actress on the face of the earth or she was telling the truth.

She cried so hard he got worried about her, about the baby. He pulled up a chair next to her and awkwardly patted her back. "Don't cry," he said. "We'll sort this out, but you've got to stop crying. It can't be good for the baby."

That seemed to penetrate into her head, because the sobs wore down to sniffles, and finally ceased altogether. She wiped her cheeks, and when she looked at him once again, there was desperation in her eyes.

"I'm so afraid," she said. "I don't know what's going to happen to me."

"For now, nothing is going to happen," Lucas replied. "You're safe here. Loretta told me to tell you that you're welcome to stay for a couple of days until you feel better."

Tears welled up in her eyes once again. "I can't believe how kind you're being to me."

He wanted to tell her that it wasn't him, that his

sister was the kind one. He was the cynical one who still didn't know whether to believe her or not.

But for the moment he decided to give her the benefit of the doubt. If she was lying, then sooner or later he would know. If she was telling the truth, then he sure as hell didn't want to be responsible for tossing a pregnant woman out on the streets all alone with no money and no memory.

"Are you hungry?" he asked.

"Starving. I can't remember the last time I ate." A half-hysterical spurt of laughter burst out of her.

"Scrambled eggs okay?" he asked as he got up from the table.

"Fine. But please, you don't have to wait on me. If you'll just show me where things are, I can do for myself." She started to get up, but he waved her back down.

"I'll take care of it, just sit tight." He got the eggs from the refrigerator and set to work making breakfast.

As he worked she stared out the window, tiny frown lines dancing across her forehead. Again he was struck by her prettiness. She wasn't screamingly drop-dead gorgeous, but rather she had a quiet, simmering beauty. He frowned and whipped the eggs more forcefully than necessary.

The last thing he needed was to be attracted to her. She obviously had a man in her life. And in any case Lucas didn't do relationships.

She continued to stare out the window as if lost

in thought while he fixed the eggs and popped in toast. Then once it was all done he placed the food on two plates, one for her and one for himself.

"Lucas?" She turned to look at him, her blue eyes troubled. "I know this sounds crazy, but I have a terrible feeling that I'm in real danger."

He set the plates on the table with a sinking sensation in the pit of his stomach. This was growing more complicated by the minute. And there was nothing Lucas hated more than complication.

JANE STARED AT HIM and tried not to notice that his dark hair had a gleaming shine to it that made it look silky soft and that he smelled like soap and shaving cream and a hint of a clean cologne. "You don't believe me, do you?"

Since the moment she'd told him that she didn't know who she was, that she had no idea what had happened to her, she'd sensed his suspicious disbelief. And she wasn't sure why it was so important to her that he accept what she was telling him.

"I don't know what I believe," he finally replied. "I think it's possible you had a fight with your boyfriend or husband or whatever, and you need a safe place to hide out until things cool off and the two of you can kiss and make up."

She reached up and touched her forehead with a frown. "I can't imagine wanting to kiss and make up with anyone who did this to me."

Did you know you could have received this book
before it hit the shops?

MILLS BOON

For access to all the latest Mills and Boon titles before they hit the shops visit www.millsandboon.co.uk

For a limited time only, we are offering you **15% OFF** your order when you enter the code 15MAY11 at the checkout. **But hurry**, this offer ends on 31st July 2011.

PLUS, by ordering online you will receive all these extra benefits:

- Be the first to hear about exclusive offers in our eNewsletter

- Try before you buy! You can now browse the first chapter of each of our books online

- Order books from our huge back list at a discounted price

- Join the M&B community and discuss your favourite books with other readers

He picked up his fork. "He'll buy you flowers or candy and swear he'll never touch you again and you'll end up going back and things will be great until the next time he loses his temper." His voice held a harshness in tone.

"I wouldn't be involved with a man like that," she exclaimed.

He raised a dark eyebrow. "How do you know?"

She felt the warmth of a blush on her cheeks. "I might not know who I am, but I know what I'd tolerate, and I'd never stay with a man who put his hands on me."

She felt a swell of tears burning at her eyes and bit them back. She'd cried herself to sleep the night before and had awakened and cried some more. She was tired of crying. "Maybe nobody hit me. Maybe I just fell and hit my head on something," she said.

"I don't think so," he replied. "Do you have bruised knees? Scraped-up palms? Anything that might indicate you'd fallen?"

"No."

"That scrape on your head doesn't look like it's the result of a fall. It looks like you were hit with something." He leaned forward and she realized his dark eyes had tiny shards of silver in them. "You know, if you're just scared and need a place to hang out for a couple of days, it's all right to tell me. You don't have to make up any stories."

"I'm not making anything up. I don't know what

to do to make you believe me. I don't know what to say to make you understand that I'm not lying."

Those dark eyes of his studied her intently. "Eat your eggs and toast before they get cold."

They ate for a few minutes without speaking, until she couldn't stand the tense silence another minute longer. "Your sister seems really nice," she said.

He nodded. "She's a sucker for people in need."

"And you're not?"

The corners of his lips turned up in a humorless smile. "I'm not a sucker for anyone or anything."

"I know your sister is a nurse, but I'm not sure exactly what it is you do."

"I own a company, Recovery Inc., with two of my friends. We were all Navy SEALs together, and when we got out of the service we opened the business."

"And you repossess cars?"

He frowned, as if the question irritated him. "Last night was not our normal kind of job. I did that as a favor for the owner of the car dealership."

"So, what is your normal kind of job?" she asked. It was a welcome relief to be wondering about him instead of wondering about herself.

"We recover items and return them to the people they belong to. But it's really not important what I do. What's important is what we're going to do about you."

"I should probably go. I'm really not your problem." She tried to ignore the terror that coursed through her at the thought of having to leave, of not knowing where she would go.

"If I let you leave under these conditions, Loretta will have my head," he replied. He stood and grabbed their plates from the table and carried them to the sink. "Our first order of business today is to get you a few things from the store. You need a change of clothing and some personal items if you're going to stay here for a couple of days."

She felt terrible. She didn't want to take advantage of either Loretta or Lucas. But no matter how much she wanted to claim back her own life, she didn't know where to begin.

"I can't believe this," she said more to herself than to him. Once again she directed her gaze out the window where the sun hid beneath a blanket of low gray clouds. She felt as if the sun was her memory, hiding someplace inside her and refusing to come out into the light.

She looked at him once again and cradled her stomach with her arms. "If it were just me, I'd leave. I'd never take advantage of your kindness."

He leaned against the counter, those dark eyes of his impossible to read. "I'll go to my place and get you a T-shirt and a jacket, and we'll head to Wal-Mart to pick up what you need."

"Whatever you buy for me, I'll pay you back. I swear I will just as soon as I figure out who I am and where I belong." She frowned and tried to ignore the headache that had begun to pound across the top of her head. "Maybe as the day wears on, something will jiggle my memory."

She couldn't imagine going day after day with no memories, with no knowledge of something as simple as her own name.

"Maybe," he replied. He shoved off from the counter. "I'll just get that shirt and jacket. I'll be right back."

As he left the kitchen she leaned back in her chair and drew a deep breath. She raised a hand and touched the scab that had formed on her forehead.

What had happened to her? Why couldn't she remember? What if a couple of days passed and she still didn't know who she was, or where she belonged? What then? She couldn't just continue to stay here forever. She could take advantage of Loretta's kindness only so long.

She dropped her hand to her belly and rubbed with a caressing motion. She thought the baby was a boy. Of course she didn't remember anyone telling her that, had no concrete memory, it was just something she knew. Like she knew that she hated peanut butter and loved pizza.

Lucas returned with the large T-shirt and a down-filled navy ski jacket. She took the shirt and returned to the bedroom where she'd slept to put it on.

Her bloodstained blouse was probably ruined. She couldn't imagine any laundry detergent that would be able to wash away all traces of the blood.

Lucas's T-shirt hung across her slender shoulders

and pulled slightly across her belly, but wearing the clean cotton material that smelled faintly of fabric softener made her feel better.

She left the bedroom and found Lucas waiting for her on the sofa. He stood as she entered the room, his gaze sliding from the top of her head down to her belly.

Self-consciously she placed a hand on her stomach. "Your shirt isn't exactly made for two," she said. "I hope I don't stretch it too much."

"I'm not worried about it," he replied, and held out the coat to help her into it.

It easily wrapped around her and along with its warmth brought that scent of him, that pleasant fragrance of clean cologne and male. She found it oddly comforting.

"Ready?" he asked.

She nodded and together they left Loretta's apartment and walked out into the hallway. "Am I keeping you from a wife or a girlfriend?" she asked as they passed his apartment door.

"No, you aren't keeping me from anything or anyone," he replied.

"What about your job? Shouldn't you be at work?"

He flashed her a quick smile. It was the first smile she'd seen from him and it shot a flutter of warmth through her. "One of the perks of owning the company is getting to pick and choose when you decide to work."

She nodded and fell silent as they walked out into

the brisk November air and headed for his car. What kind of a woman was she to be carrying somebody else's baby and feel that burst of heat at the smile of a virtual stranger?

There had been a moment when his gaze had drifted over her that she'd wished her tummy was thin and shapely, that they'd met in the grocery store or at a restaurant and were together because of a mutual attraction.

Maybe she hadn't just lost her memory, maybe she'd lost her entire mind, she thought as she slid into his passenger seat.

Stress. It had to be stress that had her thinking such crazy thoughts. The only thing she knew she could count on, at least for the moment, was Lucas and his sister. Was it any wonder she would be attracted to him?

"If you don't recover your memory sometime today, then tomorrow I'll make some discreet inquiries about missing persons reports that have been filed in the last day or so," Lucas said as he started the car. "Surely somebody you know will get worried and report you missing."

"Unless nobody cares that I'm missing," she replied.

He shot her a quick look. "I would find that hard to believe."

She released a wry laugh. "I find this entire situation hard to believe."

"Let's play a little game. I'll ask you some questions and you give me the first answer that pops into your head."

"Okay," she agreed as he pulled out of the apartment parking lot.

"What's your favorite television show?"

"The Closer," she replied without any real thought.

He nodded. "Good. And what was the last movie you went to see?"

"I don't go to the movie theater very often." She tried not to think about the tiny nuggets of information the answers revealed about herself, afraid that the nuggets would stop coming.

"What's your favorite restaurant here in the city?"

"That's easy, Café Italian on Maple Street." A buzz of excitement went off inside her. "Maybe they'll know me in there. Maybe they can tell us who I am."

"I know the place. It isn't far from where I found you last night in the car. Maybe we'll go there for lunch and see what we can find out."

Jane's excitement grew. It was possible that by lunchtime she'd know who she was; she'd at least know her name. Surely that would make it easier for her to find out what had happened to her.

"It's a place to start," he said, invading her thoughts. He pulled into the Wal-Mart parking lot and found a space near the front door. At this time of the morning the store didn't look too busy.

They got out of the car and had taken only a

couple of steps toward the door when a voice inside her head thundered.

Don't let them find you.

The words seemed to come from some separate entity inside her brain and they screamed with an alarm that froze her in her tracks.

Instinctively she reached out and grabbed Lucas's hand as fear charged through her. He curled his fingers with hers as he looked at her with concern. "Are you all right?" he asked. "Is it the baby?"

Two thoughts raced through her mind. The first was that she liked the way his big, strong hand felt around hers, and the second was that the voice she'd thought she'd heard in her head had probably been nothing more than a response to the drama of her situation.

She suddenly felt foolish. She unfurled her fingers from his and gave a small laugh. "No, it's not the baby. I guess I just had a case of nerves."

He dropped his hand to his side and studied her intently. "There's nothing to be nervous about. The only thing you have to worry about is being overwhelmed by all the choices."

She forced a smile. "That never happens with women," she said.

Once again they began to walk to the door. Surely the words that had thundered in her head meant nothing, she told herself. But what worried her was they hadn't sounded like nothing. They had sounded like a warning…but a warning of what?

Chapter Three

Once again Lucas found himself doubting the veracity of her amnesia story. Something had happened in the parking lot. He thought she might have thought of something or remembered something that she apparently didn't want to tell him.

She didn't trust him. How could he help her if she didn't trust him?

Lucas pushed the cart with one hand, took Jane by her elbow and guided her down an aisle. When he'd seen her in his T-shirt he'd realized how tiny she was despite her pregnancy. The baby weight was all up front like a ball in her belly, but everywhere else she was slender.

"If you'll just get me a blouse and a toothbrush, that should be enough," she said as they walked through the linen section toward the back of the store.

Lucas didn't know a lot about women, but there was no way he believed she could make do for a day or two with just a new blouse and the jeans she had on.

When they reached the maternity clothes, she headed directly to a clearance rack. Apparently she meant to spend as little of his money as possible.

As she thumbed through the discounted items, he spied a blue cotton long-sleeved blouse exactly the color of her eyes and plucked it from the rack. He threw it into the basket, then added an oversized blue and white sweater.

Although she hadn't mentioned it, she probably needed some underwear, too. He certainly didn't want to completely outfit a woman who might return to a husband or a boyfriend before nightfall. She had a life somewhere, with clothes and shoes and everything else necessary. Still, he didn't want her to do without the bare necessities while she was with him for a day or two.

She returned to where he stood with the cart, carrying an ugly gray T-shirt that had probably been the cheapest on the rack.

"I don't think so," he said. She looked at him in surprise. "If I'm going to be looking at you for the next day or two, I don't want you wearing something ugly."

"But it's only five dollars," she protested.

"There's a reason it's so cheap." He took it from her and hung it on a nearby rack. "What about that pink shirt there?" He pointed to a pastel T-shirt that said Baby on Board. "With another pair of slacks, you should be all right with the other things I grabbed," he said. He averted his gaze from her.

"Then we'll head to the underclothes department and you can get what you need."

She grabbed him by the arm and when he looked at her, those beautiful blue eyes of hers were once again misty with tears. "I can only hope that the father of this baby is half the man you are, Lucas."

"Don't make me into some kind of a hero," he replied with a definite edge in his voice. "I'm just doing what anyone would do under the circumstances."

As they left the maternity section and headed to the undergarments department, he wanted to tell her that he was the last person she should look at with such soft, appealing eyes, with that hint of hero worship that made him feel too warm inside his own skin.

As she picked out a package of panties, he stood at the end of the aisle and waited for her. An old woman stood at the other end of the aisle and appeared to be looking at Jane. When she saw Lucas she offered a sweet smile, then moved on to another aisle.

Jane returned to the cart and threw in her choices. Her cheeks were slightly pink as she looked at him. "I hope I'm a wealthy woman because I'm going to owe you a bunch of money."

"Don't be silly," he replied. He pointed to the nightgowns. "You need to pick out one of those," he said.

"Oh no, that's all right. Loretta gave me one to wear," she replied.

Lucas frowned, remembering when she'd stepped into the kitchen in his sister's nightgown.

"That one can't be comfortable. I saw how it pulled across your stomach. Just pick out one that will fit you comfortably."

As she moved to the rack to look at the items, he tried to forget that vision of her. That nightgown of Loretta's hadn't just pulled taut across her belly, but across her breasts, as well. Her hair had been all tousled and she'd looked achingly soft and feminine.

For just an instant as he'd held that coffee cup frozen halfway to his mouth, he'd wondered what it would be like to wake up with a woman like Jane next to him. When half-asleep, would he rub the swell of her belly and dream of the future of the baby she carried?

Jeez, what was wrong with him? He'd never thought about babies before. The last thing he'd ever wanted to be was a husband and a father. He simply wasn't cut out for either role. Jane felt just a little dangerous to him. She made him think of things he'd never thought of before.

She picked a pale pink nightgown and added it to the growing number of items in the shopping cart. He then pointed the cart in the direction of the toiletries section. She walked beside him and paused a moment to rub her lower back.

"Sorry," she said, and smiled. "Junior must be stretched out right along my spine."

Her smile torched a wave of heat through him. It was the first true smile he'd seen from her and it did amazing things to her already-lovely face. Even the scab across her forehead couldn't detract from her attractiveness.

Suddenly, he was irritated. All he wanted to do was solve the mystery of his Ms. Jane Doe and get her on her way and out of his life.

He noticed the old woman who'd been in the underwear section now at the end of the aisle where Jane stood in front of the hair care items. Once again when she saw him looking at her she smiled. She dug a cell phone out of her purse and then disappeared around the corner.

It was easier focusing on a little white-haired woman than watching Jane. He'd been too long without a woman. That was the problem. It had been months since he'd been out with anyone.

His last date had been with a friend of his partner Troy's girlfriend, Bree. Miranda had flown in from California for a weekend visit and Lucas had taken her out. She'd been perfect for him, very hot and very temporary. He frowned in irritation as he realized Jane got to him in a way Miranda hadn't. There was a softness about Jane, a sweetness in her smile, a fragile light in her eyes that pulled up a protectiveness in him he'd never felt for anyone except his sister.

"I think that's everything I should need." Jane pulled him from his thoughts as she added a hairbrush, a toothbrush and a bottle of citrus-scented shampoo to the cart.

"Then let's get out of here," Lucas said. He blew a sigh of relief as they headed for the cashier lines.

Maybe if he took her to Café Italian for an early lunch, somebody at the restaurant would recognize her and the mystery would be solved.

They fell into line behind a woman who looked as if she'd bought half the store. Jane covered his hand with hers on the handle of the cart. Her hand was warm on his skin as she looked up at him. "I can't thank you enough," she said. "I couldn't face wearing that bloody blouse all day today."

"We'll run back to Loretta's so you can change clothes, then head to the restaurant to see if anybody there knows your name."

He breathed a sigh of relief as she pulled her hand from his. "Even if somebody just knows my first name, surely hearing that will remind me of who I am."

He heard the thrum of desperation in her voice. It must be horrifying not to know even the most simple thing about yourself—your name. Until this moment he hadn't really realized that if she was telling the truth about her amnesia, then she must be absolutely terrified.

All he'd been thinking about was getting her gone as soon as possible, but he didn't want her to go unless she had her memory back.

Finally it was their turn to be checked out. As Lucas placed the items on the counter he noticed that Jane winced and rubbed her lower back.

"You want to go ahead to the car?" he asked. Maybe if she got off her feet her back would feel better.

"Are you sure you wouldn't mind?"

He held out the keys as the cashier told him his total. "Go on, I'll be out in two minutes."

She smiled gratefully and took the keys from him as he pulled out his wallet to pay the cashier. As she headed toward the exit, he put the bags of his purchases back in the cart.

As he pushed out of the exit door, he saw a van pull up. The back doors opened and two men began grappling with Jane, obviously trying to get her into the back of the van.

"Hey!" he yelled. His heart smashed into his ribs as he abandoned the cart and took off running toward them.

At that moment Jane released a scream that raised the hairs on the back of his neck and drew the attention of everyone in the parking lot. Another shopper, a burly man, began to run toward the van, as well.

Jane screamed again as she struggled to get free. The two men suddenly released her and jumped into the back of the van, which took off with a squeal of tires.

The burly man and Lucas reached Jane at the same time. She launched herself at Lucas, wrapping her arms around his neck and hanging on tight.

"Are you all right?" he asked urgently. "Did they hurt you?"

She shook her head and buried her face against his chest. Despite the fact that she wore his big, down-filled coat, he could feel the trembling of her body against him.

The big man looked at Lucas and pulled a cell phone from his pocket. "Want me to call 911?"

"No!" Jane lifted her head and looked first at the man, then at Lucas. "No, please. Let's just go home. But thank you for your help."

The man shrugged and put his cell phone back in his pocket, then headed toward the store entrance.

Another shopper, a young woman, pushed Lucas's cart to where he and Jane stood. "You aren't safe anywhere these days," she said with a worried frown on her face.

With Jane still clinging to him, Lucas pushed the basket to the side of his car. She pulled his keys from her pocket, unlocked the door and helped her into the passenger side.

He threw the bags into the backseat, then walked around to the driver door. It had all happened so damn fast. He hadn't even gotten a license plate number on the van. All he'd seen was a small symbol of some kind on the back window.

There was no way he believed that this had just been a random act of violence. Those men had been after her. As he slid in behind the steering wheel he turned to look at her. His heart still beat a rapid tattoo of alarm.

"If you have any memories in your head, if you're holding anything back, you'd better spill it now," he said as he stabbed the key into the ignition. "Otherwise we'd better figure out who you are and why in the hell those men just tried to kidnap you."

Jane stared at him as the yawning horror of what had just happened filled her with an icy chill of terror. When the van had pulled up in front of her, she'd thought nothing about it. Then the back doors had swung open and the two men had rushed her.

"I swear I don't know anything. I don't know who those men were or what they wanted with me." Her heart still beat with the frantic rhythm of fear.

A knot of tension throbbed in Lucas's lean jaw as he pulled out of the parking lot and onto the road.

She continued to look at him, needing the mere sight of him to ground her, to somehow chase away the panic that still clawed at her insides.

"I don't suppose you recognized those men?" he asked.

She shook her head. "I don't think I've ever seen them before."

"Did they say anything to you?"

"No, not a word. They just grabbed me and tried to get me into the back of the van." She shuddered as she relived the moment when they'd grabbed her arms, when they'd begun to force her toward the vehicle.

Lucas didn't say another word as they drove back to the apartment. As he drove he checked the rear-view mirror constantly and she realized he was watching to see if they'd been followed.

He didn't sign up for this, Jane thought. *He didn't*

volunteer for whatever was going on in my life. But the idea of not having him next to her terrified her.

When they reached the apartment he grabbed her by the arm and walked her inside the building, his gaze seeming to go in all directions at the same time.

"Why don't you go and take a shower and change clothes," he said. "Then we'll head to that restaurant and see if anyone there can identify you."

The idea of leaving the safety of the apartment terrified her, but she knew she couldn't just stay here and hope that her memories might magically return. Maybe being in the familiar surroundings of the restaurant would jog something loose.

She brought the shopping bags into the bedroom where she'd spent the night, then carried the clean clothes and the other items into the bathroom for a quick shower.

As she stood beneath the hot spray of water she thought of the moments when the men had grabbed her. She'd been so stunned that she'd been unable to think, and had reacted only by fighting back. She'd kicked and punched to get away, but they'd seemed determined to get her into the back of the van.

Why? Who were those men?

Don't let them find you!

The words thundered in her brain and she leaned against the porcelain wall as wave after wave of fear swept through her.

Were those men the "them" that her brain had screamed a warning about? What did they want with her? Who was she? The questions pounded her as the hot water pelted her skin.

What kind of trouble was she in?

When she was finished showering, she dressed in the new clothes, the maternity jeans feeling crisp and clean against her skin and the blue blouse fitting her perfectly. She found Loretta's blow-dryer beneath the sink and dried her hair, then brushed her teeth and pronounced herself ready for what the rest of the day might bring.

She found Lucas seated at the kitchen table, doodling on a piece of paper. He looked up as she entered, and for an instant she saw the flash of something dark, something hot in his eyes.

She might not know her own name, but she knew desire when she saw it. It stunned her and at the same time sent a shock wave of excitement through her.

There was no question that she was attracted to him, that his lean, dark good looks made her heart beat just a tiny bit faster. But she'd attempted to shove away those crazy feelings. She was carrying somebody's baby, and for all she knew she was in a happy, committed relationship with another man.

"You look nice," he said.

She wrapped her arms around her stomach. "I look pregnant," she replied, as if somehow reminding herself and him of that fact.

A corner of his mouth curled up in a smile. "You can look pregnant and nice at the same time."

"Thank you," she said, aware of the flush that warmed her cheeks.

She sat at the table across from him. "What are you doing?"

"Unfortunately I didn't get a good look at the two men who were trying to grab you, and I didn't get the license plate of the van, but I did notice a sign in the back window."

"A sign? What did it say?"

"It didn't say anything. It was a symbol of some kind. I tried to draw it to see if maybe you'd seen it before." He shoved a piece of paper to her.

She stared down at what he'd drawn—a triangle with what looked like the all-seeing eye in the center. The sight of it shot a cold, stark terror through her. She gasped and pushed it back across the table to him.

He leaned forward and covered her hand with his. "Do you recognize it? What is it, Jane? What does it mean?"

"I don't know." She felt ill, as if the cold November air had brought icy snow into her veins. "All I know is that seeing it makes me feel sick. It makes me so afraid."

She turned her hand over and twined her fingers with his, needing the warmth of his hand to banish some of the chill. "What does it mean, Lucas? My God, what was going on in my life before I lost my memories?"

"I don't know. But those men definitely had

something in mind for you." The throb of that muscle was back in his jaw.

Reluctantly Jane pulled her hand away from his. Her heart thudded anxiously as she looked at the man who had taken her in. "Lucas, maybe you should just drop me off at a shelter or something." The words came reluctantly and with a thunderous pounding in her head. "I don't know what kind of danger I might bring to you and Loretta."

His eyes narrowed. "Danger has never scared me." He leaned back in the chair. "There's no way anyone can tie you to me. I'm not concerned about danger finding you here. And there's no way in hell I'm going to drop you off anywhere until we know what's going on. I don't think those men intended to take you someplace for a nice hot cup of tea."

A river of gratitude washed over her. It would have been so easy for him to abdicate all responsibility for her and toss her to the proverbial wolves.

She cradled her stomach as the baby moved inside her. "Junior is restless," she said.

"Maybe he's hungry." Lucas pushed back from the table and stood. "Come on, let's check out that Italian restaurant. Maybe over bread sticks we'll learn your real name."

They put their coats back on, then left Loretta's apartment. "We need to stop by my place before leaving," he said.

When they reached his door he unlocked it and gestured her inside. "I'll be right back," he said, and disappeared down the hallway while Jane looked around the living room with interest.

It somehow didn't surprise her that his living conditions were spartan and as impersonal as a motel room. He'd been completely at ease in Loretta's apartment. She had a feeling he spent most of his free time there.

There was only one photo in the room and it sat on top of the television in a silver frame. She walked over and picked it up. It was a picture of him and Loretta sitting on a park bench. He looked to be around fifteen and she was nine or ten. She leaned into him, smiling up at him as if he were the greatest thing since sliced bread, but his smile looked slightly forced.

She set the photo down as he returned to the living room. "You and Loretta have always been close?"

"It's always been her and me against the world," he replied.

"What about your parents? Are they still alive?"

"No, they're both dead. But even when they were alive, Loretta and I only had each other."

She wanted to ask him more about the dark shadow that had danced over his eyes when he'd mentioned his parents. But his terse tone and frown forbade her from asking anything else.

They left his apartment and walked back out into the cold, wintry air. She got into his passenger seat and watched as he walked around the front of the car to the driver side.

As he moved, his coat blew open to reveal that he

now wore a holster with a gun. Jane's mouth went dry. She'd known she was in trouble when those men had tried to grab her, but the sight of that gun suddenly shot it all home.

He was expecting more trouble. That's what the gun meant. She only hoped they both would survive whatever happened next.

Chapter Four

The Café Italian was a popular lunch place. They had a reasonably priced luncheon menu and promised fast service for those who only had an hour or so to eat before returning back to work.

Lucas and Jane were greeted at the door by a smiling, robust man who looked as if he'd been eating pasta and garlic bread for most of his life. "Two?" he asked as he grabbed a couple of menus.

Lucas nodded and they were led to a table in the back, where Lucas sat facing the door so he could see who was coming and going. Jane took off her oversize jacket and sat across from him. "Have you been working here long?" Lucas asked the man as he handed them their menus.

"Just started a couple of weeks ago," he replied. "Why?"

"Do you recognize me?" Jane asked.

Lucas heard the desperation in her voice and wondered how she was managing to hold it all together. Certainly after the scene at the store she had every right to fall apart, but she hadn't and she'd earned a grudging admiration from him.

"Should I recognize you?" the man asked as he studied her face carefully. "Are you somebody famous?"

"No, nothing like that," she replied. "I just…I'm having some memory problems and I remember being in here and hoped somebody would be able to tell me when."

"Sorry. I'm pretty good with faces, but I don't remember seeing yours before," he replied. "I'll ask the waitresses if any of them recognize you."

"Thanks, I'd appreciate it," she replied.

As he left their table, she looked at Lucas with a disheartening frown. "I thought I'd just walk in here and everything would come back to me."

"Do you remember anything?"

She leaned back in her chair and looked around. Lucas had known the blue blouse would match her eyes, but he hadn't thought about how it might make her skin look creamy and touchable. He hadn't considered that with the top buttons unfastened he'd get a hint of cleavage each time she bent forward.

"I don't remember anything specific, but this place feels familiar. I know for sure that I've been here before. I just don't know if it was a week ago, a year ago or five years ago." She puffed a sigh of obvious frustration. "What if I never remember who I am or why those men tried to grab me?"

"It's only been a day, Jane. Maybe you're trying too hard," he replied.

She smiled. "Having a couple of goons try to grab you in a parking lot tends to make you try hard." She sighed once again and opened her menu. "The eggplant is delicious here." Her gaze shot to his in stunned surprise. "How did I know that? Why can I remember eggplant when I can't remember my own name?"

She was getting more and more agitated with each minute that passed. Lucas frowned. "I think maybe after we eat we'll go back to my place and just relax for the rest of the afternoon. Stop reaching for it and maybe it will come."

"Maybe you're right," she agreed as she closed her menu.

With each minute Lucas spent with her, more questions whirled in his head. What did that symbol mean that he'd seen on the back of the van? Why had Jane reacted so viscerally to it? And why had those men tried to grab her? What could they possibly want from her? It sure as hell hadn't been a robbery attempt. She wasn't even carrying a purse.

If the cashier had taken one more minute in loading up his purchases, if he'd stopped to look at something on his way out of the store, then they would probably have succeeded in getting her into the back of the van. The thought chilled him to the bone.

His thoughts were interrupted by the arrival of the waitress to their table. Jane ordered the eggplant and he ordered lasagna. Then Jane asked the woman if she'd seen her in the restaurant before.

"You look kind of familiar," she said. "I'm sure you've been in here before, but I don't know your name or anything."

"We knew this was probably a long shot," Lucas said as the waitress left with their orders.

"I know. I just hoped that we'd at least get a first name." She tucked a strand of shiny hair behind her ear. "So, talk to me about something else, Lucas. Tell me more about yourself." She smiled. "The good thing about being with a woman who has amnesia is that the conversation gets to be all about you."

He laughed, finding her more than a little bit enchanting. "There isn't much to tell. I'm thirty-three years old, never been married, never intend to get married. I love my work, my sister and my partners and that's about it."

"Why don't you have any intention of marrying?" she asked.

"Because I'd probably be a crummy husband and an even crummier father." He was intimately familiar with bad relationships and bore the scars of horrible parenting. That's what he knew. By staying single, by never becoming a husband or a father, he would never run the risk of repeating the mistakes his parents made.

"I don't think you'd be crummy at either," she said. But she really knew nothing about him.

"I'm just better off alone." He shrugged, slightly

uncomfortable by the conversation. "I'm happy that way."

"I know it sounds crazy, especially given this little circumstance." She patted her tummy. "But I feel like I was alone before all this." Her cheeks flushed a becoming pink. "I don't know, maybe the man who got me pregnant decided he didn't want anything more to do with me or the baby." She picked up her water glass and took a sip, then continued. "It's just a crazy feeling I have."

"Maybe you feel that way because of the circumstances," he replied. "Maybe you have a loving husband somewhere waiting, worrying about you right now."

She looked down at her hands. She had slender fingers with neatly clipped nails and wore no polish. "I'm not wearing a ring. I'm not sure how to explain it, but I just know in my heart that I'm not married."

He didn't know what to think. Certainly just because she was pregnant he couldn't automatically assume that she was married. Maybe deep down inside he hoped she was. He hoped she had a loving man in her life who was worried sick about her, a man who loved her to distraction and couldn't wait for the birth of their baby.

Although he'd known her less than twenty-four hours, he wanted that for her. And maybe he needed to believe that in order to erect a barrier between them.

There was no question that he was attracted to her.

More attracted than he could remember being to a woman in a very long time.

As the waitress arrived to serve them, he tried not to think about that attraction. He told himself it was nothing more than the way she looked at him, as if he could fix her life, as if she trusted him to make things right. Loretta was the only other woman who had ever looked at him like that.

He was as temporary in her life as her amnesia and he hoped that within another twenty-four hours she'd have her memories back and be out of his life.

Lunch passed uneventfully. They chatted about the food and she asked him questions about his partners, Micah and Troy.

He told her about how Micah had found love with Caylee when he'd gone to a private island to retrieve an airplane. And Troy fell in love with a California paparazzi favorite, Brianna Waverly, while protecting her during a kidnapping.

Brianna now ran an animal shelter not far from the Recovery Inc. office, and Lucas had a feeling it wouldn't be long before they'd begin planning a wedding.

"When we get back home I'll check in with Troy and Micah and see if they can hunt down some information about that symbol I saw in the van window," he said.

Her face paled. "Seeing it gave me a terrible feeling," she said, her voice higher than usual with obvious stress.

"Maybe if we can figure out what it means, then we'll have a clue to your identity."

"So you do believe me? You don't think I'm faking?" Those blue eyes of hers held his gaze intently.

A man could drown in those blue depths, he thought. Maybe it was because she had no past, no baggage, that her eyes were so clear, so achingly blue.

"Yeah, I believe you." It was true. At some point after those men had tried to grab her at the store, he'd realized she wasn't pretending. He'd seen the stark terror on her face coupled with utter confusion. Nobody was that good an actress.

"I'm so glad," she replied. "It was important to me that you believe me."

"Why?"

She looked at him in surprise. "Because you're helping me. Because you and your sister have already gone above and beyond for me. I don't want you to think that I'm the kind of woman to lie and take advantage of you."

He might not think she was a woman who would take advantage of him, but he had a feeling she was definitely the kind of woman who could get him into trouble if he wasn't careful.

BY THE TIME THEY GOT BACK to Loretta's apartment Jane was exhausted. "Why don't you go lie down for a little while," Lucas suggested. "You look beat."

"I am," she agreed.

"While you're resting I'm going to call my

partners and see what they can find out about that symbol. I'm friendly with the chief of police, Wendall Kincaid. I'll give him a call and see if anyone has filed a missing persons report about a pregnant woman."

She frowned. "But you won't tell the police about me?" He hesitated and she took a step closer to him. "Lucas, I don't think I'm a criminal and I have no rational reason for my fear, but the idea of going to the police makes me as afraid as the sight of that symbol did. I know eventually if I don't remember who I am we'll probably have to go to the police. But please, not yet?"

"Don't worry," he assured her. "I'm not going to go against your wishes right now. I can ask Wendall some questions, and if he asks why I want to know, I can tell him that I have an issue I'm not ready to tell him about right now. He'll respect that. But if this amnesia continues, then you're right, we might have no choice but to go to the police. Go on, get some rest."

With a nod, she turned and walked down the hallway to the bedroom where she'd slept the night before. She couldn't imagine actually going to sleep, not with the questions whirling around in her head.

Once again she found herself wondering what might have happened to her if Lucas hadn't found her in the car. He was like a guardian angel come to her when she needed somebody.

But was it normal to feel a rivulet of heat when a guardian angel looked at you? Was it normal to wonder what his mouth might feel like pressed against your own?

Hormones, she thought as she stretched out on her back on the bed. Her hormones were definitely running amok and that was the only reason for her crazy physical attraction toward Lucas.

She rubbed her stomach as she felt the baby moving inside her. Who was the father? What had happened that had sent her out into the cold in the middle of the night with a head wound?

Maybe Lucas was right. Maybe she was trying too hard to remember, and her efforts were stifling the very memories she was trying so hard to retrieve.

She closed her eyes and consciously willed away all thoughts of the moment when the two men had grabbed her arms and tried to get her into the back of the van. She drew in deep breaths and tried to empty her mind of all thought.

SYMBOLS. They were everywhere. The triangle with the eye inside it. The all-seeing eye. The all-knowing mind. Her heart crashed inside her chest as she ran down a long, dark hallway, needing to escape from it...from them.

Footsteps sounded behind her and she pressed her back into an alcove, praying they'd move on, that she wouldn't be found.

She breathed a sigh of relief as the sound of the footsteps faded away. Run! *Her brain screamed the command.* Get out!

Once again she began to move silently down the hallway, hoping she'd come to a door that would allow her to escape. She turned into another corridor and stopped, her blood cold as she saw him standing at the end.

Even though the hall was too dark for her to see his features, she knew who he was—the all-knowing mind.

SHE SCREAMED as hands gripped her by the shoulders and she opened her eyes to see Lucas. The dream fell away, but not the horror of it. She gasped as a sob escaped her lips.

"Hey, you're okay," he said as he sat on the edge of the bed. "You were just having a bad dream."

Cold. She was cold with terror and she didn't think twice about launching herself into his arms as another sob ripped out of her.

He stiffened as she pressed against him and hid her face in his chest. Then he did exactly what she needed; he folded his arms around her and held her.

In the warmth of the embrace, in the strength of his arms, any tears she'd been able to shed vanished. A dream. It had just been a dream. Or had it?

"You okay?" His voice was a rumble in her ear as she kept her head against his broad chest.

Although she found his embrace amazingly welcome, she knew she couldn't stay in his arms forever. Reluctantly she sat up and moved away from him.

"You want to talk about it?" he asked.

She wrapped her arms around her shoulders, the cold wind of fear finding her once again. "It was crazy. There were those symbols everywhere and I was in a dark hallway, trying to escape."

"Escape from what?" Lucas's dark eyes watched her intently.

She frowned, trying to make sense of the images that she'd dreamed. "I don't know. It didn't make sense. I just knew that I had to get away and then I turned a corner and there was a man standing at the end of the hall and I knew I couldn't get away." A shudder worked through her.

"Was it a dream or was it a memory?"

Jane held his gaze. It would be easy to get lost in those black-lashed dark eyes of his. At the moment she'd like nothing more than to get lost in him, to escape the uncertainty of the unknown, to feel safe and secure in his arms.

She shook herself. "I'm not sure. I don't know," she finally replied. "But if it was a memory, then what could it mean? I mean, why would I feel as if I was a prisoner trying to escape something awful?"

Lucas ran a hand through his hair. "I don't know. Maybe it was some kind of symbolism. Maybe what you were trying to escape was your amnesia."

"Maybe," she said grudgingly, although she wasn't sure what to believe. "How long was I asleep?"

He looked at his wristwatch. "About an hour or so."

He got up from the edge of the bed. "Look, I've

got some things to do. You should be fine here until Loretta gets home. She should be here by four."

She didn't want him to leave. The idea of being alone terrified her, but she swallowed the fear and nodded. "Please, take care of your business. I'll be fine." She offered him a smile that she hoped didn't look as forced as it felt.

"I'll check in with you later this evening." As he left the room, Jane felt an overwhelming need to tell him that she didn't want to be by herself, but she didn't.

She'd intruded into his life in a very big way and the very least she could do was not be a clinging vine to a man who owed her nothing just because she was overwhelmed with fear.

Fear. She slid her legs over the side of the bed and drew a deep breath. She had to get control of her fear. There were a million things she didn't know about herself, about her life, but she needed to focus on what she did know.

She and the baby were healthy, and at the moment she was in a safe place. Maybe after another good night's sleep her memory would return. Maybe during dinner tonight she'd have a sudden epiphany and all her memories would just come tumbling back.

Instead of feeling sorry for herself or afraid, maybe she needed to get her mind on something else. With this thought in mind she headed for the kitchen.

Maybe she could do something nice for Loretta

and cook dinner. Looking in the refrigerator, she spied a pound of thawed hamburger meat. Maybe a meat loaf, she thought.

Within minutes she'd gathered all the ingredients she needed to make the dish and set to work. Funny, she had a feeling she made a great meat loaf, and adding the appropriate amount of bread crumbs and seasonings came to her without thought.

She'd just popped it into the oven when she heard the sound of the front door open. "Hello?" Loretta called out.

"I'm in the kitchen," Jane replied. As Loretta came into the room, Jane felt a touch of shyness. She'd hardly spoken to the woman the night before and hadn't seen her that morning.

"You look much better than you did last night," Loretta said with a warm smile that instantly put Jane at ease.

"Maybe on the outside, but unfortunately nothing has changed on the inside," Jane replied.

"Still don't remember anything?" Loretta asked as she sat in one of the kitchen chairs and kicked off her blue clogs.

"Nothing. I hope you don't mind that I'm still here. I took the liberty of making a meat loaf for dinner."

"Mind? If you cook for me every night I might just think about marrying you," Loretta exclaimed with a laugh.

Jane relaxed and joined her at the table. "I don't

want to take advantage of your kindness. I'm hoping maybe after another good night's sleep things will become clear."

"Don't worry about taking advantage. What's important is that you give yourself some time to get your memory back. Where's my brother?"

"He said he needed to take care of some business and left about an hour ago. He said he'd check back in sometime this evening. He's been very kind to me."

Loretta smiled. "He can be a bit hard and crusty on the outside, but he's a good man." She frowned and looked as if she wanted to say something more, but instead she stood. "I'm going to go take a quick shower. I'll be back in a few minutes."

"If you don't mind, I'll go ahead and set the table."

"Mind? Knock yourself out," Loretta exclaimed, and then left the kitchen.

Jane found the appropriate plates and silverware and got the table prepared for the meal. She made a salad, opened a can of corn and got it warming on the stove top by the time Loretta had returned, now dressed in a pair of sweats and a T-shirt.

"Now, tell me about your day," she said as she put a kettle of water on the stove to boil for tea.

Jane told her about their trip to the store and the kidnapping attempt. As she related the story, that familiar cold fear seeped into her bones.

"Oh my God," Loretta exclaimed when she was finished. "You poor thing."

"Even that didn't jiggle loose any memories, but Lucas said he was going to have his partners do some research and see if they could find out what the symbol means."

"If you're in some kind of trouble, Lucas, Troy and Micah are the men to help you out. If there are answers to be found, they'll find them."

A half hour later as they ate, Loretta told Jane about Lucas's partners and the business that they owned. But what Jane wanted most of all was to learn more about Lucas.

"Your brother told me that when you two were growing up it was you and him against the world. You had a tough childhood?" she asked.

Loretta frowned thoughtfully. "Not so much me, but things were tough on Lucas. My father had anger issues and most of his rage was always directed at my brother." She shrugged. "He got through it. We both did. But it made us unusually close. Lucas was my hero when I was growing up, and throughout the years that's never changed."

"It must be nice to have somebody like that in your life," Jane said. "Somebody who will always be there for you, somebody you can depend on." A wistfulness filled her and again she couldn't help but wonder if she'd been looking for somebody like that in her life or if she'd already found him and just couldn't remember who he was.

"Yeah, the only thing nicer than having a brother like that would be having a husband like that,"

Loretta said with a laugh. "But there will be time for romance once I'm finished with medical school."

The rest of the meal they chatted about Loretta's desire to become a doctor and speculated on what Jane might do as a career. It didn't take long for them to get silly. Loretta thought Jane might be a Hollywood actress who had escaped the prying eyes of the paparazzi to have her baby in private. Of course the baby's father was a high-profile rock star who loved her to distraction, but was afraid marriage would hurt his image.

Jane offered the scenario that she'd been abducted by a space alien and impregnated and they'd erased her memories so she wouldn't bring back secrets of their planet.

The laughter felt wonderful and they were still giggling like high school best friends when Lucas walked in.

Instantly, Jane felt as if the kitchen shrank in size as he filled it with his dark energy, his bigger-than-life presence.

"Sounds like you two are having fun," he said as he grabbed a plate from the cabinet and sat at the table.

"We were just speculating on Jane's life," Loretta explained, her eyes still sparkling with merriment. "We've decided she's either a spy or a hooker going incognito."

Jane laughed again. "Your sister is a hoot."

Lucas filled his plate from the food still on the table. "Yeah, she's a regular comedian."

"What have you been doing?" Loretta asked.

"I had to go try on a tux for the wedding. Then I stopped at the office to catch up on things," he replied.

"Wedding?" Jane asked.

"My partner Micah is getting married in less than a month. I'm his best man. Good meat loaf," he said.

"You can thank Jane for dinner. She surprised me by fixing it. I told her if she cooks like this every night I might decide to keep her," Loretta said.

"You might have to keep her, at least for another day or two." He grabbed a piece of bread to add to his plate.

"I talked to Kincaid at the police station. There've been no reports of missing women filed in the past forty-eight hours."

Jane stared at him in dismay. She'd somehow hoped that a missing persons report would fill in some of the pieces.

She wasn't sure what bothered her more, the fact that strange men had tried to shove her into the back of a van or that apparently there was nobody in her life who had missed her over the past twenty-four hours.

Chapter Five

The crushed look on Jane's face touched a chord in Lucas's heart. "Maybe it's too early for anyone to have reported you missing," he said. "If you went missing not too many hours before I found you, then it's only been twenty-four hours now. Maybe tomorrow somebody will file a report."

"Maybe," she agreed. "Or maybe there was nobody in my life to file a report, nobody who misses me."

"I can't imagine that," Loretta said gently.

What must it be like to be missing from your life and believe that nobody cares? Lucas couldn't help but feel a chord of sympathy for her despite his desire to the contrary.

He listened and ate while the two women talked about babies and fashion, acting as if they'd known each other forever. The first time he heard Jane laugh, the sound shot a burst of warmth through him. She had a great, full-bodied laugh.

Who had she been before all this? Had she laughed often? Loved passionately? Did she like old movies or New Age music? Did she like quiet, intimate dinners or prefer the club scene? He frowned, irritated that he was even speculating on who she really was.

As Loretta got up to begin clearing the table, Jane rose, as well. But Loretta waved her back down. "No way. You cooked, so I do the cleanup. Just sit and relax."

Jane sat back down. She'd only been sitting a minute when a smile lit her face and she placed her hands on her tummy. "Junior is doing a happy dance." She smiled at Lucas. "Quick, give me your hand."

Without conscious thought he leaned forward and placed his hand on her belly.

Immediately he felt the undulating movement of life. A sense of awe filled him as he felt a flutter, then a sharper protrusion of an elbow or a foot. A baby, a little human life—amazing, he thought.

He jerked his hand away and sat back in his chair. He didn't want to think about babies or beautiful blondes who had smiles filled with sunshine. He refused to get emotionally caught up with the unborn baby and Jane, who would eventually remember her life and return to it.

"I've got to get home," he said, and stood, needing to escape the warmth of Jane's smile and the concern that she was all alone in the world, had somehow been all alone in the world even before she lost her memories.

"Tomorrow I want to take you to the office to meet with my partners. Micah is working to get us some information about that symbol and on the way we'll take a ride by the place where I found you. Maybe something will break loose in your head if we go back to that area."

"What time should I be ready?" Jane asked him.

"Let's say around nine?"

He walked over to his sister and kissed her on the cheek. "I'll see you later," he said.

He breathed a sigh of relief as he escaped the apartment and headed down the hallway to his own. He had no idea what it was about his "Jane Doe" that affected him so strongly.

Even throughout the last couple of hours when he hadn't been with her, his thoughts kept returning to her. What if the baby came? Who was going to take care of her and the newborn if she didn't have her memory back?

Dammit, he didn't want to feel responsible for her, and yet he did. And if he were completely honest with himself he would admit that despite the fact that she was pregnant, he was attracted to her. Never in a million years had he thought he'd find a pregnant woman sexy, but he found Jane extremely sexy.

He entered his apartment and checked his machine. No new messages. He hadn't expected any. His partners knew to get him on his cell phone and there wasn't anyone else who would want to call him. He sat on the sofa and for a moment the silence closed in around him.

The sound of Jane's laughter had found a place inside him that whispered of a loneliness he hadn't realized was there. Her warm laughter had momentarily chased it away.

What he needed was for her to wake up tomorrow and not only remember her name, but also have a family to support her, perhaps a husband who loved her.

What he really needed was a good night's sleep without thoughts of Jane intruding in his head. He grabbed a beer from the fridge and returned to the sofa, where he punched the remote to turn on the television.

As the screen filled with a sitcom he didn't recognize, he popped the top on the beer and took a deep swallow. Generally, Lucas wasn't a television kind of guy, but tonight he needed something to keep his mind off a pregnant blonde with warm blue eyes.

He focused on the sitcom and by nine had finished his beer and decided to call it a night. The next morning brought more of the same. The news didn't broadcast a missing pregnant woman report, and the moment Jane opened Loretta's door to his knock, he knew that she still didn't remember anything.

"Sleep well?" he asked.

"Actually, I slept like a baby," she replied.

She didn't look like a baby. The T-shirt she wore that pronounced Baby on Board pulled across the fullness of her breasts, and the maternity jeans they'd bought fit snug on her long, lean legs.

He could smell her, the clean scent of citrus shampoo and a fragrant soap. Every muscle in his body tensed. "You ready to leave?" he asked, his tone sharper than he'd intended.

"Just let me get a coat." She disappeared down the hallway.

She returned wearing the coat he'd loaned her the day before and together they left the apartment building. A cold wind blew from the north as they hurried to his car in the lot.

"What's the plan?" she asked once they were in the car and he'd started the engine.

"First we're going to take a ride around the area where I found you to see if that jiggles your memory," he said. "Then we'll head over to the office and see what Micah and Troy have found out about that symbol."

"I've disrupted your life. You must be sick of me already."

He turned to look at her, realizing that his sharp tone with her earlier hadn't gone unnoticed. "Don't worry about it. I didn't have much of a life for you to disrupt."

He backed out of the parking space, surprised that his own words swept that whisper of loneliness through him once again. What was the matter with him? He clenched the steering wheel more tightly, irritated by the wayward direction of his thoughts.

"Where exactly are we?" she asked as he pulled out on the street. "I mean, I know we're in Kansas City, but nothing looks familiar."

"Downtown is south of us. We're at the northern edges of the city," he replied. "The area where I found you is called Oak Grove Estates, upper-middle-class homes and a nice neighborhood. Ring a bell?"

"No." She frowned and stared out the window. "But I remember running and running before I got into that car to rest."

"Maybe we'll go by a house or a landmark that you recognize," he said. He wasn't sure what else to do. Somehow they needed to stimulate her mind to remember what had happened to her, and it wasn't happening in the safety of Loretta's apartment.

"Maybe," she agreed, and fell silent.

It didn't take long for them to reach Oak Grove. Lucas drove slowly down the street where two nights before he'd repossessed the car and held his breath for an "aha" moment from her.

But it didn't come. She stared out the window with desperation shining from her eyes. Thinking about the fact that she'd said she remembered running, he worked outward from the house where he'd found her, driving down street after street in the general area.

"It's no good," she finally said. "Nothing looks

familiar." Her voice held a wealth of disappointment. She released a weary sigh. "I'm beginning to
think I'll never remember who I am or what happened."

"You can't give up," he replied. "It's just going
to take some time, Jane. We have to be patient."

"I have to be patient, but you don't have to be," she
replied. She looked at him. "Maybe it would be best
if you did just drop me off at a motel, front me some
money and let me figure this out on my own. You
don't owe me anything. I'm not your problem. I'm just
a stranger you happened to stumble on by accident."

It would be easy to do as she suggested, just pull into
the parking lot of the nearest motel, pay for a week or
two of lodging and drop her off and forget her. But he
knew he wouldn't forget anything. She'd haunt him
forever. He'd worry about what had happened to her,
to her baby. He'd wonder where she was and how she
fared. Nope, that simply wasn't an option right now.

He shot her a quick glance and then returned his
gaze back to the road. "Don't be silly. I'm not about
to drop you off someplace and just drive away and
let you figure this out on your own." He thought he
heard a little sigh of relief from her.

"Don't worry about me, Jane," he continued.
"Sooner or later we'll find out who you are and
what's happened to you. Until that happens, I'm
here for you. I have no intention of walking away."

He glanced at her again, just in time to see her
offer him one of those amazing smiles of hers. As

he focused back on his driving, he had a feeling he was already in too deep where Jane was concerned.

THE RECOVERY INC. OFFICE was nicely decorated with two large desks and a waiting area with a leather sofa and matching chair. As Jane and Lucas entered, she beelined for the sofa and sank down to ease her aching back.

It seemed as if her baby's favorite position was sitting on her spine. Her lower back hurt most of the time.

"Troy and Micah should be here any minute," Lucas said as he walked over to the phone and punched the button to check the messages.

There was only one—a man calling about a missing cigar boat that he suspected had been stolen by his ex–son-in-law. He left a phone number with an area code Jane didn't recognize.

She felt ridiculously nervous about meeting his partners. It was as if she were Lucas's girlfriend and desperately wanted to make a good impression on his family. Of course, that was ridiculous. She was nothing more than a burden to him and it didn't matter whether his partners liked her or not.

"You want something to drink?" he asked.

"No, I'm fine," she replied.

At that moment the front door opened and a tall, good-looking man entered. Lucas introduced Jane to Micah Stone. He smiled and shook her hand warmly, then gestured her back down on the sofa.

"Lucas has told me a little about what's going on," he said as he shrugged out of his coat and hung it on the coat tree next to theirs. "I did some research on that symbol and have some things for you both to look at." He pulled several folded sheets of paper from his pocket.

As he sat on one side of her, Lucas sat on the other. She was flanked on either side by enough lean muscle and testosterone to feel as if the world could come to an end and somehow she'd survive.

"The all-seeing eye has quite a place in history," he said. "Generally it is a symbol of the protective power of a Supreme Being," Micah said. "In Mexican culture it's been used as a talisman against evil. Its origin can be traced back to Egyptian mythology and the Eye of Horus."

He opened up one of the sheets of paper and handed it to Lucas. "Did it look like this?"

Jane caught a glimpse of the picture and quickly closed her eyes. She didn't want to see it again, didn't understand what that symbol had to do with her and why it evoked such fear in her heart.

"Not exactly," Lucas replied. "It wasn't a pyramid. It wasn't like what's on the dollar bill, it was just a triangle." Micah handed him another sheet of paper. "That's it," he said.

Jane looked at Micah. "What is it?"

"It took me a while to find anything locally, but I finally found a church that uses the symbol kind of like their logo."

"A church?" Jane frowned. What on earth could a church have to do with her current situation?

"The Church of Enlightenment, to be exact," Micah said.

"And what did you find out about this church?" Lucas asked.

"Big church with a healthy, multidenominational congregation. The church owns about a hundred acres of land north of here. It's open to the public, but they have a small compound there that's a gated community of sorts."

"A gated community. That sounds rather odd," Lucas said with a frown.

"The church itself seems a bit odd," Micah said. "I didn't have time to do a lot of research. But from what information I was able to gather, the church is headed by a man known only as The Prophet, who gives the sermon each Sunday and remains a sort of mysterious father figure."

"Can you say cult?" Lucas said drily.

"I don't know about that," Micah replied. "I'd have to have a lot more information than what I have to make that kind of call."

"Just because we saw that symbol on the back of the van door doesn't mean the people who tried to grab me at the store are in any way related to this church," Jane said.

"That's true," Lucas said, his frustration obvious in his voice. "But you react strongly to that seeing eye and there's got to be a reason for it."

"Maybe I was as scared as a baby by a big hairy eyeball," she offered with a touch of humor.

Lucas laughed and shook his head. "I'm glad somebody still has a sense of humor about all this."

"You didn't notice anything else about the van?" Micah asked.

Lucas shook his head with a grim expression. "It was just a plain white panel van. Everything happened so fast." His frown deepened, as if irritated with himself for not doing more, for not seeing more.

At that moment the front door whooshed open and the third partner of the business walked in. Lucas introduced her to Troy Sinclair and for the next few minutes the three men talked about Recovery Inc. business.

As they talked she found herself watching them with interest. Loretta had told her that the three men had been best buddies when they'd all been Navy SEALs and that their close relationship had continued into civilian life.

Their friendship showed in the easy way they spoke to each other, in the way they could almost finish each other's thoughts. There was respect there, as well as the warmth of men who cared about each other.

Did she have a friend someplace? A girlfriend who she'd met for lunch or gone shopping with? A woman who had known her secrets and who had shared her laughter and her tears?

Where was that friend now? Was she worried about Jane? It was going on forty-eight hours that

Jane had been missing from her life. Didn't anyone care? A wave of despair rushed through her.

It was only when she heard her name that she focused on the three men once again. "I checked with Wendall. There have been no missing persons reports in the last twenty-four hours that match Jane," Lucas told his partners. "I plan on checking in with him again tomorrow morning."

"He didn't ask why you wanted to know?" Micah asked with a lift of one dark eyebrow.

"He asked. I didn't tell him," Lucas replied. "Jane has a feeling that in going to any authorities she could be putting herself in more danger than she's already in."

All three men turned to look at her and she felt the heat of a blush in her cheeks. "I can't explain it," she said. "I know it sounds irrational, but the idea of going to the police terrifies me."

"With what happened yesterday at the store, I'm willing to give it some time before going to the police, but I've told Jane if she doesn't recover her memories soon, eventually we might not have any other choice than to go to the authorities," Lucas said.

Even though Jane knew he was right, a shiver of dread worked through her at the thought. Why was she afraid of the police? Was she some kind of criminal? She couldn't imagine that being the case.

As she'd told Lucas when they'd first met, she might not know who she was, but she knew *what* she was. She'd bet her life she'd never been in trouble with the law in her life.

It was almost noon when they finally left the Recovery Inc. offices. The November air had chilled while they'd been inside and there was a faint scent of impending snow.

Thanksgiving was two weeks away. Would she be home by then? Would she be having turkey and stuffing surrounded by friends and loved ones, or would she still be struggling to figure out who she was and where she belonged?

Minutes later she and Lucas were back in his car and headed to Loretta's. "I'll drop you off at the apartment. Then I'll be back around dinnertime," Lucas said.

She didn't ask where he might be going or what he was going to do. She knew there was nothing more they could do to get her memory back. At the moment it seemed as if all she needed was some time. But how much time would it take before Lucas was sick of her and her problems?

It was a silent drive back to Loretta's. "You've gotten quiet," Lucas said as he turned the key in Loretta's door.

"I was just thinking about Thanksgiving and wondering if I'd be home by then." She leaned against the wall in the hallway. "Do you and Loretta have a big feast that day?"

"Actually, we do. It's the one holiday that Loretta never works. She does the turkey and stuffing and makes sweet potatoes and pies and we invite some friends over."

He took a step closer to her and raised a hand and touched her cheek. "I'll do everything in my power to make sure that you're home for Thanksgiving," he said softly.

His warm fingers lingered on her cheek and Jane's breath caught in her chest. There was a look in his eyes that made her think he was going to kiss her and she was stunned by how much she wanted him to.

She raised a hand to capture his, not wanting him to draw away from her, but rather wanting him to fall into her, to wrap her in his arms and pull her as close as he possibly could.

She closed her eyes as he came closer, his mouth mere inches from hers. She leaned forward, wanting...needing the contact with him. And then his mouth touched hers.

Hot and tender, his soft lips plied hers in a kiss that didn't just warm her mouth, but sizzled a wave of warmth through her entire body.

It wasn't until he pulled her closer and her tummy bumped into him that he jerked back from her. "Sorry. That was inexcusable." He drew a deep breath as if to steady himself.

She took hold of his arm. "I can excuse it," she said. "In fact, if you wanted to do it again, I wouldn't have any problems excusing you." She couldn't believe her forwardness, but it wasn't just gratitude she felt for him, it was a white-hot attraction that had her half-giddy.

She was afraid she might have offended him, but he gave her a sexy half grin that only increased his appeal. "That was very nice, but we can't lose sight of the fact that there's probably a man in your life." His gaze shot pointedly down to her stomach.

"I don't think so," she said. "I can't explain it, Lucas, but I think I was alone before all this began."

He sighed and tucked a strand of her hair behind her ear, then opened the door to Loretta's apartment. "Get some rest," he said. "I'll see you later this evening."

He turned and nearly ran down the hall away from her. How foolish was she? A pregnant woman with no memory making passes at a hot guy who'd already said he had no interest in getting married or becoming a father.

How foolish was she to think that he'd even want to kiss her again. With a new depression settling over her shoulders she turned and went into the apartment.

Chapter Six

The kiss had been a major mistake. The taste of her sweet, lush lips haunted Lucas for the remainder of the day.

He'd left Loretta's apartment, gone straight back to his car and headed out to the Church of Enlightenment compound. He had no idea if it had been somebody from the church who had tried to grab Jane at the store, but the fact that the church used the seeing-eye symbol as a kind of trademark was the only lead they had.

The Church of Enlightenment was located at the very northern edges of Kansas City, about ten miles from the neighborhood where Lucas had found Jane in the car.

It seemed unlikely that Jane would have been able to walk ten miles in her condition that night, but he wasn't willing to rule out the possibility altogether. There were stories in the news all the time about people accomplishing all kinds of impossible feats when in danger.

The church itself was a huge building with amazing stained-glass windows and a sign across the door that welcomed all who came for spiritual nourishment.

He didn't bother going inside; in fact, didn't even leave his car. What interested him more than the church itself were the buildings in a gated area behind it.

There was a massive three-story home, several other low, flat buildings, a construction site with a foundation poured and fields as far as the eye could see. All of it was surrounded by tall, sturdy fencing designed to keep people out.

There was no question that religion could be big business, but this particular church didn't seem to be affiliated with any others or have an organized base. He made a mental note to ask Micah to see if he could find a list of the board of directors or whatever governed the money obviously flowing into this church.

He pulled up to the gate, but there was no guard on duty and the heavy iron fencing was locked.

Surely this couldn't have anything to do with Jane, he thought. Even if he were able to get a list of names of all the people in the congregation, there was no way he could pinpoint who had been responsible for the attack at the store.

It just didn't make sense. Maybe the sign he'd seen in the back of that van had nothing to do with this church. He just couldn't make the pieces fit.

He left the church and went back to the Recovery

Inc. office where Troy was inside working on the financial records for the company.

The two men talked about Jane and both agreed that time was what she needed most of all. Eventually something would trigger her memories, and in the meantime there wasn't much any of them could do.

While Lucas would love to know who had tried to grab her and why, the odds of figuring it out were not in his favor.

It was nearly four when Lucas left the office. But instead of heading home, he drove to the Sandbox, a bar and grill he frequented on a regular basis.

It was dark and smoky and the perfect place for a man to sit and drink a beer without being bothered by anyone. Even though Lucas had been coming here for years, he knew nothing about the bartender except that his name was Joe and he poured a perfect Scotch and soda.

Joe nodded to him as he took a stool at the bar and in the blink of an eye Lucas had his drink in front of him. He curled his fingers around the cold glass as he thought once again of kissing Jane.

He didn't know her real name, but he liked her sense of humor. He liked the fact that despite everything that had happened to her she hadn't melted down into a hysterical mess.

She represented everything he didn't want in his life, a woman who would want a husband, a woman beginning a family. Kissing her had been a major mistake. Even if she were single and as alone as she thought she might be, he had absolutely nothing to offer her.

Her mouth had been tempting before he'd tasted it, but with that single taste, his desire had winged out of control. He'd wanted to back her up against the wall and explore her mouth further. He'd wanted to cup her full breasts in his hands and feel their warmth, then take her hips and press them against his.

He clenched the cold drink glass tighter. She was vulnerable at the moment, and he'd be all kinds of a bastard to take advantage of that vulnerability.

Still, the thought of kissing her again filled him with an anticipation he hadn't felt for a very long time, and that bothered him. She bothered him in a way no woman ever had.

He finished his drink, then nursed a second one until just after seven, reluctant to share the evening meal with Loretta and Jane. Instead he filled up on nuts and pretzels, and wound up making small talk with a salesman from New Jersey who was in town for a convention.

Darkness had fallen when he finally left the Sandbox and headed back to his apartment. After sitting in the smoky confines of the bar, he wanted to shower before checking in with Jane and Loretta.

The minute he opened his apartment door he sensed something amiss. He froze in the doorway and looked around the living room, every muscle in his body on alert.

Lucas was an orderly man. Troy and Micah often teased him about having more than his share of obsessive-compulsive disorder when it came to his living space.

He pulled his gun as he saw that the magazines in the middle of the coffee table had been moved a fraction of an inch to the right and the papers at his desk weren't quite in the same position they'd been in before he'd left.

Even the picture of him and Loretta wasn't in the exact same place that it had been before he'd left that morning. Close, but no cigar.

Somebody had been in here. He gripped the gun more tightly and moved stealthily across the living-room floor. A glance into the kitchen showed nobody there. Then he headed down the hallway toward his bedroom.

His closet door was open just an inch. He knew he'd closed it completely after he'd gotten his clothes out that morning. He had an obsession about open doors and cabinets, and always made sure they were closed after he used them.

Somebody had been in here and it was obvious they hadn't wanted him to know about their presence. They'd been good. Somebody less observant would never have known anyone had been inside the place. But he knew, and the thought sent a cold chill through him.

It took him only minutes to know that there was nobody inside the place now. But somebody had been there. The words went around and around in his head.

He stood in the center of the living room, his thoughts racing to make sense of it. Why would anyone want to snoop around his apartment? Nothing appeared to be missing so it hadn't been a burglary.

Jane.

Her name thundered in his head. Had this been about Jane? Perhaps it was somebody looking for her or evidence of where she might be?

He hadn't gotten a license plate number from the van the day before at the store, but had somebody gotten his? And had that somebody used that information to find out who he was and where he lived in hopes that Jane would be here?

Time to move, he thought. He stared at the photo of himself and his sister. It wouldn't take a lot of digging for them to learn about Loretta.

A question here or there to one of the people in the apartment complex and they would know that Lucas and Loretta were siblings. It wouldn't take a rocket scientist to suspect that Lucas might have stashed Jane with his sister.

What was going on? Who was Jane and why did these people want her? What in the hell was going on?

He returned to the bedroom, where he packed a duffel bag, then left the apartment. A glance around the hallway showed nobody around and he hurried to Loretta's and let himself in using his key.

He dropped his duffel just inside the front door

and headed for the kitchen where he could hear the sound of Jane and Loretta's laughter.

The two women were seated at the table. The dinner dishes had been cleaned up, but they each had a piece of cake in front of them. Jane had a glass of milk and Loretta had coffee. Both of them looked relaxed and happy.

"Lucas!" Jane said as he walked into the room. Her eyes shone with a bright warmth that stirred something inside him. "I was wondering if you were going to show up this evening."

"Have you eaten?" Loretta asked.

He nodded. "Loretta, were you in my place today?"

"No, why?" She looked at him curiously.

"Jane, you need to pack a bag. I've got to move you out of here."

The warmth in her eyes fled and was replaced with fear. "Why? What do you mean?"

"What's happened?" Loretta asked as she stood from the table.

"Somebody was in my apartment today. I think they were snooping around to find Jane." Jane's eyes widened at his words.

"But surely nobody knows she's here," Loretta said.

"Maybe not yet, but eventually they'll figure it out. They probably saw the picture I have of the two of us together. If they figure out who you are, eventually they'll check to see if she's here."

Jane got up from the table. "I'll go get my things." Her voice was slightly shaky.

"Wait, Jane." Loretta placed an arm around Jane's shoulders. "I'll get you an overnight bag." Together the two women left the kitchen.

Lucas returned to the living room to wait for Jane, his mind still filled with possibilities and suppositions.

Right now the only thing he could do was act defensively, try to minimize risk without knowing exactly from what direction the danger might come.

He picked up his own bag as Jane and Loretta returned to the living room. Jane had on her coat and clutched a small black bag. "Where are you taking me?" she asked. There was a wealth of dread in her voice.

"A safe place," he replied.

"The safe house?" Loretta asked and he nodded.

Jane looked at him curiously. "I'll explain on the way," he told her, then looked at his sister. "I'll call you."

"Am I in danger?" Loretta asked.

Lucas frowned. "I don't think so. It's apparent whoever was in my apartment wasn't looking for a confrontation of any kind. They got in and out while I was away."

Jane grabbed Loretta's hand. "I hope I haven't brought danger to your doorstep. I'm so sorry about all of this."

"Don't worry," Loretta assured her. "Hasn't Lucas told you I'm tough?"

"Just make sure there's no sign that she was ever here in the apartment," Lucas said as he opened the door and peered down the hallway. Seeing nobody around, he motioned Jane out the door.

Neither of them said a word as they headed for the door that would lead outside into the cold, dark, early-November night.

When they reached the door, Lucas told her to wait, then stepped out and looked around. Unfortunately the darkness made it difficult for him to see if anyone was hiding in the shadows, cloaked by the night.

He drew his gun, unwilling to be surprised without the protection of his weapon. He stepped back inside the door and grabbed Jane's arm. "Stay right next to me. We're going directly to my car."

He felt the tremble of her body as he pulled her close against his side. He felt bad that she was scared, but better scared and on guard than oblivious and vulnerable.

He didn't breathe again until they were both safely in his car. As he started the engine once again he scanned the area, looking for any threat that might come out of the darkness.

Nothing. He saw nobody lurking about, nobody sitting in a nearby vehicle. But that didn't mean they weren't there.

Pulling out of the parking lot, he kept his gaze focused on the rearview mirror, looking for any other car that might follow.

Even though he saw none, he didn't feel safe, wouldn't feel safe until they reached the house and he was certain that nobody had followed them there.

A tense silence filled the car as he drove, constantly watching the rear- and side-view mirrors. He was grateful for her silence as he needed all his concentration on the road.

He drove down neighborhood streets, turning first left, then right at random in an effort to identify whether they had a tail or not.

For thirty minutes he drove first one direction, then another and finally felt comfortable that nobody was following them. His tense muscles began to relax and the adrenaline that had pumped through him from the moment he'd walked in his front door ebbed slightly.

"The safe house is a ranch house out in the country," he finally said, breaking the silence that had filled the car. "It's owned by a dummy corporation that can't be traced back to Recovery Inc. The only people who know where it is are my partners and their girlfriends, Loretta and Wendall Kincaid, the chief of police. You'll be safe there until we can figure all this out."

"The only way we're going to get anywhere is if I get my memories back, and that doesn't seem to be happening," she said, her frustration obvious. "I'm sorry, Lucas. I'm so sorry about all of this."

"There's no need for you to apologize," he assured her. "This won't be the first time Recovery Inc. has helped somebody in trouble."

He frowned and tightened his hands around the steering wheel. Twice in recent months the safe house had been used, first by Micah, who had hidden out there with Caylee while they fought false murder charges brought against them both. Then the ranch house had been used by Troy to keep his girlfriend, Brianna, safe when a stalker had been after her.

Both men had found love while in the safe house, but there was no way Lucas would fall victim to the same thing. He glanced over at Jane, who had her fingers splayed across her belly, as if to protect the life within.

She belonged somewhere, to somebody. And even if she didn't, he told himself he wasn't interested in any kind of a relationship with her and the baby she carried.

It didn't matter that he'd liked kissing her, that he definitely wouldn't mind kissing her again…and more. Even though he didn't know her real name, he had a feeling that Jane was a forever kind of woman, that she'd want the picket fence and a husband by her side. She'd want family barbecues and a brother or sister for the baby she carried.

She definitely didn't strike him as the type who would be ready for an affair with no strings attached and no promises of forever. He reached up and rubbed the back of his neck, where he could feel the ridge of an old scar.

An ancient wave of anger welled up inside him as he dropped his hand back to the steering wheel. A vision of his father entered his mind.

Lucas couldn't remember a time when Roger Washington's face wasn't twisted and red with rage.

He couldn't remember a kind touch, a loving glance. All of Lucas's memories of his father were filled with pain, both physical and mental.

That was his legacy. And that was what Lucas would never take a chance of passing on. He couldn't be a bad husband if he never married. And he couldn't be a brutal father if he never had children.

The safe house had brought love to his two partners, but there was no way in hell Lucas would allow himself to fall victim to the same emotion.

JANE STARED OUT THE WINDOW at the dark landscape. They'd left the city behind and were traveling on roads with no streetlights. The houses were discernible only by the faint spill of light from windows, and they were getting farther and farther apart.

Two days ago, if Lucas had driven her out here in the middle of nowhere she would have been terrified. But in the two days she'd spent with him she'd come to trust him implicitly.

The idea that she'd brought danger to the young woman who had opened her home and her heart to her broke Jane's heart. She'd die if anything happened to Loretta because of her.

Who were these people? And why, oh, why couldn't she remember anything? She desperately needed her memory. She needed her identity to make sense of everything that had happened.

She sat up straighter in her seat as he turned down a narrow gravel road. Eventually they came to a clearing where she could see the dark outline of a house with tall trees on either side.

Where would this all end? she thought with despair. What if the people who had tried to grab her at the store somehow found her here? Then where would she go?

"Stop worrying," he said as if he could read her thoughts.

She cast him a nervous smile. "I can't help it."

He pulled up in front of the house, killed the engine and turned to look at her, his eyes dark and glittering in the faint illumination from the dashboard. "You'll be safe here. And who knows, maybe in the next couple of days your memories will come back."

"I hope so," she said fervently. She changed positions in the seat, her back aching with a dull throb. "That night when you found me in the car and I realized I had some sort of amnesia, I was sure that once I got a good night's sleep I'd wake up and everything would be all right. But I've had two good nights of sleep now and still nothing."

"It's only been a couple of days," he said. He pulled the keys from the ignition and turned off the lights. "Come on, let's get settled inside."

As they got out of the car, the unusually cold wind seemed to blow right through her, chilling her to the bones. But she knew it wasn't the wind that made her cold; rather it was fear of the unknown.

She felt somewhat better when they were in the house and Lucas had turned on the lights. The living room was pleasant, although decorated as impersonally as a motel room.

"The kitchen is in here," he said. "I'll head out first thing in the morning and get some groceries." The kitchen was large and airy and decorated with bright yellow accents.

From the kitchen he led her down a hallway. "You can stay in here," he said as he stopped at the first doorway. "The bathroom is across the hall. I'll stay in the bedroom in the back." He set her overnight bag on the double bed. "Don't look so scared. You're going to be just fine."

The warmth of his deep voice helped ease some of the tension that had tightened her muscles since the moment he'd walked into Loretta's kitchen and told her to pack a bag. She shrugged off her coat and tossed it on the chair just inside the bedroom door.

"I just wish I knew what was going on," she said softly. She sat on the edge of the bed and rubbed her lower back with one hand.

"One thing you don't have to worry about is support from me," he said. "If I wasn't in until the end before, I am now." His eyes narrowed. "They made a big mistake when they came into my apartment and invaded my privacy." He frowned. "Are you all right?"

She nodded. "Just a little backache. It's no big deal."

"It's not labor pains, is it?"

She nearly laughed out loud at the horrified look on his face. The tough ex–navy SEAL with a gun on his shoulder looked scared to death at the idea of a baby's birth.

"No, it isn't labor," she assured him. "Just a backache. It will probably be gone by morning."

"Then I'll just say good-night," he said. "If you need anything I'm just down the hall." He disappeared from the doorway.

She wanted to call him back. She wanted him to stay with her throughout the long, lonely night, hold her in his arms to keep away any nightmares that might try to rear their ugly heads.

Instead she got up from the bed and closed the door, then pulled her nightgown from the bag. It was after nine and she was tired. She took her nightgown and toothbrush into the bathroom across the hall and changed, then brushed her teeth and stared at her reflection in the mirror. "Who are you?" she asked the woman who stared back at her.

With a tired sigh she turned away from the mirror. Even though she was exhausted, she feared the night to come.

Even more fearful was the idea that she'd sleep soundly and wake up the next morning with nothing changed, no memories returning.

Lucas had told her he was in until the end, but she knew if too much time went by he would start encouraging her to go to the police. And although she didn't understand it, that idea horrified her.

Did she have a husband who was a cop? An abusive man she'd run to escape? Or was she wanted by the law and running from a prison sentence? There were so many questions without an answer in sight.

As she left the bathroom she heard the faint sound of Lucas's voice coming from the back bedroom and assumed he was on the phone with somebody. Perhaps telling his partners of this latest development, she thought.

She turned off the light and got into the unfamiliar bed. Lying on her back, she watched the shadows of tree limbs dancing in the moonlight on the ceiling and tried to empty her mind of the million questions that played there.

She must have fallen asleep because the next time she opened her eyes, the sun was shining through the window and the scent of frying bacon and fresh coffee hung in the air.

She kept her eyes closed, for a moment fantasizing that it was her husband in the kitchen preparing a morning meal for his beloved pregnant wife. And after breakfast, he'd rub her aching back with loving hands as he whispered how much he loved her.

Squeezing her eyes more tightly closed, she tried to summon an image of the man, but all that came to her mind was a vision of Lucas.

Her mouth burned as she remembered the taste of his lips, the fire they had ignited in her, a flame of desire. She'd only known him for a couple of days and yet she was more than a little bit crazy about him.

Was it possible she didn't want to go to the authorities because she knew that would be the end of their time together?

It was a shameful thought and it pulled her out of bed and across the hall for a shower—a cold shower to cool thoughts of Lucas and his sinfully soft lips.

Once she was dressed, she felt better prepared to face whatever the day might bring and the man who was precariously close to owning her heart.

"Ah, I thought I heard you up and about." Lucas greeted her as she walked into the kitchen. She stopped short and for a moment forgot how to breathe.

He stood at the stove, clad only in a pair of jogging pants that rode low on his lean hips. His black hair was boyishly tousled, but there was nothing boyish about his broad muscled chest or the stubble of dark whiskers across his jaw. He looked hot and she felt his heat warming every part of her body.

"You hungry?" he asked.

"You have no idea," she muttered more to herself than to him.

"I have to admit I'm not the best of cooks, but I figured I could rustle up some bacon and eggs. Sit and I'll get you a glass of juice," he instructed.

She slid into a chair at the table and tried to look at anything but him. "You must have gotten up and out early."

"There's a twenty-four-hour grocery store not far from here. I got up at dawn and got enough supplies in for a couple of days. How do you like your eggs? I'd recommend scrambled."

She smiled. "Scrambled is fine."

He turned toward the refrigerator and she saw the scars on his back. They were faint, but discernible, and crisscrossed the expanse of his back. "Lucas, what happened to you?" He whirled around to face her. "Your back. What happened to your back?" she asked.

A myriad of emotions played across his features before they finally settled on calm acceptance. He turned back to grab a carton of eggs from the fridge. "My father happened to me," he replied after a long hesitation.

She stared at him for a long moment as his words sank in. "He beat you?" Her heart ached for him as she realized that must have been what he'd meant when he'd told her it had always been him and Loretta against the world.

"Just about every day of my life until I turned eighteen and joined the navy." He cracked several eggs into a bowl and offered her a tight smile. "He was a miserable bastard who for whatever reason decided early in my life that I was the source of his misery."

"Did he drink? Was he drunk when he beat you?" She couldn't imagine a parent doing that to a child unless he was out of his mind on drugs or alcohol. And even then it was unimaginable.

"No. He was always stone-cold sober whenever he beat me."

"What about Loretta? Did he beat her, too?"

"Never touched her." He poured the egg mixture into an awaiting skillet. "Maybe he instinctively knew that if he did, I'd kill him." He said the words matter-of-factly and Jane wondered what kind of scars had been left behind that couldn't be seen with the naked eye.

"Loretta was only about five years old the first time she crept into my room after I'd gotten a beating." He pushed the button on the toaster. "She had a wet washcloth and placed it over my forehead, then held my hand until I finally went to sleep." He smiled again, this smile with more warmth. "Even then she was taking care of the sick and wounded. After each and every beating I got, it was Loretta who came into my room to bring me water or rub salve on my back."

"What about your mother? Where was she when all this was happening?" Jane asked.

"She was sitting in her chair, or making dinner or watching television. She was emotionally disengaged. She neither encouraged him nor stopped him."

"Did your father beat her?" she asked.

"Not that I remember. She didn't seem particularly afraid of him. She just didn't seem to love Loretta and me enough to fight for us. For a long time after I was grown I wasn't sure who I hated more, him or her." He picked up a spoon and stirred the eggs and smiled at her once again. "Don't look so stricken, Jane. I survived and I'm probably stronger for it."

The toast popped up, and as he buttered it, Jane's heart opened wider to him. There were other ways to gain strength than to survive a horrendous childhood, she thought.

"I can't imagine being hit by my parents," she finally said. "My mother always said she could tell when I was fibbing because I'd tug on the end of my hair, but I was always punished with a time-out or grounding, never hit."

She looked at him in surprise. "I remembered that." She frowned and concentrated on the faint memory that stirred inside her head. "My mother's name was Bernice, but everyone called her Bernie."

"And what was her last name?" He stared at her intently.

She reached for it, trying desperately to put a last name to the woman's face that filled her mind, but it was no good. The vision fell away and no matter how hard she tried she couldn't summon it again. She shook her head. "No, it's gone." She sighed in frustration.

"It's okay," he assured her as he ladled the food on plates. "It's a good sign that you had even a single memory. Maybe that means they'll all start coming back." He placed her plate in front of her. "And it's good information to know, about the hair-tugging," he teased.

She laughed and picked up her fork. "I can't imagine ever lying to you. You're the only one I trust completely right now."

"I'm the only one you know right now," he returned as he joined her at the table.

"True, but I have a feeling if there were a dozen people in my life, you'd still be the one I trusted most. In fact, I'm thinking when my little boy is born, I'll name him Luke, after you."

Any teasing light that had warmed his eyes vanished. "Don't, Jane."

"Don't what?" she asked.

"Don't make me into some kind of a hero." His eyes grew hard and a knot pulsed in his jaw. "I'm just the man who is stuck with you until we can figure out where you really belong."

She stared at him for a long moment. She might have lost all her memories, but she still remembered what it felt like to be hurt.

Chapter Seven

"I'm heading in to the office to meet with Troy and Micah," Lucas said three days later as Jane sat at the kitchen table, drinking a glass of orange juice. "I should be back by dinnertime."

He needed to check in with his partners and stop by his sister's place, but more than anything he needed to escape from Jane and the tension that had built to intolerable proportions in the last three days of isolation.

She nodded. "I'll have something ready for dinner."

It had quickly become habit that she cooked dinner and they both did the cleanup afterward. The domestic nature of their time in the house was definitely starting to get under his skin.

"Thanks," he replied. "Lock up behind me. I'll see you later." He grabbed his coat and pulled it on, then walked out the front door and into the unusually cold, gray day.

There was a taste of snow in the air. The weathermen on the news the night before had talked about the possibility of an early snowstorm. Just what he needed—to be snowed in with the woman who was slowly driving him out of his mind.

He started the car and as he waited for the engine to warm up, he stared at the house and thought of the woman inside.

She'd been unusually quiet, and he knew she'd been hurt by his words at breakfast that first morning. But he'd needed to ground her in reality. She'd looked at him as if he were the man he wished to be instead of the man he feared he was, and that had scared him.

They'd spent the three days playing cards and Monopoly to pass the time. She was good at poker, but lacked the killer instinct to win at the board game. She'd teased him about closing cabinet doors and meticulously arranging things in an orderly fashion, and he hadn't taken offense. In truth, he found the teasing charming.

They were no closer to finding out who might be after her, but more memories had resurfaced. She'd remembered a high school dance and a trip to the Kansas City Zoo. She'd also remembered her father's funeral and then burying her mother two years later. They were bits and pieces of a life returning in brief glimpses that had yet to reveal the information they most needed—her name.

Still, he knew now that it was probably just a

matter of days before her memory completely returned and then she'd be out of his life for good.

What he didn't understand was why the idea of never seeing her again bothered him more than a little bit. Each evening as they'd sat in the living room watching television, his attention had been focused on her.

He loved the way she lifted her hair off her neck when she got too warm, how she unconsciously rubbed her tummy as if caressing the baby inside her.

The sound of her laughter filled him with a particular kind of joy he'd never felt before, and the worry that flirted darkly in her amazing eyes made him want to move heaven and earth to take it away.

He put the car into gear and pulled away from the house. Definitely time for some distance. How on earth had she managed to get so deep inside him in such a short space of time?

Unlike his sister, he'd never had a particularly soft spot for strays or the vulnerable, and yet something about Jane touched him in a way nobody ever had.

He tightened his hands around the steering wheel. He needed to get a grip. He glanced over to the small brown bag on the passenger seat. Inside was a drinking glass that Jane had used the night before.

He'd sneaked the glass into the bag and brought it out to the car last night after she'd gone to bed. He had a friend at the crime lab who could print it and run her through the AFIS. If she had a criminal record or had ever been fingerprinted for anything, the Automated Fingerprint Identification System would find her. He'd considered doing this before, but had dismissed the idea, hoping the situation would resolve itself.

He hadn't told her what he was going to do, knew that it would only add additional stress to an already-stressful situation. There was no question that he was intrigued by her adamant refusal to go to the police. At least by checking her fingerprints, within the next twenty-four to forty-eight hours he'd know if she had a record. And if she did, then they'd know her name.

Before dropping the glass off with his buddy, before checking in with his partners, he wanted to see Loretta. By the time he pulled into the apartment complex, the gray sky had begun to spit snow.

Today was Loretta's day off, and despite the fact that it was nearly ten o'clock when he knocked on her door, she greeted him still clad in her pajamas and with a coffee mug in hand.

She ushered him into the kitchen, where he poured himself a cup and sat at the table across from her.

"I heard the weatherman mention snow today and decided it was a good day to stay in my pajamas," she said. "How's it going? How is Jane?"

"Okay. She's started getting some memories back, although nothing about who she is or what happened to her. She's remembered fairly inconsequential things."

"But that's a good sign," Loretta exclaimed.

"That's what I told her. That's what I keep telling myself, that it's just a matter of time before she remembers everything."

"I kind of miss having her around." Loretta took a sip of her coffee and then continued. "She was good company. She has a great sense of humor. I like her."

"Yeah, well, it won't be long before she's back where she belongs."

"Maybe she shouldn't go back where she belongs," Loretta said. "I mean, she ran away for a reason."

Lucas frowned with a touch of irritation. He didn't want to think about that. He had to hang on to the idea that someplace out there Jane had a safe place to go and people who cared about her. "I'm just ready for this all to be over. I need to get back to my life."

Loretta crooked one of her dark eyebrows upward and smiled ruefully. "What life?"

"Ha, ha, very funny," Lucas replied drily.

"I'm not trying to be funny. You have my life and you have your partners' lives, but you don't have much of one of your own."

"It's a little early in the morning for a Dr. Phil moment," he replied. "Have you seen anyone suspicious lurking around the apartment building over the past couple of days?"

"No, and I wasn't finished talking about you,"

she replied. "Seriously, Lucas, at least it was nice to see you interacting with Jane. You like her. I know you do. I could tell by the way you looked at her. I know she probably has a life to get back to, but it's all made me think about how much I wish you'd find some nice woman to be a part of your life."

"I don't need anyone in my life," he replied. "Besides, you're one to talk. When was the last time you had a date?"

"Actually, I have one this Friday night." She smiled smugly.

Lucas leaned back in his chair and narrowed his eyes. "With who?"

"He's a really nice guy who works as a lab tech at the hospital. We've been spending our breaks together for the last month or so, and he finally asked me out."

"What's his name?" Lucas asked.

She shook her head. "Oh no, you don't. You are not going to check him out through whatever nefarious means you might have. I'll tell you his name on the day of the wedding."

Lucas stared at her in stunned surprise. "It's that serious?"

She laughed. "Not yet. But I am serious about you staying out of it." She leaned forward and covered one of his hands with her own. "I love you, Lucas, but you have to give me a little breathing room to find my own way when it comes to romance."

He knew she was right. "Just be careful. Make

sure you go someplace where there are other people." He bit his tongue before a full-blown lecture could escape. "And have a good time."

She smiled gratefully. "Thank you. I plan on it."

"I've got to get out of here," he said with a check of his watch. "I've got some errands to run before I get back to Jane." He stood, drained his coffee cup and carried it to the sink. "Call me Friday night when you get home, okay?"

"It might be late." She got up from the table to walk him to the door.

"That's all right. I'll sleep better knowing you're home safe and sound."

She walked with him to the front door. "You'll let me know what happens with Jane?"

"As soon as I know anything," he replied.

"Good. I'd like to keep in contact with her. She's a terrific woman, memory or no memory."

Minutes later as Lucas drove to the lab, he felt a new depression settle across his shoulders. His partners were both building new lives with women that they loved, and it was obvious Loretta was excited about her date on Friday night. Things were changing. Everyone seemed to be moving on with their lives while Lucas was being left behind.

He shoved the ridiculous thought from his mind as he pulled into the parking lot of a small café across from the Kansas City Crime Lab.

The lab itself was housed in a low, long brick building, but he'd arranged to meet his friend at the

Cornerstone Café, which was usually filled with people from the lab grabbing a bite to eat.

He spied Justin James seated at a booth in the back the minute he walked through the door. Loretta described Justin as the hottest science nerd on the face of the planet. Lucas didn't know about hot, but he knew the man ate, slept and breathed forensic science.

Justin raised a hand as he saw Lucas approach. With his other hand he picked up a cinnamon roll the size of New Jersey and took a bite.

"Sugar and science," Lucas said as he slid into the booth opposite the blond-haired man. "It's nice to see some things never change."

Justin shrugged. "As far as I'm concerned, change is vastly overrated. Now, to what do I owe the honor of this meeting?"

Lucas set the paper bag on the table. "This is a drinking glass. You should be able to lift a decent set of prints from it. I'd like you to run it through the AFIS and see if anything pops up."

"And what's in it for me?" Justin raised one of his blond eyebrows.

"Two dozen glazed from the bakery of your choice," Lucas replied.

"Done. It will take about twenty-four hours. I'll call you with any results."

"I appreciate it," Lucas said.

"Gonna tell me what this is all about?"

"Nope." Lucas signaled the waitress for a cup of

coffee. "And I'd prefer this to stay between you and me."

"I figured that without you saying," Justin said.

"How's work at the lab?"

"The one thing good about working in a crime lab is I never worry about job security. As long as there are bad people in the world, my job is relatively safe."

The two men visited briefly about work, sports and the weather; then Justin stood to get back to work and Lucas left, as well.

He checked in with Troy and Micah at the office, then decided to head back to the safe house and Jane. The snow was coming down in earnest and he turned on his wiper blades against the fat, wet flakes that obscured his vision and began to cover the street and grass.

He'd only gotten a block or so from the office building when he noticed a dark sedan two car lengths behind him. He turned down a residential street and watched his mirror. The sedan followed, and just behind it another black sports car.

Lucas turned again and watched as the sedan fell back and the sports car got behind him, tag-teaming him in an attempt to hide the fact that they were fol-lowing him.

A surge of adrenaline filled him as he increased his speed and fishtailed around another corner to make sure that his assessment of the situation was correct. The two cars followed.

He stomped on the brakes and stared into the

rearview mirror at the front license of the car that nearly rear-ended him. JMV-237.

"JMV-237. JMV-237." He repeated it several times until he was sure he had it memorized; then he stepped on the gas and tightened his grip on the wheel as he set about losing the tails.

They were good. But he was better.

He rocked through the streets like a NASCAR driver, taking turns too fast for the road conditions and breaking the speed limits in his effort to evade them.

It took thirty minutes to finally ditch them. Still he drove aimlessly for another thirty minutes, constantly checking his mirror to make sure he'd lost them for good.

When he was confident that he wasn't being followed any longer, he headed to the house and Jane as he wondered again who the hell she was and why people were after her.

HER BACK HAD BOTHERED HER throughout the day. Jane was seated on the sofa with a pillow from the bedroom behind her for support when Lucas came inside.

Instantly she could tell that something had happened. She straightened. "I didn't hear you pull up out front," she said.

"I didn't. I pulled around to the back and parked in the garage." He sat on the chair across from her, energy rolling off him in waves. "I've got Troy and Micah dropping off a rental car later this evening."

"What happened?"

As he told her about being followed from the Recovery Inc. office, a new frustration coupled with a familiar fear edged through her.

"Who are these people and what do they want with me?" she cried in desperation.

"I don't know, but I'm hoping we'll have the name of one of them before the night is over. I got a license number of one of the cars that was following me and I put in a call to Wendall Kincaid."

"The chief of police?" she asked. As always, the idea of the police knowing anything about her made a nervous flutter in her stomach.

"Don't worry. I told him the driver of the car rear-ended me and I need his name to file an accident report." Lucas raked a hand through his hair and leaned back in the chair.

He looked exhausted, and a wave of guilt swept through Jane. "Maybe we should go to the police," she said, and heard the slight tremor in her voice. "This is getting so complicated and I'm sure you're sick to death of me."

He smiled, but she could tell it was slightly forced. "I'm not sick of you. I am sick of not knowing what's going on. I could maybe understand some crazy nut being after you...a stalker boyfriend or husband...but this isn't just a single individual. It's a whole group of people."

"Maybe I really am a spy," she said. "That's one of the things Loretta and I came up with. Of course we also thought I might be an undercover rock star or a high-class madame."

A whisper of a smile curved his lips and she saw him starting to relax. "I guess it's better to be a high class-madame than a low-class one."

She leaned back against the pillow once again. "I have discovered one important fact about myself today."

"What's that?"

"I don't like soap operas. When you feel like you're living one, the last thing you want to do is watch one."

"Your back still hurting?" he asked as she adjusted her position against the pillow.

She nodded. "It's just a dull ache. I think carrying around this baby weight is pulling on my spine. But it's fine. I'm fine. I made a pot of stew for dinner, but it's still simmering and won't be ready for another hour or so."

"That's all right. I'm not hungry. If you don't mind, I'm going back to the bedroom to make some phone calls. I'm expecting a fax soon and the machine is back there." He got up from the chair and she watched him disappear down the hallway.

As always when he left, he seemed to take some of the energy from the room, from her. She rubbed her stomach as she thought of the new events that had taken place.

The license plate number he'd managed to get was the first real clue they'd had that might yield answers, and she was surprised to realize she was conflicted about it.

On the one hand she wanted her life back, whatever that life might be. She hated the idea that she was taking advantage of Lucas and keeping him from his own life, but on the other hand she didn't want to tell him goodbye.

Was she reluctant to let go of him because she had nothing else to hang on to? Perhaps if she were completely truthful with herself she'd accept that that was part of it. But what was more difficult to accept was the fact that she didn't want to leave him because she was falling in love with him.

It was crazy. It was positively insane. She was carrying somebody's baby. She didn't even know her own name, but she knew what was in her heart and if felt like love.

She didn't believe that Lucas felt as if he was stuck with her, as he'd said at breakfast the first morning in the house. She wasn't sure what he felt about her. But if that kiss they'd shared and the odd moments when she felt his gaze lingering on her were any indication, he definitely felt something toward her that wasn't just a reluctant responsibility.

Twice she got up from the sofa and went into the kitchen to stir the stew, then stood at the window and watched the snow. It had finally tapered off to flurries, leaving behind less than an inch on the ground.

She'd returned to the living room and was back on the sofa some time later when Lucas came back into the living room and handed her a sheet of paper with a driver's license copied on it.

"Recognize him?" he asked as he sat next to her on the sofa.

She took the sheet of paper from him and stared at it. Charles Blankenship. He was fifty-eight years old, weighed two hundred pounds and was five feet eleven.

He had a severe, square jaw and brown eyes, his salt-and-pepper hair was cut military short and he wasn't smiling for the camera.

She frowned thoughtfully. "He looks vaguely familiar, but I don't know from where." She handed him back the sheet of paper. "Who is he?"

"One of the cars that followed me was registered to him. I think first thing in the morning I'm going to pay Mr. Charlie Blankenship a visit."

"I want to come with you."

"I'm not sure that's a good idea," he replied with a frown.

"It's the only idea we've got," she protested. "His picture looks familiar. Maybe seeing him in person will finally jiggle my memory. Besides, I'm not worried about my safety as long as I'm with you. It's my life, Lucas. Please let me be a part of things."

He stared at her for a long moment, and in the depths of his dark brown eyes she saw the same emotion that she'd seen moments before he'd kissed her. It was a yearning that made her breath catch in her throat and dried her mouth with sweet anticipation.

He leaned forward, as if drawn to her by an invisible thread, and she parted her lips, wanting him to kiss her again, needing to feel his warm, soft mouth against hers.

Abruptly he stood. "You think that stew is ready now?" His voice was deeper than usual.

She released her breath and nodded. The moment was broken, but it gave her a crazy new hope, the hope that somehow when this was all finished they might be together.

They had just finished eating when Troy and Micah arrived with the rental car. Jane made a pot of coffee as the three men sat at the table and Lucas caught them up on his chase that afternoon.

He showed them the faxed copy of Charles Blankenship's driver's license, but neither of them had any idea who the man was or why he'd be following Lucas.

"It has to be Jane," Lucas said. "They're looking for her."

She turned around from the sink as she felt the weight of three pairs of eyes on her. "I wish I could explain it. I wish I knew what was going on."

"Our plan is to talk to Charles Blankenship in the morning and ask him why he was following me," Lucas said as Jane joined them at the table.

Micah looked at her. "And you still don't want to go to the cops?"

She hesitated before replying. No, she didn't want to go to the police, but she also knew if that's what Lucas wanted her to do, then that's what she would do.

"Not yet," Lucas replied for her. She smiled at him gratefully. At least he wasn't so sick of her that he was willing to throw her to the dogs. Not yet.

"For whatever reason, Jane feels as if she'd be putting herself at risk by going to the cops and we're hoping before that becomes our only option her memory will return."

Micah nodded and tapped the picture of Charles Blankenship with the tip of a finger. "Want me to see what I can dig up on this guy before morning?"

"That would be great," Lucas replied. "You're better than anyone I know at digging up facts about people."

Micah grinned at the compliment, then looked at Troy. "We'd better get out of here so I can get to work."

The four of them rose from the table and walked to the front door. "Micah, Troy, thank you for all your help," Jane said. "I'm sure Lucas knows how lucky he is to have friends like you that he can depend on."

A niggling depression weighed her down as she told the men goodbye and went back to sit on the sofa as Lucas walked out with them.

She'd been missing almost six days and still nobody seemed to be looking for her. Why wasn't somebody worried about her? Why didn't anyone care that she was missing?

Was she so unimportant in this life that she could disappear for days…for a week…forever and nobody cared?

Chapter Eight

The house was quiet. Jane had gone to bed an hour earlier and Lucas sat at the kitchen table, worrying about everything he'd learned during the course of the evening.

Justin had called to tell him that there had been no hit on Jane's fingerprints, so that had been a bust.

And Lucas had almost kissed her again.

He frowned and stared out the window. He'd wanted to kiss her again so badly it had ached in his chest and burned in his blood.

Thank God he hadn't followed through on the impulse. Nothing good could come from him kissing her again.

Still, even now the scent of her remained in his head, the citrus-clean fragrance of her shampoo coupled with a faint, floral, feminine scent that drove him half-mad.

He hadn't just wanted to kiss her, he'd wanted to touch her skin, rub her belly and feel the kick of her son against his palm. The son she said she was going to name after him.

If he looked deep within himself, he had to recognize that he'd been touched by her words, and yet horrified at the same time. He didn't want a kid named after him and he definitely didn't want a woman looking at him with such trust, with something that looked like love.

His cell phone vibrated in his shirt pocket and he pulled it out, grateful for the disruption of his thoughts.

"Ready for a little bit of information?" Micah asked.

"Whatever you've got." Lucas leaned back in his chair.

"Charles Blankenship is an insurance salesman. No criminal record, nothing to indicate he's anything but a good, upstanding citizen. He's married and has two grown children, one grandchild. No financial issues, the usual credit card debt and a car loan, but nothing out of the ordinary."

Lucas bit back a sigh of frustration. "I was hoping for something different, something that might explain his interest in Jane."

"The only thing I discovered that I think you'll find interesting is that he's on the board of directors of the Church of Enlightenment."

A bolt of adrenaline flashed through Lucas, sitting him up straighter in his chair. "What?"

"The board consists of eight men and two

women. Charles is one of them. I don't know what it means, Lucas, but I'm going to do a little more digging into this church."

"Yeah, thanks. I'd appreciate it," Lucas replied thoughtfully. "I don't get it, Micah. Why would a church want Jane?"

"I don't know, buddy. We can't be sure it has anything to do with the church. The worst thing you can do is jump to conclusions without solid evidence. Right now, the fact that this Charles was chasing you and that Jane has an aversion to his church's logo could be nothing more than coincidence."

"And you really believe that?" Lucas asked drily.

"Not for one minute," Micah replied. Lucas could hear the grin in his buddy's voice.

Long after the two men hung up, Lucas remained at the table, trying to fit together pieces of the puzzle of Jane.

Was it just a coincidence that the logo the church used inspired an irrational fear in Jane and that the man who had been tailing Lucas was a member of the board of that church?

Why would a church be after Jane? It was the question that kept niggling at his brain. None of it made sense. Maybe Charles would be forthcoming in the morning when Lucas had a little visit with him. Yeah, right, and maybe tomorrow it would be warm enough to swim.

He got up from the table and checked the back

door to make sure it was securely locked, then turned out the lights and walked through the dark living room.

He checked the front door and headed down the hallway, but he'd only taken a couple of steps when he heard the sound of crying coming from Jane's room.

Just walk on by, he told himself. She had plenty of reasons to be sad at the moment, but there was nothing he could do to solve her problems, nothing he could say to ease her fears.

Just walk on by.

Steeling himself, he passed her bedroom. The door was just barely cracked open and the soft sound of her weeping seemed to thunder in his head. It sounded so achingly pitiful.

He got as far as his bedroom door, then stopped. There was no way he could just go to bed with the sound of her crying in his head.

With a reluctant sigh he turned back around, knowing it was foolish, but unable to stop. He paused just outside her door and then knocked softly. "Jane? Are you all right?" He pushed the door open far enough that he could peek into the room, but the room was too dark for him to see her.

"No. I'm not all right."

He heard the rustle of the sheets; then the bedside lamp turned on and there she was, clad in a pale pink nightgown with her hair all tousled around her head and her eyes shiny with tears. She sat up and the sheet fell to her waist, exposing her delicate collarbones above the neckline and the thrust of her breasts against the thin material.

He remained in the doorway, afraid to breathe, afraid to move. She looked so achingly lovely despite her tears.

"What's wrong?" he asked, then grimaced. "Stupid question, right?"

She gave him a watery smile, but it held for only a moment before tears began to trek down her cheeks once again. "I'm being a baby," she said. "I've just been lying here wondering why nobody misses me, why I haven't been reported missing. People are after me and I don't know why and my back hurts so much and I don't have anyone to rub it for me. I'm going to have this baby all alone and I might never know who I am."

He tried to maintain a barrier around his heart. He didn't want to feel her pain, didn't want to get pulled into her despair, but it was impossible not to.

Before he realized what he was doing he found himself standing next to the bed where the sweet scent of her eddied in the air.

"I can't tell you why nobody has missed you, Jane. I can't tell you why you have people after you. But you won't have that baby alone. I'll make sure of that."

Someplace in the back of his mind he knew he was making a promise he didn't intend to keep, but at the moment all he wanted to do was stop her tears, bring that beautiful smile back to her face.

"And if you need somebody to rub your back, then all you need to do is ask," he heard himself saying.

Her lips trembled slightly as she looked up at him. "Would you? Just for a minute or two? I'd appreciate it so much." She scooted over and turned on her side, her back to him and her long, blond hair a spill of shiny strands against the pillow.

He tentatively sat on the side of the bed, his brain screaming that he was making a huge mistake, but his body didn't appear to be listening.

She pulled down the sheet, exposing the length of her, the long nightgown the only barrier between them. He could see the curve of her waist, the flare of her hips and her rounded buttocks as his heartbeat sounded in his ears.

He reached out and laid his palm against her lower back and she released a sigh of sheer pleasure. The warmth of her skin radiated outward through the thin material, and as he began to rub the area, he tried to stay focused on the fact that it was supposed to be a therapeutic massage and nothing more.

"Hmm, that feels so good," she said, her voice a soft whisper.

Lucas didn't reply. He couldn't. His breath was caught in his chest, making speech impossible as desire welled up inside him. He tried to tamp it down, but it refused to dissipate and instead seemed to grow bigger, stronger inside him.

As he rubbed her back with one hand he reached

with the other and touched a strand of her hair. It was luxuriously silky, just as he'd expected. He closed his eyes against a new wave of want.

It's just a back rub, he tried to tell himself. And yet it felt as intimate as anything he'd ever experienced. Her heat, her scent seemed to fill him up. Her tiny mewls of pleasure scorched through him.

His jeans grew tight at his groin as he felt himself responding to her. For God's sake, what was wrong with him? She was pregnant. She didn't even know her name. This whole thing was completely inappropriate. But nothing his brain told him seemed to be making a connection with his body.

He knew he should stop and run from the room, that he was being sucked into a desire greater than any he'd ever felt before. And yet he continued rubbing her back and caressing her hair, trying to tell himself that he was only doing what she needed, not what he wanted.

She moaned and stretched with pleasure. The sound shot a new surge of electricity through his veins. He had to stop, before things spiraled out of control.

Get out, a voice screamed in his head, but he didn't. He couldn't. He was caught…trapped by his own desire to continue.

Instead he worked his hands from her lower back up to the center of her back, then to her shoulders, using just enough pressure to ease but not hurt her tight muscles.

"I can't tell you how good this feels," she said, her voice slightly husky. She turned a bit so that she could look at him, and the curve of her jaw begged for an exploration by his mouth, her lips tormented him as they curved into a soft smile.

"You give a great massage," she said.

He dropped his arms to his sides and stood. "Better?"

The smile fell from her face and she eyed him with an intensity that halted his heart for another long beat. "Better," she replied. She sat up and grabbed his hand. "Don't go, Lucas. Lie here with me and talk for a little while. I don't feel like being alone right now." She patted the bed next to her.

Suddenly he couldn't think of any place he'd rather be than spending a wintry night in bed with her. *No big deal. We're just going to talk,* he told himself.

Still, as he stretched out on the mattress that was still warm with her body heat, he wondered what in the hell he was doing.

IT FELT RIGHT for Lucas to be next to her on the bed. Jane leaned up on one elbow and gazed at him, taking in each and every detail of his features. She loved the length of the lashes that framed his dark eyes and the quirky smile that eased some of the darkness that clung to him. Dark whiskers shadowed the lower half of his jaw and they only added to his rugged, slightly dangerous attractiveness.

"You're staring at me," he said, looking decidedly uncomfortable.

She reached out and placed her palm on his cheek. "I like looking at you," she replied. "You have a nice face, Lucas Washington, but you have the eyes of an old soul."

"Growing up with a father like mine, I guess I aged quickly," he replied. "And if I wasn't a man when I joined the navy, I quickly became one."

She dropped her hand from his face and frowned thoughtfully. "I can't imagine what you went through. Even though I don't have any real specific memories, I think I had a happy childhood."

"I'm glad. I'd like you to have happy memories from your childhood. I can tell you this—you don't have a criminal record of any kind."

She looked at him in surprise. "How do you know that?"

He looked slightly sheepish. "I took a glass you'd used to a buddy of mine who works in the crime lab. He got your fingerprints off the glass and ran it through the system. You weren't in there."

"Why didn't you tell me you did that?"

"I just told you." He smiled. "I didn't want to tell you before I knew the results."

"That's definitely a relief. But what would you have done if I was some sort of criminal?" she asked curiously.

"I guess I would have had to handcuff you and turn you over to my friend Wendall," he replied with a teasing light. "Of course, it's possible you're just a very smart, good criminal and have never been caught."

She moved closer to him, reveling in the scent of him, the warmth of his body radiating out to her. She didn't particularly want to talk. What she wanted was for him to wrap her in his arms. She wanted to feel his lips against hers once again. She wanted to caress his bare skin. She wanted things she shouldn't want, things she was afraid to want.

As she looked at him she forgot what they'd been talking about. All she could think about was how much she wanted a man like Lucas in her life. No, that wasn't true. She wanted Lucas himself in her life. Not just during this time of uncertainty but always.

Of course that was impossible. He'd let her know in every way that he didn't want any kind of lasting relationship. And why would he want a woman carrying another man's child? A woman who was in some kind of trouble?

Still, that didn't stop her from wanting him now. Tomorrow she might wake up with all her memories intact and she'd be on her way back to her former life. But she had tonight. Was it so wrong for her to want to be held, to want to feel loved? "Kiss me, Lucas," she said. "Wrap me up in your arms and kiss me."

His eyes widened and then narrowed. "That's probably not a good idea."

She might have thought he just didn't want to if it wasn't for the pulsing knot in his jaw, the burn in his eyes and the tension in his body.

He wanted her. She felt it radiating from him, saw it spark in the depth of his eyes. She'd heard it in his husky voice.

"I don't care." She reached out and placed her hand on his broad, firm chest. "I know the score, Lucas. I'll probably be out of your life within a matter of days, but that doesn't stop me from wanting to kiss you tonight, right now."

The words were barely out of her mouth as his lips touched hers. Feather-soft, they plied hers with heat. But a soft, gentle kiss wasn't what she wanted. She wanted more. She wanted hard and hot and breathless. She wanted overwhelming and mindless.

She leaned into him, opening her mouth to him, and he responded, swirling his tongue with hers as he pulled her into his arms.

Even with the bulk of her belly, she fit neatly in his arms, as if she belonged, as if she'd never been in another man's arms.

She knew he was aroused. She could tell by his accelerated breathing, by the way his arms tightened around her. His mouth left hers and he trailed kisses down the length of her neck as she ran her hands across his back. She could feel the ridges of his scars and she wanted to kiss them, to somehow caress them away.

Even though she desperately wanted him to make love to her, she knew that wasn't an option. Although she realized sex was usually okay for pregnant women, she'd also heard that in the later stages of pregnancy having sex might induce labor. She didn't want to take that chance, no matter how slim it might be. But she wanted to give him pleasure.

She began to pull up his shirt from the waist, wanting it off, needing to feel his bare skin beneath her fingers. He pulled away from her, and his chest heaved with his rapid breathing. "What are you doing, Jane?" His low, hoarse voice shot a thrill through her.

"I want to love you, Lucas. I want to run my hands across your bare skin. Let me." She touched his shirt. "Take it off and let me love you."

He seemed to freeze, his only movement the rise and fall of his chest as he held her gaze. For a single agonizing moment she thought he was going to spring from the bed and run from the room, from her. But instead he sat up and pulled his shirt over his head and tossed it to the floor.

When he lay back down she placed her face against his chest, loving the warmth of his skin, the rapid beat of his heart beneath her ear. She ran her hands down the length of his chest and he moaned in response.

Her mouth followed her hands, nipping and kissing the heated skin as his hands tangled in her hair. She loved the taste of him, the scent of clean male that clung to him, and when she reached the waist of his jeans she knew she wanted all of him.

Giving pleasure was as exciting, as stimulating as getting it, Jane thought, especially when you were giving it to somebody you cared about.

It didn't take long before Lucas was clad only in his briefs and her caresses and kisses grew more fevered. There was no other thought in her mind but him.

At the moment the past and the future didn't matter. It was just the two of them in the intimacy of the moment. It was she who pulled at his briefs, and when he kicked them off, she wrapped her fingers around his hard length as his mouth found hers in a kiss that seared her to her toes.

She stroked him as he gasped in pleasure against her mouth. She knew that Lucas was a man she'd never forget, that he had etched her heart with an indelible mark that time and circumstance would never erase. And she wanted to be somebody he would never forget.

She felt the rise of his release in his pulsing hardness and moved her hand faster, wanting to take him over the edge, to give him a night with her to remember.

And when he reached the peak, he cried out her name. The only regret she had was that it wasn't really her name, that she might never hear her real name from his lips.

Afterward he got out of bed without a word and

left the room. Instantly, worry rippled through her. Had she offended him with her aggressiveness? Was he angry about what had just happened?

She crept from her bed and went across the hall to the bathroom, heard the sound of running water and realized there must be another bathroom in his master bedroom.

She returned to her bed and lay in the dark, worried about the consequences of what had just happened. Did he think she was terrible? That she was nothing more than a tramp who would fall in bed with anyone?

Moments later he returned to her room, slid back into bed and pulled her into his arms. It was only then she breathed a sigh of relief.

"You realize that was incredibly stupid of us," he finally said.

"It didn't feel stupid," she countered. "It felt wonderful." She raised her head from his chest to look up at him. "Oh, Lucas, you don't have to worry about me expecting more from you than you can give. Everything that has happened to me feels like an out-of-body experience, but I know what just happened between us has nothing to do with real life."

She sighed and dropped her head to his chest once again, where she could hear the solid beat of his heart. "I don't know anything about my past and I certainly can't guess what my future might hold. I just wanted to be with you tonight…a single night in the limbo that has become my life."

He leaned up slightly and turned out the bedside lamp, then tightened his arms around her. "Maybe we'll know more when we confront Charles Blankenship in the morning. For now, get some sleep."

She closed her eyes, and for the first time since all this began, she wasn't afraid. She felt protected and warm with Lucas's arms around her and it took her only minutes to drift off to sleep.

The dream began almost immediately. She was in a church and there were flowers everywhere, filling the interior with sweet fragrance. There was joy in the air and the people in the pews all wore smiles.

Three men stood at the altar, all of them clad in black tuxedos with crisp white shirts and turquoise bowties.

It was a wedding. The groom stood with his back to her and as she gazed at him, her heart filled with happiness. As the traditional wedding march began she started down the aisle, her long, white, silk dress swishing around her legs.

Her heart thudded and she wanted to run to him, to start their life together right now. Lucas, her heart sang, as she stopped herself from running to his side.

Finally she reached where he stood and he turned to look at her, a smile on his handsome face. She froze.

Not Lucas. The man who reached for her hand,

*the groom, was a man she couldn't remember ever
seeing before.*

She woke with a gasp, her heart thundering a
frantic beat. She opened her eyes to the darkness of
the bedroom, aware of Lucas's slow, even breathing
as he slept beside her.

A dream, she told herself. It was nothing more than
a crazy dream. And yet even as she said those words
to herself, she knew the truth. It hadn't been a dream.

It had been a memory.

Chapter Nine

"Anything about the house look familiar?" Lucas asked as he pulled into Charles Blankenship's driveway the next morning. He looked over at Jane, who frowned thoughtfully as she looked at the two-story beige house in front of them.

It was just after ten on another gray, cold day. Breakfast had been awkward. He hadn't been able to get the night before out of his mind.

"No," Jane replied. "It doesn't look familiar at all. I don't think I've ever been here before."

Her hands were clasped tightly in her lap and he could feel her tension. He'd tried to talk her into not coming with him, but she'd been adamant.

"It's my life, Lucas," she'd exclaimed stubbornly, "and if seeing this man in person makes me remember everything, then it's worth any risk."

The problem was Lucas didn't know exactly what risk this might entail. What if Charles Blankenship was some kind of crazy maniac?

They were in his car. Lucas hadn't wanted any-one to get a look at the rental car. He figured Charles had already seen his vehicle, so it made sense to drive it here.

Once again he turned to look at Jane. "When I get out of the car I want you to scoot across and get behind the wheel," he said. "If anything goes wrong, if I get hurt, then I want you to get the hell out of here. Drive back to the safe house and call Micah or Troy."

Her eyes widened and she reached out and grabbed his hand in hers. She squeezed tightly as she held his gaze. "Surely you aren't expecting anything like that?"

"I don't know what to expect," he replied. He pulled his hand from hers. "We don't know what these people are capable of, but I need to know that you'd do exactly what I told you. If anything goes wrong you drive away and don't look back. Promise me, Jane."

He could tell it was a promise she didn't want to make, but as she placed her hands on her stomach and rubbed, she nodded. He knew she would do it for her baby, if not for herself. "I promise," she replied softly.

Lucas opened the car door, and the cold wind slapped his face as he got out of the car. His coat was open, allowing him fast access to his gun if he needed it.

He walked to the front door, then turned to make sure Jane had done as he'd asked. She was in the driver seat, her wide eyes watching him closely.

At least if anything bad happened she'd be able to pull out of the driveway and get the hell out of Dodge. He turned back around and knocked on the door.

This might be a foolish move, but they were stymied, and for the first time since this had all begun he felt like he was playing offense instead of defense.

He knocked once again and the man himself opened the door. Clad in a pair of dress slacks and a long-sleeved white shirt, Charles Blankenship couldn't quite hide the look of surprise that flashed across his blunt features before he schooled them into the curious interest of a stranger. "May I help you?" he asked.

"Yeah, I'd like to know why yesterday evening you chased me through the streets of Kansas City," Lucas said. He didn't intend to waste time playing games with this man.

Charles's gaze shot over Lucas's shoulder to the car, and again a flash of surprise lit his eyes, quickly masked as he looked back at Lucas. "I don't know what you're talking about," he bluffed.

"Oh, I think you do," Lucas replied.

The two men stared at each other for a tense space of time; then Charles sighed and ran a hand through his salt-and-pepper hair. "You cut me off and it made me mad. I'm not proud of my actions. Chalk it up to road rage," he said.

Irritation burned in Lucas's gut. "That wasn't road

rage," he said as he took a step closer to the door. "You were following me. You know the woman in the car?"

"Does she know me?" he countered with a touch of belligerence.

Lucas considered his options. He could tell this man the truth, that Jane didn't have her memories, and see what happened next, or he could bluff. He opted for something in between.

"She hit her head and she's having some memory issues. She doesn't specifically remember you, but she thinks you look familiar. Her memories are coming back every day, and if she remembers that you hurt her, I'll come back here and make you sorry. Got it?"

"There's no need to threaten me," Charles exclaimed.

Lucas offered him a tight smile. "Trust me, that wasn't a threat, that was a promise."

"Look, I don't know that woman, and I already told you I acted badly yesterday. You cut me off and I allowed my anger to take control. It was a simple case of road rage and nothing more. I'm sorry. There, I've apologized. Now get off my porch before I call the police."

"If I see your car anywhere around me, I'll be the one calling the police," Lucas replied as he backed away from the door.

He returned to the car, still watching the door, not willing to turn his back on the man. By the time he reached the car, Jane had scooted back into the passenger seat.

He got in and backed the car out of the drive, a new sense of frustration tying a hard knot in the pit of his stomach.

"I'm not sure exactly what I thought would happen, but this accomplished absolutely nothing," he said as he pulled away, his focus as always divided between the road ahead and the rearview mirror.

Jane reached out and placed her hand on his forearm. Even through the bulk of his coat he could feel her heat, and his irritation grew.

"I'm sorry," she said. "I'm sorry I didn't recognize him."

"You can't do what you can't do," he replied, grateful as she pulled her hand away.

He was also grateful for her silence as they drove back to the safe house. He needed to think, not about what had just transpired with Charles Blankenship, but rather how much longer he could continue to do this, to be responsible for her, to be around her twenty-four hours a day.

The lovemaking of the night before had definitely messed with his mind. Waking up this morning with her spooned against him had been overwhelmingly nice.

Her hair had been a sweet tickle beneath his nose, and the warmth of her body had pressed intimately against his own.

For a few minutes he'd simply remained there, imagining what it would be like to wake up with her every morning for the rest of his life, reluctant to leave her side.

Things were spiraling out of his control. He was spiraling out of control. He was getting too close, wanting things he knew weren't good for him, weren't good for her.

And he wasn't the only one. She was getting in too deep, as well. He felt it in her most simple touch; saw it in her eyes whenever she looked at him; felt it in his heart, in his soul as she'd caressed him the night before.

They couldn't continue this indefinitely. It might take weeks or months for her memory to completely return. There was no way he could do a couple more weeks, let alone a month or two with her. He had to figure out how much longer he was willing to give her and how he was going to tell her that sooner or later he was going to bail.

Once they were back in the house she went to her bedroom to rest and Lucas paced the kitchen, too restless to sit.

The fact that Charles Blankenship had lied to him wasn't surprising. What he'd really hoped was that Jane would see the house or the man and all her memories would come tumbling back.

Charles had lied when he said he didn't know her. He'd lied about everything. Why?

What had happened to her? What had been so terrible that she'd not only run away, but had also shoved the memories of her entire life into the darkest recesses of her mind?

By the time she got up from her nap and joined him in the kitchen, he'd fried burgers and had opened a can of baked beans for dinner. He added a bag of chips to the table and they sat down to eat.

They talked about inconsequential things, the weather, an article in a magazine she was reading, how Kansas City was growing by leaps and bounds.

They didn't talk about men in white vans or all-seeing eye symbols or lost memories. Although the conversation remained pleasant, in the back of his mind Lucas was trying to figure out how to tell her that he was reaching the end of his rope, that it was time they considered going to the authorities for help.

They cleared the table together and a knot of tension formed in his chest when she stood close enough that he could smell her. Memories of the night before stirred in his mind. She'd been soft and warm and giving. She'd been hot and sexy and amazing.

While she'd made love to him last night, it was easy to imagine a time when she would no longer be pregnant and could indulge herself in complete lovemaking.

"You're very quiet this evening," she observed as he put the last plate into the dishwasher. "I did most of the talking during dinner."

"I guess I'm all talked out," he replied. He dried his hands on a hand towel and then turned to look at her.

She must have seen something in his expression, for she leaned against the countertop and released a sigh. "You aren't just talked out, you're Janed out," she said softly. There was not only a whisper of pain in her eyes, but one of fear, as well. "Is this about what happened between us last night?"

"Maybe a little," he said honestly. "Don't get me wrong. It was great…you were great, but it shouldn't have happened."

"I'm glad it did." She lifted her chin as if in defiance. "At least it's one good memory I'll carry with me always."

And so would he, he thought. "It still shouldn't have happened. We don't know what your situation is in your real life, but you know mine. The longer we're together, the more the lines blur between reality and fantasy. I can't be the man in your life, Jane. I don't want to see you get hurt."

"I realize that," she replied, but he thought he heard a touch of wistfulness in her voice. That cinched the deal as far as he was concerned.

He steeled his heart for what he was about to do. "Forty-eight hours, Jane. If you don't get your memory back in forty-eight hours, I'm calling Wendall and we're filing a report."

Once again a dark fear edged into her eyes, but she nodded her head. "All right." She turned and left the kitchen.

Lucas remained standing at the sink, fighting the impulse to run after her and tell her he'd changed his mind.

Forty-eight hours and then she would no longer

be his responsibility. Forty-eight hours and he'd have his life back. What he didn't understand was why the thought didn't fill him with joy.

TWENTY-FOUR HOURS.

The next evening those words whirled around and around in Jane's head, making her alternately sick with fear and beyond sad.

She knew once Lucas turned her over to the police she'd probably never see him again, and that thought ached inside her with a force that was shocking.

She was in love with him. It was as simple and as heartbreaking as that. And when the next twenty-four hours passed she would have to tell him good-bye forever.

As she glanced over at him, her heart swelled and she felt the unwelcome burn of unshed tears. She was on the sofa and he was on the chair nearby, his attention seemingly focused on a crime drama playing on television.

Do not cry, she commanded herself firmly. The last thing she wanted to do was weep and make him feel bad. He'd already gone far above and beyond for her.

She couldn't be hurt or angry with him for wanting to get back to his real life. She couldn't be upset that he didn't love her back enough to want to offer more than he already had.

"I'm going to get something to snack on. You need anything?" he asked when the show ended and he got out of his chair.

Just you, a little voice whispered inside her head. "No, I'm fine. I'm just going to catch a little of the news. Then I'm going to bed." *And tomorrow I'll be gone,* she thought.

As he disappeared into the kitchen she placed her hand on her tummy and wondered what would become of her. Would the police place her in a women's shelter until they could figure out where she belonged? What would happen to her if she never regained her memories?

She focused on the television, her speculation about the future too painful to think about. "More wintry weather ahead," a pert blond newscaster said with a smile. The smile fell and she offered the camera a concerned expression. "A drive-by shooting ends in a young man's death. And police are asking for your help. Have you seen this woman?"

Jane's breath caught in her throat as a picture of her filled the screen. "Lucas," she managed to gasp.

"Details after the break," the blonde said, and a commercial came on.

Lucas appeared in the doorway. "What? What is it?"

She pointed to the television. "It was me. There was a picture of me on the news."

He looked stunned. "What did they say?"

"Details after the break," she replied.

He sank down next to her on the sofa, his attention riveted to the screen. Jane's heart thundered, hurting her chest with the intensity of the beat.

The commercial seemed to last forever, and then

the news returned. The top news story was of a drive-by shooting that had left one teenage boy dead. Jane felt as if she were in agony as she waited for the story that would change everything for her.

There were two more news stories before a picture of her filled the screen. "And now this," the newscaster said. "Concerned family members are looking for this woman. Her name is Julie Montgomery and she's eight months pregnant. She's been missing from her home for the past week. Anyone with any information should call the TIPS hotline." She gave the appropriate number and then they cut away to the weatherman.

Jane sat in stunned silence. Julie. Her name was Julie Montgomery and she had concerned family members looking for her. She rolled the name again and again through her mind. She wasn't sure whether to laugh or cry.

"It suits you," Lucas said softly. "Julie is a nice name."

She turned to look at him. "What happens now?"

"I guess I make a phone call." He pulled his cell phone from his pocket. "You have people who care about you, Julie. It's time you returned to them."

Even though she knew he was right, she was surprised that she didn't feel more relief at the knowledge that she was on her way home—wherever that might be.

"Are you calling the TIPS hotline?" she asked.

"No, I'm calling Wendall. I want to get the name

of the people who reported you missing. Before I turn you over to just anyone, I want them vetted. We need to make sure they're really who they claim to be."

As he stood and punched in numbers on his phone, she thought about what he'd just said. It hadn't occurred to her that it was possible the people who were after her might pose as concerned family members.

She trusted Lucas to see that she wasn't in danger, that the people who were looking for her had only love and concern for her well-being in their hearts.

It was impossible for her to glean any information from Lucas's end of his conversation with Wendall Kincaid. Lucas listened more than talked initially, then spent several minutes telling Wendall about how he'd stumbled upon her and her bout of amnesia.

It seemed to take forever before the men hung up. Lucas set his phone on the coffee table and turned to look at her. "You were reported missing by a Robert Montgomery, who identified himself as your brother-in-law."

"My brother-in-law?" Julie once again placed a hand on her pregnant stomach. She knew there was a man somewhere out there that she'd married. She'd dreamed of him the night after she'd made love to Lucas. She just hadn't told Lucas about that particular memory. "Did he say anything about my husband?" The last word seemed to catch on her tongue.

She had a husband. So why had her brother-in-law reported her missing instead of her husband?

"Wendall only had sketchy information and Robert Mongomery's phone number. Maybe your husband is out of town or in the military. I'll call Robert and set up an initial meeting with him for tomorrow morning. I'll have Troy or Micah sit with you in a car. If Montgomery doesn't come with proof of his relationship to you, then you won't be meeting him at all."

"I'm not sure why I'm so crazy nervous," she said with a small laugh. "This is what we've been waiting for and I know I should be happy, but to be honest, I'm scared."

He reached out and took her hand in his. "That's natural. Even though these people are probably loving relatives, you have no memory of them. We know that there are people after you for some reason or another. It's only normal that you'd feel apprehensive."

She squeezed his hand and leaned against him. She closed her eyes as she drew in the familiar scent of him. He smelled like safety, like passion and home. A lump crept into her throat and again she felt the burn of tears at her eyes.

"I won't see you again after tomorrow, will I?" she asked softly.

"I'm sure we'll run into each other sooner or later," he replied.

They both knew it was a lie, and she loved him even more for pretending that they might maintain some sort of relationship once this was all over.

They remained seated on the sofa for a long time, not speaking, just being with each other. He finally stood and grabbed his cell phone from the coffee table. "First I'm going to call Micah and have him do some digging into Robert Montgomery's life. Then I'm going to make arrangements for the meeting in the morning," he said. "You might as well go on to bed. Get a good night's sleep."

He smiled, but the gesture didn't reach the darkness in his eyes. "Just think, by this time tomorrow night you'll be back where you belong."

She forced a smile to her lips as she stood. "Good night, Lucas," she said. What she couldn't say to him was that she felt in her heart—in her soul—that she belonged with him.

As she headed down the hallway to her bedroom, the tears she'd fought back for the last several minutes began to fall. She should be deliriously happy. She finally knew her name, and tomorrow she'd be reunited with family members, but all she could think about was that after tomorrow she'd never see Lucas again.

Chapter Ten

Micah and Troy were at the safe house at nine the next morning. They all gathered around the table to see what information Micah had managed to dig up on Robert Montgomery.

Lucas couldn't help but notice that Jane's hand trembled slightly as she poured herself a cup of coffee. Julie, he mentally amended. Her name was Julie and he wished there were some way for him to take away her obvious anxiety.

She looked particularly pretty with her hair falling in soft waves around her shoulders and her cheeks flushed with color. She wore the blue blouse he'd picked out for her at the store, and it made her eyes pop.

If all went well he'd be back in his own apartment tonight and Julie Montgomery would only be a fond memory. He tried to summon the joy he'd expected to feel at the idea of getting his life back, but found it curiously absent.

"So, what did you find out about Robert Montgomery?" he asked Micah, determined to focus on the matter at hand and not on matters of his heart.

"He's a forty-four-year-old businessman who owns a lucrative gift shop on Oak Street. He's been married for ten years to a woman named Martha. They live in a small home off North Maple Street. No children, no criminal record for either of them. On paper they look like good, upstanding citizens." He unfolded a sheet of paper and laid it on the table in front of Julie. "Look familiar?"

Lucas could see that it was a copy of a driver's license for Robert Montgomery. The photo depicted a burly man with sandy-colored hair and blue eyes that seemed to jump right off the page.

She studied the photo for a long moment, then shook her head. "No," she replied. "He doesn't look familiar at all, but that doesn't mean anything. I do have amnesia," she added drily.

"Now you want to hear what I dug up about you?" Micah asked.

She sat back in her chair in obvious surprise. "All right." She shoved a strand of hair behind her ear with a shaky hand.

"You're thirty years old and you worked as an elementary school teacher until two years ago when you married David Montgomery, Robert's younger brother." He paused a moment as if to give her time to digest the information.

"Third grade," she said with a touch of surprise

in her voice. She paused a moment, then nodded and smiled. "Yes, I taught third grade." The smile wavered as she continued to look at Micah. "Where's my husband?"

"Dead. I'm sorry, Julie. Your husband was killed almost eight months ago during a mugging," Micah said softly.

Lucas's heart fell at this bit of information. So, there was no loving husband for her to return to. She was alone just as she'd felt she was despite having no real memories.

She sighed and nodded once again as her hands lowered to her stomach. "Somehow I knew it." She turned to look at Lucas. "I told you I thought I had been alone before all this happened."

"You own a home near Robert and Martha's house," Micah continued. "But after your husband's death you apparently moved in with them and put the house up for sale." Micah leaned back in his chair. "That's all I could get in the short amount of time I had."

"At least I know more now than I did when I woke up this morning. Thank you," she said.

"So, how are you going to work this?" Troy asked.

Lucas looked at his watch. "In thirty minutes I'm meeting Robert and his wife at the Calico Café. I told him last night on the phone to bring proof of his relationship to Julie, pictures and documents or whatever he had. I explained to him that she was having some memory problems. I'd like you and Micah to stay with Julie in one of your cars until I feel comfortable that it's okay for her to enter the restaurant. Then I'll call one of you on your cell and you can bring her in to meet her family."

He turned to gaze at Julie. Her anxiety was through the roof. Her lower lip trembled slightly and he wanted nothing more than to cover it with his own, hold her until her trembling halted. "It's going to be okay, Julie. It's time for you to be with people who care about you, people who will watch over you."

He hesitated a moment, then added, "If you feel alarmed, then you don't have to go with them. We'll bring you back here." He told himself that was the last thing he wanted, that it would be best for everyone involved if she returned to her rightful place.

"Thank you," she replied. "I'm sure it's all going to work out just fine." She raised her chin a notch, and at that moment Lucas thought she was one of the bravest women he would ever know.

"Then we should get out of here," Troy said.

They all rose from the table and went into the living room, where they grabbed their coats. Julie went down the hallway to the bedroom where she'd been staying and returned a few seconds later with the small black overnight bag packed with everything she had.

"I'm ready," she said with a lift of her chin despite the tremor in her voice.

Minutes later they were on the road, Lucas in his rental car followed by the others in Micah's car. As he drove, Lucas's mind filled with the sound of Julie's laughter, the pleasure of morning coffee with her bright smile across from him at the table.

The taste of her filled his mouth, and the scent of her seemed to ride the air. A wave of sadness suffused him, shocking him with its heavy weight.

He could have loved her if he was a loving kind of man. *Which I'm not,* he reminded himself. He could never be the man she wanted, the man she needed. He reached up and touched the scar on the back of his neck to remind himself of where he'd come from. She and her baby were much better off without him.

Surely her extended family would take care of her, see that both she and the baby were happy and healthy. He had to believe that. And eventually she'd find some special man to share her life with her, the kind of man she deserved.

Lucas turned into the parking lot of the café as Micah drove on by. He would park someplace up the street until Lucas called him to bring Julie.

He found a parking space near the front door and got out of the car. The wind seemed colder, but it was also filled with the scent of bacon, eggs and strong coffee.

As he entered, a quick glance at the diners told him that Montgomery hadn't arrived yet. He took a booth next to a window with a view of the parking lot and ordered a cup of coffee from the waitress. He might have ordered a full breakfast if his stomach hadn't been so tied in knots.

When the coffee arrived he wrapped his fingers around the mug and told himself once again that this was a happy occasion. It was what they'd been seeking—Julie's identity and the place where she belonged.

He'd only been sitting for about five minutes when he saw a beige sedan pull in and Robert Montgomery get out of the driver's side. An attractive woman with dark hair got out of the passenger side and together they headed toward the café.

This was it. The moment Lucas had wished for, the chance to get rid of Julie once and for all and get back to his own life. No more safe house, no more intimate breakfasts or back rubs that went too far.

As Robert and Martha stepped inside, their gazes swept the area. Lucas raised a hand to motion them over as he stood.

"Lucas Washington?" Robert had the deep, rich, booming voice of a radio personality.

Lucas nodded and the two men shook hands. Robert introduced his wife and then they all sat back down in the booth. Robert placed a manila folder in front of him.

"Where's Julie?" Martha asked, her gaze darting around the room.

"I wanted to meet the two of you first," Lucas said. The waitress arrived at the table and both

Robert and Martha ordered coffee. When the coffee was served, Lucas explained to them how he'd found Julie and about her amnesia.

"Oh my goodness," Martha exclaimed when Lucas had finished his story. "That poor girl. She's all right? The baby is all right?"

"Physically she's fine, but she's still struggling with some memory issues," Lucas replied. "Which is why I asked you to bring proof of your relationship to her. Since she can't remember you, I want to make sure you're who you really say you are."

"Of course," Robert said. He opened the folder in front of him and handed Lucas a photo. It was a wedding picture. Julie was the bride, a handsome blond man was the groom and on either side of them were Robert and Martha. "That was the day my brother married Julie," he said. "We were thrilled that he'd found such a lovely woman to share his life with, and we were eager to welcome her into our family."

She was a beautiful bride, Lucas thought as he studied the picture. And a little over a year after this happy photo had been taken she had become a pregnant widow. He handed the photo back to Robert.

"It's been almost ten days. Why didn't you report her missing sooner?" he asked. Micah had told him that according to the neighbors Julie was living in Martha and Robert's home. Why had it taken so long for them to realize she wasn't there?

"She told us she felt like she wanted some time

alone, that she was going to stay at her house for a few days," Robert explained. "We thought maybe she just needed some space. Our home isn't huge, and we were kind of on top of each other." He frowned. "She doesn't remember any of this?"

"No," Lucas replied. There was absolutely no reason for him not to trust the two people in front of him, but he couldn't explain the faint thrum of apprehension that worried him.

Maybe it was nothing more than the fact that he hated the idea of Julie leaving. Or perhaps it was the knowledge that she had no husband, no father for the baby she carried.

This was definitely more difficult than he'd thought it would be. He hadn't expected that handing her over and telling her goodbye would feel like a loss.

JULIE NEARLY CAME UNGLUED when Micah's cell phone rang. The last thirty minutes had been the most agonizing she thought she'd ever spend.

She leaned over the back of the front seat as Micah answered. When he clicked off, he looked at her in the rearview mirror. "Buckle up, it's a go."

So, Robert Montgomery had passed the Lucas test and she was about to be reintroduced to family members whom she'd been close to before whatever event had stolen her memories.

She leaned back and fastened her seat belt as Micah pulled away from the curb where they had been parked and headed toward the café.

"You okay?" Troy asked.

"Nervous, but okay," she replied. Her heart felt as if it might pound right out of her chest and the baby did a sudden somersault as if sensing her anxiety.

"You know Lucas would never put you in a dangerous situation. Both Micah and I can tell that he cares about you."

Troy's words created a ring of pain around her heart. He might care about her, but not enough to want to be a part of her life. Once her picture had appeared on the evening news he'd certainly wasted no time arranging to get rid of her.

She frowned. That wasn't fair. Lucas believed he was doing what was best for her, and even though it pained her, she knew she had to somehow push him out of her heart.

As Micah pulled up in front of the café, Troy got out to escort her inside. She grabbed her overnight bag from the seat next to her in one hand and grabbed his arm with the other.

She was so nervous her legs felt wobbly beneath her. Maybe she'd take one look at Robert and Martha and all her memories would instantly return. She wanted that. Even though they'd found out her name and knew bits and pieces of her life, she wanted, needed her memories back.

As they entered the café she immediately spied Lucas. Martha Montgomery rose as Julie approached the booth, and when Julie got close enough the older woman pulled her into a hug.

"Oh, Julie, dear. We've been worried sick about you," she exclaimed.

Julie held herself stiffly in the stranger's arms, but as the hug continued she felt herself begin to relax. They weren't strangers…they were family, she reminded herself.

As Martha released her, Julie slid into the booth next to Lucas, surprised to discover that Troy had disappeared.

"Julie, honey, we know this is difficult for you," Robert said. "Lucas has explained about your memory issues. But I'm sure once we get you home, you'll be just fine. The baby's crib is all set up and we're eager to get you settled back in where you belong."

"Before that happens, there's something you should know," Lucas said. "Somebody tried to grab Julie and shove her in the back of a van at the store the other day. You have any clue why that might have happened?"

Martha and Robert exchanged pointed glances as Julie felt a new tension coil in her stomach. "My brother, God rest his soul, was a good, but troubled man," Robert said. "He had a weakness for drugs and gambling. At the time of his death, he owed money to people who don't easily overlook debts." He turned his attention from Lucas to Julie. "Part of the reason we had you move in with us was that you had been receiving threatening phone calls from these people. I guess they got tired of making phone calls and decided to get more aggressive."

Julie looked down at the table as she tried to process this new information. Her husband had been a drug abuser and a gambler? She could only guess that the marriage hadn't been a happy one. Was that why she'd forgotten it, forgotten David?

"The problem," Robert continued, "is that Julie doesn't have any money. Another reason we decided to move her in with us was so we could sell her house and get her out from under that payment. Our plan was for her to live with us until the baby was born, and then she could go back to teaching and get on her feet."

"There was no life insurance policy on her husband?" Lucas asked.

Robert grimaced. "My brother cashed it in months before his death. He left Julie nothing."

"Why don't we order some breakfast and chitchat a bit about more pleasant things?" Martha suggested.

Julie was grateful for the suggestion. Hopefully it would give her a little more time to feel comfortable with the people who intended to take her home with them.

Lucas motioned for the waitress and they all ordered. While they ate, Robert and Martha told her a little more about her life with them.

With each moment that passed, a weary acceptance filled Julie. Robert and Martha appeared to be kind, well-meaning people. There was no reason for her not to leave with them.

Except that she didn't want to leave the man

seated next to her. Lucas was quiet during the meal, as if he'd already disconnected from the situation, from her.

Love me, her heart wanted to plead. Ask me to stay with you. Don't send me away with people I don't remember. Don't send me away at all. But all too quickly they had finished eating and it was time for her to leave.

There was nothing to stop her from going with them. They'd had the documentation to prove that they were who they claimed to be, and Julie knew it was time for her to get back to whatever life she'd forgotten.

As they reached the sidewalk outside, Robert and Martha started toward their car as Lucas grabbed Julie's arm. "She'll be right there," he said, indicating they should go on.

She looked up at him, wishing for things he couldn't give, yearning for an ending different than the one she was getting. "They seem like really nice people," she finally said.

He nodded, his gaze intent on her, and for just a moment she thought she saw something wonderful in the depths of his eyes, something warm and caring, something that looked like love. "You're going to be just fine, Julie." He said the words forcefully, as if trying to convince himself as well as her. He reached up and tenderly tucked a strand of her hair behind her ears, then stepped back from her.

"So I guess this is goodbye." Her throat grew

thick with emotion. She finally felt free to say the words that burned in her heart.

His strong jaw clenched and his eyes darkened. "I know through this whole thing I've been your lifeline, but once you get your memories back you'll realize what you feel for me is nothing more than gratitude."

Was he right? Did she feel so strongly about him because she was lost in a sea of the unknown? Was the love she felt for him nothing more than gratitude masquerading as something deeper?

"Julie, I told you not to want anything from me, that I'm not cut out to be a husband or a father."

"I know. I just don't understand why you'd say that about yourself. You have all the qualities it takes to be a wonderful husband and father." She wanted to touch him, but his eyes grew even darker and he took another step back from her.

"You have my cell phone number if you need anything. Goodbye, Julie." He shoved his hands in his coat pockets, a distinct dismissal of her, of any hopes she might have had to the contrary.

"Goodbye, Lucas," she replied. She tightened her grip on her overnight bag, then turned and headed toward Martha and Robert's car.

Her heart sat like a heavy boulder in her chest. Robert opened the back door of his car with a reassuring smile and she slid in. As he pulled out of the parking lot, she turned and gazed back at Lucas, who hadn't moved from his position on the sidewalk.

Her last impression of him was that he looked as alone as she felt, and that somehow this was wrong, all wrong.

"I'm sure you're exhausted from all this drama," Martha said. "All of this can't be good for the baby. We're going to make sure you get plenty of rest and healthy meals."

Julie offered her a weak smile. "I am tired," she admitted. But not from anything other than the difficulty in telling Lucas goodbye.

She stared out the window and watched the passing scenery, her thoughts still on the man she'd just left. There was no way she believed that her feelings for him were mere gratitude. She knew what she felt in her heart, and it was love.

"Are you warm enough back there?" Robert's voice pulled her from her thoughts.

She met his piercing blue gaze in the rearview mirror. "I'm fine," she assured him. Fine. Everyone seemed to be using that word a lot when it came to her and her future. You're going to be just fine, Lucas had told her. But she didn't feel as if she'd ever be completely fine again.

She sat up straighter and frowned as she noticed they were driving north. She could have sworn Robert and Martha lived south of the café where they had met.

"Are we going home?" she asked, a strange feeling of dread welling up inside her.

"We're taking you right where you belong, dear," Martha said.

Julie's sense of dread grew bigger, a faint alarm ringing in the back of her head. Then she saw it just ahead of them—the Church of Enlightenment. Even though she couldn't remember coming here, didn't recognize it from memory, she knew what it was.

"What are we doing here?" she asked. She unfastened her seat belt as Robert pulled the car up to the gate that led into the inner compound.

He clicked a remote button on his dash and the gate opened. At the same time Julie tried to open the back car door, somehow knowing that she needed to escape.

But the door wouldn't open. Panic welled up inside her. Why was she locked in like a prisoner? Why were they bringing her here? Oh God, something was wrong. Something was terribly wrong.

As Robert pulled through the gate and it clunked shut behind them, Julie's memories came rushing back. And with them came the knowledge that she was in grave danger.

Chapter Eleven

Lucas watched them pull out of the café parking lot as his heart twisted in a way he'd never felt before. She was better off without him. Robert and Martha Montgomery seemed like fine people, and eventually Julie would find another man, one who would be a great husband and a terrific father. She was better off without him, and he was better off without her.

Even as he told himself this, he hurried to his car and got in, driven by an impulse he didn't understand. He wanted to see the house where she'd live, the place where she'd bring her baby after he was born and get on with her life.

He drove several car lengths behind them, not wanting her to see him. He didn't want her to think that he was coming after her, that he'd changed his mind and wanted to take her home with him.

It didn't take long for him to be confused by the direction they were traveling, and with his confusion came a spark of concern.

The farther north they drove, the more concern Lucas felt, and when the Church of Enlightenment came into view, the concern transformed to a screaming alarm.

He stepped on the gas in an effort to catch up to them, but before he could, their car disappeared behind the security gates. He braked and stared at the seemingly impenetrable gate that surrounded the buildings within.

Why had they brought her here? During their conversation nobody had mentioned the church. Julie had been terrified by the symbol of the all-seeing eye that the church used as its emblem. Why would they have brought her here? What did they— what did Julie have to do with the church?

He ran the conversation they'd shared over break-fast through his head again and again, seeking some-thing he'd missed, a clue he'd somehow overlooked.

In retrospect the only thing that sounded odd was the idea that goons would be after Julie because of her husband's drug and gambling debts. Julie had no money. The goons would have nothing to gain by going after her, and they sure wouldn't try to grab her in the middle of the day in a busy parking lot.

She was in trouble. He'd handed her right over to danger. He slammed the steering wheel with the palms of his hands, then grabbed his cell phone from his pocket and called Chief Kincaid. Wendall answered on the second ring.

"Wendall, it's Lucas. I need your help."

"What's up?"

"Can you meet me in fifteen minutes in front of the Church of Enlightenment?"

Wendall must have heard the thrum of urgency in Lucas's voice, for he didn't ask any questions. "I'll be there."

"And Wendall, could you bring a couple of officers with you?"

There was a momentary pause. "Are you in danger?"

"No, but I think somebody else is," Lucas replied.

"On my way."

Lucas dropped his cell phone on the seat next to him and backed away from the security gate. Instead he pulled to park in front of the church, his heart pounding with a nauseating intensity.

Why was she here? It didn't make sense. He glanced at his watch. He felt as if each minute that passed was an hour as he waited for reinforcements to arrive.

What he wanted was to talk to Julie, to assure himself that she was okay. He'd like to storm the fence, either ram his car through it or climb over it. But he knew that if he was arrested for destruction of personal property or trespassing, he wouldn't be any help at all to Julie. *If she needs help,* he reminded himself.

He supposed it was possible the Montgomerys had brought her here to visit a friend, or to worship before taking her home. He tried to convince himself that those scenarios were possible, but he remained unconvinced.

Once again he checked his watch. God, could the minutes move any slower? With nervous energy screaming through him, he unfastened his coat and placed a hand on the butt of his gun.

He'd kill for her.

The thought shocked him. As a navy SEAL he'd killed before, but that had been war, cases of kill or be killed. It wasn't something he'd enjoyed, nor had he ever expected to do it again in civilian life.

But for Julie and her unborn son, he'd do whatever it took to protect her, even if it meant killing again.

He breathed a sigh of relief as a patrol car pulled in beside him and Wendall got out. Wendall Kincaid was good-looking, dark-haired and the youngest and most popular chief of police in Kansas City's history.

Although he frowned on some of Recovery Inc.'s methods, he'd become a friend to all three of the men. "What have we got?" he asked.

As Lucas began to fill him in on what was going on, he saw a frown etched deeper and deeper into Wendall's forehead.

"What do you want from me, Lucas?" Wendall asked when Lucas was finished explaining everything. "Julie is a consenting adult and she went willingly with these relatives of hers. There isn't much I can do about that."

"But they told me they were taking her home," he protested.

Wendall shrugged. "So they had a change of plans. No crime has occurred here."

Lucas grabbed Wendall by the shoulder. "Maybe not yet, but I'm telling you this isn't right. Julie would never have willingly come here. Just check it out. Make them bring her out here to talk to me. If she tells me this is where she wants to be, then I'll walk away and not bother her, not bother you again."

Wendall frowned once again. "Let's go check it out," he said.

Lucas dropped his hand from Wendall's shoulder and breathed a sigh of relief. "Thanks, man. I won't forget this."

Minutes later Lucas, Wendall and Officer Ben Branigan approached the locked gate. It was Wendall who found a buzzer that Lucas hadn't noticed before. He rang it and a moment later a man's voice replied. "This is private property, please state your business."

"This is Chief of Police Wendall Kincaid. I'd like to speak with Robert Montgomery," Wendall said in a voice that rang with his authority.

Lucas's chest was filled with such a cold, hard knot that he found breathing difficult. He told himself to relax, but it wasn't happening, wouldn't happen until he knew with a gut certainty that Julie was okay.

The resulting silence seemed to last a lifetime, but finally Robert's deep, familiar voice boomed out of the hidden speaker.

"What can I do for you?"

"I want to talk to Julie," Lucas shouted over Wendall's shoulder.

"I'm afraid, Mr. Washington, that Julie doesn't wish to speak with you," Robert replied smoothly.

"I really must insist that we see Julie," Wendall said.

Once again his words were met with a long silence. Lucas could feel his heartbeat not only in his chest, but banging at his temples. Was it possible that she didn't want to see him? That he'd hurt her by sending her off where she was supposed to belong, even though hurting her was the last thing he'd wanted to happen?

"There's nothing wrong with Julie except that she's stressed and wants some peace and quiet. I see you have an officer with you," Robert said. "I'll allow him to come in and speak with Julie. Perhaps he can convince her to come out and talk to you, but I won't force her to do anything she doesn't want to do."

Wendall looked at Lucas, who in turn looked at Officer Branigan. He shrugged. "I'll go in and talk to her," he said. "I don't have a problem with it."

"Okay," Wendall said into the speaker. "Officer Branigan will come in and speak with Julie."

Minutes later a tall, burly man approached the gate from the inside. He offered them a friendly smile, as if it was business as usual to have the chief of police standing at the gate.

"Officer Branigan? You can come on in." He opened the gate and allowed the cop inside, then closed and locked the gate once again.

Branigan turned and offered Wendall and Lucas

a thumbs-up signal. Lucas tried to tell himself that surely if anything was wrong the people inside wouldn't want an armed cop in their midst.

Lucas looked at Wendall, "Don't you think it's damned suspicious that they wouldn't let us in?"

"Maybe," Wendall agreed. "But I have no jurisdiction to just barge in. At least they allowed an officer in to speak with him."

Still, Lucas couldn't get rid of the feeling that Julie was in some kind of terrible danger and needed his help.

JULIE SAT ON THE EDGE of the bed in an attractive bedroom with an adjoining bath. Under other circumstances she might have appreciated the fine mahogany furniture and the beautiful tapestries that hung on the walls.

But as beautiful as the bedroom was, it was nothing more than her prison. And it had been her prison for a month before Lucas had found her shivering in the back of that car.

She remembered everything now, her marriage to David, his unexpected death and the fact that her brother and sister-in-law were monsters.

Robert was the prophet, the father figure behind the curtain who preached in anonymity on Sundays to a congregation who desperately wanted to believe in something different than what traditional religion offered.

More than anything, she remembered that they

wanted her baby. She wrapped her arms around her belly and looked around the room for the hundredth time since being locked inside.

The room was located on the third floor. Although there were two windows, there was no way she could chance jumping. She would probably kill herself. But more importantly she could hurt her baby.

There was nothing to use as a weapon, no way for her to fight the people who held her captive. She squeezed her eyes closed tightly against the tears that threatened to fall. She refused to cry and she refused to think about Lucas, knowing if she did she would start crying and never stop.

Her husband, David, was dead. That much had been true. He'd been the victim of a mugger who had stabbed him to death. And Robert and Martha *had* taken her into their home days after the funeral.

Over the next couple of months, things had been going okay.

Robert and Martha had embraced her and her unborn child with love and support—or so she'd thought. David had told her when they'd married that Robert couldn't have children of his own, that a childhood illness had left him sterile. Both Martha and Robert had seemed to have made peace with the fact that they would never have children.

It had been at the beginning of her seventh month of pregnancy that everything had changed. She'd started talking to Martha about the possibility of moving to a new town. Maybe in another state after the baby was born. She wanted a fresh start. She'd been brought here and held prisoner. Robert had told her his plan for her and her child.

She jumped to her feet as the door opened and Robert walked in, along with a uniformed police officer. The sight of the officer should have produced a sense of relief in her, but instead it stirred a new fear.

She'd seen him before. Here, in her prison. He was a member of Robert's wicked board, a man seeking wealth and power and definitely not on the side of law and order.

"We have a little problem," Robert said. "It seems your boyfriend has brought the chief of police to check on your welfare."

Lucas was here? Oh, thank God, he'd come for her. Her heart swelled with hope. "Just let me go, Robert. I won't say anything to anyone. I won't press any charges against you. Just let me go and you'll never hear from me again."

Robert smiled at her indulgently. "I've worked too hard, too long to do that, Julie. The child you carry will be mine. He will herald in a new world for the Church of Enlightenment. He will be the new Prophet and offer hope to all."

"Why don't you tell the truth, Robert?" she said angrily. "This isn't about the church and hope. It's about money and power."

Robert's smile grew. "There is that," he agreed. "It's amazing how much money people will cough up if they think it means their salvation. For the new prophet they'll give up their property, their retirement funds. We'll build our own little community here with people working for the church and we'll all get wealthy. Right, Ben?"

The police officer nodded. "Can't get wealthy working for the man," he replied.

"You'll burn in hell," Julie exclaimed.

"Perhaps," Robert agreed easily. "But what a life I'm planning before I die. The best of everything for the new prophet's father on earth." His smile fell and his blue eyes grew icy. "But before any of this can happen we have the little problem of your Romeo and his friend at our gates."

"I have a feeling they aren't going away until they see that she's okay in person," Ben said. "She needs to tell them everything is all right."

"And I'm not about to do that," Julie replied fervently. Lucas, her heart cried. Please save me from this nightmare.

"I think you will," Robert countered confidently. "I think you're going to go down to the gate and tell them that you have all your memories back and this is where you want to be."

"And why would I do that?" she demanded.

Robert reached into his pocket and pulled out a photo and held it out to her. Reluctantly she took it from him and gasped in alarm.

It was a picture of Loretta, taken as she was entering the hospital where she worked. "We can get her anywhere, anytime we want. Same with your boyfriend. Neither of them will know who to fear. They'll never see us coming. If you don't cooperate with us, Loretta Washington is a dead woman. And after we kill her, we'll get Lucas. We would have taken you sooner from Loretta's apartment, but as we made our plans, you disappeared. Besides, it's much better this way. We don't need any police problems."

A dull roar resounded in Julie's head. She believed him. She believed every word he said. They would find Loretta and they would kill her, and eventually they'd get to Lucas, too.

She held both Loretta's and Lucas's lives in her hands and there was no way she could sacrifice them for herself. They had both been so kind to her, a stranger in need and she wouldn't reward their kindness by placing them at risk.

"All right," she finally said, then grimaced. "I'll do whatever you tell me to do, just leave them alone."

Robert took the picture of Loretta from her and tucked it back in his shirt pocket. "I thought you'd see things my way." He grabbed her by the arm, making her skin crawl with his touch. "Just keep in mind, if you screw up, you're putting a bullet in their heads. Make this problem go away, Julie."

As he led her out of the room, Julie's heartbeat was a dull throb in her chest. There would be no magical rescue for her. She was going to have her baby here and she had no doubt that Robert would see to it that she didn't survive the birth.

As they walked down the long hallway that led to the stairs, she remembered the hall from her nightmares. She'd run this way on the night she'd escaped.

As she slowly walked between Robert and Ben, she remembered that night. She'd been told of Robert's plot for her baby, and when Gemma Walker, the old woman who brought her meals, had come in to serve her dinner that night, she'd shoved past her.

Gemma had hit her on the head with the serving tray, resulting in the wound on her forehead, but Julie had managed to slip by her. That night she'd gotten out of the house, and through some amazing good luck had found the security gate unlocked.

She wouldn't get a chance for escape again. They reached the front door of the house, but before they walked outside Robert provided a coat for her and himself.

It didn't matter to her whether she wore a coat out into the cold afternoon or not. No cotton or nylon fabric could warm the icy core inside her.

As they left the house and walked across the long expanse of concrete toward the security gate, Robert squeezed her arm. "It's in everyone's best interest for you to look happy."

She gave an imperceptible nod. He didn't have to tell her what needed to be done, she knew. Still, the minute she saw Lucas at the gate, it took every ounce of her self-control to keep herself from crying out for him, to keep from launching herself over the gate and into his arms.

Instead, as Robert released his hold on her arm she summoned all the inner strength she could find to get through the next few minutes.

"Julie." Lucas's voice was filled with raw concern as he took a step toward her. The tall, dark-haired man standing beside him held him back.

"Julie, I'm Chief of Police Wendall Kincaid," he said. "Lucas here seems to think you're in some sort of trouble."

Her heart was a sick thud in her chest as she pasted on a bright smile. "In trouble?" She looked at Lucas. "No, I'm not in trouble. In fact, everything is better than it's been in days. Lucas, I've got my memories back. It was amazing. The minute we pulled through the gates here, they all came tumbling back to me."

Lucas's eyes were filled with doubt as he stared at her intently. "And you want to be here?"

"I'm safe here, Lucas," she replied, relieved that her voice didn't tremble, didn't waver, but sounded strong and normal. "Martha and Robert brought me here to keep me safe from the men who are after me because of David's debts."

"Really, Mr. Washington, you're looking for drama where there is none," Robert said smoothly.

"Lucas, I really appreciate everything you did for me," Julie said. "But I'm fine now." She hoped the smile that curved her lips didn't look as plastic as it felt.

Wendall looked at Lucas, who still stared at her with an intensity that made her heart ache. "And this is where you want to be?" Lucas asked.

"Absolutely," she replied; then she reached a hand up and deliberately tugged on the end of her hair.

"Are we done here?" Robert asked with a touch of impatience. "It's cold and Julie is weary." He placed an arm around her shoulder and she fought the shiver of revulsion that tried to take hold of her at his touch.

"I guess we're done," Lucas said flatly. "Sorry to bother you all. Julie, I hope things go well for you." He turned and headed back to his car, followed by Wendall and Ben.

"You did very well, my dear," Robert said as he guided her back toward the house.

Julie barely heard him as she felt the last of her hope flutter away. She'd tried to tell Lucas that she was lying by the tug of her hair, but obviously he hadn't gotten it.

She glanced backward just before she went back into the house and saw Lucas's car driving away. It was over, done, and she was helpless to fight Robert and his minions.

She hadn't been able to save herself, but at least she'd saved Lucas and his sister. Still, as Robert led her back up the stairs to her room, she began to weep for Lucas, for her baby and for herself.

Chapter Twelve

She'd lied.

When she had said she was fine and where she wanted to be, she'd been lying. She'd definitely pulled on the ends of her hair when she'd said those words.

"My mother said she could always tell when I was fibbing because I'd tug on the end of my hair." Julie's words reverberated around and around in his head. She'd been trying to signal him, to let him know that she was in trouble.

Lucas hadn't even gone half a block from the church when he pulled out his cell phone and punched in a number. "Meet me at my place in fifteen minutes," he said to Micah.

"What's going on?"

"I'll tell you when you get there. And call Troy. I want him there, too."

Lucas hung up, tossed the phone on the seat next to him and stepped on the gas pedal, eager to get to his apartment and plan a course of action.

He knew there was no point in talking to Wendall. Julie was a consenting adult. She'd told them all that she wanted to be in the compound behind the church. Without any more evidence to the contrary, Wendall's hands would be tied.

Besides, going through legal channels for help could take days, and even then he'd have to convince Wendall that a pull on the hair had been a signal instead of a simple gesture.

But Lucas wasn't bound by law. He'd seen all the evidence he needed to see in the simple tug of her hair. Rage balled up in his chest as he thought of Julie afraid and alone with people who meant her and her unborn baby harm.

He still didn't understand what they wanted with her, why they would take her to the compound and hold her there against her will, but he didn't need a reason to go in and get her out.

He also didn't know if she'd lied about having her memories back or not. But it didn't matter. Nothing mattered except getting her out of that place and away from those people. Guilt ripped through him. He'd handed her over to them. He'd sent her back into danger.

It was almost two in the afternoon by the time he reached his apartment. Micah and Troy were already in the parking lot awaiting his arrival.

They didn't speak until they were in the apartment and then Lucas told them what had transpired at the church compound.

"I don't know what's going on there. I don't know why they're holding her, but we have to get her out," he said. "I know she's in danger." He thumped his chest with his fist. "I feel it here."

He was grateful that neither of his friends tried to dissuade him from his belief. In any case it would have been a waste of time. With or without them, Lucas intended to get Julie out.

"What do you have in mind?" Micah asked as he leaned forward in his chair at the kitchen table. His eyes glittered with the call to war. There was nothing Micah and Troy enjoyed more than action.

"A covert operation," Lucas replied. "We go in under the cover of night and we don't come out unless we have her with us."

Micah sat back and frowned thoughtfully. "What do you know about the house where she's being held?"

"Not much. It's a three-story mansion. I don't know how many people are inside. I don't know if she's being held under armed guard. I'm not sure what we'd be walking into."

Troy smiled. "Wouldn't be the first time," he replied.

"I'll see if I can get a copy of permits and maybe a floor plan of the place this afternoon," Micah said.

"And I'll do a little reconnaissance work and see if I can tell how many people might be inside and whether they're armed or not," Troy added.

Lucas nodded, gratitude swelling in his chest.

"Why don't we coordinate back here at seven tonight and make final plans?"

Troy and Micah left immediately, and Lucas paced the confines of his kitchen, his thoughts filled with Julie. It was only now that he recognized the depths of his feelings for her.

He loved her.

He'd never allowed himself to fall in love with any woman, but somehow Julie had gotten under his defenses, touched places in his heart that had never been touched before.

He had no illusions. There was no happily ever after for them. His loving Julie didn't magically absolve him of the issues that would forever keep him a solitary man.

But he wanted her safe. He wanted her healthy. And eventually he hoped she'd be happy. He knew in his gut that none of those things were going to happen as long as she was in that house. He had to get her out and then he could walk away from her with no regrets.

The late afternoon and early evening hours crept by with agonizing slowness. Lucas got on his computer and tried to find out everything he could about the Church of Enlightenment, seeking answers to questions he didn't even know how to pose.

He did a Google search of the names of the few people he knew from the church—Charles Blankenship, Robert Montgomery, Martha Montgomery and of course, Julie. Charles Blankenship had a Web site devoted to his family with nothing inflammatory or unusual about it. He could find nothing on Robert and Martha except a special interest article in a local newspaper about Robert's gift shop.

He found the article about David's murder. It had occurred as the man had left an ATM. The case was never solved. His obituary mentioned that he was survived by his older brother, Robert, and his wife, Julie, but Lucas already knew that.

All in all, the computer time was a bust and once again Lucas took to pacing the kitchen, his head whirling with crazy thoughts and emotions he'd never felt before.

By the time seven o'clock arrived, Lucas was like a cat on a hot tin roof, filled with a nervous energy that begged to be directed into action.

He changed his clothes, opting for a pair of black jeans and a long-sleeved black turtleneck that would allow him to blend into the night.

When Troy and Micah arrived they were dressed similarly, and they didn't come empty-handed. They brought stun guns, rope and grappling hooks for rappelling. More importantly, they brought their stealth and clandestine methods and expertise as ex–navy SEALs at getting in and out without detection.

For the next four hours they plotted and planned. Micah had somehow gotten hold of a floor plan of the house, and they speculated in what room Julie might be held.

Troy had counted eight men going in and out of the house who he thought might be armed. But why would a church-owned establishment need armed guards?

By midnight they were all champing at the bit, ready to take on an entire army to save one beautiful pregnant woman. It was decided that they would park their cars a mile away near the fields that served as a backyard to the home. There they would scale a tall chain-link fence.

They would spread out and each find a way into the house. There was no need to plan the specifics, each would do whatever necessary to gain entrance. The goal was to get in and out without encountering anyone, but if they did, they each knew how to take out a threat without making a sound.

They would go in at twelve-thirty and hopefully rendezvous back at the safe house with Julie in hand by one-thirty.

"I just want to tell you both how much I appreciate this," Lucas said as they left his apartment. None of them had spoken of the fact that before the night was over there was a possibility they could be in jail—or dead.

Troy clapped Lucas on the back. "In until the end," he said.

It was what they'd said when they'd served side by side, and in that moment Lucas realized how rich his life was in having these two men as friends.

They left Lucas's apartment complex, each in his

own vehicle, and within minutes were in position about a mile away from the compound.

None of them spoke as they ran toward their objective.

They scaled the fence that thankfully wasn't electrified. The minute they split apart and Troy and Micah disappeared into the darkness of the night, Lucas's thoughts were solely on Julie.

Was she still okay? Had they harmed her since he and Wendall had appeared at the gate to check on her welfare? So many hours had passed since then. It was possible they were already too late. He couldn't dwell on that. The idea that she might be hurt—or worse—would destroy him.

He moved like a shadow in the cold night, his feet skipping over the frozen earth without making a sound. Troy would head to the left side of the house, Micah to the right and Lucas would take the rear. Somehow they would get inside. It was what they were trained to do.

With every step he took he saw her again and again, tugging on that golden strand of hair, her lips curved into a pleasant smile as she'd lied to him and told him she was where she wanted to be.

Be safe, Julie. His heart thundered the words, and it was in those moments as he ran toward the house, as his heart beat the frantic rhythm of fear, that he was struck again by the depth of his love for her.

She was the woman he'd want in his life if he were the man he wanted to be instead of the man he feared he was. Hopefully he could rescue her, get her to safety and then love her enough to let her go.

The moon cooperated with the mission, hiding its light behind a thick layer of clouds, and as Lucas approached the dark, quiet house, his heartbeat slowed and his anxiety level dropped.

He called it mission mode, when all thoughts left his head and he was filled with a cold calm. All emotion fell away, replaced by the steely determination of a soldier.

There wasn't a single light on anywhere in the house that could be seen, and yet even with the hidden moon overhead there was a faint illumination.

Where are you, Julie? They all had agreed that she was probably being held on the second or third floor.

He reached the side of the house and looked up, but there was no clue as to which of the dozens of windows she might be behind.

A faint crunch of icy grass came from the side of the house. Lucas flattened himself with his back against the building just as the dark outline of a tall, thin man came into view.

A guard, Lucas quickly surmised. He walked at a leisurely pace, letting Lucas know he had no clue that their security had been breached.

Still, Lucas knew his safest course of action was to take the man out. He narrowed his gaze as the guard drew closer, making a wide circle around the back of the house.

If he saw Lucas, then he might get an opportunity to alert others before Lucas could neutralize him. Lucas stopped breathing, hoping, praying he wouldn't be seen.

Crouching for attack, he waited until the man had his back to him; then he sprang.

It took less than five seconds to get the man in a sleeper hold and render him unconscious. As he fell to the ground, Lucas quickly taped his mouth closed and tied his hands and legs, then dragged him away from the house and into the field beyond.

Moments later he sprinted back and once again eyed the house. *Now to find a way inside,* he thought. His mission-mode calm slipped away as he thought of Julie, and prayed that they would get to her in time.

JULIE LAY IN BED in the darkened room, sleep the furthest thing from her mind. Tonight was her last night on earth.

Robert had told her when he'd left her room earlier that tomorrow she would be undergoing a cesarean section. She knew that they would take her baby and she would die. There was no way they could allow her to live. She was a loose end, a liability in their crazy plan.

She closed her eyes and rubbed her tummy. Robert would raise her son as his own, and groom him to usher a congregation from a good, religious group to a dangerous, powerful cult. When Robert had first told her his plan, she'd asked why it had to be her baby. He'd told her it was the bloodline that mattered. If anyone in the congregation questioned that the child wasn't of his own bloodline then he'd have DNA proof. He'd promised his congregation a child of his blood, and a nephew would fit the bill just fine.

With the hours that she'd had to think, she'd realized that it was possible that Robert had killed his brother, her husband.

Robert had known Julie was leaving David and that she'd just discovered she was pregnant at the time of David's death. It was possible he'd feared that she'd leave David and disappear into another life with her son. And Robert wanted her child.

If what she believed was true, then Robert had taken a gamble. He'd wanted a child of his blood to fill the position of the son he'd never had. Julie and David's baby fit the bill. Still, if he'd killed David and she'd miscarried, he would never have gained the child he desperately wanted—needed—to complete his plan.

None of that mattered now. It was over. Robert was going to succeed and she was going to die. At least her regrets were few.

Although the pain of knowing she would never see her son, never hold his sweetness in her arms and watch him grow into a man, was too hard to bear, in every other area of her life there weren't many things she regretted.

She'd loved.

A vision of Lucas filled her head. With all her memories now intact she knew that what she'd felt for him hadn't been just gratitude. She loved him with a sweeping depth that she'd never felt for the man she'd married.

And she'd been loved.

She didn't care what Lucas said, he had loved her, too. Unfortunately his love for her hadn't been strong enough.

She knew it had to do with his father, with the miserable childhood he'd suffered. There was no way a child could go through that kind of experience and not be changed at the very core.

If only he could see himself through her eyes and embrace the man he was, a loving, giving man who might have made her life complete.

Her only regret was that she and Lucas had never gotten the chance to make love for real. She would never feel his hips against her own, the weight of his body on hers as he buried himself deep inside her.

Too late now.

She closed her eyes, begging for sleep to come and take her away from her thoughts. She had almost drifted off when a faint thud sounded just outside her door.

She shot up to a sitting position, her heart thundering alarm. What was that? Were they coming for her? Had they decided to take the baby now, tonight?

Her weary acceptance of what was to come disappeared as an unexpected adrenaline filled her. At that moment she realized she did not intend to go easy.

She would scratch and claw and fight whoever came inside to take her baby. She would kick and gouge and scream bloody murder even if it didn't help. She'd make sure she hurt them before they killed her.

She slid out of bed and grabbed the bedside lamp. With a single pull she yanked the cord from the plug in the wall. It was a tiny thing, by no means a lethal weapon, but she crept to the door and held it up over her head.

Her arms shook and her heart pounded so hard she felt half breathless as she waited to see if anyone would enter. Seconds ticked by and she began to think that maybe she'd imagined the noise she'd heard in the hallway.

She froze as she heard the scrape of a key in the lock, then the squeak of the knob slowly turning. As the door creaked open she tightened her hands on the base of the lamp.

As the dark figure stepped into the room, she crashed the lamp down on him, crying out in frustration as she realized she'd missed his head and hit him on his shoulder.

He whirled around and grabbed her by the shoulders, his big, strong fingers biting painfully tight into her tender flesh. She screamed and was instantly backhanded with a slap that nearly sent her to her knees.

"Shut up," Robert said. "If you scream again I'll

knock you unconscious." He batted the lamp out of her hand and grabbed her. "Let's go. We're moving out of here. Security has been breached."

He jerked her out into the dim hallway, where only faint night-lights lit the area. It was like her dream, the long hallway and the eerie lighting. Only this time she wasn't running alone, she was being dragged by the man who wanted her dead.

It was only as they stepped out of the bedroom that she realized he had a gun, and her heart once again knocked so hard against her ribs it nearly took her breath away. "If you make a sound, I'll put a bullet in your brain," he whispered as he pulled her up against him.

What was happening? Why was he moving her out of her bedroom in the middle of the night? And why was he doing it at gunpoint?

They moved slowly, passing dark rooms with open doors. Where was he taking her? It was obvious he was moving in the direction of the back staircase that would eventually take them into the kitchen of the large house. In the kitchen was a door that led to the garage.

Was he moving her completely out of the house? Was he taking her someplace where a doctor awaited to cut her baby from her and toss her dead body on some deserted city street?

She might have fallen to the floor in utter despair if they hadn't passed another room. As she glanced inside she could have sworn she saw the movement of a dark, silent shadow just inside the door.

Her heart skipped a beat and a tiny flicker of hope ignited inside her. Lucas? Her heart cried his name. Was it possible he had caught her attempt to signal him when she'd pulled on the end of her hair?

Had he realized she'd been lying to him when she'd told him everything was all right? Or had she simply imagined that dark form in the room because she desperately wanted to be rescued? Or had the dark shadow simply been one of Robert's henchmen?

Closer and closer they got to the stairs that would lead them down and out of the house. Knowing that if he managed to get her outside, nobody would ever know what had become of her, she dragged her feet, making it difficult for them to make forward progress.

When they passed another dark room and she thought she saw the shadowy figure of a man, she wondered if she was losing her mind, if the stress of the situation had her seeing phantoms.

She never heard them coming. The phantoms seemed to jump out of the very woodwork, two behind them and one in front of them, blocking their way down the hall.

She also didn't see the blow that sent the gun flying from Robert's hand. Everything happened in a blur. One of the shadows grabbed her, and the minute she was pulled against his chest she knew it was Lucas.

Tears sprang to her eyes, and she might have wept with relief if it wasn't for the sound of running footsteps coming from the opposite end of the hallway.

Lucas shoved her behind him and turned to face the next challenge. Somebody turned on the hall lights, and as Julie cowered against the wall, her hands protectively splayed across her belly, all hell broke loose.

Lucas and his partners faced off against Robert and the two other men who had appeared in the hallway. As Robert dove for the gun he had dropped, Lucas jumped on his back while Troy and Micah began hand-to-hand combat with the others.

"Take her and go," Micah yelled as he rendered his opponent unconscious, then jumped on Robert's back.

Lucas rose, his features set in grim lines as he grabbed Julie by the hand and pulled her toward the stairs. They raced downward as fast as she was capable of going. They wouldn't be safe until they were out of this house, away from this compound.

Down the two flights of stairs they flew, and when they reached the kitchen they burst out the back door. Julie hadn't realized she was crying until the cold air slapped her wet cheeks.

"Wait," she said, and stopped in her tracks. Even though she knew they needed to get out of there as quickly as possibly, the run down the stairs had winded her. She bent over slightly and drew in deep gulps of air.

She gasped in surprise as Lucas scooped her up in his arms and continued across the field toward the high fence in the distance. She buried her head in his shoulder, awed by his strength, by the chance he had taken to come in to get her.

It was only when they reached the fencing that he set her back on her feet. Troy and Micah grinned at them from the other side of the fence. "What took you so long?" Micah asked, and pulled apart a section of the steel links that had been cut away.

"I stopped to smell the roses," Lucas replied drily. Julie stepped through the hole in the fence and Lucas followed.

"I'm taking her right to the police station," Lucas said. "I suggest you two lie low until we see how this all plays out. Any casualties?"

"Nothing that a little time and a few bandages won't heal," Troy replied.

"Call Wendall and tell him to meet me at the station," Lucas said to Troy, who nodded.

"Let's move," Micah added. The two men headed for their vehicles, and Lucas and Julie raced for his. Within minutes they were driving away from Julie's nightmare and Julie was telling him everything she remembered, everything that Robert had planned.

Lucas said nothing, he just listened until she was finished telling her story. By that time they were in front of the police station.

As he turned off the engine of his car she placed a hand on his arm. "Lucas, before we go inside, I need to tell you something," she said.

"What's that?" His gaze was enigmatic in the spill of light from the nearby police station.

"In the hours tonight as I contemplated my own death, the one thing that kept me strong was my love for you. Not gratitude, Lucas. Love. I love you, Lucas Washington, and if you look in your heart I know that you'll see that you love me, too."

"It doesn't matter what's in my heart," he said, his features looking starker, more sharp than usual as a pulse knotted in his jaw. "I told you from the start of this that I don't want a wife."

He started to open his car door, but she stopped him by grabbing his arm. "Is it because of the baby? You can't love a baby that isn't yours?"

"Of course not," he replied without hesitation. "I could love a baby—I could love your baby, but I told you I don't want to be a husband or a father."

"Why not? What are you afraid of, Lucas? Why would you deny yourself the joy of a woman who loves you? A family who could fill your life?"

"We don't have time for this," he said impatiently.

"That's one thing I realized as I was waiting to die," she exclaimed. "The only real thing we have time for on this earth is to love and to be loved."

He stiffened. "I will not repeat the mistakes of my father," he said in a voice that trembled with suppressed emotion.

"No, you won't," she agreed. "Because you are not anything like your father. Oh, Lucas, why can't you see yourself as I see you, as your sister sees you? How long will you allow the shadow of your father to keep all light from your heart?"

A headlight beam from an arriving car bathed Lucas's face in stark brightness. "That's Wendall. Let's go inside." Before she could stop him he opened his door and got out of the car.

For the next several hours Julie sat with Chief Kincaid and a prosecuting attorney in an interrogation room where she told them everything that had happened from the time of her husband's murder to the present. She now knew why she had been so terrified of coming to the police, and she told Wendall of Officer Ben Branigan's involvement with Robert's plans.

Lucas had disappeared. She assumed he was being questioned in another room. Several times Wendell left and was gone for long minutes only to return for more questioning.

She was completely wrung out by the time Wendall called a halt to things. "I've arranged a room for you at a nearby hotel for the next couple of days," he said. "You'll be under guard until we can sort all this out."

He smiled for the first time since they'd begun the questioning process. "Don't worry, Julie. We'll make sure you and your unborn baby are safe now."

She nodded wearily. "Can I see Lucas now?"

He looked surprised. "Lucas left here some time ago. He told me to tell you goodbye for him. Now, let's get you settled in for the night."

Numb. She was numb as Wendall escorted her from the room and introduced her to Officer Clay

Samuels, who would be taking her to her hotel and standing guard for the next twelve hours.

He left without saying goodbye. He'd made sure she was safe, he'd listened to her tell him that she loved him, but ultimately he'd made the choice to walk away from her. She had a horrible feeling that she would never hear from, never see him again.

Chapter Thirteen

"Want more coffee?" Loretta asked Lucas as she got up to pour herself another cup.

"No, thanks, I'm fine. What are your plans for the day?" he asked once she'd joined him at the table.

"I'm going shopping for a dress to wear to Micah's wedding," she replied. "And then I'm meeting Joe for lunch."

Joe was the coworker she'd had a date with, the coworker Lucas suspected might eventually become his brother-in-law. Even as she said his name her eyes took on a new sparkle.

"When do I get to meet this guy?" Lucas asked with a touch of impatience.

"I don't know—not yet. We'll see how things go in the next couple of weeks," she replied with a smile. "What do you have planned for the day?"

Lucas glanced out the window, where it was yet another cold, gray day. "I'm not sure. I'm kind of at loose ends." For the last week he, Micah and Troy had kept a low profile, not even going into the Recovery Inc. offices as they waited for the dust to settle following their raid on the Church of Enlightenment compound. The D.A. had decided not to press any charges against the men who had rescued Julie.

"I heard they made some more arrests yesterday," Loretta said, as if she knew his thoughts.

He nodded and focused back on her. "That makes fourteen. I spoke to Wendall late last night and he told me he thought they'd arrested everyone that had anything to do with Julie's case."

"And they'll all be charged with kidnapping?"

"Among other charges." He picked up his coffee cup and took a sip, trying not to think about Julie. He wasn't even sure where she was now, told himself it was enough just to know that she was safe.

According to what Wendall had told him the night before, they had recovered enough information off Robert's computer to see that he'd spend most of the rest of his life behind bars. He'd kept a diary, filled with plans and sermons he would give his congregation to welcome in the new little prophet.

It never failed to amaze Lucas how stupid criminals could be when it came to their computers and what they typed in, believing that they wouldn't get caught, that nobody would ever see their incriminating records.

They'd also managed to find the doctor who had been going to take the baby from Julie and allow her to die. Martha Montgomery had been a weak link, and according to Wendall, was spilling her guts in hopes of cutting a deal with the prosecution.

"Troy proposed to Brianna," he said, once again to get his mind off the thoughts of the woman who had haunted him for the last week.

"Good for him," Loretta replied. "Did they set a date for the wedding?"

"Not yet, although they're thinking sometime in the spring." And they all lived happily ever after. The words that ended every fairy tale flittered through his head.

Micah would soon make Caylee his bride, Troy and Brianna would follow and begin a family and eventually Loretta might marry her Joe.

"The only real thing we have time for on this earth is to love and to be loved." Julie's words whirled around in his head.

"You've invited them all for Thanksgiving dinner?" Loretta asked.

He nodded and stood abruptly. "I've got to get going," he said, needing to do something, anything that would keep him too busy to think. He carried his cup to the sink just as Loretta's phone rang.

She answered as he washed out his cup and put it in her dishwasher. By the time he turned to face her, she'd already hung up.

"That was Julie," she said. "She's in labor and on her way to the hospital." Loretta looked at him expectantly.

A rush of crazy emotions blew through him. *"You won't have that baby alone. I'll make sure of that."* Wasn't that what he'd told her? Wasn't that what he'd promised her?

It hadn't been a real promise, he tried to tell himself. It had just been a statement made in the heat of a moment.

As he stood there, frozen in place, Loretta's look of expectation turned to one of faint disgust. "You're a fool, Lucas. I know you love her and I know what's holding you back. In a million years, under a million circumstances, you could never be like him."

She grabbed her purse from the countertop. "You're my hero, Lucas. You always have been, but a hero isn't afraid of loving somebody. I'm going to the hospital, because Julie needs somebody with her. I'm not the person she really wants, but I guess I'll have to do."

She marched out of the kitchen without a backward glance, and a moment later Lucas heard the slam of her front door. He remained standing in the stillness of the kitchen, alone as he'd always been, alone as he should be.

JULIE FELT THE GRIP of another contraction coming on and tried to breathe slowly and evenly as she succumbed to the pain that would eventually usher in the birth of her son. She panted as the pain slowly eased away.

"Three minutes apart. It won't be long now," the

nurse said cheerfully. "You're doing just fine, Julie. I'm going to check in with the doctor. I'll be right back."

As she left the room Julie turned her head to look out the hospital room window. The gray, overcast skies could do nothing to detract from the joy of the knowledge that in a short period of time she'd have her baby boy in her arms.

The only thoughts that might have stolen a tiny bit of joy from her were of Lucas. She tried desperately to keep him out of her mind.

For the last five days while she'd been alone in her hotel room, Lucas was all she'd been able to think about. She'd almost wished she could call back her amnesia and forget everything that had happened from the moment he'd found her in the back of that car to when he'd walked out of the police station without a backward glance.

Unfortunately, selective amnesia didn't seem to be in her power, and thoughts of what might have been had haunted her throughout those days and nights.

With yesterday's arrests, Chief Kincaid had told her that he thought she was no longer in danger. Everyone she remembered being part of the plot to steal her baby was now in jail.

Last night she'd moved back into the house she'd shared with David. She would live there until it sold, then hopefully she'd have enough to cover a couple of months of living expenses. Next fall she intended to return to teaching.

The future was an open book filled with potential and all she had to do was stop thinking about a particular black-haired, dark-eyed man who had stolen her heart.

She'd called Loretta several times during the past week, finding solace in the friendship that the two had built in the brief time they'd spent together. In none of those conversations had Lucas's name come up.

As she felt another contraction beginning to build, she clenched her fingers into the sheets as tears blurred her vision. They weren't tears of pain, but rather ones of disappointment. She'd called Loretta, but she hadn't shown up yet.

I can do it alone, she told herself as a whimper escaped her lips. She knew she was strong, perhaps stronger than most women. She'd just endured an ordeal that few would ever experience and she'd come out of it okay.

She closed her eyes as the pain shot through her. Another whimper slipped from her mouth, this one a little bit louder. She was vaguely aware of somebody coming back into the room and suddenly her hand was clasped in a bigger, stronger one.

Her eyes flew open and she gasped as she saw Lucas, his dark eyes radiating with her pain. "Breathe, Julie," he said softly.

She closed her eyes as his hand squeezed hers tightly and she breathed, riding the wave of pain more easily just knowing he was with her.

When the contraction subsided, she looked at him once again. Was he here because Loretta had insisted he come? Because he'd made her a promise and Lucas was a man of his word?

She was afraid to hope for anything more. "I'm naming him Luke," she said with more than a touch of defiance. "And if you don't like it you can just lump it."

He raised a dark eyebrow with a teasing smile. "Lump it?"

"You know what I mean," she replied. "What are you doing here, Lucas?"

He pulled up a chair next to the side of her bed and sat, then once again took her hand in his. "Somebody very wise once told me that the only real thing we have time for on this earth is to love and to be loved."

Her heart skipped a beat as she eyed him cautiously. "That still doesn't answer my question."

The teasing smile that had curved his lips faltered and it was with complete seriousness that he gazed at her. "As crazy as it sounds, I think I fell more than half in love with you the minute I saw you in the back of that car. You knew I was in love with you. Loretta knew I was in love with you. Even I knew it. But you scare the hell out of me."

"You're an ex–navy SEAL. Nothing should scare you," she protested.

"Not being the man I want to be has always scared me," he replied.

"But you're the man *I* want you to be. You're the man I want in my life forever. Oh, Lucas, don't you see?" The last word rose an octave as a new contraction ripped through her.

It seemed to last forever and was followed by another one almost immediately. The doctor swept into the room and smiled at Lucas. "Ah, I see we're all here—mommy and daddy. And very soon we'll have little junior here with us."

Julie knew she should correct the doctor, tell him that Lucas wasn't the daddy, that he was just here because he'd made a stupid promise.

She should tell the doctor that Lucas would be here only long enough to see the birth of the baby and then he would disappear from her life once again.

But she couldn't tell him, she couldn't speak a single word as waves of pain tore through her. Lucas grabbed her hand, his eyes shining overly bright as the doctor got into position at the foot of her bed and told her to push.

"Push, Julie. Let's get this baby born," he said.

She bore down with a low scream as tears blurred her vision. The tears were a mix of pain and joy. *Come on, son,* she begged as she stopped bearing down and tried to catch her breath.

"You're doing great, Julie," Lucas said as he swept a strand of her damp hair away from her face.

"Again, Julie," the doctor said. "Push."

"Come on, honey, that little boy wants to be born," Lucas said. "Push."

She did. Over and over again she grunted and pushed to give birth.

"That's it," Lucas exclaimed. "You are so beautiful," he exclaimed as he swept her damp hair away from her forehead. "You're the bravest woman I know."

"I can't do it anymore," she exclaimed in exhaustion.

"Yes, you can," Lucas replied. "I love you, Julie, and I love that baby. Now, push!"

Although his words and actions of love were welcomed, in the back of her mind she knew not to embrace them into her heart. The ability to think fell away as she gave herself into the gripping pain of birth and the knowledge that this moment with Lucas wouldn't last forever.

NIGHT HAD FALLEN and outside her hospital window the sky was filled with stars. It was as if the clouds had parted to reveal the beautiful starlit night sky just for little Luke.

He lay in her arms, sleeping soundly, and snuggled against the reassuring sound of her heartbeat. Love swelled up inside her as she kissed the top of his little bald head.

She'd slept most of the afternoon, exhausted by the birth. A nurse had awakened her a little while ago and told her it was time to feed her boy.

The birth itself now felt like a dream, the memory of pain gone beneath the overwhelming joy. Had she dreamed of Lucas when in the throes of childbirth?

Immediately after little Luke had made his appearance, Lucas had done a vanishing act, and she hadn't seen him since. She really hadn't expected anything else. He'd fulfilled his promise that she wouldn't have the baby alone, and now he owed her nothing more.

"We're going to be just fine," she whispered to Luke. "We're going to have a wonderful life together."

Once again she turned her head to look out her window. No point in wishing on a star for a man who refused to make a commitment despite his pronouncements of love for her.

Instead, she wished for a long and happy life for her son, a world filled with laughter and love. She would give him that. She would give him all the love she had in her heart.

A sound from the doorway drew her attention. When she turned her head to see who was there, her breath caught in her chest.

Lucas stood just inside the room. In one hand he held a huge bouquet of flowers, and in the other arm he gripped the biggest teddy bear she'd ever seen.

"I didn't think I'd ever see you again," she said.

"Yeah, I didn't think you would, either." He placed the flower arrangement on a nearby table, the teddy bear in a chair and then moved to stand beside her bed.

In the dim lighting of the room his eyes glowed as he gazed at her. "I thought I could walk away from you—from him—but I can't. For the first time in my life, my love is bigger than my fear."

He sank down in the chair next to her, as if his legs wouldn't hold him up any longer. She didn't say a word, afraid that in doing so she might break the moment.

"I've done nothing but think about you since I left the police station a week ago. The last week has been the longest in my life, but I was determined to stay away from you. Then Loretta told me you were in labor and I knew this was where I needed, where I wanted to be."

He paused and reached for her hand. "I'm not my father and in a million years I could never be my father. I've wasted too many years of my life worrying about what I might become instead of recognizing the kind of man I am."

"I've been trying to tell you that," she finally said, her heart more full than it had ever been in her entire life.

He grinned sheepishly. "You should know by now that I'm hardheaded." His grin disappeared and he leaned forward, his eyes shining with a suspicious moisture. "I love you, Julie, and I want a life with you, with Luke. I want to be the man in both of your lives."

"Lucas Washington, if you don't kiss me this minute I think I might die," she exclaimed.

He grinned, that sexy smile that swelled her heart even bigger. He stood and bent over, capturing her lips in a kiss that flamed through her with a wealth of new promises.

When the kiss finally ended, he drew back from her and gently tucked a strand of her hair behind her ear. "You'll be home for Thanksgiving, Julie. You and Luke will be home with me."

As the stars twinkled outside the window, Julie felt the fire of a comet in her soul, but she knew it was nothing more than the sweet warmth of love.

* * * * *

INTRIGUE..

2-IN-1 ANTHOLOGY

HITCHED!

by BJ Daniels

Jack needed a cover to solve a decades-old mystery. And Josey offered him the perfect one: if she would agree to pose as his wife for a week…

CLASSIFIED COWBOY

by Mallory Kane

Texas Ranger Wyatt never forgave himself for a witness disappearing on his watch; now anthropologist Nina's in danger, he's determined not to let history repeat itself.

●●●

2-IN-1 ANTHOLOGY

THE BABY'S BODYGUARD

by Alice Sharpe

With a threat looming over Hannah's family, Jack steps in as her baby's bodyguard while battling his growing desire for the woman he believes betrayed him.

TO CATCH A KILLER

by Kimberly Van Meter

Working with his ex to hunt a murderer, Matt never expected Kara to reveal her own little secret. And, now his newfound daughter's in danger, Matt's sworn to protect her.

On sale from 20th May 2011
Don't miss out!

Available at WHSmith, Tesco, ASDA, Eason
and all good bookshops

www.millsandboon.co.uk

0511/46a

INTRIGUE...

0511/46b

Kaylee has one addiction: her boyfriend, Nash.

'Twilight fans will love it'

RACHEL VINCENT

my SOUL to Keep

SOUL SCREAMERS

A banshee like Kaylee, Nash understands her like no one else. Nothing can come between them. Until something does.

Demon breath—a super-addictive paranormal drug that can kill. Kaylee and Nash need to cut off the source and protect their human friends—one of whom is already hooked.

But then Kaylee uncovers another demon breath addict. *Nash.*

Book three in the unmissable Soul Screamers *series.*

www.miraink.co.uk

Join us at facebook.com/miraink

Love and betrayal.
A Faery world gone mad.

Deserted by the Winter prince she thought loved her, half-Summer faery princess, half-human Meghan is prisoner to the Winter faery queen. But the real danger comes from the Iron fey— ironbound faeries only she and her absent prince have seen.

With Meghan's fey powers cut off, she's stuck in Faery with only her wits for help. And trusting a seeming traitor could be deadly.

_TC

"To say that I met Nicholas Brisbane over my husband's dead body is not entirely accurate. Edward, it should be noted, was still twitching upon the floor…"

London, 1886

For Lady Julia Grey, her husband's sudden death at a dinner party is extremely inconvenient. However, things worsen when inscrutable private investigator Nicholas Brisbane reveals that the death was not due to natural causes.

Drawn away from her comfortable, conventional life, Julia is exposed to threatening notes, secret societies and gypsy curses, not to mention Nicholas's charismatic unpredictability.

2 FREE BOOKS
AND A SURPRISE GIFT

We would like to take this opportunity to thank you for reading this Mills & Boon® book by offering you the chance to take TWO more specially selected books from the Intrigue series absolutely FREE! We're also making this offer to introduce you to the benefits of the Mills & Boon® Book Club™—

- **FREE home delivery**
- **FREE gifts and competitions**
- **FREE monthly Newsletter**
- **Exclusive Mills & Boon Book Club offers**
- **Books available before they're in the shops**

Accepting these FREE books and gift places you under no obligation to buy, you may cancel at any time, even after receiving your free books. Simply complete your details below and return the entire page to the address below. You don't even need a stamp!

YES Please send me 2 free Intrigue books and a surprise gift. I understand that unless you hear from me, I will receive 5 superb new stories every month, including two 2-in-1 books priced at £5.30 each and a single book priced at £3.30, postage and packing free. I am under no obligation to purchase any books and may cancel my subscription at any time. The free books and gift will be mine to keep in any case.

Ms/Mrs/Miss/Mr _____ Initials _____

Surname _____

Address _____

_____ Postcode _____

E-mail _____

Send this whole page to: Mills & Boon Book Club, Free Book Offer, FREEPOST NAT 10298, Richmond, TW9 1BR